WALK OF SHAME

THE COMPLETE SERIES

BY: VICTORIA ASHLEY

Justine -
Enjoy your men!

♡

Victoria Ashley

WALK OF SHAME COMPLETE SERIES
Copyright © 2015 Victoria Ashley
All rights reserved.
Cover by CT Cover Creations
Cover Photography: Sara Eirew
Model: Mike Chabot
Edited by Charisse Spiers
Formatting by Perfectly Publishable

SLADE
Copyright © 2014 Victoria Ashley
Cover by CT Cover Creations , Stock photo ©123RF.com
Edited by Charisse Spiers
Formatting by Perfectly Publishable

HEMY
Copyright © 2014 Victoria Ashley
Cover by CT Cover Creations, Stock photo ©123RF.com
Edited by Charisse Spiers
Formatting by Perfectly Publishable

CALE
Copyright © 2015 Victoria Ashley
Cover by CT Cover Creations, Stock photo ©123RF.com
Edited by Charisse Spiers
Formatting by Perfectly Publishable

SLADE

WALK OF SHAME #1

VICTORIA ASHLEY

CHAPTER ONE

Slade

IT'S DARK.

I love it with the lights off. She insisted on teasing me this way. My arms are tied behind me, my naked body bound to a chair. Goose bumps prickle my flesh as she softly blows on my hard cock, almost breaking my willpower. Her lips are so close, yet not close enough. I insist on teasing *her* this way.

"Na ah, not yet, baby."

She tilts her head up, her blond hair cascading over her shoulders as her eyes lock with mine. They're intense, desperate. She's silently begging me with her eyes, asking me to let her touch me already. I'm used to this. She needs to learn that when you're in my house we play by my rules. "Slade," she whimpers. "Come on already."

"Look down, baby." She tilts her head back down and runs

her tongue over her lips as she eagerly looks at my cock; no doubt imagining what it tastes like in her mouth. "That's it. Don't move."

I lift my hips, bringing the tip of my head to brush her lips. "You want me in your mouth?"

She nods her head and lets out a sound between a moan and a growl. Damn, it's such a turn on.

"How bad do you want it? I want to fucking hear it?"

Her nails dig into my thighs as she growls in aggravation. "More than anything. I want it so just give it to me, dammit. You already know how bad I want it."

A deep laugh rumbles in my throat as she scratches her nails down my legs in an attempt to hurt me. What she doesn't realize is that I welcome the pain. I get off on it.

"Is that all you got, pussycat?" I tease. "If you want my cock, you're going to have to do better than that."

She looks angry now; determined. Standing up, she points a finger in my chest. "You're the one tied up. This is supposed to be my game. Why do *you* have to torture me and make me wait?"

Biting my bottom lip, I nod for her to move closer to me. When she gets close to my face, I slide my tongue out and run it over her lips, causing her to tremble as I taste her. "Show. Me. How. Much. You. Want. Me."

Straddling me, she screams and slaps me hard across the face before yanking my head back by my hair. If I could get any harder, I would.

Fuck me.

"Now, that's what I'm talking about." I press my stiff cock against her ass, showing her just how turned on I am. Then I look her in the eye. "Show me what you can do with your mouth. First impression is always the most important."

A mischievous smile spreads across her face as she slithers her way off my lap and down between my legs. Gripping my thighs in her hands, she runs her tongue over the tip of my dick before suctioning it into her mouth. It hits the back of her throat, causing her to gag. She doesn't care; completely uninhibited. She just shoves it deeper.

Fuck yeah.

I moan as she swirls her tongue around my shaft while sucking at the same time. It feels fucking fantastic. "I told you it's worth the wait, baby. Just wait until I get inside you. It feels better than it tastes."

She pulls back and licks her lips. "Then why don't you show me. My pussy has never been so wet." She stands up and bends over in front of me, exposing her wet lips. I can see the moisture glistening from here; beckoning to suck me inside. She smiles as she runs her fingers over the folds as if she's teasing me; testing me. "You like that?" she asks seductively, tantalizing me. "You want this tight little pussy all for yourself, you greedy little bastard?"

I nod, playing into her little game. She seems to think she's in charge.

"Well, come and get it." She inserts her fingers into her mouth and sucks them clean, before shoving them into her entrance, fucking me with her eyes. Her ass moves up and down in perfect rhythm as she purrs. "I'm waiting." She shoves her fingers deeper. "I want to see those muscles flexing as you ram into me. I want you to . . ."

Well you won't be waiting for long.

Breaking free from my restraints, I stand up, grab her hips and flip her around before slamming her back up against the wall. "What were you saying, baby?" I growl into her ear. I grip both of her ass cheeks and lift her as she wraps her legs around my waist, squeezing. "I'm not sure you can handle what I have to offer." I grip her face in my hand before leaning in and biting her bottom lip, roughly tugging. "You're finally about to get what you've wanted. I just hope you don't have shit to do for the next few days because this might get a little rough. Last time to make your escape, because once I start there's no stopping until you're screaming my name loud; so loud it fucking hurts my ears." I search her eyes waiting to see if she's changed her mind; nothing but raw heat and lust. She still wants it. She's brave. No girl walks into my bed and walks out unscathed. So, she'll get it. I lift an eyebrow. "Okay, then."

I take wide strides across the room to my king-sized bed and toss her atop the mattress. Before she can blink, I am between her thighs, spreading them wide for me. I run my tongue up her smooth flesh, stopping at intersection of her thighs and clean shaven pussy. "You ready for me to make you come without even touching you?"

I begin blowing my cool breath across her swollen, wet pussy. She thrusts her hips up; no doubt her hungry little pussy wanting more and just as I'm about to show her my skills, there's a knock at the damn door.

Bad fucking timing.

Gritting my teeth, I shake my head and look toward the door. "Give me a sec." I step down from the bed and motion for Lex to cover up. When she's done, I call for Cale to come in. "Okay, man."

The door opens right as I'm reaching for my pack of cigarettes and switching the light on. My dick is still standing at full alert, but I could care less. This shit head interrupted my night. If he doesn't like seeing my dick hard, then he should have known better than to come up to my room in the middle of the night.

Stepping into my room, Cale takes notice of my hard on and quickly reaches for the nearest item of clothing and tosses it on my dick. I look down to see a shirt hanging from it. I shake it off. "A little warning next time, mother fucker. I'm tired of witnessing that shit."

SLADE

Lighting my cigarette, I laugh and take a drag. "Jealous, prick?"

Ignoring me, he walks past me when he sets eyes on Lex. She's been coming to the club for a while now and she's sexy as hell. All of the guys have been trying to get with her, but she's wanted nothing but my cock this whole time. He raises his eyebrows and slides onto the foot of my bed. "Damn, Lex. You get sexier every time I see you."

Gripping the sheet tighter against her body, Lex growls and kicks Cale off the bed. "Go fuck off, Cale. I don't want your dick."

Jumping up with a quickness, Cale reaches for my jeans and tosses them to me. "I don't want to fuck you, Lex. I want to pleasure you. This dick is special." He nods toward me. "Unlike Slade's."

"Fuck you, Cale. What the hell do you want?"

He turns to me after smirking at Lex. "The club just called. We gotta go."

"It's not my night to work, man. Isn't Hemy working?" I take a long drag of my cigarette, letting the harsh smoke fill my lungs as I close my eyes. I really need to release this tension. I will fuck her in front of him if I have to. It wouldn't be the first time I've fucked in front of an audience. "I'm a little busy right now." I dangle Lex's thong from my finger. "If you can't tell."

Not getting where I'm going with this, Cale pulls out his phone and starts typing something in it. "We need to go now. There's a bachelorette party and the chicks asked for us specifically. You know what that means. Plus, Hemy is getting eaten alive right now."

Oh shit. I didn't think it was possible, but my cock just got even harder.

"Well, then I guess we better get started." I put out the cigarette, push past Cale and slide under the sheet. I reach for the condom on the nightstand and rip the wrapper open with my teeth. "This is going to have to be a quick one," I mumble before spitting the wrapper out and rolling the condom over my erection.

9

Lex looks at me questionably and nods to Cale. "You're going to have sex with me while he watches?"

I smirk as I flip her over and shove her head down into the mattress. "If he doesn't get out of my room, then yes, I'm going to fuck you while he watches." I peek over my shoulder at Cale and he lifts an eyebrow, his interest now peaked. "You've got three seconds and the counting started two seconds ago."

Pointing to Lex, he starts walking backwards while chewing his bottom lip. "As much as I'd love to watch you get fucked, I'm out. This dude gets too wild and I'll probably hurt myself just watching." Picking my wallet up from my dresser, he tosses it at my head, but misses. "Hurry your ass up. I'm changing my shit right now and then we need to go."

Lex moans from below me as I grip her hips, pull her to me and slide inside her. She's extra wet for me, making it easy to give her a good quick fuck. "You're so fucking wet. You were craving this cock weren't you?"

"Dude," Cale complains from a distance; although, I can still feel his eyes watching us.

"Your three seconds were up." I thrust my hips, gripping her hair in both my hands. "Mmm . . . fuck." *Damn that feels good.* "I'll be out in a minute."

"Leave, Cale!" Lex moans while gripping the sheet. "Oh shit! You feel even better than what I've been told. So thick and oh shit . . . it's so deep."

"Damn, that's hot."

"Out!" Lex screams.

"I'm out. I'm out." Cale backs his way out, shutting the door behind him. The truth is, if it weren't for Lex kicking him out, I could've cared less if he stayed and watched. I'm not ashamed.

Knowing I don't have a lot of time, I need to get this chick off fast. That's my rules and I don't have many. She gets off, then I get off. There is no stopping in between for me. Once I start, this is a done deal.

I can feel her wetness thickening. "You've gotten wetter. You like him watching, huh?" I yank her head back and run my tongue over her neck before whispering, "I would've let him stay; let him watch me as I fuck your wet pussy. Does that turn you on?"

Before she can say anything else, I push her head back down into the mattress and slam into her while rubbing my thumb over her swollen clit.

Her hands grip the sheets as she screams out and bites down on her arm, trying to silence her orgasm.

Slapping her ass, I ball my fist in her hair and gently pull it back so her back is pressed against my chest. "Don't hold it back. I want to fucking hear it. Got it?" She shakes her head so I thrust into her as deep as I can go. "Show me how it feels."

Screaming, she reaches back and grabs my hair, yanking it to the side. This makes me fuck her even harder. "Oh yes! Oh God! Slade, don't stop."

Reaching around, I grab her breast in one hand squeezing roughly and bite into her shoulder, rubbing my finger of the opposite hand faster over her slick clit. Her body starts to tremble beneath me as she clamps down hard on my cock. "Oh, shit. Stop, I can't take it. It feels so good, Slade."

I grip her hips and brush my lips over her ear. "You want me to stop?" I pull out slowly, teasing her. "You don't want this cock filling your pussy?" I shove it back in, causing her head to bang into the wall. "Huh, do you want me to stop?"

She shakes her head. "No, don't stop. Shit, don't stop!"

"That's what I thought." I push her completely flat on her stomach, holding my body weight with one arm as I grip the back of her neck and fuck her with all my strength. I want her to remember this because it's the only time she'll be getting my cock and we both know it. It's how I work.

She's squirming below me, shaking as if she's in the middle of another orgasm. "Slade! Oh shit!"

A few thrusts later and I'm ready to blow my load. Pulling out, I bite her ass and stroke my cock as I come.

The relief gives me a high; a fucking drug that I can't get enough of. Nothing else makes me feel this way. Actually, nothing else makes me feel. This is it for me.

My own personal hell.

CHAPTER TWO

Slade

CLOSING MY EYES, I TILT back my second shot of Whiskey. *That's it*, I think, moaning as it leaves a raw, burning sensation in the back of my throat. It's what I need; what I crave.

After rushing Lex out of my room and listening to Cale ramble on about one of his old friends crashing with us for the next week, I need this damn rush; the alcohol pumping through my veins, weakening my demons. Hell, I might even go for another one just for the numbness.

Fuck it. Why not.

Holding up my empty shot glass, I nod at Sarah to come my way. She instantly drops what she's doing to come to me. "Give me another one."

Snatching my empty glass away, she smiles and nods over to Cale and Hemy working their shit on the girls in the back corner.

"Shouldn't you be over there showing them how it's done?" She laughs while pulling out a bottle of Jack and filling a new shot glass. "They're both looking a little tired and worn down. You know how bachelorette's are; last night of freedom and all."

I turn around in my stool and look at the two idiots. Cale is standing on a couch grinding his cock in some girl's face while wiping sweat from his forehead. Hemy has some girl on the floor, rolling his body above hers, but he's moving in a rhythm slower than the music.

Tired? How the hell can they . . .

"Yeah, well give me another shot and then I'll show them what's up."

"I'm sure you will, Slade. Keep slamming these back and I might be showing you what's up later." She pushes the shot of Whiskey across the bar and I grab it. "Go ahead. Drink up." She winks.

Smirking, I hold the glass to my lips. She already knows how I work. "We've already had our night, Sarah." I tilt the glass back and run my tongue over my lips, slowly, just to remind her of how I pleasured her. This causes her to swallow hard and her breathing to pick up. "It was hot as fuck too." I slide the glass forward and stand up. "But it goes against my rules."

Her eyes linger down to the very noticeable bulge in my jeans. She smiles while running her finger over the empty glass. "Good to know I can at least still get you hard."

I toss down a twenty and start backing away. "Baby, you get every man hard." I point to the awkward looking guy that has been staring at her since I sat at the bar. "Especially that dude."

She glances at the scrawny dude with glasses and forces a smile. He smiles back and leans over the bar, awaiting conversation. "I so hate you, Slade," she growls and I love it. Growling turns me on.

"That's all right. I'm used to it."

She tosses a straw at me and I knock it away with my hand before turning around and making my way over to the bachelorette party.

The girls are tossing back drinks; some of them standing on tables while a few of them are watching from afar. Those are usually the married ones; the good girls. That's all right though, because I don't need to touch them to pleasure them. They'll still get off.

As I'm about to show my boys up, to my right, I notice two girls dancing and minding their own business. Instantly, my focus goes to the curvy body that is swaying back and forth, drawing my cock to instant attention. It's so seductive it makes my cock hurt.

Skin tight blue jeans mold to her every curve, making me imagine what it would be like to run my tongue over that tight little ass; to taste every inch of her.

Letting my dick do the talking, I walk up to the dance floor, grab the drink out of her hand and set it down on the table beside me.

She looks pissed off, but that's all right. Pissed is sexy as hell on her. It makes me want her more. Her eyes stray from the table I just set her glass on and land on my stomach. Then my chest. Then, slowly, up to my face. She swallows and a look of lust flashes in her eyes. She wants me and I haven't even done anything yet.

Holy fuck. She is beautiful.

My eyes trail from her long blond hair that stops just below her breasts up to her red pouty lips. Damn, I want to suck those between my lips. She's looking at me through long, thick lashes and even in the dimmed lighting; I can see that she has two different colored eyes. I can't make out the colors, but I can see the shade difference.

So fucking hot.

"Umm . . ." She smiles and runs her hand through her hair.

"Can I help you with something? We kind of have a private party going on here."

Taking a step closer, I lean in and brush my lips over her ear. "Yeah, I can help you with something," I whisper. "I can help you with a lot of things."

Her breathing picks up and I already know that I have her. It's that simple. "I'm sorry, but I don't even know you." She takes a step back, but her eyes trail down my body before coming back up to meet my face. She looks nervous. I love that. I can teach her a few things. "And I was drinking that."

I watch her with a smirk as she reaches for her drink and pretends to give me a dirty glare. It's not working on me though. I already know her body language and she's already let it slip that I do something to her. "I can give you something better than that."

Her tiny nostrils flare as her eyes rake back down my body, stopping on my fucking crotch. If that's what she wants then I'll give it to her. "Sorry, but I'm not interested. I'm just here for a friend's party."

She likes games. Good thing, because I like them too.

Closing the distance between our bodies, I cup her cheek in my hand. I bring my lips close to hers while looking her in the eyes. Her breath hitches as I press my body against hers and bring my eyes down to meet her lips. "Are you sure about that?"

Her lips begin to move as if she's about to respond and I have the sudden urge to suck them into my mouth; to own them. She's breathing heavy and I can feel the heat radiating from between her thighs that are pressed against my leg while I rub my thumb over her cheekbone.

I feel myself leaning closer until my bottom lip brushes hers. "You're fucking beautiful."

She takes in a quick burst of air and takes a step back. "Umm . . ."

"Slade!" A drunken female shrieks from behind me.

Shit. I hate shriekers.

Exhaling, I turn my head, but keep my eyes glued to the beautiful blond in front of me. For some reason, I don't want to take my eyes away.

Those lips. Fuck me, I want to fuck them. I want them wrapped around my cock.

"About time you got here." A dark haired woman with huge fake tits bounces in front of me and grabs my hand, pulling me away from the beauty in front of me. I see blondie's eyes glance down at my hand, but she quickly turns her head away and clears her throat as if embarrassed. "My favorite piece of eye candy is here." She throws her arms up and starts screaming while pulling me away. "Look everyone. It's fucking, Slade," she slurs.

Smiling to blondie as she watches me, I mouth, "You're mine later."

Her lips part and I can tell she just swallowed. I have her thinking about it. It's written all over her face. Her friend starts nudging her in the side until finally she pulls her eyes away from me and smiles nervously at her friend.

Shit, I've gotta have her. I won't stop until I do.

Spinning on my heel, I pick the brunette up by her hips and sit her down on the chair in front of us. She spreads wide for me and presses her hands against my chest as I step between her legs and slowly grind my hips to the music.

Placing one hand behind my head, I grip her neck with my other as I close the space between our bodies, grinding my hips in a slow, seductive movement as if I'm slowly fucking her.

She moans from beneath me as I let her hands explore my chest and abs. The women here like to touch and I like to give them what they want. It's my job to please them and I'm damn good at it.

"Take it off!" A few girls start screaming.

"Let us see your body. Come on!"

Absofuckinglutely.

Pulling the brunette's chin up, I look her in the eyes as I slowly pull my shirt over my head and toss it down beside me. Most women love it when I make them feel like I'm stripping just for them. It makes them feel special.

She bites her bottom lip as her hands go straight for the muscles leading down to my cock. The girls can never get enough of it; of both.

As much as I'm enjoying getting these women off, there's one woman in particular I want to get off and I'll be damned if I'm going to let her leave here unsatisfied.

CHAPTER THREE

Aspen

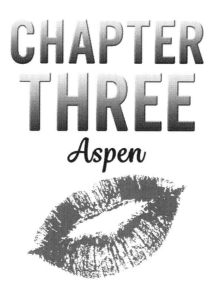

KAYLA KEEPS NUDGING ME TO get my attention, but for some reason I can't seem to drag my eyes away from the jerk-off that is practically dry humping some girl in the corner. She loves it too; over there moaning and rubbing her hands all over his body as if she's about to have an orgasm. How gross. Have some damn class. We aren't in the middle of a damn porn.

A stripper? I shake my head and snort. *A sexy as hell one too. Who the hell does he think he is getting that close to me?*

The bad part of it is, I think he may just be the sexiest man I have ever laid eyes on. Messy black hair that falls over his deep blue eyes and the perfect five o'clock shadow that surrounds a set of full lips. I can't forget that body of pure muscle that you could easily see through that firm fitting white T-shirt he had on. Now, it's off and . . . *crap.* He has me so worked up, I can barely breathe.

This is embarrassing.

Our lips were so close I could almost taste him. I imagine he probably tastes minty and fresh; perfectly refreshing. For some stupid reason, I had the urge to run my tongue over those full lips. They just looked so soft and inviting; calling me to feel them, suck them. The way he was looking at me; holy shit, it was like he was tasting me in a way I have never been tasted. I liked it. Dammit, why did I like it?

"Um . . . Aspen. Hello. Am I talking to my damn self? Snap out of it."

I suck in a deep breath and pull my eyes away from Mr. Sex himself. "What? I'm listening." I bring my eyes up to meet hers, but they quickly stray back over to *him* as I pretend to pay attention to her.

Brushing her burgundy locks over her shoulder, she rolls her eyes at me and grabs my hand. "Come on. Let's just get closer so you can drool over sexy stripper boy up close. There's nothing to be ashamed of. Stop being so shy. We're here to have fun."

I huff and pull my hand out of her grip. There's no way I'm going over there and giving him the pleasure of seeing me watching him. I'm only here because Paige is getting married. Hell, I'm not even watching *Cale* and I've known him for years. I'll just stay where I'm at. No thank you.

"I'm good, Kayla. I'm not getting in the middle of that orgasm fest. It's pathetic." I hold my drink up and grin. "This is all the pleasure I need while I'm here. Simple as that." I take a huge gulp as my eyes once again land on him and *oh God, that ass.*

His jeans are now hanging half way down his ass, showing his muscular butt cheeks through his white boxer briefs. The busty woman in front of him is desperately tugging on the front of his jeans, working on pulling them down his body. I don't blame her. I want to take them off with my teeth.

Crap, my mind is in the gutter.

Placing his hands behind her head, he pulls her face down by his crotch as he starts grinding his hips up and down in perfect rhythm to the song playing. It's a slow, seductive song that makes me think about sex. Yup, I'm definitely thinking about sex now.

Just as I think he's about to actually let this woman publicly suck his dick or something, he grips her by the hips and pulls her up to her feet. Slowly, he makes his way behind her and his eyes land on me and they stay there, locked with mine.

What the . . . why? Stop looking at me.

I tug on the collar of my white blouse and without meaning to I start fanning myself off. He smiles at this, knowing exactly what he's doing to me. He's doing this on purpose.

Cocky jerk.

Bending the girl over, he grips her hair in one hand and pulls her neck back while grinding his hips on her ass. His eyes bore into mine as he shakes himself out of his jeans and lets all of his sexiness consume us. Yes, he is damn sexy and he knows it. That just pisses me off more. His legs are thick and muscular; covered with random tattoos and every muscle in his body is well sculpted.

Now that he's facing me it's easy to see his defined chest and abs flexing as he moves with the music. The muscles leading down to his briefs are staring at me, flexing with each sway of his hips; calling out to be touched and licked. *Mmm yes. I want a taste . . .*

Holy hell, he's in shape; like a fitness model. Plus, he has random tattoos inked across his chest, sides, lower stomach and arms as well. Hell, he has tattoos all over and it makes him even hotter. They glisten as the perspiration forms on his skin.

He's staring at me, while practically having sex with this girl with his clothes on. Still, I'm standing here watching as if it were me.

What is wrong with me?

I feel myself start to sweat and get a tingling sensation between my thighs as he bites his bottom lip and starts thrusting hard and deep while his eyes devour me. Well, at least I imagine it would be really deep. I can't deny that I bet it would feel so good.

He must notice me sweating because he laughs a little and steps away from the girl that is still bent over with her ass in the air. Ignoring all the girls screaming for him, he starts walking with meaning; unstoppable. With each step, he gets closer and closer to me.

My body is shaking just from his presence and my breathing picks up. I hate my body right now.

His eyes are intense; telling me he wants me as his. A part of me almost wants to give in just from that look alone.

My eyes slowly leave his eyes, searching my way down his muscular body and landing right on his hard dick.

Oh. My. God.

You can see everything through his tight briefs. The thickness of his dick and even the shape of its head. The whole package. He's so . . . hard.

Stopping in front of me, he smirks and tilts his head down toward his cock. My eyes are betraying me. *Damn bastards.* They won't move away. "You know, it's against the rules, but I would let you touch it if you wanted to."

Shaking my head, I pull my eyes away and slam back the rest of my drink. This is my third one and I'm a lightweight; probably not a good thing. I take a step back as he takes a step closer. Clearing my throat, I ask, "Touch what?"

Reaching out, he grabs my hand and places it on the V of muscles that lead down to his briefs, slowly sliding it down his sweaty, slick body. "My cock," he whispers.

My body clenches from his words and I hate it. Yanking my hand away, I grab Kayla by the arm and slam my empty glass down onto the table beside me. I need to get out of here. "Thanks for the offer, playboy, but I'm here to meet a friend and like I said, I'm not interested."

Smirking, he takes a step back as Cale slaps him on the shoulder. "Dude, back away from our temporary roommate. You're freaking Aspen the fuck out, Sir Dick a lot."

I see the smile in his eyes as if he's got me right where he wants me now and he looks like a man that always gets what he wants. Running his tongue over his bottom lip, he backs away slowly, keeping his eyes on me the whole time, until disappearing back into his crowd of fan girls.

Cale gives me a quick hug and apologizes. "Sorry about him. Just ignore him and you'll be fine." He starts backing away and smiles. "We'll catch up later, I promise."

"All right, pretty boy," I call out. "Better hurry and get back to your crazy fan girls."

Cale is the definition of pretty. Short blond hair, striking green eyes and the sweetest dimpled smile you'll ever see. I will never understand why my sister has never hooked up with him.

Turning to Kayla, I let out a deep breath and instantly turn red with embarrassment as she starts laughing. "What!" I yell.

She smirks and pretends like she's giving a blowjob.

"Stop that! You dirty, bitch." I push her shoulder and she laughs. "I need another drink."

She turns toward Slade, dancing his dick off in the middle of some girls. "I would need a drink after that too. Holy shit! That is one fine piece of ass." She starts pulling me towards the bar. "Plus, you need to get your mind off a certain someone," she says to remind me. "Relax a little."

"Yeah," I breathe. "Probably so. I'm not going to let it bring me down this week."

When we reach the bar, the pretty bartender smiles at me and shakes her head.

Wondering if she's laughing at me for some reason, I take a seat on the stool in front of me and give her a hard look. Slade has me all kinds of feisty at the moment and I can't believe he's Cale's roommate. Not good. "What?" I narrow my eyes at her as she reaches for an empty glass.

Scooping up some ice, she looks over my shoulder and laughs again. "Honey, no one turns Slade down. Are you insane? That is one piece of ass that you don't want to miss out on. Trust me."

Trying my best not to look behind me, I fail. I should kick my own ass. I glance over my shoulder to see Slade staring at me while using his shirt to wipe the sweat off his chest. He slowly moves it down his body as if teasing me.

Crap! He even looks sexy doing that.

I growl under my breath and ignore what she just said. Obviously, he's a man whore. "Just give me another drink, please. Make it strong."

The bartender tilts her head and goes about her business. Thank goodness because I really don't want to think about that half naked, sexy asshole anymore.

"Right on," Kayla says happily. "It's a good thing I'm driving your ass around."

"Probably a very good thing right now," I say softly, trying to get my thoughts in check.

After setting eyes on the sexiest asshole I have ever seen, I have a feeling I'm going to need help if I'm going to be in the same house with *him* for the next week.

Crap, I'm in for a ride.

CHAPTER FOUR

Slade

MY NIGHT WAS MADE WHEN Cale said those three little fucking words. *Our temporary roommate.* Apparently, she lives in Rockford and is planning to stay here in Chicago as a bit of a break from home. He wouldn't tell me why and I could care less. It's none of my business. I don't mind sharing my bed; although, Cale will probably offer his to be nice.

That damn pussy.

The look on Aspen's face when she realized she'll be spending the next week in the same house as me was fucking priceless; a dead giveaway that she finds me tempting.

Damn, my cock is hard.

Pushing my cock down, I adjust my jeans and moan.

"Dude, what the shit!" Cale looks over from the driver side and scowls. "Don't tell me you're thinking about fucking her."

Playing stupid, I cross my hands behind my head and laugh. Of course, I'm thinking about fucking her. "Who?"

Cale lets out a long huff and pulls into the driveway. "Fucking, Aspen, you dipshit. She doesn't need you messing with her right now."

I push the car door open and step out before slamming it behind me. When Cale catches up to me, I laugh and lean against the door as a little red Chrysler Sebring pulls up behind my truck. Since I've had a few shots, I made Cale drive us home. I never drive after I've had a few drinks. One of my small list of rules, I never break. They were created for my own good.

"Every girl needs me messing with her; especially that one."

I nod toward Aspen as she steps out of the car looking like a fucking Victoria's Secret model. The sexy, curvy kind that you want to run your tongue over every inch of flesh and savor the fucking taste. You don't just want this woman for dessert. You want her for breakfast, lunch, and dinner too. Any average guy would. Good thing I'm not your average guy.

Aspen

OH HELL. WOULD SOMEONE PLEASE make him stop looking at me like that? He stares at me; burning his eyes into my body, like he's about to rip my clothes off and pound me against a wall somewhere. It's so distracting.

Don't let him get to you. Don't let him get to you.

Taking a deep breath, I close the car door behind me, wave to Kayla and start walking to the porch of Cale's two bedroom home. I've been here before as a guest, but it was back before Cale had a roommate. I have known Cale for years because he and my sister were best friends growing up. He's a good guy and I love him like a brother. I was excited to come here, but now . . . I'm not so sure.

Before I can even step onto the porch, I can see Slade's eyes burning into mine. Hell, I can almost feel them. They're so dark and broody. Is everything about this guy so intense?

I bet sex is.

Mentally slapping myself, I shake off the thought and walk over to Cale. He wraps his arms around me and squeezes me in his usual hug. "Oh man. I've missed you," I say. "Thanks for letting me crash here. You have no idea how much you are helping me out."

Shaking me roughly, he lets go and kisses my forehead. "I missed you too, gorgeous. My house is yours whenever you need it. No need to even ask. You know that."

When I turn back to Slade his eyes look me up and down, branding me into the portals of his memory. He's undressing me with his eyes like he's formulating a plan of attack in his mind; the ultimate predator. I feel it; everywhere. He knows it too. He's a pro at this game.

Now that we're in the lighting of the porch, I can see a scar on his right cheekbone. He catches me staring and lets out a little growl before turning and opening the door to let us in.

I follow behind Cale, in a hurry to get this night over with. I'm so tired I can barely keep my eyes open. I want to ask where I'm sleeping, but I'm afraid Slade might have too much fun with that.

I take a glance around the house to see it looks exactly the same as before: Black furniture, black curtains, sixty inch TV with a huge surround sound. Pretty much everything manly. This place really needs a woman's touch; just not mine.

"So . . ." I lift my eyebrows at Cale, hoping he gets the hint as Slade walks into the kitchen. He doesn't. He just looks at me and raises his eyebrows back in question. One of the things I've learned about Cale is he never gets the hint, ever.

"What do you want to do now?" As the words leave Cale's lips, he then glares over at Slade as he walks back into the living room, shirtless, with a bottle of Whiskey pressed to his lips. "Oh boy."

Slade pulls the bottle away from his mouth and smiles a devilishly sexy smile that makes me wet. "You don't need to ask her that. She wants to come up to my room so I can bend her over my desk and fuck her."

I wrinkle my forehead in shock and anger at him being so outspoken and straight forward.

Seriously!

Taking the only thing I can think of in my outburst of anger, I toss my phone at his head; better that than my favorite heels. He dodges just in time and leans against the couch. The muscles in his arms and stomach flex as he holds the bottle up and takes another swig. "You're a real piece of work. Do you know that?"

"So I've been told," he says stiffly. "You haven't seen anything yet. The next time you're ready to inflict pain, you better be ready to follow through. I'll show you what a real fucking piece of work I am, then."

"You asshole! I will . . ." Bending over, I reach for my high heel and almost fall over. Cale reaches for my arm and steadies me. We'll see what he says when I stab him with my stiletto.

"Whoa, whoa." He turns to Slade and gives him the nastiest look I've ever seen on Cale's pretty face. "Dude, I told you to leave her alone. If she kicks your ass, that's on you. Then, I'll kick your ass just for pissing her off."

I feel my nostrils flare in anger as I find myself checking out Slade's sexy body. His faded jeans are fitted and hanging low on his slender waist. I swear I could kill him just for being so sexy. *That asshole.*

"All right. Your loss, Pen."

Without glancing back, he heads for the stairs and I watch in utter shock as he holds my phone up, smiles and tosses it to me. "You're going to make hating you easy," I growl. "And don't call me Pen, man whore."

"I've heard worse," he says calmly. "Oh and I texted your friend Kayla and asked her to join me tonight."

That prick!

Pulling my eyes from his muscular back, I turn to Cale and growl. Yes, I growled. I am so pissed, I could scream at poor Cale.

"I'm sorry. I'll get his ass in check by the morning." Leading me toward the back of the house, he rubs my shoulders and kisses the top of my head. "You can take my room. I cleaned the sheets for you last night. I'll sleep on the couch so you don't get mauled like a bear in your sleep."

Thankful, I exhale and give his muscular frame a hug. I would kiss him if it wouldn't be so weird. "Thanks. I appreciate that. I hope there's a lock on the door now." I look at him with a raised eyebrow, remembering the image of me walking in on him getting sucked off by some girl once. That was awkward.

Laughing, he pushes me into the room and starts closing the door as he takes a step back. "Don't worry, he won't come into my room. He's just being an ass because he's used to all the girls wanting him. I'll keep my eye on him." He rubs his chest and yawns. "I'm crashing."

"Goodnight," I mumble.

As soon as Cale is out of the room, I clutch my phone in my hand and scroll through my text messages. I take a deep breath and exhale when I see that he was lying about texting Kayla. For some reason that pissed me off. The thought of him having sex with her is not something I want to picture.

I strip down to my panties and bra and make a quick phone

call while hopping into Cale's bed.

The phone rings a few times and just when I think it's about to go to voicemail, he picks up.

"Hello," Jay yells into the phone. I can barely hear him over the loud music. My heart sinks just knowing what he's up to.

"Jay, are you busy?" I ask with a sigh.

It takes a second before he answers and all I can make out is a female giggling. "Yeah, Aspen. I'm a little busy right now."

I don't say anything for a few seconds. I just listen to his heavy breathing and the sound of her whispering and then giggling. I feel like puking.

"All right. I just wanted to say goodnight." I grind my jaw, trying my best not to cry.

"Okay, goodnight. I'll try to talk to you tomorrow night. Right now is just bad timing. You should really be sleeping by now."

"Yeah." I sigh. "You're right. I am pretty tired. Talk to you later."

Pulling the phone away from my ear, I hit the end button and curl myself into Cale's nice warm blankets. What I wouldn't give to be wrapped up in someone's arms right now. I make myself sick just for wanting it. I just really need an escape from myself right now.

What a shitty night.

CHAPTER FIVE

Slade

SITTING ON THE EDGE OF my bed, I run my hands over my face and close my eyes. I didn't sleep for shit as usual and I have a headache from hell. I've been sitting here, awake for the last two hours, but I can't seem to bring myself to move from this spot. It's eating at me deep today. The pain; it's fucking killing me. Some days are harder than others and I really need to work to get my shit in check.

I let out a deep breath and slip on a pair of my boxer briefs before making my way down the hallway and downstairs. The house is still dark and I can hear Cale snoring from the couch. I'm not surprised, because I'm always the first one up. Like I said, I'm not much of a sleeper. It's the one thing that comes difficult for me.

After slamming back a glass of water, I slip into the bathroom and close the door behind me. I stand there, staring at my reflection in the small, darkened room. The only light shining through is from the small beam coming from the slightly part-ed shades. It's just enough lighting to let my eyes fall on the scar across my cheekbone. It's not very big.

Fuck, it should be bigger.

Placing my hands in front of me, I grip the sink and lean over it. I feel my breathing pick up as the emotions swarm through me; awakening the madness that I keep buried deep. I have an urge to put my fist through this mirror to stop the pain, but I won't. My hands are already scarred up enough. Anger and rage only douse the pain, but doesn't stop it.

I get distracted when I hear a noise coming from the hallway and then the bathroom door is pushed open. I slowly tilt my head to the side to see Aspen standing there in only a T-shirt.

Shit. She is damn sexy.

She takes a step back when she notices the look on my face. I would too. I'm a monster. The concern in her eyes makes my heart skip a beat and I have no idea why. She doesn't even know me, but she's looking at me as if I'm transparent; seeing straight through to my damaged soul. I don't like it one bit.

"I'm sorry." She pulls her eyes away from mine and tugs on the hem of her T-shirt, causing my eyes to trail down her legs and my grip on the sink tightens. "I didn't realize anyone was in here. It was dark and the door wasn't shut all the way."

Pushing away from the sink, I get my emotions in check and walk toward the door. If I wasn't feeling like shit, I would hit on her right now and tell her all the things I want to do to that beauti-ful body. I should, but I can't. I've let my inner thoughts take over and pull me down; remind me of the piece of shit that I really am. I know it, everyone else knows it and I've accepted it.

"It's cool. I was just going to take a shower, but I'll let you have it first." I wait for a response. When she doesn't say anything,

SLADE

I stand and turn, now standing in front of her. I grip onto the top of the doorframe and look her in the eyes. I can't tell which one I like more; the blue one or the deep green one. They're stunning. "It's all yours if you want it."

Her eyes dart down to my chest and she swallows before shaking her head and turning away. "It's fine. I can wait. I was just going to take a quick shower and see if Cale would run me to Kayla's. It's not a big deal. He's still sleeping anyways. I'll just go and let you-"

"I'll take you," I say, stopping her mid-sentence while gripping the doorframe tighter. "I have to go to the club here in a bit anyways. I'm filling in for Sarah behind the bar for a few hours."

She looks a bit surprised and not sure if she wants to take me up on the offer. That bothers me for some reason yet I don't know why. "It's fine. You don't have to. I'll just wait. You were already in here anyways."

Releasing the doorframe, I take a step closer and slowly run my hands down her sides, tracing every curve through the thin material. *Fuck, she feels so good.* My hands stop amidst her hips and I squeeze, pulling her body to press against mine. My cock hardens against her stomach and she sucks in a deep breath, but doesn't pull away. A part of her wants this and the more I look at her, the more I fucking want her; a distraction. Fucked up or not, I can't deny that I *need* this distraction, addiction, necessity or whatever else you may want to call it. I've gotten used to the harsh judgments of my lifestyle.

"We can take a shower together." I brush my lips over her neck and whisper, "I can dirty you with my body and then clean you with my tongue."

She tilts her neck and allows me to run my tongue up it as if that's the pass code to her arousal. She likes it. I can tell by her soft moans. "Have you thought about what my cock will feel like inside you?" I suck in her earlobe and bring my hands down to cup her

33

ass. It's the perfect fit. "I want to fuck you. I want you to know what it feels like to have me deep." I lick my lips and breathe into her ear. "Inside you."

Her chest pushes out as she takes a deep breath. "I don't even know you." She places her hands on my chest and backs away. "Plus, I don't like you. Now, if you don't mind. *One* of us has to take a shower first. You or me? Pick one."

She presses her legs together and I can tell she's trying to hide that I have her pussy aching for my touch. She's wet and ready for me. I don't have to check; I just know. That's okay 'cause my cock wants it just as much.

Enjoying watching her squirm, I smile and lean into the doorframe. "I'm going to take care of that for you."

Her eyes watch mine as I look down at her black panties that are barely peeking out from under what I assume is one of Cale's old shirts. For some reason, the thought of stripping her out of another man's shirt turns me on; gives me a rush knowing I can.

She watches me intently, but doesn't say a word as I grab the bottom of the T-shirt and slowly lift it over her head and toss it behind me. She's standing there in just her thong and bra. Her breasts are plump and firm, squeezed into a tiny black bra to match her panties; her cleavage playing peek-a-boo. My cock instantly strains to break free from the material as I imagine dropping to my knees in front of her and devouring her fucking pussy; the perfect breakfast.

Running my hand up her tight little stomach, I press her up against the wall with my hand above her head. "Touch yourself for me."

She's hesitant at first, but nervously licks her lips as she slides her hand down the front of her panties, her eyes never leaving mine.

"That's it. I bet it feels so fucking good." I press into her with my body as I squeeze her hip. She takes her eyes away from mine, so I grab her chin and pull her face to meet mine. "Don't turn away. Look at me while you touch yourself." I lick my lips in satisfaction as she does what I say. "Does your pussy feel good, baby?"

She nods her head and places her bottom lip between her teeth as she starts moving her hand up and down.

"I bet. Now imagine it were my fingers fucking your tight little pussy and rubbing your swollen clit. So thick and firm, filling you up as I pleasure you." Her hand quickens as she closes her eyes and moans. "That's it. You like the thought of me pleasuring you, don't you? Fuck yourself harder. I want to fucking hear your pussy wet for me."

Her breathing picks up and she begins shaking as if she's about to have an orgasm. She stops abruptly and opens her eyes, staring into mine. "What the hell am I doing?" Pulling her hand out of her panties, she places her hands against the wall behind her and looks down at my hard cock with longing. I can see the want in her eyes, but she's fighting it for some reason. "I'm not doing this. This is beyond messed up."

Grabbing her hand, I lift it and slowly suck her wet fingers into my mouth, tasting her. I suck her fingers clean while looking her directly in the eyes. *Oh fuck*. My cock just got harder. "Damn, baby. You taste so good. I can fucking taste your frustration and need. Why not let me ease that frustration; show you what it's like to have me taste you, suck you, and fuck you."

I smile against her fingers before placing my hand in the back of her hair and pulling her mouth towards mine. Just as I'm about to kiss her, she turns her head away and sidesteps around me. "Don't call me baby and I shouldn't have done that. Now get out so I can take a shower."

She looks away embarrassed as I lick my lips one last time, tasting her on my mouth. Without saying a word, I turn around and walk out of the bathroom.

I could tell by the nervous look on her face that even she can't believe she just did that in front of me. I could also tell by the look in her eyes that she wanted me to stay. She wants me and I'm going to show her it's okay to have me.

TWO HOURS LATER AND HERE I am, leaning against my motorcycle, watching with satisfaction as Aspen exits the house with a look of frustration. She looks so tense and . . . unpleased. Sickly enough, this pleases me.

Judging from her hour long shower, I would say she definitely couldn't please herself without my help. That only gives me more reason to want to please her. To show her how I can make her feel.

Crossing my legs in front of me I smile as she approaches and gives me a look so dirty, I might just need another shower. I don't think she understands what that look does to me. It's so damn sexy. "Did you have a good shower?" Tossing my helmet up, I catch it and hold it out for her to grab. "I would've finished you off; gave you the best orgasm of your life."

"Shut up," she growls. Rolling her eyes she exhales while looking at the helmet in my hand. "Seriously? You want me to get on that? Why not take the truck?"

Since she refuses to take the helmet, I slide it on her head and rev the engine. "Just get on. I don't have all day."

She shakes her head once before throwing her leg over the motorcycle and hopping on behind me. "You think this shit is funny, don't you? What you did back there."

I look over my shoulder at her sullen face and smirk. "What?"

"You know what I'm talking about. Don't play stupid, *Slade*," she growls. "You did that on purpose."

"What did I do? I want to fucking hear it."

She gives me a dirty look and runs her tongue over her teeth in frustration. "Nothing. Nothing at all, okay."

"All right. Then, I apologize for doing nothing at all. Happy?"

She lets out an exasperated huff before grabbing my shoulder with her left hand and placing her other hand behind her, keeping her distance. "Let's just go. Kayla is waiting on me."

"Grab my waist," I say firmly. When she doesn't make a move to grab me, I reach for both of her arms and wrap them around my waist. She stiffens as if she doesn't know what to do. "Keep your arms around me. Got it."

If she's not worried about her safety then she can walk. It's as simple as that.

"Fine. Let's just get this over with." Locking her fingers around my waist, she tilts her head to the left. "Go down to the light and make a left. Then go ten blocks and make a right. All right. Be careful too. I want to actually make it there before she has to go to work."

Swallowing back my remark, I take off causing her to squeeze her arms around me for safety. I smile to myself, feeling the awkwardness in her touch. She definitely needs to loosen up and give into her needs.

After a few minutes of riding in silence her arms finally start to relax and I can feel them inching higher, getting closer to my chest.

Every time I make a turn or pass someone, I can hear a little gasp from her as my muscles tighten from below her hands. She's trying hard to hide it, but I can tell she wants to explore. It gives me a fucking rush.

About five minutes later, we pull up to a little white house to see her friend outside waiting on her. The red car from the other night is sitting in the driveway and it makes me wonder why she didn't just ask her friend to pick her up if she hates me so much.

As soon as I stop the bike, she jumps off and takes my helmet off as fast as her fingers will allow her. She tosses it in my lap and scowls. "Thanks for the ride, jerk."

Smiling at her and her hot little friend, I slide the helmet on my head. "Anytime." I look down toward her pussy. "And thanks for the show." I wink and she looks away embarrassed. I can feel her eyes burning into me as I take off. Hell, I don't mind. She can undress me with her eyes anytime she wants.

WHEN I PULL UP AT the bar, it's completely empty. I toss my cigarette and jump off my motorcycle while looking around, preparing myself. This is a shit shift and you don't make crap at this time. The bar opens at eleven, but really the business doesn't take off until late at night when the entertainment comes in.

I don't mind doing Sarah favors, though, because she has a young child and I want her to be able to be there for him when it's needed. That shit is very important. If anyone else asked me to cover this crap shift, my answer would be hell no.

Now, I'll be stuck here for the next few hours practically talking to myself and hoping for someone to stop in and entertain me. Not my idea of a good day. It gives you too much time to think.

Hilary has already been here and has left. I can tell as soon as I unlock the back door and walk in. The lights are all turned on and the bar is set up and ready to go.

Hilary is the owner. She's an older woman, maybe in her early fifties. She only stops in once a day and usually it's when no one is here. She's good at what she does, though, and helps out whenever she can. I really like her as a person and a manager. She treats us well.

A couple hours into my shift, a woman around my age, mid-twenties, finally comes into the bar and takes a seat in front of me.

I've seen her in here a few times before and I have to admit that I've thought about taking her home. She's a natural redhead with a small freckled nose, full lips and a nice set of breasts. She looks sexy as fuck in those tight little suit skirts. She has to work in some office somewhere. I like the thought of dirtying her. She looks like she needs a good fuck to relieve some of the tension she is carrying around.

Taking a seat in front of me, she smiles and sets her purse down beside her. "I'm taking a quick break from work. Give me a drink of your choice. Anything will do." Her eyes rake over my body as I reach for a glass and come her way. There's a look saying she's looking for what I call the fuck and fly; short and hard. It's more of a business exchange between two people. I'm used to the look; prone to it. "I'm going to cut to the chase, okay. I don't have a lot of time, but I have a little time." She smirks while watching me with desperate eyes.

I'm listening . . .

Reaching for a bottle of Jack, I pour it half way up and add a splash of coke and a little lime juice. It may be a little strong, but she looks like she can handle it. She looks like she can handle a lot of things.

Setting the drink down in front of her, I lean over the bar as she reaches for my shirt and pulls me to her. "I've heard a lot of good things about your *dick*. I need to release some tension and I want you to *fuck* me. Can you do that? Nothing more. I'm a very busy woman."

I let my lips brush over her ear before whispering, "For the things I do, you would need a lot more than just a little time." I place my hand behind her neck and pull her closer to my lips. "I would tie you up to my bed, blindfold you and devour your pussy with my tongue. Then when I was done, I would stand you up against my wall, bind your hands above you and fuck you until you can't walk. I would tease you slowly at first to learn your body and what it wants. Then I would fuck you so hard and thoroughly you will never want another cock. I don't think that is what you're looking for. Trust me, it's not easy moving on to just a quick lay after that."

A throat clears from nearby.

"I see you're still on the prowl, son."

Gritting my teeth, I pull away from the redhead and bring my eyes up to meet the one man I wish I could stay away from: my father. He's more like the devil in a fucking suit. He's standing there as if he's so fucking perfect and can't do any wrong. It pisses me the hell off.

"What are you doing here?" I begin finding things to do; pretending to be busy. The last thing I want to do is deal with him at the moment.

Stepping up to the bar, he fixes his tie and takes a seat. "Do I need to have a reason to come see my son? We haven't spoken in over two months."

Walking over to stand in front of him, I lean down and get in his face. "We both know why too. Don't come in here acting as if it's my fault. Get out of here with that shit."

"Son, calm down." Pulling out his wallet he searches through it. "I'll take a Scotch on the rocks."

Rolling my neck to keep my tongue in check, I make him his drink. I set it down in front of him and lean against the register while watching him sip on it.

He makes a sour face while setting the glass back down. "I see not much has changed since the last time we've talked." I watch him with anger while he adjusts his tie as if he's better than me. "When will you realize this lifestyle isn't going to change anything? It won't make things better."

Gripping the counter, I lean over the register and turn my head away. I can't stand to look at him. "Don't even say it. I don't need to hear this shit. I'm fine with my life. Why don't you get back to yours and stop worrying about mine? Don't fucking judge me."

We both look over as the redhead slams back her drink and stands up. "I'm out, boys." She looks at me and winks. "Maybe another time."

I don't say anything. I just watch as she leaves. I'm glad, because she doesn't need to hear this.

"You don't think I'm concerned about my son? That I don't see that you've thrown your life down the drain? It pisses me off." He takes another sip and then scoots it across the bar. "You're better than this. Just because-"

"Don't you fucking say it," I growl out at him in warning and shake the counter.

"I'm just telling you that there's still meaning in your life and you need to find that again. The pain will never go away. I get that but-"

"Fucking stop! Do you understand me?" My voice comes out firmly. "Don't you say another word about it. It's done. Over. I've moved on."

Looking me in the eyes, he stands up and picks up his glass for me to see. "This is what you call moving on? A career as a bartender that strips on the weekends and has meaningless sex with any tramp you can slip your dick into. No, son. This is not moving on. It's fucking numbing the pain."

Grinding my jaw, I swing my hand across the counter, knocking over the bottle of Scotch along with a bunch of other items like limes, straws, and cocktail napkins.

"You just don't know when to stop, do you? This is why we don't talk. This is why I stay away. You won't let me live." Turning to leave, he stops and throws down some money. "No, I'm trying to help you live and stop being a piece of shit. Get your shit together before it's too late. You're twenty six years old for fucks sake. Act like it."

I hear him walking away, but I refuse to look his direction and show him just how worked up I am. He always fucking does this; acts as if he knows what I'm going through or how the fuck I feel and *should* feel. No one does.

Fighting to catch my breath and calm down, I lean over the bar and grip the front of my hair in my hands. I feel like going fucking mad right now. Today is not a good day to think about this shit.

I'm pissed. Pissed at my father and pissed at myself for knowing he's right.

Picking up a bottle of Vodka, I toss it across the room at the wall. It shatters against the wall, leaving the clear liquid dripping on the floor. It doesn't do shit to calm me down though. So, I just stand there and stare at the ceiling.

"Well . . . I see it's extremely busy in here today."

I look over with narrowed eyes to see Aspen walk in. She's no longer wearing her clothes from yesterday. Now, she's wearing a pair of faded jean shorts and a white tank top that shows the pink outline of her bra. She must've had her clothes in Kayla's car. She looks . . . good. This look fits her.

Exhaling, I stand up straight and gesture around me. "Yeah, really busy. I hope you're not here for a drink because I might not be able to handle making you one," I say sarcastically.

She leans against the front of the bar and starts fingering the remaining napkins. "I'm here because Kayla had to go to work and Cale isn't home. I don't have a key to get in and he didn't pick up the phone." She looks down at the mess by my feet and then looks up at me. "I suppose you could use a little company anyways."

"I guess," I mumble. "Doesn't look like I have much of a choice." I reach for a glass and scoop it full of ice. "Want a drink?"

"Just a Sprite will be fine. I only drink when I'm out at parties. It's kind of my thing. I'm a lightweight."

I watch her as she sits down in front of me and chews on her lip. "Are you nervous?" I study her reaction to the question that is making her cheeks turn red.

Shaking her head, she reaches for the glass after I finish filling it and pulls it to her lips. "Why would I be nervous? You think you make me nervous? No. You just make me mad. Those are two different things."

Nodding my head in agreement, I say, "You're not the only one."

I'm used to it. Hell, I'm pissed at myself most of the time.

She laughs under her breath and sticks the tip of the straw into her mouth. "I bet there are a lot of pissed off women running around this world due to you. I just get that vibe."

Challenging her, I lean over the bar and pull the straw out of her mouth with my tongue, being sure to get close to her mouth. "Oh yeah," I whisper. "What kind of *vibe* is it that you get from me?"

Backing away, she watches my mouth as I chew on her straw. She clears her throat and averts her eyes when she sees that I notice her staring. "A bad one," she replies.

I stand up and spit out the straw when I see Cale walk in. "Dude, what are you doing here?" For some reason the thought of him being here to pick Aspen up pisses me off.

"Sarah called and said she won't be able to make it to work at all today because her son's doctor appointment is taking longer than she expected. Figuring you wouldn't want the full shift, I offered to come in until seven."

He walks up behind Aspen, wraps his arms around her and squeezes. "Hey, gorgeous. What are you doing here?"

She places her hands on his arms and smiles. "Hey, pretty boy," she says teasingly. "I couldn't reach you earlier so I had Kayla drop me off here."

Looking up from behind Aspen, Cale gives me a concerned look. "Yeah, so your dad stopped by this morning, but judging from the look of this place he's already been here too," he says looking down at the ground.

"I don't even want to hear it. Thanks for the fucking warning."

Cale releases Aspen and steps behind the bar. "I didn't say shit. He must've figured it out on his own. It's pretty simple to find your ass."

A few guys walk in and take a seat next to Aspen at the bar. I notice the preppy, clean cut one staring at her with a creepy ass smile and I have the urge to shove my fist down his throat.

He better not try to pick her up. She doesn't need a guy like that. She needs one that is going to fuck her good and please her so good that it hurts. He looks like too much of a pussy to handle her.

"Hey," he says to Aspen. "Alex."

Cale starts talking to me, but my attention stays focused on *Alex* to be sure he doesn't sign his fucking death wish.

"Aspen." She shakes his hand and then looks away uncomfortable.

Cale nudges me as he goes to approach the guys. "Get your ass out of here. I got it from here. Hemy will be coming in around four so it's all good."

"Huh," I mumble. I pull my eyes away from Aspen and look up at Cale.

"I got it, man. Aspen can hang out here while I work so she doesn't have to be at the house by herself. I'm sure you have shit to do."

Looking back toward Aspen, I notice the creepy guy has somehow gotten closer. Cale is taking their drink order and he doesn't even notice. Seriously?

"No, man. Aspen is coming with me. I don't have shit to do."

Aspen looks up and watches as I clock out.

"Come on. We're leaving."

She looks at me for a second as if she didn't hear me right.

Grabbing my helmet, I walk around to the other side of the bar and reach for her hand, pulling her up to her feet. "Let's go."

Cale and the creepy dude give me a weird look, but I could care less. I'm not leaving her here with that fucking preppy douche.

Aspen looks like she's about to say something until I look her in the eyes and clench my jaw. Instead, she turns beside her to look at Cale. "I'll see you when you get home."

He gives me a warning look before turning to Aspen. "Don't let this dick get to you. If he does, let me know." He turns back to me and scowls. "And don't worry, asshole. I'll clean up your mess."

Waving him off, I walk her out of the bar. When we get to my bike, I toss her my helmet while straddling my bike. "Get on."

CHAPTER SIX

Aspen

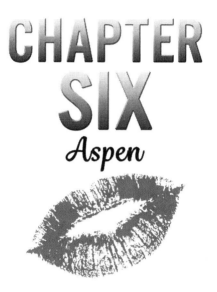

SITTING ON THE BACK OF Slade's motorcycle with my arms wrapped around his waist is the last thing I thought I'd be doing right now. Just earlier I wanted to rip his hair out and choke him, but I have a feeling he might like that type of thing. I might even like doing it to him. That's the sad part.

Since leaving the club, we've been riding for the last hour in dead silence. I have a feeling he needs this at the moment and hell, I do too. It's relaxing having the cool breeze hit against your skin as you ride with no worries; not knowing where you're going or where you'll end up at. The only problem is - it feels like it's about to rain. I can smell it and almost taste it.

Yup, here it comes. Perfect timing.

Holding on tighter, I bring my body closer to his as the rain suddenly hits, pouring off the helmet and soaking my shirt. It's cool. Cooler than I expected, giving me instant chills. My nipples harden as the fabric of my now wet shirt rubs against them. Maybe it wasn't the best idea to go with lace today.

Slade tilts his head up, takes a deep breath and slowly releases it. I can feel his body tensing beneath my arms and I feel myself unintentionally squeeze tighter as he makes a quick right. He rides down a path hidden beneath the trees until finally making a stop in the middle of nowhere.

Grabbing for my hand, he helps me off the bike before he quickly hops off and yanks his gray T-shirt over his head and holds it above me. He slowly backs me up until we're standing below a huge tree, hidden from the rain.

He's standing there soaked, looking at me through long, wet lashes. He has the most amazing blue eyes I have ever seen. I want to pull my gaze away, but I can't. I'm hypnotized. As much as I hate to admit it, he's so damn beautiful; dangerously beautiful. His black hair is wet and slicked back from the rain. It's thick and slightly long. I love that. The focal point is those lips. *Oh God, those lips*. The rain is falling on them, beading, and dripping down. With each drop that falls, it causes him to keep using his tongue to dry them. It's so damn distracting.

"Here. Use this." I pull my eyes away from his lips and take hold of his shirt, holding it above my head. "It's not a damn umbrella, but it will help."

He turns away and walks out into the open, but stops to stand in the pouring rain. I watch as he runs his hands over his face, the rain pouring over his head and arms while soaking his jeans. His bare chest is moving up and down as if he's trying to fight some deep emotions and with each move, his muscles flex, making me very aware of his sex appeal. It's confusing. I don't know if I want to hug him, slap him or fuck him. All I know is that I definitely want to be doing something to him.

After a few minutes of him just standing there, I walk away from the safety of the tree and hold his shirt above both of our heads. By now, it's completely drenched and not serving much of a purpose, but I don't take notice. Someone else has captured my attention. I'm standing on the tip of my toes, trying my best not to lose my balance and fall into him.

It takes him a moment, but he finally turns around. Looking me in the eyes, he reaches for his shirt and throws it down beside him. His eyes are intense; dark. "I need to finish what I started," he growls. He takes a step forward and I take a step back, but his stride is wider than mine. He leans in close to my ear and whispers, "I've been craving your pussy all fuckin' day. That sweet smell from earlier has my mouth watering for another taste."

He doesn't even hesitate before grabbing me by the hips and picking me up. It's as if he already knew I was going to let him do what he wants to me. It angers me, but I have to admit it has me so turned on I don't think I could say no if I tried.

I want to say something; protest or scream no, but I don't. I should, but I won't. I'm too wrapped up in what he's about to do to me. I'm not thinking clearly. My thighs are moistening with every look at his beautiful body and every filthy word that exits his mouth.

He walks toward his black motorcycle with me wrapped around his waist. Just thinking about the way he made me feel this morning without even touching me has me so turned on that I can already feel the ache between my legs just waiting to be released; pulsating to be filled by his dick. It's new to me. It's what *he* does to me.

Setting me down beside his motorcycle, he places one hand on my waist while working the button on my wet shorts with the other. I try to look at his face to see what he's feeling at the moment, but its void of any emotions. He's hard to read and it gives me an adrenaline rush; a need to figure him out.

His hands are working fast to pull my shorts down my legs and lift my feet out of them. Even with them being wet, he is a pro at stripping me out of them. He's good at getting what he wants and it makes me wonder if he's just as good when he gets it.

Standing here almost naked, I feel myself panting as he balls my thong in his hand and yanks. The thin strings rip apart, baring my throbbing pussy to him. My first thought is to cover myself up, but he lifts me up and sets me down so I'm straddling the back of his motorcycle.

I feel my legs spread wider as he runs his hands up my thighs and licks the rain from his full lips. Sitting here right now makes me feel dirty, but a part of me really needs this right now. Maybe letting him pleasure me will be enough to take my mind off things for the moment; not worry about what a certain someone is doing.

"Oh, fuck." He grips my thighs and bites his bottom lip. "The taste of your sweet pussy has been on my tongue all day; teasing me and making my fucking cock hurt. You better hold on tight while I devour your pussy; taste you in ways you've never been tasted."

Gripping my thighs, he pulls me closer to the edge of the motorcycle and runs his tongue up my thigh while grazing my flesh with his teeth. I can already feel myself squirming on the wet bike, trying not to slip off. My heart is going wild in my chest, making it hard to breathe.

Oh. My. Goodness.

"You like that, don't you," he asks against my thigh. "I bet you're already imagining what it's going to feel like when I run my tongue up your wet little pussy." He bites into my thigh and pulls me closer so my legs are over his shoulders. It hurts, but feels so good at the same time. My breathing picks up as he nibbles a little harder. "You like it when it hurts, baby?" He pulls away and lets the rain fall against my swollen clit. It has me wishing his mouth was there instead, to ease my ache.

Just touch me already . . .

An aching pleasure runs throughout my body, causing me to tremble as he inches his way up to my inner thigh, right beside my pussy and bites down onto my skin. I shake my head and squirm out of his reach in an attempt to get away. I can't handle it. It's too much. He feels my pull and yanks me back down by my thighs so I reach out and yank his hair making him look up at me. "Not so rough, asshole. Don't make me regret this anymore than I already do."

"Fuck," he groans out. He closes his eyes and moans. *Oh my, that moan. So deep and rough.* "Pull my hair again and I will fuck you instead of just licking you. Got it?"

Knowing that I'm pushing my luck with him, I release his hair and grip onto the bike handlebars behind my head. I'm already too far to turn back now. I want his tongue, but that's it. Nothing more. This is it. Just one time. Just . . .

"Oh shit," I moan out as his tongue slides up my pussy, slowly and teasingly. "This can only happen once. You know that, right?" I fight to catch my breath. "This is wrong in so many ways."

He looks up from between my thighs with a sly grin. He's a dirty little snake that has me in his grips and he knows it. "Yeah, but it feels so fucking right, doesn't it?"

I don't answer. I don't want to. All I want to do is close my eyes, lean back and let his tongue work its magic to release the tension I've had built up since this morning. When he sucked my wetness into his mouth and tasted me, I almost gave in right there and let him have me. It took every bit of strength to fight my urge to pull him into the shower and let him have his way with me; to take me just once.

His tongue works slowly at first to spread the moisture up my folds. He's being gentle and teasing me, making me want more. His rhythm is precise and in control as if he knows the exact spot to work me up. He's slowly building me up, knowing I'll want more at the end. He's good; a pro. He's in control of his game and it makes me want to knock him down a notch; tease him a little.

I catch myself moaning as he slides his tongue down further and shoves it into my pussy as deep as it will go. He's fucking me with his tongue. The feel and the thought is enough to almost bring me to climax . . . but I fight it. I'm not ready yet and I have a feeling he won't let me get off so easily anyways.

After a few seconds he slips his tongue out and slides it up and over my clit before sucking it into his mouth. It feels so good I have to reach out and grip his hair again. I feel myself pulling and the harder I pull the better his tongue pleases me. He gets off on this and I plan to use this to my advantage.

I yank his hair to the side and he sucks my clit so hard that I scream out in pleasure and almost fall over, but he catches me. I can feel him growling against my clit and it deepens the pleasure and makes me want more as he holds me steady. "Oh shit! Oh shit!"

"Fuck this shit! I want to fuck you so bad and make you scream louder while I'm pounding your tight little pussy. It's so hot hearing me pleasure you." Standing up, he runs his tongue over his lips and places both of his hands on his bike, hovering above me. "You want me to fuck you?" He runs his tongue up my neck and stops at my ear. "Just say the word and I'll end that throbbing ache between your legs. I'll fuck you so good that my cock will be the only one you ever fucking think about again. Let me show you."

I shake my head and place my hand on his chest. "No. Dammit, Slade." I give him a shove, but against his firm body, it doesn't even make him budge. It only makes me want him more. "I don't need you to fuck me and I don't want you to. Just finish what you started, dammit."

Wiping the rain off his face, he spreads my legs wider and places his thumb over my clit and starts rubbing. "Why? Are you afraid it will feel too good? You scared that I might please you better than anyone else can?" I look at him and swallow while trying to pretend his words aren't having the effect on me that they are. "My cock will feel so good in that tight little pussy." Grabbing the back of my head with one hand, he shoves a finger inside me and sucks in his bottom lip. I moan and take a deep breath, feeling the thickness of his finger move in and out, making my body feel hot and tingly. "See how wet I make you."

Closing my eyes, I moan and grip onto his wet hair. I have the urge to pull it and push him even further. I want his finger deeper. I need to get off. "You're an asshole for doing this and you know it," I say between deep breaths.

"Oh yeah, baby," he breaths into my ear. "Fucking show me how much of an asshole I am and I'll show you how good I am at pleasing you. You want me to please you; you have to fucking work for it."

What an asshole.

"Fuck you!" I scream as I dig my nails into his back, wanting to hurt him. "You're such an asshole."

He freezes and looks me dead in the eyes, clenching his jaw muscles. His eyes look fierce and I start to wonder if maybe I shouldn't have done that.

"I'm-"

"Don't finish that," he cuts me off.

Without saying another word, he lifts me up off the motorcycle and holds me up high enough for me to squeeze my thighs against his face. I can feel his lips brushing my clit and it already makes me want to lose control.

Oh shit.

Gripping my ass in his hands, he squeezes while his tongue works on catering to the aching throb between my legs. I grab onto his hair as I arch my back and scream. I scream so loud that it hurts. It actually hurts. My heels dig into his back as I continue to hang here while he pleasures me. He doesn't seem like this is straining him at all.

I have never felt anything so good in my life. This is definitely not what I was expecting. I feel the heat surging through my body and I can tell that I'm almost there. I'm so damn close that it hurts. "Shit, it feels so good. Don't stop, Slade. Faster . . ."

He grips me tighter and sucks my clit into his mouth right as my body trembles in his arms and I'm brought to climax by his tongue. *Damn, that magical tongue. I'm so damn ruined.*

"Holy shit, Slade. What did you just do to me?" I suck in a deep breath and release it. My heart is pounding so fast that I'm starting to feel dizzy. "Put me down, dammit. Put me down."

He runs his hands up my legs before grabbing my waist and helping me down to my feet. His eyes bore into mine as I take a step back and reach down for my shorts as fast as I can.

I feel like such an idiot for letting him get me off. I don't even like this guy. He's a jerk; nothing but trouble. The fucking devil in disguise, looking to taint my soul and consume my every thought. *I really need to get out of here.*

He leans against his bike, giving me a cocky look as I quickly slip my shorts on and wipe the water off of my face. "I'm ready to go. Take me back to the house."

Without saying a word, he reaches for his helmet, slips it on my head and jumps onto the bike. I grab his hand as he offers it for help. "What about your shirt?"

"Fuck it. I don't need it." I feel his chest rumble as he laughs under his breath. "What about your panties?"

"Screw you, Slade."

He revs up the engine, makes sure I'm holding on tight and then takes off.

THE RAIN STOPPED ALMOST IMMEDIATELY after we left. The ride back was in total silence. Exactly how I expected it to be. By the time we get back to the house, all I want to do is get as far away from *Slade* as I can. I feel so stupid for letting him work me up the way he did and catch me in a moment of weakness.

All it does is show him that he's right; he gets whatever he wants. I told myself I wouldn't let this happen, that I would be good this week and take some *me* time to figure out my life. So much for that. I feel like such a failure for being so careless.

I quickly hop off the motorcycle and slide the helmet off my head. Slade stays seated and watches me as I hand him the helmet. I can't help but to notice how sexy he looks shirtless on that damn motorcycle. Those tattoos and that damn perfect body. I hate it. No one should be allowed to look that devilishly sexy. "You're not coming in?" He slides the helmet on his head and adjusts the crotch of his jeans.

He turns away, takes a deep breath and reaches into his pocket. "Here's the key. I'll be back tonight."

I reach for the key and swallow. For some reason I don't want him to leave. Yeah, I wanted to get far away from him, but I wanted him to at least be in the house. "All right then," I say aggravated. "And just so you know, that is never happening again. Got it? Stay as far away from me as you can. You got to me in a moment of weakness. It won't happen again."

He grips the handles, clenches his jaw and watches as I walk away. I don't know why he even bothers waiting. I'm sure he's ready to get as far away from me as I am him. That's probably a good thing. The two of us being around each other is nothing but bad news. He's no good for me.

Letting myself in the house, I go straight for Cale's room and fall face first onto his bed. I'm so pissed at myself that I scream like a child. I'm twenty three years old and I still have no control over my life. I need to stay far away from Slade before he makes everything more difficult.

I knew he was going to be trouble from the second I laid eyes on him at the club. I just knew it. Heck, even his name screams trouble. Slade Merrick. Enough said.

CHAPTER SEVEN

Slade

I'VE NEVER HAD A WOMAN act as if *me* pleasing *her* disgusted her. This is a fucking first. I can't say that I like it. As a matter of fact, it pisses me off. She knows damn well that she enjoyed it. I bet she's never had someone make her scream that loud before; make her come on contact. She's just afraid to admit it; afraid to give into her needs; afraid that I'll fuck her too good. That has to be it.

With the way she has me feeling at the moment, the last thing I want to do is go and exist in the same house as her just to have her avoid me and act as if she doesn't want it as much as I do. I'm not down for that shit right now. I need to get some things off my mind; cool off a bit.

Out of habit, I end up at *Walk of Shame*. Pulling my motorcycle in the back parking lot, I yank my helmet off before slamming it down on my seat and shoving my motorcycle. Cale and Hemy better be ready to keep the drinks flowing, because I have a feeling that I will be here for a while.

Stay far away from her. Yeah, I'll fucking stay far away.

I push my way through the back door, walk over to my locker and grab a shirt. I get ready to put it on, but say *fuck it* instead. I'll end up without it on by the end of the night anyways. I toss it down and make my way into the bar.

I notice that the crowd is finally starting to show up. Perfect fucking timing. There should be plenty of entertainment to keep me busy.

As I approach the bar, I see Cale sitting on the edge of the bar talking to a group of women. They all seem to be laughing; fucking entertained.

He nods and jumps off the bar when he sees me. "Dude, why the hell do you look so pissed? I thought you were going to keep Aspen company until I get off?"

Leaning over the bar, I grab for the nearest liquor bottle and reach for an empty glass. "Yeah well, she's not the easiest to entertain. I'm pretty sure she'd rather be alone right now."

Cale tilts his head back with a dirty look as he watches me pour a drink. "Yeah . . . or maybe it's just you she doesn't want to be around."

"Fuck off, Cale. I'm not in the mood today."

"Yeah, well nothing new there."

Slamming back my drink, I set the empty glass down on the bar and take a step closer to Cale so we're face to face. I want to see him when he says it. "What the hell is that supposed to mean?"

Looking away from me, he sighs and takes a step back. "You know what I mean. You're just not the same person you used to be. You're my best friend, but seriously, you need to . . ." He huffs and grips the towel over his shoulder. "Never mind. I've got work to do."

"Yeah. Me too. I have *a lot* of fucking work to do." I pour another drink and make my way over to one of the empty couches. Lucky for me, everyone seems to be in the back room with Hemy so I can get a few minutes to myself.

I set my drink down on the table next to me and lean forward with my head in my hands and my elbows resting on my knees. I just can't get over the fact that I'm so pissed off at this woman. This morning my past consumed my thoughts and now the fact that this woman angers me like nothing else has taken over; has me completely worked up. The bad part is, the more she angers me the more I want to slip between those thighs and take it out on her.

I disgust her? Nah, fuck that.

I reach for my glass and tilt it back. I need to get my mind somewhere else. The liquor won't do anything but numb it, but numbing is what I'm used to. It's what keeps me going. My cock starts to harden at the thought of a needed release. *Right on schedule.*

"What's up, dick."

I tilt my head up at the sound of Hemy's voice. He looks down at me and holds out a bottle of Whiskey. I can't help but to laugh a bit when I notice he's standing there wearing nothing but an American flag wrapped around his waist. He has claw marks all over his skin from the women grabbing at him. He loves it just as much as I do. He's a dirty mother fucker; like me. "What's up, man?"

"Not shit. You look like you need another one of these." He pours my glass back up to the top and leans against the arm of the couch. "You here to help me work the ladies tonight or what? It's a small crowd. A private party."

I look up at the small group of women that have started rounding up in the back room. Most of them look slutty and will-ing. I'm sure the thought of *me* fucking *them* doesn't disgust them. Most of them will probably be begging. How can I pass that shit up?

"Yeah." I take a gulp of my drink and watch as a few of the ladies wave over at us. "Why not. I have nothing better to do."

Hemy slaps my shoulder and stands up. "Finish that shit up and get your ass over there then. There's a certain someone that is asking for you." He starts backing away. "She has huge tits and a big fucking appetite. I'm pretty sure that's your type."

I can definitely deal with that. There's no shame in having a huge sexual appetite. I need a woman that can handle me. I like to fuck and I like to fuck dirty. The fact they get the ultimate pleasure in return is just the icing on the cake. If my cock is what does the trick, then why the fuck should I stop? It's not my fault I'm so good with it.

Taking a few more minutes to myself, I finish my drink and prep my brain by entering into fuck mode. It's what keeps my mind from going places it shouldn't while my cock is in charge. I stand and make my way over to the back room, ready to get out of my head.

Hemy has a group of women, groping his ass, legs and chest, while a few of the other women are waving money around and screaming. This is what we're used to; what we live for.

My eyes scan the room of women, until they fall on the one I'm looking for; the brunette from the other night. She's standing across the room in a tiny white dress that is hugging her every curve. She's by far the most attractive woman here and the perfect distraction.

Stepping up behind her, I brush her hair behind her shoulder and whisper, "I'm here. Now what the fuck are you going to do with me?"

She turns around in my arms and bites her bottom lip when she notices I'm shirtless; less clothes for her to take off. Her eyes look hungry. "I have a few things in mind." Her eyes rake down my chest and I can tell she's been wanting me for a while. Most women do.

"You want my cock?" I run her hands down my chest and abs until it lands on my erection; always ready when I need it to be. "I'll let you have it under one condition. There are no exceptions." I wait for her to look me in the eyes to be sure she understands me. "It's yours for one night and one night only. No bullshit after. Enjoy it and move on. I need to get off and I'm pretty damn sure you do too. Are we clear?"

She lets out a soft moan and nods as her hand gropes my thick cock, moving up and down over my slightly damp jeans. The look in her eyes is pleading for me to take her right here in front of everyone. She's about to tackle me right now and ride me right here in the open. Hell yeah, it's a huge turn on.

"Even better," she whispers. "I just want one taste. I've been waiting for this opportunity for a long time." She strokes my cock through my pants. "A *very* long time."

Seeing that Hemy has the room handled, I pick the leggy brunette up and walk forward until her back is against the back wall and we have a little privacy. She moans as I slide my hand up her dress and rub my thumb over her lacy thong, teasing her through the thin fabric. "Well, it's worth the fucking wait. Trust me." Wrapping her hair around my hand, I pull her head back, exposing her neck to my mouth and graze it with my teeth as I shove my finger into her entrance. It's so wet that I can feel it dripping down my hand. "You like that, huh?"

She moans next to my ear before biting my earlobe and tugging it with her teeth. "Oh yes. I love it, Slade. Don't stop."

I move my finger in and out, slowly at first before going faster and deeper. Her legs tighten around my waist as she moans out and starts breathing heavily. "This isn't shit. Just wait until I shove my thick, hard cock in there." I bring my lips up to meet her ear.

"You're going to be screaming. You like to scream?"

"Mmhmm." Grabbing my face, she attempts to pull me in for a kiss, but I turn my head out of her reach. "Come on, baby. You're not even going to kiss me? I want to taste those lips." She leans in again and I lightly pull on her hair, stopping her an inch from my face.

"No kissing." I freeze as I hold her up against the wall angry with myself. I still have the taste of Aspen on my lips and I'm being a greedy fucking bastard. I don't want to share her taste with anyone.

What. The. Fuck.

"You know what. Never mind." I release her thighs and she slides down my body, landing hard on her feet. "I'll take care of myself. I'm pretty fucking good at it."

She gives me a stunned look before fixing her dress and combing the knots out of her hair. "Are you serious, you ass?"

"Yeah. I'm fucking serious." I push away from the wall and head for the door. When I look over at Hemy, he's standing there with his hard dick swinging everywhere. We don't usually get fully nude, but on occasion if no one else is paying much attention, we end up baring it all. He does it the most. He has the bad ass biker look down so when women see him stripping, they go crazy over it. Shit, one of the girls is practically sucking his dick right now. They seem to love the hard steel of his piercings almost as much as his dick itself.

Heading back over to the bar, I take a seat in front of Cale and grip the bar. I really need to get my shit together. "Three shots of Jack," I say stiffly. "Actually, make it four."

Cale reaches for the shot glasses and lines them up in front of me. "I'm guessing I'll be giving you a ride home."

"Yeah. Your guess is fucking right."

Yeah, and as soon as I get home, I'll be taking a shower to

wash this day away.

"So what is Aspen doing then? She didn't want to come hang out here?" He looks up from pouring the shots. "She doesn't get pissed off easily. It must be a *Slade* thing."

Not really caring to hear what he has to say, I grab the first shot and slam it back before wiping my mouth off with my arm. "How do you know this chick anyways? She's not even from around here."

Now it looks like he's battling a demon of his own. I know that look well. I wear it with pride. "I was best friends with her sister, Riley, growing up. Riley Raines. They used to live here back when we were all kids."

Okay. I've heard him mention that name before. I can't remember for shit why, though. There must be something about these sisters that make a man go nuts.

Aspen fucking Raines. What a sexy name.

CHAPTER EIGHT

Aspen

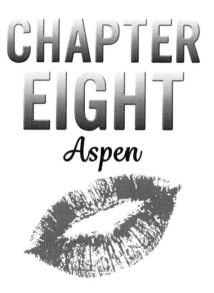

STUPID, PIECE OF CRAP, NO good vibrator . . .

I toss what I thought was my handy dandy vibrator down beside me and roll over on my stomach, shoving my face into the pillow. I'm so frustrated, I could scream. This cannot be happening. Gripping the plush pillow, I smother my face deeper and curse my damn vagina.

Is it broken? Seriously. I mean my vagina. Not the vibrator. The vibrator definitely had some kicking power left in it. I think that cocky, sexy, asshole broke it. Obviously, my vagina has decided it wants the best and has gone on strike until it gets it. I've never had this problem before him. Why now?

Rolling back over, I sit up and grab my panties, pulling them on with a sigh. A very frustrated sigh. After the orgasm I had yesterday, I'm ruined. No other orgasm I'll ever have will compare to it and it makes me so angry. It seems I've lost the control over my vagina. I've spent the last hour just trying to have a small orgasm; any orgasm and nothing. Trust me, I've tried both ways and what were the results? Nada . . . it's completely numb now.

It's definitely time to throw in the towel. It's not happening. Maybe I just need to make some breakfast, relax and try again later. I think I just have too much on my mind.

Yeah. That's it. I'm just mentally frustrated.

I stand from the messy confinements of the bed and grab my t-shirt from the wad of clothes on the floor, pulling it on. Exiting the room, I walk past Cale snoring on the couch and dodge my way into the kitchen. The boys didn't get in until at least two a.m. There's no way they will be waking up anytime soon. I'm surprised that I'm even up to be honest. I didn't sleep for crap. It was an endless night and a part of me wants to just crawl back in bed and force myself to sleep.

One minute I was checking my phone and the next minute I was checking the driveway. Not sure why I cared so much about when they were getting back but it seemed to drive me nuts. I haven't even gotten to spend any time with Cale and I've been here for three days. So far Slade has been my only real entertainment.

Lucky me . . .

My stomach starts growling as I begin to search through the fridge for something to cook for breakfast. Digging through the contents, I end up with a roll of sausage, a pack of bacon and some bagels. My mouth is practically watering just anticipating the taste. At least there's *something* in this house to look forward to.

Half way through cooking, everything starts to go horribly wrong. If I thought I was flustered before, this just confirms it. The bacon is popping grease everywhere and the stupid sausage is stuck to the bottom of the pan. The whole kitchen is full of smoke. It would be really embarrassing if the smoke detector went off right now. It's pathetic. I just can't seem to concentrate . . . on anything.

"Ow, damn!" I jump back when I get popped with bacon grease *again*. That shit really hurts.

"What the hell are you doing?"

I turn around to the sound of Slade's deep, raspy voice. He's standing there shirtless in a pair of low hanging jeans, showing off the muscles right above his . . . penis. His body is slightly damp as if he's just taken a shower, but I know he hasn't. I would've heard the water . . . I think. What is it about a wet man that is so sexy?

His eyes are dark and intense; looking at me as if he wants to either strangle me or just fuck me really hard. I can't really tell. I get a rush of excitement from both. That's really messed up.

Clearing my throat, I turn back around and start scraping the sausage off the bottom of the pan as if it's not a big deal. I just pretend I didn't mess breakfast all up. The last thing I want to do is see him standing there half naked, looking disturbingly delicious while judging my cooking skills. He looks tastier than this damn food. That's not what I need right now. "What does it look like I'm doing?" I ask, not bothering to hide my irritation.

When he speaks again his voice is right behind me, sending chills up my spine. His body is now pressed against mine, but not in a sexual way; in a way that makes my heart jump a little. Just a little. "Burning down the damn house. I hate to tell you this, but I left my fireman suit at work. I'm not prepared for this shit this early in the morning." He reaches for the spatula and hisses in my ear. "Now move out of the way."

Not budging, I reach for the spatula but he pulls it out of my reach. "I can handle it. Shouldn't you be sleeping or I don't know . . . kicking some skank out of your bed. I'm pretty sure you had a *late* night."

Giving me a stern look, he grabs me by the hips, picks me up and sets me on the counter. His lips are brushing my ear when he says, "I kicked her out last night. No girl sleeps in my bed. Ever." My heart sinks from his harsh words. He turns around and turns off the stove before throwing the spatula down. "If you needed my help then you should have asked. Is there anything you *can* do on your own?"

Narrowing my eyes at him, I get ready to jump down from the counter, but he steps right in front of me and stands between my legs blocking me. "What kind of a question is that? Is there something *else* you assume I can't do on my own?"

Running his hands up my thighs, he looks me dead in the eyes and smirks. "Yeah. Get off. I do believe you needed my help there as well."

"Fuck off, Slade. I don't need you to get off. Trust me." I place my hands on his chest and give him a little shove. Damn him; his body is pure muscle. "I can do it fine by myself. Now move."

He slides his hands up my shirt, lifts my body up and grips my ass in his hands. The skin on skin contact causes my breathing to slightly pick up. "Is that right?" Pulling me closer to him, he squeezes my ass and runs his lips up my neck. "Not from the frustrated sounds I heard coming from Cale's bedroom this morning. Those were definitely moans of frustration and not pleasure. Trust me. I know the difference." He slides his finger under the fabric of my panties and instantly I can feel the need for him to be inside me. He isn't even touching anything but the crevice between my leg and vagina.

What the hell?

Gaining my composure, I pull my neck away from him and shove him until he's out of my way. "You are so infuriating. Why are you such an ass?" I hop down from the counter and start walking away. "I'll clean this mess up later. I'm not in the mood to eat-"

"Get dressed and meet me outside in ten minutes," he says

trampling over my words.

I stop when I get to the doorway and turn around to face him. "And why the hell would I do that?"

"So we can eat breakfast." He pushes the pan across the stove and picks up the spatula, tossing it in the sink. "Be ready by the time I'm dressed."

"Yeah. You're funny," I huff. "I'm good. I'm going back to bed."

"Suit yourself, but I can hear your stomach growling from over here. Stay if you want. I just want to satisfy your . . . hunger."

He walks past me and then jogs up the stairs. The muscles in his back flex and the deep scratches in his skin stand out, making me hate my damn body again for the reaction it gets from him.

Son of a bitch . . .

AGAINST MY BETTER JUDGMENT, I'M sitting across a booth from Slade with a piece of bacon hanging from my mouth. We both just sit here in silence eating breakfast and I'm thankful for that. I really don't feel like chatting with him. Not that he seems like the chatty type person. Actually, he's pretty far from it.

"Are you going to sit there and play with that bacon all day?" He takes a bite of his hash browns and then leans against the back of his booth. "It has to taste better than that crap you were catching on fire when I walked in."

Rolling my eyes, I point my bacon at him and start waving it as I speak. "I wasn't catching it on fire, dammit. Why are you-"

The bacon slips out of my hand and hits him on the cheek, causing me to stop and cover my mouth to keep from laughing.

Watching me stifle my laughter, he grabs for the piece of bacon, smiles and takes a bite out of it. "You think that's funny, huh?"

I nod my head and laugh. "Yeah. You should have seen the way your eye twitched when it hit you. It was pretty damn hilarious."

"I bet," he replies before shoving the remainder of it in his mouth. "Now eat. I have things I have to do today."

"Yeah. Like what?"

He takes a drink of his coffee and then holds the mug under his lips. "Lots of things. Some of them include: work out, run, grocery shopping, clean the house and then go to work tonight. The things that adults do. In between, I plan to just ride and get away. Get out of my fucking head and breathe a little. *That's* what I have to do."

I look at him a little stunned. For some crazy reason I just didn't take him as the responsible type. I expected that Cale took care of the things around the house. I have to admit, it's pretty sexy. I almost like this side of him.

"I'm done anyways." I reach for my purse and get ready to pull out my wallet, but he reaches over and snatches my purse away. "Umm . . . my purse."

Shaking his head, he sets my purse down and pulls out his wallet. "Never expect to pay when I ask you to eat with me. I asked you because I wanted to treat you to breakfast." He pulls out two twenties and sets them on the table. "Let's go then."

He stands up right as the waitress walks over. She's a young woman, maybe in her early thirties. She looks a bit stressed out as she keeps looking back at the counter. "You guys are all set?" She picks up the money and her eyes go wide when she looks at the tab. "Sir, it's only fourteen dollars. Let me get your change."

Looking over at the counter, he watches the two kids that our waitress has been sitting with in between her running around like crazy. "No, ma'am. Keep the change." He pulls out another twenty, drops it down and grabs my hand. "Have a nice day."

I don't even get to see the woman's reaction because he pulls me out of the diner too quickly and then jumps into his truck without another word.

I keep wanting to say something, to maybe get a reaction out of him, but I can't think of what to say. I'm still stunned speechless by his generosity back at the diner. He did seem distracted while we were there. I noticed he kept looking away from the table as if something was catching his attention. Now, I know why.

"Slade," I say softly. "That was a really nice thing you did for that lady back at the diner."

He looks away from the road with a distraught look on his face. He looks like he's beating himself up over something. "Yeah, well she needed it more than me. Those kids shouldn't have to be at the diner while she works her ass off for three dollar tips. It's not right. They don't deserve that."

I sit here and watch him as he drives. He seems a little worked up and I can't help but want to comfort him. I don't even know why. The urge just comes out of nowhere. His side profile is strikingly beautiful and the act of kindness that I just witnessed makes him even more beautiful.

Without thinking, I reach out and grip his knee, running my hand up and down his leg for comfort. He stiffens at first and glances down at my hand with a surprised look, but doesn't say a word. He just drives in silence, keeping his eyes on the road. For some reason, I keep my hand there the whole way home.

I rub and massage his leg while looking down at my small hand on his muscular thigh. It feels good under my touch; natural. It isn't until we get back to the house that I feel his muscles fully relax.

When he stops the truck and pulls the key out the ignition, he looks over at me and then down at my hand. He's silent for a moment, his body still.

"I need to get ready to go running. I think Cale has the day planned for just the two of you." He lifts my hand off his knee and sets it on my own lap. "I'll see you later."

I nod my head as I watch him jump out of his truck and walk over to the door. Why is a part of me feeling down for him? Maybe it's because I feel there's something more to him than I thought. That maybe he is a real human being after all.

Hopefully Cale keeps my mind busy today. I think I need the distraction.

CHAPTER NINE

Aspen

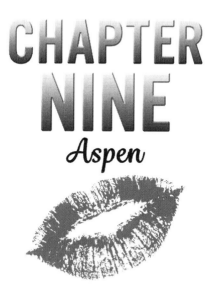

IT'S BEEN TWO DAYS SINCE I let Slade go down on me in the rain and I've been working as hard as I can to avoid him. Well, besides yesterday morning and the brief moment we shared in the kitchen earlier today. He set a full plate of breakfast down in front of me before popping a piece of bacon in his mouth, smiling and walking away. No words were exchanged. The only other inter-action between us has been heated stares from across the room. When I say heated, I mean hot enough to scorch me; to heat me straight to my core.

The thought alone is almost enough for me to get off. He's so intense, I'm not sure I can handle being in the same room with him for longer than five minutes without getting wet; panties soaked kind of wetness. I'm not used to that kind of want and need. It scares me. Not to mention, I'm still a little shaken up from our diner experience. I can't quite figure him out. It's eating at me.

". . . Aspen. Hey! Are you even listening?"

"Huh?" I look up from the pile of makeup in front of me to see Kayla hovering above me. I give her a forced smile and reach for the mascara. I've never had a problem with paying attention before. "Yeah, sorry. I was just thinking."

She leans over my shoulder and grabs for my red lipstick. "See. Now that's your problem. You think too much. You better not be thinking about-"

"I'm not," I cut her off. I don't even want to think about it. I've been in Chicago for four days now and haven't spoken to Jay since the first night. The only thing I'm missing back home right now is cutting people's hair and interacting with my clients. Other than that, I don't even want to think about my life back home. "I'm not worried about him. It's something else," I mutter. "Someone just makes me so angry and I don't understand why I am letting it get to me so much."

She gives me a knowing look and yanks my hair to the side. "Tell me all about it. Did you sleep with someone? Was it Cale or that sexy hunk, Slade?" She drops down beside me and watches as I coat my lashes with mascara. "I want details before we get to the club. You've been spending a lot of time with Cale. Hell, you could melt butter off the both of them. If I was single I'd take both on at the same time."

I roll my eyes at her and push her out of my space. "Neither one. I haven't slept with anyone." I look up at her and my eye starts twitching. My stupid nerves are getting to me and giving me away. "What?" I say as her eyes widen as if she's just figured something out.

Shit.

"You may not have had sex, but you did something sexual." She shoots to her feet and yells, "You, dirty little slut. You better start talking."

I stand up and adjust my short red dress. The material is so thin, it makes me feel naked. It barely covers my breasts and hangs just a few inches below my ass. I can't even wear a bra with this dress. Kayla picked the dress out this afternoon when we went shopping. It's the first real time we've had to spend together since I've been here. Her job and family life keep her too busy. I envy her. I want that in my life.

"Maybe I did," I mumble embarrassed. "That's all you're getting because I'm not having you embarrass me tonight." I look around Cale's room until I spot my black, leather strapped stilettos. I grab them, buckle my feet in and head for the door. "Ready?"

She takes a bite of her jerky stick and grabs for her purse. "More than ever. Alex is letting me cut lose tonight. Don't be surprised if you see my hands all over that biker looking stripper. Hot damn, he is fine. I swear he looks more like he belongs in a motorcycle club than a strip club. Lucky for us, he's in the strip club. Now, let's go."

I must not have paid much attention last time I was there because I don't remember seeing him. The only one that got my attention was Slade. My mind was too clouded that night and I was working hard to keep to myself. Well, not tonight, dammit. I'm out to have a little fun.

WHEN WE ARRIVE AT THE club, it is jam packed. We literally have to squeeze our way through the door and over to the bar. I've never seen such a group of crazy women before. I can't even see the guys because they're buried somewhere in the way back behind screaming women. I'm already starting to sweat just from rubbing against bodies.

As soon as we get close enough inside, I see Sarah is tending the bar along with two other women I have never seen. They all seem to be enjoying themselves, despite the crowd - they have waiting on them for drinks. I admire them. I'd be freaking out right about now.

Sarah notices me when we get closer and gives me a smirk as if she remembers me from that first night. I'm surprised that out of a crowd of people, she would remember me. I'm definitely not one to stand out in a crowd. "Hey, gorgeous ladies," she says with a wink. "What can I get you girls tonight?"

"Something strong," Kayla yells out over the music. She smiles and leans over the bar. "For the both of us. Especially her."

I nudge her in the side, causing her to yelp and move away from me. "Ignore her." I smile and grab for my purse, pulling out some cash. "Just give me a Vodka and cranberry. Easy on the Vodka."

Sarah smiles and reaches for two glasses, setting them down in front of her. I hadn't noticed before, but she's actually quite beautiful. Long amber hair and big blue eyes that make you feel comfortable and at ease. I'm sort of glad she's here. "So, you ladies are back for more of the boys of *Walk of Shame*, huh. Well, I don't blame you." She scoops the glasses full of ice and starts reaching for the bottles of liquor. "I'm guessing you're here for Slade." She looks up at me and runs her tongue over her teeth as if she knows without a doubt, that she's right. "Nice choice, honey."

The more she talks, the more curious I get about Slade. She talks about him and the others as if she's had them all. I'm not sure how to feel about that. I'm not even sure I should feel *anything* about it. "So, what do you know about these boys?" She slides our drinks in front of us and waves at someone behind us.

"I know they like to fuck." She throws her towel over her shoulder and leans across the bar so that she's closer to us. "And

I know they're good at what they do. You won't find any better. Trust me." She winks at me and smiles.

Sipping my drink, I look beside me to see Kayla is hanging on every word out of Sarah's mouth. I've never seen her so curious. She's practically sitting on top of the bar ready to jump on top of Sarah. "So, you've been with all of them?"

"Kayla!" I can't believe she just asked that.

"What! I'm just curious." She grins and leans in closer. "So . . ."

Sarah just laughs as if the question doesn't bother her at all. She looks proud, as if her answer makes her feel good about herself. "I've been with two of them. Best experience of my life. Both at the same time and it was hot."

Okay, now I'm curious. *What! Two at the same time?*

"Details?" Kayla's mouth asks what I'm too afraid to.

Sarah raises her eyebrows and jumps up to sit on the bar in front of us. She's really enjoying this. To be honest, I'm a little nervous. "All right, you asked for it." She grins at Kayla and then over at me as I watch her with curiosity.

"Well, it was Hemy and Slade. We were at a party at Cale's house. I had been hitting on Slade all night but he was in one of his drinking binges so he wasn't really up for it. I finally gave up and was having sex with Hemy in one of the rooms down the hall. Slade walked in, drunk and looking for pussy. I've learned that look well. Hemy was laying on the bed with me riding his cock and without stopping, just looked at him.

At first I thought he was going to kick Slade out, but then he asked him if he was going to just stand there or join. I about died when Slade came stalking in and kneeled behind me on the bed, pulled his pants down, rolled a condom on and slipped inside my ass. I will never forget that feeling. Two cocks filling me at once. They never touched each other, but it was so hot. The only bad thing is, Slade has sort of a rule. He never sleeps with the same girl twice and my one chance wasn't even alone with him. Doesn't matter, he won't budge on his stupid rules."

Why does that bother me? I'm not sure I'm liking this, but I stay and listen anyway.

Sarah makes a face as if just remembering something else. "It wasn't until later that I found out Hemy swings both ways. Talk about sexy. You haven't seen anything worth seeing until you see two sexy as hell men kissing each other. I'm telling you, it's hot. Hemy just likes to fuck. Doesn't matter if it's male or female; although, I don't think he's much for taking if you know what I mean. Being with Hemy and Slade at the same time was by far my best sexual experience, but being with Hemy and this other guy came in close second."

By the time she's done, I'm sitting here with my mouth open. Should I be turned on by this? I'm not so sure, but I definitely am; almost jealous.

"So, what about Cale?" Kayla looks over at me while taking a sip of her drink. "I bet that boy likes to get it on too."

"Kayla, I don't need to hear about Cale. That's just weird. He's like a damn brother to me." I look up at Sarah, hoping she's done with her story. I'm not so sure I can hear any more of this, especially right before I'm going to be seeing the boys practically naked.

Sarah shrugs her shoulders and grabs for a couple glasses when she notices some girls returning back to the bar with empty ones. "He's a little tougher to take down if you know what I mean. All I know about Cale is that he doesn't sleep with women. He only pleasures them and lets them pleasure him. I don't know why. All I know is that all of these women are hoping to be the lucky one that gets him to go all the way. I don't know. I would definitely take him for a ride. I heard he works wonders with his tongue. I've never experienced it firsthand, but the women around here talk. When you're a bartender, you get all of the latest scoop. It's part of the reason why I love my job so much. That and those fine as fuck men. I can get off just by watching them. I can't say that about many men."

She pushes the drinks in front of the other women, then comes back to us. "All I know is that you don't come to *Walk of Shame* unless you're looking to fulfill your darkest, wildest fantasies. This place is dirty. The boys are dirty; addictive." She slaps her hand down on the bar top and laughs. "Well, have fun, ladies. Gotta get back to work."

I swallow hard and look away from Sarah while trying to process everything that just came out of her mouth. I guess when you're hot as hell and surrounded by a sexual lifestyle, it doesn't really matter who's watching or joining in. Slade . . . seems to like sex more than the average male and pleasures like a pro . . . like an addict. Still, the sexiest man I have ever laid eyes on. He's definitely trouble and I need to keep my mind off him.

"Oh. My. God." Kayla grabs my arm and starts pulling me through the crowd. "Did you hear her? Hemy must be the other stripper I was telling you about. That's insanely hot."

"I don't know, Kayla. This place seems pretty wild. You heard her. The boys are dirty. You better be careful before you find yourself in a position you don't want to be in."

She stops and turns to me. "What? Like you?"

"I don't want to talk about it." Pulling away from her, I push through the crowd, just wanting to get away and my heart instantly stops when I lay eyes on . . . *him*. Slade is standing shirtless with a pair of leather pants hanging low on his hips, holding a water bottle above his head.

His head is tilted back as the water drips down his flawless body and his hand works its way down where it cups his dick while he practically fucks the air. He thrusts and grinds his hips while a couple of women are on their knees in front of him.

His body is slick, sexy and hypnotizing; it's hard to breathe as I watch him move to the slow, seductive song. I can feel Kayla standing beside me and even her breathing has picked up.

"She wasn't kidding when she said these boys are dirty and addictive," Kayla breathes while grabbing my arm and pulling me against her. "Look beside Slade." I pull my eyes away from Slade to see a very attractive guy with long dark hair, brushed behind his ears. "That sexual predator there is Hemy; totally fuckable and I want to be his prey. I can't stop imagining him kissing another sexy guy now. Oh man, that would be so hot. I would pay good money to see that. I don't know why, but it has me turned on right now."

I focus my attention on Hemy in hopes it will distract me from Slade's smooth, very wet body. It helps a little. Hemy is very sexy in the mysterious, dark way. His dark hair falls just above his shoulder and he has a beard, but not an overly long unattractive one. It's just enough to scream that he's a bad boy with dark secrets, much like Slade. His body is perfectly sculpted and he too is covered in random tattoos. Even his neck has tattoos. He definitely screams bad and dirty.

Kayla and I watch as he moves his hips up and down, grinding in some thick woman's face. The woman keeps reaching out and scratching at his chest, causing Hemy to thrust her face away with his crotch. He's wearing nothing but a pair of low hanging leather pants, just like Slade. These boys are definitely killing it with those pants. They don't leave much up to the imagination since neither of them are wearing briefs underneath. I can tell from across the room. I don't even want to check on Cale. This is too dirty and sexy.

"You like looking at Hemy," a deep voice growls in my ear. "If he turns you on that much, I would let him watch as I fuck you. Maybe he could jerk off as you scream for me to let you come."

Swallowing hard, I pull away from Slade and turn around to

face him. There's no humor in his eyes, just pure want and need. "Yeah. Maybe I do like watching Hemy." For some reason, I want to tease him; see what kind of reaction I can get out of him. "I can't stop imagining how hot it must be to see him kiss another sexy guy." I lick my lips and smile over at Kayla as she lifts her eyebrows, probably wondering where I'm going with this. "It's definitely got me turned on."

Slade tilts his head while wiping his hands down the front of his wet body. He's looking at me with a cocky grin that makes my legs go weak. "Does that make you wet?" He steps closer to me and without grabbing me, rubs his lip over my ear. "Does it make you think about . . . fucking?"

I nod my head and exhale. *Holy hell, he smells so damn good.* The sweat is only making it more tempting for me to run my tongue over his every muscle and taste him on my tongue. "Mmm . . . very much."

He stands up straight, sucks in his bottom lip and then turns to Hemy. "Dude, get your fucking ass over here."

Wait. What is he doing?

Hemy grabs his shirt and wipes it over his chest before running over to stand in front of us. He's even sexier up close. Full lips with a piercing off to the side, amber eyes and a sexy smile. "What's up?" He looks over at me and a dark look takes over his eyes. It's a sexy, mysterious look that says he wants to ravish me. Maybe he really is into sex more than Slade. That's hard to believe.

Slade notices me staring at Hemy and growls. "You better fucking enjoy this." He looks to Hemy and gives him a hard look. "Don't get any fucking ideas, man."

Hemy nods his head confused. Hell, I'm confused.

Next thing I know, Slade steps up to Hemy, grips his hair and presses his lips against his. I watch as their lips move in sync with each other's. Slade even makes sure to use his tongue a little just to give me a show.

Hot damn! This is so sexy. Instant wetness.

Slade pulls away from the kiss and grabs for my hand. Before I know what he's about to do with it, he presses it to Hemy's rock hard dick. It feels so thick in my hand and I somehow forget how to breathe. "See what my tongue does to people?" He presses my hand harder against Hemy's erection and starts moving it up and down his thin pants. That's when I notice he must have a couple piercings down there as well. It makes my heart beat faster at the thought. "This is what I do to people," he growls.

I pull my hand away while fighting to catch my breath. I am so turned on right now that I can barely stand it. I'm heated to the core and I feel that if my thighs rub together that I will have an orgasm right here in front of everyone.

That was sexier than I expected. Why did seeing Slade kiss another guy only make me want him more? Is it because I know he did it for me or because he wants to have me that bad? Crap, I was not expecting this.

Hemy looks at me and takes a step closer. I can't help but to look down at his erection. I can't believe that Slade put my hand on his dick. I'm so embarrassed and turned on at the same time.

Slade puts his arm across Hemy's chest and stops him from getting any closer. "You can go now," he growls.

Hemy gives me one last look, smirks and walks away.

I look Slade in the eyes as he places his hand behind my neck and yanks me to him. His other hand slithers down the front of my body and stops on the inside of my thigh. "I'm not even touching your pussy and I can feel the wetness on your thighs." He bites his bottom lip and leans into my ear. "Be ready for me to take care of this later."

Then he turns and walks away. He seriously just walked away.

"Kayla," I growl out as she smiles at me. "Don't say a word. I will strangle you right now."

Kayla throws her arms up and backs away from me as she watches Hemy from across the room. "You're so damn lucky," she breathes. "That was so damn hot."

Yeah, lucky me.

Both of the men have gone back to their screaming fans, giving us all a show. A dirty, erotic, breathtaking show.

Maybe coming here was a bad idea. Yeah. Definitely a bad idea.

CHAPTER TEN
Slade

THE FRUSTRATION IS SLOWLY BUILDING. It's been four days since I've had sex and after watching Aspen give me heated looks from across the room, I decide it's time to get her in on a little action; show her what I can do. I can't take her shit anymore. This is a fucking record for me and I need to release this shit and soon. She wants me and we both know it. I just need to prove that I know it.

I walk over to her and place my hands on her hips, running my hands up her curves as her friend watches me with a huge grin. Even her friend can see what my touch does to her. She's eyeing us up, giving Aspen the nod; the one that says she's about to sit back and watch; her own private show.

Backing her up, I nod my head to Hemy and he kicks the chair that's sitting behind Aspen closer to us. He already knows what I plan to do. I'll have to remember to thank him for looking out for me later.

I can hear the surrounding women screaming and getting excited as I guide Aspen down to the chair and place both her hands on my stomach. The women fucking love this chair and so will she. I'll fucking make sure of that.

She gives me a nervous look as I stand between her thighs and start grinding my hips to the beat of the music while slowly undoing the top of my pants. We wouldn't usually do this in such a big crowd, but I want her more than anything I've wanted in a long damn time. Even if that means fucking her right here, I will do it with no shame.

I pull my pants down my hips just enough so the head of my cock is exposed to her. Her eyes widen as I push her hands down further and lean down into her ear. "Like I said, it's against the rules." I suck in her earlobe as I guide her hand over my bare skin and squeeze her hand over my head. "But I want you to touch it."

Her breathing picks up as her hand starts caressing my cock through my thin pants. Each time her hand touches the head, I close my eyes and moan and so does she. It feels so fucking good that I could bend her over this chair right now, slide that dress up and fuck her; no regrets; just pure erotic sex. I don't mind giving a good show; displaying what I fucking do best.

"That's it. You like touching my cock with everyone watching? Does it turn you on to know you're the one sitting in this chair, groping my hard cock? All these women would kill to be doing this." I grab her hand and help her to smear my pre cum over the head of my dick. "See how bad I want you, Aspen?" I pull her hand away from my erection and bring it up to her lips. "I tasted you. Now it's your turn."

She leans her head back and closes her eyes as I brush her fingers over her lips, giving her a taste of what she does to me. It's so dark in here that I doubt anyone can see that the head of my dick is on display. She must feel the same way because she seems to be enjoying it as much as I am.

She moans and licks my taste from her lips as she rubs her hand up my erection, pulling me closer. She loves my taste. I can tell by the way she licks her lips once more, savoring the taste before opening her eyes as if she's just noticed the crazy crowd of women surrounding us. "Slade." She pulls her hands away from my body and runs them over the side of her dress, embarrassed. "I'm not doing this. Especially, right now. I told you to stay away from me, dammit," she says breathless. "I meant it."

Standing up, she pulls her dress down and pushes me out of the way. "Go fuck yourself," she growls.

She says one thing, but her eyes say another. I think I'll listen to her eyes. They don't lie as much as her sexy mouth. Biting my bottom lip, I bring my body against hers and pull one of her legs up to wrap around my waist. Then, I lean her back and slowly grind my hips against her aching pussy while tugging on her hair. I've been imagining this for fucking days. It would almost be too easy for me to just pull her panties aside right now and slip right inside her. The thought causes me to moan against her lips.

I can feel her leg tighten around me as her body starts trembling beneath my touch. I know and she knows that she's about to have an orgasm right here in front of everyone. It pleases me, knowing it's from my doing. I can get her anywhere and she knows it.

Thrusting my hips, I move slowly to be sure she can feel the head of my cock rubbing against her clit through her thin panties. I want her to imagine just how much better it would be if it were inside of her; deep inside of her and filling her to max.

I pull her neck up and grind my hips one last time right as her body starts shaking and her breathing comes out in short quick bursts. "I told you my cock feels good, baby. It's going to feel even better inside you, claiming you."

Pulling out of my grasp, she gives me a heated but angry look before slapping me right across the face. The contact stings, making my dick even harder for her. I've done her in and she fucking knows it. She can barely even stand right now and it has me so turned on, I may not even make it through the rest of the night without having to release this tension. "I hate you sometimes. You're such an asshole, Slade."

The women start screaming and throwing money as she walks away and dips into the bathroom. They all want their turn, but all I want is to finish what I started. She's mad, but it's not at me. It's at herself for wanting me. It's written all over her face; enough for everyone to see.

I'M STANDING THERE WIPING MY sweat off when Hemy leans in next to me and whistles while looking across the room. "Hot dayum. She is one fine piece of ass. I think we need to tag team that shit later. You can bend her over and fuck her while she sucks my cock. I saw how worked up you got her while you were dancing for her. She needs a good fuck."

I bring my eyes up to see Aspen leaning over the bar, tugging on the back of her tight little dress. Damn, those legs are enough to hypnotize a man and almost make him forget where the fuck he's at and why he's there in the first place. Just one look at her and I can't deny that I want that all to myself.

"That, asshole, is all mine. I've already gotten a taste and I'm not sharing." I reach for the nearest shot glass and slam it back, closing my eyes as the slight burning sensation slides down my throat, giving me a temporary feeling of relief. It's nothing strong enough though. Not even enough to give me a buzz.

"Well, good luck with that shit, bro. It seems that asshole at the bar thinks otherwise." He pauses for a second as I open my eyes and look up. He points and grips my shoulder. "She doesn't seem too happy. You better take care of that shit before I do."

I growl as some drunken asshole grabs her by the hips and attempts to pull her into his lap. I can see, even from back here that she isn't into it. "Shit! I'll be right back. Start without me." I slam the shot glass down and take off towards the bar. I am so heated right now, I could break this mother fucker's jaw.

I can slightly make out what they're saying as I get closer and I am right. This asshole is definitely drunk. Not a good move on his part.

"I said no, asshole." Aspen reaches for his hand and tries prying it away from her waist while looking out in the crowd as if searching for someone. Neither one of them seem to take notice of me approaching. That's cool with me. I'm still going to fuck him up.

"Come on, baby." The guy ignores her and tightens his grip on her, pulling her down to his lap. This only pushes me further. "Look at that fine ass. I want it in my lap. We could go somewhere more private if you want."

Swinging her arm back, she elbows him in the face and stomps on his foot. "I said, let go!"

The guy stands up, pushes her and grabs his nose that is now dispersing blood. "You fucking bitch. I will-"

Anger boiling up inside me, I reach for the back of the guy's head and slam it down onto the bar beside him as hard as I can. The guy groans out in pain, obviously not expecting it as he reaches for his hair to try to release it from my tight grip.

Yeah, well suck on that, mother fucker.

"Fucking touch her again and I will break both your arms and make your small fucking dick unusable. Got it?" I lean in next to his ear and slam his head down onto the bar again to get my point across. Then I whisper, "Never touch what is mine again."

I look up with the guy's hair still wrapped in my hand and am not surprised to see all eyes on me as I stand there breathing heavily. It's not often fights happen in here since the majority of population is women. My bad, but he fucking asked for it.

Aspen is looking at me with a heated look as if by hurting this prick turned her on. *Well, fuck me.* It turned me on too. I didn't know she had it in her. I like seeing her hurt someone. It's hot; especially, while she's wearing that sexy little dress.

Licking my lips, I push the asshole's head down, release his hair and walk toward Aspen. Placing one hand on her hip, I look behind her right as her friend is approaching. "Aspen won't be needing a ride." I look up at Cale as he gives me a concerned look, just now realizing what happened. "Give me the fucking keys," I growl out.

Digging in his pocket, he looks to Aspen. She doesn't take notice because she's too busy still looking at me with a very confused look on her face. She doesn't know whether to slap me or jump on me and ride me. I'll take either one. "What the fuck, man. You're not even going to finish your shift?" He tosses me the keys, already knowing my answer, and I quickly reach out and catch them.

"Nope. I have better shit to do. Take care of this asshole. Get him out of here." Grabbing Aspen's hand, I drag her past the curious crowd and out of the bar. Once outside I swing my truck door open, pick her up and set her inside.

She still hasn't said a word and I know why. She knows she's finally lost the war within herself. I'm about to fuck her and even she can't deny the sexual tension between us. It needs to be dealt with and there is only one way; to fuck and to fuck hard.

The look that she's giving me is enough to push me over the

edge. I'm trying to be respectful, but I may just say fuck it and take her here and now before we can even make it back to the house.

Fuck me.

CHAPTER ELEVEN
Slade

LEANING AGAINST THE SIDE OF the truck, I pull out a cigarette, light it and take a long drag. That mother fucker is lucky I don't go right back inside and shove my fist down his fucking throat. I never want to see that shit again. I can't. I just fucking can't.

I hear the sound of Aspen's heels hit the pavement beside me, but right now I'm too pissed to even look up. I'm standing there staring at my shoes, trying to keep my cool. If she opens her mouth right now, there's a huge chance I will bend her over and fuck her right now. I have way too much shit going on in my head; not to mention that asshole inside has just pushed me over the edge.

"Did you enjoy that?" Her voice comes out soft, but with a hint of anger. I'm not surprised. After what I did to her in front of everyone, I'm sure she wishes it were me she elbowed in the face. "You just can't resist messing with me and pushing my buttons, can you? I don't get it."

I take another drag, close my eyes and exhale. I need another moment before I even attempt to speak. Right now, I feel like a fucking animal released from its cage and about to pounce on its prey. The intensity of me wanting her is eating at me.

"You didn't have to save me from that idiot. Besides, it looked like you were pretty *busy* over there trying to juggle the slut squad. I have a feeling you're a damn pro at it by now."

Okay. One more drag and I'm good to go.

I take one more hit, toss the cigarette down beside me and pin her against the side of my truck. She looks up at me with a shocked expression, but doesn't say a word. Her eyes just keep jumping back and forth as I stare into them. "I did enjoy it." I lean into her ear and rub my bottom lip up her neck. "Just admit it, you did too. You think you can hide it, but I can smell it all over you." I slowly run my hand up the inside of her thigh, stopping below her panty line. "And feel it."

I am not a patient man and I've been waiting too many days for this. She better be ready. I'm about to pour all my frustration into her body because she's the reason I'm about to explode.

"You can't fucking hide it anymore and we both know it," I growl. "You want to kick my ass and fuck me at the same time. Well guess what," I whisper. "I'm fucking waiting."

I hear her breathing pick up before she places her hands to my chest and pushes as hard as she can. It only makes her angrier when her shove has no effect on me. She leans her head against my truck and exhales. "How do you know it's for you, huh?" I move my hand higher and cup her mound in my hand, causing her to close her eyes and moan out. "It could . . ." She moans again as I start rubbing her through the thin fabric. It's getting hard for her to find her words now. I like that. "Be for someone else. How do you know," she growls questioningly.

Sliding my finger under the fabric of her panties, I shove it into her very wet pussy and grab the back of her neck. "This is how I know," I assure her. "The way your breathing picks up and your body trembles under my touch." I shove my finger deeper, causing her to raise her hips and thrust against my hand. "Do you feel that, Aspen? Your body is ready to be fucked. It needs to be fucked by me. No. One. Else."

I grab both her hands and hold them above her head while pushing my thigh between her slightly parted legs. It feels so good between her thighs. So warm and . . . wet. "You want me to fuck you, baby?" I gently place my hand on her throat as I lean in and pull her bottom lip into my mouth and suck it, hard. She lets out a soft moan and nods her head as her lip slips from my grip. "Tell me you want me to fuck you. I want to fucking hear it."

Looking at me, she doesn't say a word, but the look in her eyes says it all. She lowers her hand down the front of my body, down my abs and grabs my erection in her hand. It feels so huge under her touch and I can tell by her little gasp that she feels the same way. I close my eyes and moan as she starts stroking it through the fabric as if she fucking owns it. Damn, that's such a turn on. It's all hers if she wants it.

Her hands start working on the button of my pants as she leans in and bites my nipple. She's breathing hard as she looks up at me. I'm so fucking turned on right now that I can barely contain myself. I feel like a fucking virgin about to get pussy for the first time.

What. The. Shit.

I press my body against hers and grab her legs one by one to wrap them around my waist. We both just stand there silent, looking into each other's eyes before I slam my lips against hers and claim them. I can't take it anymore. I need a fucking taste. I suck and tug, before slipping my tongue between her parted lips and sucking her tongue into my mouth. I never thought kissing could be such a turn on, but damn her lips feel so good against mine. I have to admit that I've wanted to kiss her since that day in the bathroom.

"You still haven't said it, Aspen," I groan against her lips while rubbing her hand over my hard cock. "You feel how big it is for you?" Her legs shake around me as her hand caresses my erection. "Just say the word and I will drive us back to my house and fuck you so damn thoroughly that this cock . . ." I force her to squeeze my dick as I thrust and bite her bottom lip. "Will be the only thing your body craves."

"Dammit," she hisses while pulling her hand away from my dick in a panic. "It's happening again. Put me down." She pushes at my chest and forces me to drop her to her feet. I have to catch her when she almost twists an ankle because of her high heels. "Just take me back to the house. In case you forgot." She jumps into the truck as fast as she can and slams the door closed behind her. "I'm pissed at you. Shit!"

"Nothing new there," I point out.

I smirk to myself while walking over to my side of the truck and jumping in. I'm no fool. She can play hard to get if she wants, but in the end she and I both know that as soon as we get back to the house and walk in that door, I will have her riding my cock as if her life depends on it. Her body is getting desperate and so is she. Right now she hates me and is fighting against wanting me. Well, she'll hate me even more after she sees what my body can fucking do to her.

We ride in silence, but I notice her press her legs together every few minutes while glaring over at me. She can't seem to sit still and she looks as if she's about to scream. Sexual frustration is one of those bittersweet things. It claws at you until you release it and there is only one way to do so; to fuck and fuck hard. I can tell she's trying hard to keep her eyes away, but they keep scanning over my body, imagining it being on top of hers. This seems to piss her off even more.

Reaching over, I force her legs apart and slide my hand up her thigh. I slowly inch it further up her smooth skin until I feel the wetness between her legs. Then I stop. I want to see what her reaction is. I want to see how badly she needs me to release her.

She gives me a dirty look, but spreads her legs wider for me as if waiting for me to go further. I could pretend to be surprised, but I'm not. In the end, the throbbing between their legs wins out over the voice of reason in their heads. When I don't make an attempt to move, she grabs my hand and pushes it away. "You're an ass. Do you know that?" She presses her legs closed and looks out the window. "Stop screwing with me just because you think you're God's gift to women. You're gorgeous and you have a rockin' body, so what. Stop using that against my weakness. You're the only person that can piss me off this way."

She turns to look me in the eyes and her frustration is so sexy, it hurts. Yanking her legs apart, I pull her closer to me and rub my thumb over her swollen clit. I really need to get her off because by the time we get back to the house, I won't have the patience. I'm going to want to fuck her as soon as we step through the door. Her pussy has been the only thing on my mind since I tasted it for myself.

She moans as I start rubbing small circles against her body, teasing her. I start out slowly at first before moving at a faster rhythm. She starts rocking against my hand, getting more desperate the faster I go.

"oohhh . . . keep going." She rocks faster. "It feels so good. Why do you have to be so good at this?" She moans out in pleasure while pulling at her hair.

"It's a fucking blessing. Trust me," I groan while trying to keep my eyes on the road. "You ready to come yet?"

She nods her head and grips onto the headrest behind her. "Yes. I'm ready. I'm so ready," she breathes.

"Ask me to make you come then."

She runs her tongue over her teeth in anger before digging her nails into my arm. "Will you make me come? I want you to make me come. It feels so good when you do it."

I slip one of my fingers inside while still rubbing her clit with my thumb. She moans and digs deeper into my arm, trying not to scream. "That feels good, doesn't it? You like my finger filling you, huh? Just wait until I ram my hard cock in there." I shove another finger inside her and start moving them in and out.

"Oh damn, you're so tight, baby and so wet. Damn, it's running down my fingers." I shove my fingers deeper, while moving my thumb faster. "So fucking tight. Oh shit. Scream for me, baby. Show me what I do to you."

I feel her body start to shake before she clamps down around my fingers. She lets go of my arm and grips the seat while screaming. She arches her back as I shove my fingers in one last time. "Stop! I can't take it," she breathes. "Don't move. Just . . . don't. Move."

It takes her a few seconds to catch her breath. I don't blame her. That was one intense orgasm. I'll be surprised if she'll be able to walk after that shit. I slowly pull my fingers out and suck them into my mouth, tasting her as she watches me with hooded eyes. She likes it when I taste her.

Fuck me.

As soon as the house comes into view, I pull off to the side of the road and slam the truck into park. "Fuck this!" Pulling the keys out of the ignition, I hop out of the truck, slam the door behind me and rush over to her side. I can't wait any longer. I need to be inside her before I fucking explode. I won't nut until I get a feel inside her.

I yank her door open and reach inside to pull her out. Before her feet can hit the ground, I have her wrapped around my waist and I'm heading for the door. I practically bust the door down while slamming my lips against hers, both of us breathing heavily while fighting for air.

I don't even bother shutting the door behind us as I walk us over to the stairs. I set her down on the staircase and spread her legs before ripping her thin panties from her body. My eyes slowly trail from her breasts, down to her pussy as I bite my bottom lip and moan. "It's so fucking beautiful."

I force my body between her legs and press my lips against hers again. She's kissing me with such anger and frustration that it only makes me want her more. "I want to slap you so bad right now," she breathes. "I hate the way you make me want you."

"Well, I fucking love it." I grab the top of her dress and rip it open, exposing her breasts to me. I knew she wasn't wearing a bra. I could see her hard nipples even in the dim lighting of the bar earlier. She gets ready to say something; to yell at me about her dress until I suck her left nipple into my mouth, causing her to moan out instead. "You want me inside you, don't you? Just fucking admit it."

Moaning, she grabs me by the hair and yanks my head back. "I hate you so much for making me want you. Me wanting you is the last thing I need."

"Well you don't hate me enough. 'Cause if you did, then you would fuck me; punish me. I want you to slap me, scratch me, bite me and pull my fucking hair. If you hate me, then punish me. I want to feel your fucking hate; drown myself in it. Then I want lick the hate right off your fucking body and taste it."

She yanks me up by my hair so that our faces are almost touching. Then she looks me in the eyes before slamming her lips against mine and digging her nails into my back. A burn remains in their wake, but I love the pain.

I can't fucking take it anymore. This shit is happening. I rip her dress the rest of the way off so she's lying fully naked beneath me. She looks embarrassed at first, but then relaxes as she watches me undo my pants, pull them off and reach for my cock. I stroke it for a second to see how much she likes it. Her eyes look heated as she watches me.

I stroke it a few more times before pulling a condom out of my pocket, ripping the wrapper open with my teeth and rolling it over my erection.

Not wanting to wait another second, I grip the back of her neck while sliding inside of her. We both moan as I slowly push it in all the way and stop to give her body time to adjust to my thickness.

"Fuck, you are so wet for me."

We're both panting now as I press my lips to hers and fuck her while backing her up the stairs. We get higher with each thrust until we're at the top of the stairs.

Pushing into her, I pick her up and she grabs onto the top of the door frame while I roll my hips in and out, fucking her as hard as I can.

Her grip tightens on the door frame as I grab her hair and yank back while pushing deep. "Fuck, you feel so damn good." I thrust into her hard and long, causing her to pull on the door frame, almost ripping it off. "You're so tight. Damn, my cock can hardly fit inside you."

The only sound around us is the sound of our heavy breathing and our sweaty bodies slapping together as I pleasure her. It feels so fucking good, but I want to get her in my bed.

"Let go of the door frame," I breathe in command. "Grab onto my hair, baby."

Squeezing her legs around me, she lets go of the door frame and grips onto my hair. Her hands rub the back of my head as if she enjoys touching me and wants more. It almost makes me want more. "Slade," she moans. "I'm going to hate myself after this."

Slamming her against the wall, I thrust into her while biting her neck. "Well, until then you can fucking enjoy it."

The louder she screams, the harder I fuck her. I've been waiting for this for too long and I'm going to make sure she never forgets the way my cock makes her scream. I want her to crave my fucking cock; to never think of another one besides mine and how it fucked her so good she couldn't think straight, let alone walk. I want my cock to own her fucking pussy.

We somehow make it to my bedroom door. I hold her against it, never stopping my assault on her body while turning the knob and pushing it open as I thrust in a steady rhythm. She grips me tighter when she realizes that there's nothing behind her to support her any longer. I love having her hang on me and touch me all over. Her hands are roaming my body, taking it all in and I love it. It only proves more that she has been wanting me as long as I have wanted her.

I take a few steps inside before tossing her on my bed. I quickly jump on behind her and flip her over so her ass is up in the air, facing me. I grab her by the hips, run my tongue up her pussy, then thrust into her slow and hard.

She grips the blanket and moans as I reach around and play with her clit. "You want to come again, baby?" I rub it faster, while pushing into her, filling her to the hilt.

She nods and pushes against me with her ass.

"Show me how badly you want me to fuck you then, Aspen. Fucking take your hate and frustration out on me. Show me and

I'll make you come again."

I pull out of her and flip her over so she's looking up at me from her back. Her legs are spread wide as she takes a few deep breaths and then sits up. "You want to see my hate?" She grabs me by the hair and jumps at me so we both fall off the bed with her on top of me. "You're not the only one that has frustration to get out."

Straddling me, she slaps me across the face and then grabs my hair before sinking onto my cock and biting my ear.

Holy shit.

I'm so fucking turned on that I could bust my load right now, but I won't. This is going to last as long as I can make it. This feels too good to stop.

Grabbing her by the hips, I close my eyes and moan while she rides me. "Bite me again and I will pick you up, bind your hands behind your head and fuck you so hard that it hurts."

I don't know if she thinks I'm only messing around or if she really just wants it hard, but she bites into my ear again and tugs on my hair.

I flip her over so that I'm between her legs. Then I look her in the eyes and smirk. "You fucking asked for it."

She lets out a little yelp as I pick her up, hold her hands above her head and slam her into the wall. "Fuck me, Slade," she moans. "I want your *big* dick deep inside of me. I want to see how long you've been wanting me. I want to know that I'm not the only one that's been suffering."

Hearing her say those words releases some kind of beast inside of me. I've never wanted to fuck someone so hard in my life. She knows just the right things to trigger me and get what she wants. She wants me to make her scream again. I can't hold back. Pleasing her turns me on more than anything.

Shit!

Thrusting back into her, I place one hand around her throat while holding her hands above her head with the other. I push in so hard and deep that she screams and scratches at my hands. She wants her hands freed to punish me and I want the same.

I release her hands and they immediately find my back and scratch long and deep as my movements pick up. I feel her starting to tremble and I know she's getting close. Our lips meet each other's and I grab her face, forcing her to look me in the eyes as I make her come.

She moans and screams against my lips so I suck her bottom lip into my mouth and move fast and hard to finish myself off.

It only takes her kissing me hard and pulling my hair before I find myself busting my nut deep inside her still throbbing pussy. We both moan as I release myself as deep as I can. I'm not used to releasing myself inside anyone and the sensation is fucking fantastic. I usually pull out, but this felt too good to even think about it.

We stand here for several seconds, looking each other in the eyes before I pull out of her and set her back down on the floor.

I rub my hands over her face before leaning in and kissing her. She freezes at first, but then grabs the back of my head and slowly caresses her tongue with mine. It's soft, slow and hot. The most intimate kiss I've had in years. I'm not sure how to react.

I pull away from the kiss and back away from her. She watches me with a strange look in her eyes before turning away from me and placing her hands over her face.

She sighs before speaking. "I'm going back downstairs before Cale gets home. I'm sorry. This should never have happened."

I yank the condom off my dick and toss it onto one of my old shirts. I just stand there and watch as she walks toward the door. Before I can stop myself, I say, "Wait."

She stops and waits for me to walk over to her. Stopping in front of her, I cup her face and pull it up so I can look her in the eyes. I just have to look into them and see how I make her feel; see that I pleasured her beyond belief. "Your eyes are the most beautiful fucking thing I have ever seen."

She swallows hard as her eyes dance back and forth before she closes them, as if embarrassed. "In case you're wondering, no I didn't lose a contact. I was born this way, alright? I'll save you trouble from the silly question."

"I wasn't even going to ask you that. I noticed your eyes from the very first time I laid eyes on you. They've never changed. I'm not as stupid as some people. They're beautiful. Don't let anyone else make you think any different."

She laughs and it's the most beautiful sound I have heard from her. I've never heard her laugh before and it's nice to see this side of her. "Yeah, well I'm glad you're smarter than most. I would hate to have another reason to hate you. I already have too many to count." She pauses to push my shoulder and smile. "And thank you. Now I have one less reason to hate you. It's a start."

This makes me laugh. "Is that right?" I pick her up by her hips and set her on my desk. "I can show you a few good reasons not to hate me." I pause as I lick my lips. "Oh yeah. I already have."

She punches my chest, but this time it's playful and not out of pure hate or fuck me anger. I catch her fist and bite it to tease her. "You're such an ass. Do you know that?"

I nod my head and bite her harder while smiling up at her. She laughs and starts tickling me when I don't let go. "Ouch! Let go, Slade." She laughs and tickles me harder.

I didn't realize I was ticklish until now. I find myself squirming until I finally release her fist and let her jump down from the desk. She smiles at me and clears her throat. "Okay . . . I'm going now. Goodnight."

"Why not just sleep in my bed?" I grab her body from behind and pull it close to mine. I have no idea what I'm saying or doing.

All I know is that it's late and I'm tired as shit. "Let Cale have his bed tonight. I'm pretty sure he's bringing some chick home. He's going to need the privacy."

She hesitates before spinning around in my arms. "You don't mind me sleeping in your bed?" Her eyes narrow as she watches for my reaction.

For some reason, at the moment, I don't. "Nah. Tomorrow you can go back to hating me from a distance. Tonight, you can hate me from my fucking bed. I promise it's a lot more comfortable than Cale's damn bed."

I watch her as she walks past me, smiles small and crawls into my bed. She doesn't say another word. She just looks up at me and keeps her eyes on me until I crawl in beside her and flip the lamp off. It only takes a few minutes before I crash out.

IT'S THE MIDDLE OF THE night and I try to roll over, but I can't. That's when I realize that there's a body draped over mine. My eyes shoot open and I sit up in a panic, causing Aspen to move but not wake up. I forgot she was in my bed.

I don't know what the fuck I was thinking when I asked her to sleep in my bed with me, but it's so unlike me. It must've been the adrenaline of finally getting her to have sex with me. That's my only excuse.

Stepping out of bed, I search for a cigarette in the darkened room, open the window and light it. I really need to get my shit together. My whole body is shaking and I'm covered in sweat.

I take a huge drag, close my eyes and let the harsh smoke fill my lungs before releasing it. I have to admit that she looks fucking beautiful lying there naked on my sheets and the thought of slipping back inside her is eating at me. It felt good. A lot better than I expected it to. I had never been so turned on in my life.

Fuck!

I put my cigarette out on the windowsill and take a deep breath while running my fingers through my hair, to keep from punching something. I need to get the fuck out of here. I need to go down to our gym and work this shit off. Like now.

Fucking get a grip, Slade.

CHAPTER TWELVE
Aspen

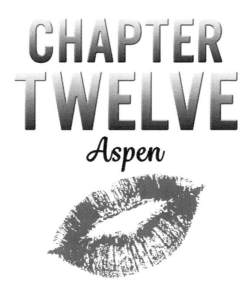

ROLLING OVER, I LAZILY OPEN my eyes and stretch; a very long, hard stretch. It only takes me a few seconds for my eyes to focus and remember where I'm at: Slade's room. Panic sets in and I sit up straight, pulling the sheet over my naked body. I was sleeping so well that I forgot where the hell I was at. Not a good thing. Not good at all.

Shit! Shit! Shit!

I back up against the wall and look around to see I'm alone in the big, quiet room. Slade must have gotten up in the middle of the night and left. A part of me is glad. The last thing I want to do is face his smug ass and listen to him rub in the fact that he finally got what he wanted; not to mention that is was great. It was the best I've ever had and I can't deny it. My body already gave me away.

I tried so hard to resist. I really did, but he's too good. He's damn good at getting what he wants and he knows it. He knew I would eventually cave in and put my hate and frustration into fucking him. It's what he wanted. He likes it rough and meaningless. Well, that's exactly what he got.

While mentally cursing to myself, I jump out of his bed and look around for something to put on. I really need to get out of his room before he comes back. I don't want to see him right now. I can't.

Shit. Why did I let him rip my dress?

Cale is probably downstairs sleeping on the couch and there's no way I'm going down there naked and risking him waking up to see me. I really doubt he needed the bedroom like Slade said. I think Slade just wanted another thing that he could be in control of. Well, I'm sick of him being in control. I'm out of here.

I rush over to the closet, almost tripping over the sheet, but I catch myself just in time and untangle it from my legs. Reaching for the handles, I slide the doors apart and step into his very big and neat closet. I'm surprised to see how organized he actually is; shocked actually.

I walk all the way to the back in hopes I can find an old shirt that he will never miss. I don't know how he would react to me wearing one of his good shirts. When I get to the back my eyes land on a huge row of business suits; very expensive looking business suits.

What. The. Hell.

I run my fingers across them while counting inside my head.

. . . 6, 7, 8, 9, 10, 11, 12, 13, 14. Fourteen suits! Why so many?

I look up to see there are more suits stacked up on the top shelf of his closet. I don't understand what kind of stripper slash damn bartender needs so many suits. Nice ones at that. These look and feel very expensive.

Pulling my eyes away, I take a step back and look around.

There are stacks of shoe boxes with expensive brand names lined up under the hanging suits. Then, to my right there is a whole rack of ties. There is definitely more to Slade than I know; more than what he shows us. I'm definitely curious.

Gripping the sheet tighter, I walk back toward the front of the closet and look up at the shelf when I notice a pile of plain black shirts stacked on top of each other. I'm pretty positive he won't miss one of these.

I reach up and try to pull the bottom one out from the stack, but am not having much luck. I'm all the way on my tip toes and I can still barely get it in my reach.

Come on . . .

My fingers pinch the thin fabric and I tug, pulling the whole pile down with it, along with a shoe box. The shoe box lands on its side with the lid knocked off, causing a bunch of pictures and letters to fall out. I quickly struggle to gather the belongings and stuff them back inside before Slade comes back. The last thing I want him to think is that I'm snooping through his things. He definitely would not be happy about that.

After getting everything stuffed back inside, I am just about to replace the lid when a photograph catches my eye; one that has me very curious. I set the lid down beside me and reach into the box. My eyes scan the ultrasound, checking out dates, names and any other thing that may give me a clue as to why Slade has it stacked away in his things.

Helena Valentine, December 2011.

The baby is huge. It has to be at least eight months gestation. It's from over two years ago. It makes me wonder if this child is his. I really cannot imagine him with a child. It doesn't seem like him.

Setting the photo aside, I dig a little deeper into the box to find photos of a very beautiful pregnant woman. She has long, blond hair, sun kissed skin and a flawless smile. She looks happy; like the happiest woman on earth. She's holding her swollen belly, showing it off to the world as if she's the proudest woman in the world.

In a few of the photos, Slade is in the pictures with her, but he looks different; much different.

He's clean cut with short black hair, no tattoos and the most beautiful smile I have ever seen. I also notice that the scar on his cheek isn't present in the pictures. He looks so happy; nothing like the Slade I see today. He's laughing in almost every single one of them and even kissing her belly in one. He's wearing a suit in a few of them. He looks very professional and handsome.

I hate to feel like I'm prying, but it makes me wonder where this Helena is at. Where is this baby? Did he leave her and now regrets it? Is she still around, but a dark secret that he doesn't want anyone to know about? There are so many possibilities that my head is spinning. I feel lightheaded trying to piece it all together. Slade may be a lot of things, but I don't take him for reckless abandonment.

I'm sitting here just staring, in a daze, when all of a sudden I feel someone standing above me. My heart sinks to my stomach when I look up and see the hurt look in Slade's eyes. He's looking back and forth between me and the box. I instantly drop the photos and hold my breath, not knowing what to expect.

He's standing above me with his jaw steeled and his fists balled at his sides. His body is slick with sweat and his hair is dripping with water as if he's just worked out. His eyes are quick to change from hurt to pure anger and rage. I've never seen someone so angry.

"What the fuck are you doing in here?" He grips the door frame and squeezes as hard as he can. His muscles flex so hard that his arms are shaking and his veins are popping out. "Did I say you could go through my things?"

I scramble to my feet and grip the sheet against me. "No. I wasn't trying to snoop. I was looking for a shirt to-"

"Yeah. I can fucking see that. It must have been by fucking accident then. Am I right?" His jaw clenches even harder as he reaches for my arm and pulls me to him.

He looks me in the eyes for a second and I almost see them soften; a glimpse of hope that he wants to talk to me and let me in. I can't help what comes out next. "Where are they? Did you break her heart and leave her? What about your child?"

He takes a deep breath and backs us out of the closet before slamming the doors behind me and punching the wall. "Get the fuck out!" He reaches in his dresser, grabs a shirt and tosses it to me. I catch it while trying to keep my composure. "There. That's what the fuck you were looking for. Now. Get. Out."

I clutch the shirt against my body and watch as he leans over the dresser and takes a long, deep breath. He stays in the same position for a moment before knocking everything over to the floor and then pushing his dresser over as well.

He doesn't say another word to me. He just stands there looking the other direction, his body tight and his breathing heavy.

"I'm sorry," I stammer. "I-"

"I said get out," he says firmly. "Leave the sheet and go. I won't look at you. Just go." His voice rumbles as he grips his hair in his hands before reaching for his pack of cigarettes.

I can't stop watching him. My hands shake as I drop the sheet, quickly throw his shirt on and run out of the room, shutting the door behind me. I fall against the door and take a deep breath as I hear him breaking things and screaming from the other side. I didn't even know he was capable of feeling anything. I guess I was wrong. He's definitely feeling right now.

After a few seconds, I pull myself together enough to walk away. I don't know why, but a part of me wants to stay. A part of me wants in even though I know that will never happen. I want to see this part of him that I never even knew existed.

I quickly reach for my ripped dress and ball it up in my arms while running down the steps, past the couch and to Cale's door.

It's still dark and quiet so I doubt that he saw me. I quickly turn the knob and push the door open only to stop dead in my tracks when I set eyes on a naked Cale getting his dick sucked by some chick. He looks up while gripping her hair as if my presence doesn't even bother him.

"Holy shit!" I cover my eyes and fall against the wall. "I didn't know you were in here."

Cale lets out a soft chuckle. "Calm down, Aspen. You act as if you've never walked into this situation before." He moans before speaking again. "Your phone's been going off. It's on the dresser."

Keeping my hands over my face, I maneuver my way into the room and over to the dresser as quickly as I can. "I'll be right out. Shit!" I grab my phone and then quickly turn and rush for the door. Right as I'm about to walk out, Cale's voice stops me.

"You caved in," he says softly. "I hope you know what you're doing."

Without turning his way, I take a deep breath and exhale. There's no denying it. The proof was left on the steps. "I do. Trust me."

I step out of his room and shut the door behind me. My heart is going crazy right now and I'm in total shock and a little grossed out. I can't believe that girl didn't even stop sucking that whole time.

Seriously though!

I take a seat on the couch and take a look at my missed messages. My heart sinks when I see Jay's name across the screen. He called twice and sent a text message.

I touch the screen and go straight to the message.

This is a lot different than I expected it to be, Aspen. I actually miss you here. I'll see you in two days.

Swallowing hard, I drop my phone down beside me and lay down across the couch. Any other day, I would be jumping to respond to his message. Well, not today. I just don't have it in me. The need is not there.

CHAPTER THIRTEEN
Slade

FUCK! THIS IS GOING TO be a shitty day . . .

I take a long drag of my cigarette and hold it in while leaning my body weight against the side of the building. I've been outside smoking for the last twenty minutes and I have a feeling it's going to take a lot more than just this shit before I'm able to collect myself enough to go back inside. My head is all fucked up.

I can feel my hands shake as I exhale and cross my arms over my chest to calm my breathing. My nerves are so shot today that I'm surprised I even made it out of bed to begin with. My mind hasn't stopped spinning since I kicked Aspen out of my room this morning.

What the fuck?

I toss my cigarette down, turn around to face the building and punch it repeatedly. What I wouldn't give right now for a fucking release; some kind of distraction. My mind is in such a haze I don't even notice the crackling of bones and splitting of skin. Does it hurt? Hell yeah, but physical pain I can deal with. I'm not good at dealing with *this* shit. The pain shooting through my hand does little to rest the demons inside my head. All it does is piss me off more.

I look up with guarded eyes when I hear some voices nearby. A few girls in passing; laughing and talking amongst themselves. The voices keep getting closer. I'm standing off towards the back of the building next to a dark alley that separates two buildings. It's not very often people come back this way. It's usually my safe place; a place where I can think.

"Is that you, gorgeous?"

A slim figure rounds the building and my eyes are quick to scan it out. Every single inch of it. A pair of long, slender legs lead up to firm thighs, followed by a curvy set of hips hugged by a barely there dress and a firm set of breasts. I know those breasts anywhere.

My eyes continue to marinate in the hot as hell female I recognize as the sexy redhead from the other day. She's no longer dressed in work attire. The perfect example of a little sugar and spice, that's for damn sure. She's in far less now.

Fuck me.

She smiles when she notices me checking her out. She's definitely enjoying giving me a good show and I'm enjoying the view. She found a damn good time to give it too. "Sarah told me I could find you back here. You busy?" She works her lips together, smearing her red lipstick while putting her cigarette out on the bottom of her heel. "I have some *extra* time tonight and was hoping I'd find you."

Wiping my bloodied fists on the back of my pants, I step closer to the temptation in front of me and look her up and down, taking her all in. "Are you sure you have enough time for me? This may take a while. A long fucking while."

Looking over her shoulder, she sends her friends off with a wave of her hand before turning back and flashing me a seductive smile. Her demeanor turns serious while checking out the bulge in my jeans. "I definitely have time for you."

She steps toward me, places her hands on my chest and backs me up against the building. I know exactly where she's going with this and I can't deny I need exactly that.

I pull out another cigarette and light it as she drops to her knees and starts unbuckling my belt followed by my jeans. She works fast at pulling them down my hips while rubbing my erection with her free hand. "Mmm . . . you're a big boy, aren't you?" She pulls my briefs down, letting my cock spring free from its restraints. Her eyes go wide as she licks her lips. "Definitely a big boy. I'm going to have fun with this one."

I close my eyes and take a drag as she moves in and closes her lips around my cock. She moves in a slow rhythm, swirling her tongue around while moving her hand up and down my shaft. She's a pro at this. The combination of the nicotine mixed with the suction is just what I need at the moment.

I moan as she starts moving faster. It feels fucking fantastic, but I'm not feeling the release that I should. This pisses me off.

Taking another hit, I inhale it long and deep while grabbing the back of her head and pushing it further down so my head hits the back of her throat. She grabs my ass and starts sucking faster; enjoying it.

I move my hips back and forth, fucking her mouth, matching her rhythm; looking for a release that isn't coming. Not even close.

Dammit! *I've had enough of this shit.*

Tugging her hair so she knows to stop, I pull out of her mouth, bend down and pick her up to her feet. I toss my cigarette down.

"Bend over." I place my hand on her back and push her forward so her ass is in the air. Beautiful. She looks over her shoulder at me, waiting. "This isn't doing what I need it to do, sweetheart. I need to bury my cock deep in your pussy for the release I need. You better be ready to take it deep and hard." I bend over her and speak in her ear while pulling her dress up. "I have a lot of frustration to work out. Just a one-time release."

I turn her around so she can place both her hands on the building for support. She's going to need it. I slap the right exposed cheek, hard. She yelps and I press my front to her back. "You like that," I ask as I hook my thumbs under her panties and inch the tiny thong over her hips, letting them fall to her feet. Pushing back, I reach in my pocket for a condom.

My jaw clenches as I stare down at her slick pussy just waiting for me to ram my cock in it; to give her the same release I'm needing. For some reason, I don't feel the same rush as usual. As a matter of fact, I don't feel shit.

"Fuck!"

I toss the condom packet at the building and rub my hands over my face. I am beyond frustrated with myself at the moment. This is not fucking good. Sex has always been my way to cope. If I don't have that what kind of pussy am I? What the fuck am I supposed to do now?

She looks over her shoulder to see my face before she quickly stands up and pulls her dress down. She looks disappointed as fuck. "What the hell is wrong? Are we doing this or not?"

I shake my head while pulling my jeans back up and exhaling. "Not." I buckle my jeans and then turn to walk away while redoing my belt buckle. I need to get my ass busy with something. Fucking shots or something. Anything to numb this shit.

I storm my way back into the bar and over to Sarah. "Give me a fucking shot; the strongest you got . . . and quick." I sit my ass on a stool and watch as she reaches for a glass. She flashes a knowing smile while setting it down in front of me and eyeing me up and down. "What, Sarah?"

She shakes her head and pours me a shot of Whiskey. "Looks like you're not the only one here to drink your mind away." She nods behind me and leans over the bar. "Look behind you by Hemy."

I grab my shot and spin around in my stool while slamming it back. The sight in front of me makes my heart race.

What the hell?

"How long has she been here?" I push the shot glass in front of Sarah and stand up. "Another one. Fast."

Sarah sighs and pours me another one. "She got here right after you went outside. She's already had three shots of Vodka and a Vodka and cranberry." She watches as I slam back the second shot before speaking again. "She looks like she's having some fun with Hemy. My guess is . . ." She smirks at me and grabs my empty glass out of my hand. "That you already fucked her. Women always seem to go looking for the next guy to make her feel *wanted*."

"Yeah, well we both know she isn't getting it with that mother fucker. He's worse than I am. Shit."

I can already see Hemy working his bad boy charm on Aspen and even from across the room, it looks as if it might be working. The truth is, if Hemy wants to fuck someone he will fuck them one way or another. It's how it works with him.

He's over there with his jeans unbuttoned, slowly pouring water down the front of his chest while looking her directly in the eyes and fucking the damn air. From my angle I can see her hands reach out to touch his stomach. I'm not sure I'm liking this shit.

Making my way across the room, I step up behind Aspen and grab her arm to turn her around. It takes her a few seconds before she even registers that she's looking at me. The drinks are clearly setting in and I'm wondering just what the hell her reasoning is for being all over Hemy. "What the fuck are you doing here?"

Aspen laughs, clearly unfazed by my tone and yanks her arm out of my reach. "I'm getting a strip tease from Hemy. What does it look like?" She reaches for Hemy's jeans and pulls him closer to her. "Don't stop dancing on account of that asshole," she says with a scowl.

Hemy raises an eyebrow to me and smirks as he notices my eyes trail down toward her hands that are working their way down to his hard dick. She's clearly trying to push my buttons.

"Don't come over here and try to ruin my fun just because you're having a bad day. Clearly you have some shit to deal with." She runs her hand over Hemy's cock while looking at me. Hemy seems to fucking like this. "Maybe Hemy isn't as big of a dick as you." She laughs and looks me in the eyes. "Well, he definitely has as big of a dick as you. Maybe he knows how to use it just as good."

Okay. Now I am getting extremely fucking pissed. I don't like seeing her rub his fucking cock one bit. It makes me want to kick the shit out of Hemy. Well, that's a fucking new feeling. "Too bad you won't be finding out. You're fucking going home. Now."

She yanks her arm away from me as I reach for it. "The hell I am. I'm having fun with Hemy. He's so damn *sexy*." She steps closer to Hemy and caresses his chest and abs. "And I bet those piercings feel . . . good. I've heard some hot, hot stories about him. Maybe I want to try him out. Have a little fun of my own for once."

Hemy goes to reach for her waist, but I place my hand to his chest and push him back. "Back the fuck up, man." My jaw steels as I look him in the eyes to let him know just how fucking serious I am. "Not a good time to fuck with me."

Hemy gives me a hard look before backing away and finding

the closest chick to start grinding on. We may push each other's buttons, but we've figured out in the past just how far to push each other. We're not going that fucking route again.

"Are you serious?" Aspen reaches for her purse and starts heading for the door. "I really cannot stand you. First you fuck me and then you throw me out like trash and now you ruin my fun. What the hell goes on in your twisted mind?" She moves faster as I fall into step behind her. "Huh? Huh? What?"

"None of your business. All you need to know is that you're acting like a fucking fool. If you think Hemy will treat you any better than me, then you're fucking mistaking. He will take you home and call over a buddy while they both fuck you until you're sore. Then they will wake up and fuck you again. You will still end up alone in the end results. Hemy is not going to make things any better."

She yanks the door open and rushes outside before turning around to yell at me. "So, what the hell does it matter? It seems that no one wants me. I'm not enough for anyone. Might as well just fuck them all then. I'm so tired of it. So tired of everyone treating me like I'm worth nothing but sex. What is so wrong with me?"

I watch as she turns around and stomps over to her friend's car. She struggles with unlocking the door while trying to balance on her heels. "Don't you fucking get in that car." I stride over and yank the keys from her hand. "You're not driving."

She reaches for the keys, but I hold them up high so she can't reach them. She slaps my chest and pushes me. "Give. Me. The. Keys."

I shove them in my front pocket and push up against her until her body is pinned against the car. "No. You're not driving. You're fucking drunk." I pin her hands above her head as she struggles against me. "And you are fucking enough. We're all just fucking assholes. You need to know that."

She stops struggling against me and looks me in the eyes. I see a hint of her there but I can tell that she's pretty close to wasted. After a few seconds, she pulls one of her arms free and reaches into my pocket digging for the keys. I feel her hand brush over my cock and it instantly gets hard. "Give it to me, dammit."

I yank her hand out of my pocket and pin it back against the car while roughly pushing my body against hers. "I said you're not fucking driving. I'll call us a cab. Try reaching for those keys again and I will fucking tie your ass up with my belt."

"Why the fuck do you care? Now you want to be the good guy?" She laughs and pushes me away with her knee. I back off and give her the space she needs. She looks hurt now. I can't deal with that. "Get off me. I'll be over here." She starts walking away. "In the bushes waiting."

I don't understand why, but I just want to get this woman home and in bed; in my fucking bed.

BY THE TIME WE GET back to the house, the full effects of the shots must have kicked in. She's slurring her words and laughing at absolutely nothing at all. It almost makes me want to laugh, but I'm too fucking annoyed to enjoy this.

She laughs even harder as I pick her up and throw her over my shoulder. "My ass is showing." She starts tugging on her dress and squirming in my arms. "My thong! My thong!"

I slap her ass to stop her from moving. "No one cares. We're the only ones here and I have already seen your ass."

"Yeah. And a *whole* lot more." She begins pulling up the hem of my shirt, revealing my back. She inserts the tips of her fingers under the waistband of my jeans, lightly caressing my ass. It kind of tickles until she digs her nails into my skin and scratches upward.

"I want to see more of you. Strip." She continues to scratch up my back, hard, causing me tip her back up.

I grab her ass cheeks in my hands and she instantly wraps her legs around my waist. She bites the skin on my neck playfully as she reaches for my belt. I start walking up the stairs toward my bedroom. "Take it off, dirty stripper boy," she says teasingly. "I love your body. It's so *sexy*. I just want to lick it and taste."

As turned on as I am by her biting me and trying to strip me, I keep my fucking cool and toss her on my bed before walking out of my room and slamming the door behind me. I can't let this shit happen for two reasons: number one, she's drunk. Number two, it's against my fucking rules.

Shit. I need a cold shower.

I take my time in the shower before quietly making my way up the stairs and to my room. When I walk in, I notice right away that she is sleeping. She's managed to strip out of her dress and heels and is now wearing one my favorite shirts. I have to admit, I like seeing her in it. She looks beautiful; like a fucking angel.

I reach for a cigarette and light it while pacing around my room and watching her sleep. She looks so fucking peaceful lying there. A part of me wants to crawl into bed next to her and hold her in my fucking arms, but the smarter part of me is reminding me of what a horrible idea that is. So instead, I dig out my favorite picture of Helena, grab the chair and pull it next to the window and sit.

I stare at the picture until my eyes blur. I haven't looked at this in almost a year. It hurts. It hurts so fucking badly that I can't breathe . . . but there is something making it a little easier. Someone that makes me want it to be easier. That thought scares me.

I must sit there for about an hour, in the dark with my hands wrapped in my hair before I hear her mumbling and moving around. When I look up, I see that her eyes are opened and she's staring right at me.

"Talk to me, dammit," she says.

I feel an ache in my chest at the thought of talking about it. I've been holding in my emotions for so long; for too long. Maybe it's time to get it out. She'll be gone in a couple days anyways. Maybe this will help ease some shit in my head.

Here goes fucking nothing . . .

I jump to my feet, toss the picture on the bed and try to hold back the tears. "Her name *was* Helena Valentine. She was my fiancé and was carrying my child."

CHAPTER FOURTEEN

Aspen

OH. MY. GOD.

I feel an ache in the pit of my stomach and a part of me feels like puking. *Was. He said was.* I blink a few times to focus my vision before reaching for the picture next to my feet and rubbing my thumb over it. It's moist and the color is smeared. It wasn't like that last time I saw it.

"I really don't want to talk about this, but it is starting to take every fucking thing in me to keep my shit together. I do everything I can to keep my mind busy. It's getting pretty fucking exhausting. I don't think I can take it anymore."

I look up at Slade and suck in a deep breath while taking in the pained look in his eyes. They're wet and I can tell it is taking everything in him to not cry. I can't even speak. I don't want to. I'm afraid to hear more. I'm scared to hear what he went through.

It's silent as he starts pacing. The silence is getting me so nervous that my stomach hurts. Not that the liquor helps any . . . but I feel totally sober now; wide awake and alert.

"I loved her with everything in me," he finally says. "I would have never left her or my child. Don't ever think that. It sends a flood of rage through my body. I may be a piece of shit now, but I wasn't always this way." He looks up toward the ceiling and rubs his hands over his face, clearly frustrated with himself. "We dated all throughout high school and I had known her since I was ten. She was my best fucking friend and I never had the courage to tell her how I felt. I went years holding it in, afraid that she would reject me and it would ruin our friendship."

He stops pacing, pulls out a cigarette and lights it before continuing. "She meant more to me than that. I couldn't lose her. I wouldn't allow it. Our freshman year I watched her date numerous assholes that always broke her heart. She always came to me for comfort and I was always there to take care of her. I promised her I always would be and I keep my fucking promises. One night after some asshole put his hands on her, I kicked the shit out of him and told her I couldn't take seeing her hurt anymore."

He takes a long drag of his cigarette and looks out the window as if trying to picture it all in his head. His voice is starting to break and I can tell this is tearing him up inside. I hate this.

"I told her I loved her; that I was *in* love with her. She was shocked as hell when I told her. I still remember that look on her face before she leaned in and kissed me harder than I had ever been kissed in my whole life. It was as if she were desperate; as desperate as I was. Come to find out, she had been in love with me the whole time and she was afraid of the same thing I was. From that day on she was mine. I took care of her." He turns to look at me. "And I never fucking hurt her. She was my life. I would have given my life for hers."

He places his hand over his face and looks down at the ground. I can't be sure, but I think I see tears falling. He puffs his cigarette and clenches his jaw. "If I could trade places with her I would, dammit. Fuck!"

He crouches down, resting his elbows on his knees with his face buried in his hands. "It should have been me. We were both in that fucking car. Not just her. Both of us, dammit!"

He starts shaking his head back and forth, hitting his head against the dresser behind him, as the tears come out steadily, dripping down his face and arms. "I didn't want to go anywhere that night. I tried so hard to get her to just stay where we were. It was New Year's Eve and all though I wasn't drinking, I knew others were. I told her. I fucking told her I didn't want to drive her home with all the crazy people that would be out that night, but she was eight months pregnant with our baby girl and she kept complaining she was uncomfortable and needed to go home to sleep. Finally, I caved in." He looks up toward the ceiling. "I'm so fucking sorry, Helena. I should have said no and put my foot down. You may have been pissed at me, but you and Hailey would be here right now. I would be taking care of you both; protecting you."

His body starts shaking as he looks back down at the ground and breaks down. He's crying so hard that I can't help the moisture building up in the corner of my eyes just from watching him. My heart aches for him. He's been holding all this pain in. That's not healthy for anyone. Not to mention the fact that he blames himself. No one should have to bear that pain.

I stand up and walk over to stand in front of him, but he doesn't look up from the ground. He just takes a quick drag and exhales. "The car killed her on impact; broke her neck. Dammit! All it did was throw me around a little." He brushes his fingers over the scar on his face. "I still remember holding her until the ambulance came. It felt like forever before they got there. I knew she wasn't breathing, but I . . . I just kept on yelling at her to hold on; that her and Hailey were going to be okay, but the blood . . . it was everywhere. Her seat was soaked in it, but I never let myself believe that Hailey wouldn't be born. I refused to give up hope."

He stops and chokes back a sob before whispering, "My life ended that night, along with theirs."

Without thinking, I drop down on my knees in front of him and place my hands on his arms, but he jerks away. I grab his arms again and pull them away from his face. He looks up at me through wet lashes while dropping his cigarette and putting it out with his knee. "You can't blame yourself for that night, Slade. Please, stop blaming yourself. You did everything you could to take care of them."

His nostrils flare and his jaw muscles flex as tears roll down his blotchy face. His eyes are distant and his whole body is shaking under my touch. His pain is too much to handle. All I want to do is help ease it.

I grab his face and rub my thumb over his scar as a tear slides down my cheek. He still hasn't said another word. He just looks numb now; dead inside. He's staring at me as if he's a bit surprised by my comforting him. "It's okay for you to talk about it. It's okay to let it out and ask for help to carry some of the burden. Let me help you." He starts shaking his head as he closes his eyes, tears still falling. "I know you miss them. That is nothing to be ashamed of. Nothing at all. Okay, dammit? The world should know how much you love them. Don't let the memory of your family die out because you're too afraid to talk about it; to remember. You shouldn't live life that way."

He clears his throat and looks blankly at the wall across from him. "Every day is a struggle for me to get by. Just the thought of losing them takes the breath right from my fucking lungs. It hurts so fucking bad. I never thought a day would go by that I wouldn't have Helena by my side. We spent every day together. Even as kids. It's not easy to just move on with life after losing the biggest part of you; like losing a vital organ. After that day, I just shut down. I gave up. Every day I feel like I'm fucking dying, over and over again. I can't fucking breathe, Aspen. I can't."

Feeling my heart break for him, I wrap my arms around him and pull him to me as tightly as I can. To my surprise he doesn't push me away. Instead he snuggles his face into my neck and wraps his arms around my head, letting the tears fall. So, I sit here and hold him for a while until the tears stop. It feels like forever, but I refuse to let him go. He needs someone. All of this pain has been consuming him and he's been living his life by numbing himself to the world; getting out of his own head.

Quite a bit of time passes, but finally, he pulls away from me and stands up. He doesn't even bother with wiping his face off. He just lets the last tear fall; unashamed. "You should get some rest, Aspen." He looks me in the eyes for a moment before picking me up and walking over to his bed. He stops in front of it and gently places me atop the mattress. "It's really late. Cale should be home soon. You can just crash in here."

He takes a seat at the edge of the bed and places his face back in his hands while yawning. I sit up and crawl over to him to place my hand on his shoulder. It's tense and he's still slightly shaking. "You should get some rest too. I am fine on the couch." I swallow hard while looking at his solid muscles though his snug shirt. They keep flexing as if he's struggling with something; as if he's fighting frustration. "I can stay if you need me to, though."

He turns around, wraps his arm around my waist and pulls me to him before laying back on the mattress. He gently brushes my hair away from my neck and snuggles up against me with his face against the side of my neck. His breathing is soft and warm against my flesh. It gives me goose bumps. "I need you to," he whispers.

My heart skips a beat from his words and I find myself wrapping my arms around him for comfort and to pull him closer; as close as I can get him. For some reason, being in his arms this way is making it hard for me to breathe. I have never seen this side of him and I'm afraid the feeling is too good for me not to want more. Right now, being in his arms makes me feel special. He's opened up to me in a way that I doubt he has with anyone else in a long time. This feeling makes me happy.

WHEN I WAKE UP, SLADE is gone. Just like he was the last time I stayed in his room. Except this time, I know he stayed the whole night because he never let me go. He held me so tight that I could barely move. Being in his strong arms made me feel safe and at home; something I haven't felt in a while. It confuses me.

I sit here for a while waiting for Slade to return, but he doesn't. It's been, I don't know, maybe twenty minutes or more since I've noticed him gone. A part of me worries that he's still suffering from the pain of last night and maybe he left to numb the pain. I've noticed the way he uses alcohol to numb the pain because, well, I did it last night. Pain gets the best of us all at some point.

I tiredly crawl out of bed and make my way down the stairs. When I pass the couch, I see that Cale is asleep on it. He must've assumed I was in his room when he got home late last night. Well, he was definitely wrong.

When I get to the bathroom door I stop, because it is slightly cracked open, but the lights are off. Last time this happened, Slade was behind that door and I'll never forget that look in his eyes when he saw me standing there. I'm not sure I can face that again. It made my knees weak.

Working against my nerves, I push the door open and take a

step inside. Slade is standing there in a T-shirt and a pair of white boxers briefs. He's leaning against the sink while staring up at the ceiling. He looks lost in thought.

I hesitate before speaking. I'm not sure he wants to be bothered.

"I . . . I just wanted to check and make sure that you're okay." I step further inside and he turns to look at me. The look in his eyes is different this time. I can't tell exactly how, but just different. He doesn't speak; just clenches the sink and then lets go. "Do you need anything?"

He slowly walks toward me, his eyes focused on my face. His expression is calm and relaxed. I've never seen him like this. His hands reach out and he softly caresses my cheek before bringing his eyes down to my lips. "Yeah," he whispers. "You."

"What-"

My words are cut off when he tangles his fists in the back of my hair and gently presses his lips to mine. He kisses me soft, but with a want that makes my heart speed up. My lips part enough for him to slip his tongue inside and swirl it around mine. When this man kisses like this, he doesn't just kiss you, he owns you.

His muscles flex around me as he pulls me closer to him and slowly backs me up against the wall. I find my hands desperately seeking his body; just wanting to touch him in any way I can. Right now, we couldn't possibly get any closer, but I'm still trying; he's trying.

"I love the way your mouth tastes," he whispers against my lips. "I haven't wanted to kiss someone this much . . . in a very long time." He tugs on my bottom lip with his teeth before sucking it into his mouth and releasing it. "With you, I can't get enough of it."

Desperate for more of him, I slam my lips against his and dig my nails into his strong back. I feel him growl against my lips before he picks my legs up and walks to the right, stepping into the shower. He sets me back down on my feet while grabbing my hip and pulling me against him.

With his lips still pressed against mine, he reaches over and turns the shower on before guiding us both under the water. He continues an assault on my lips; kissing me so hard it's a little painful. The stubble from his lip scours my smooth skin, but at the moment I couldn't give a damn.

The water is cold at first, causing me to jump back, but he squeezes me tighter to him and causes a friction between our bodies. The radiation of body heat warms me up and it only makes me want him more.

His hands work slowly, pushing his T-shirt up my thighs as he works his beautiful lips against mine; teasing me in a way I have never been teased.

Every time his tongue caresses mine, I feel myself clenching my thighs to keep from going crazy. His touch and the taste of him is driving me mad; not only making my body want him, but crave him. Now I see why Hemy was so hard. This man is so erotic.

Both of us are drenched; our wet clothing plastered against our bodies as we stand here trying to catch our breath. He's now looking me in the eyes as he reaches for my thong with both hands and drops to his knees, gently guiding them down my legs as if I'm delicate and he's trying not to break me.

I place my hands on his shoulders and look down at him as I lift my feet out of them. After he tosses my panties aside, he looks up at me while running his hands up my thighs, followed by his soft lips. My whole body quivers from his touch and my breathing picks up as he gets closer to the ache between my thighs.

Just when I think he's about to pleasure me, he stops and stands up while wiping the water from his face. The bathroom is still slightly dark, but I can still see the steely blue of his eyes and the intensity in them is so great that I find myself grabbing the back of his head and slamming my lips back to his for more. They can't get enough; I can't get enough.

I feel his erection press against my belly as he cups my ass cheeks and squeezes. He picks me up and presses me against the wall. My legs wrap around his waist on instinct. His stiffness against my pussy sends a surge of pleasure and need throughout my body, causing me to moan out against his lips.

"Why does this feel so good," I ask breathless.

He runs his hands up my side and speaks against my lips. "Because it's with me," he breathes, "And I want you in a way I never thought I'd want anyone again. There is something about you that is different."

Pressing my body tighter against his, he rubs my pussy against his erection, making me want to scream out, even through the wet fabric. It feels so big and firm and it is still confined inside the cotton of his briefs. I've never wanted a man like this before. I want to touch him bare; undress him and pleasure him.

Loosening my legs, I slide down his front until I am standing on my two feet. I drop to my knees; my eyes level with his hard cock that is begging to be released from its cage. As I take hold of it in my hand, I picture what it felt like inside me and with that vision I lose control, having no other option than to release it from his briefs, so I do by hooking my small fingers underneath the elastic band. Pulling outward, his cock springs free, allowing me to pull them down his legs until they pile up at his feet.

His cock is standing at attention, commanding to be touched. It's the most beautiful cock I've ever seen. I run my hand up and down his shaft, brushing the tip of his penis once in a while to tease him. Each time I do this, he moans and bucks forward.

"Touching you drives me crazy," I whisper. "I want to feel you." He takes my hand and pulls me to my feet, pressing me against the wall. He touches my cheek with the tips of his finger, brushing my wet hair off my face. He lightly traces the seam of my body, stopping at my thigh and clenching it in his palm before pulling it upward to rest around his waist.

He brushes his finger of the opposite hand over my entrance, slightly dipping inside and running it up my folds before sticking it inside and slowly moving it in and out. He's good at pleasuring me and he damn well knows it. "Mmm . . . yeah. Touch me, Slade." I run my tongue up his wet chest, then up his neck, making my way to his ear. "I love you inside me," I whisper.

Pinning me against the wall with his sculpted body, he presses deeper inside, quickening his pace at an angle like a hook. Each time he slams inside, he hits a spot and it feels amazing. I can't help but to vocalize the way it makes me feel. "That's it. Don't stop. Please don't stop."

No man has ever made me come with his hand before, but I can feel it starting. I'm beginning to zone out as the feeling of bliss takes over my body. "You like my fingers inside you, baby? Do you want my fingers to make you come or do you want my cock?"

As the last syllable escapes his lips, he stops as I'm on the verge of orgasm. He looks me in the eyes with those magnificent blue eyes waiting on an answer. "I want your cock, Slade. I want you to fill me completely."

I feel his chest rumble before he grabs the bottom hem of the large T-shirt, pulling it off in one quick motion. "I need you naked for this," he says in a voice that makes me want to come right now. Placing his palms over my ass cheeks, he trails down both of my thighs with a quickness, picking me up and pressing me against the wall, aggressively. I love this side of him.

His eyes lock with mine as he lowers me to his erection and slowly eases it inside of me. I close my eyes and moan as I feel his thickness stretching me to accommodate his girth. He holds me there for a minute, being sure that I'm okay before he slowly starts moving me up and down his cock allowing the wetness to spread. He's taking me for another ride, despite the fact it's against his rules and I'm definitely not blind to this. It gives me a rush like nothing else and is hot as hell.

We both moan with each thrust; not able to get enough of this pleasure. It's beautiful, raw and erotic just like him.

Feeling him raw, inside of me, has my adrenaline pumping so hard that I forget how to breathe. I'm not sure if I want to. I just want to feel this moment for what it is and never forget it.

I slowly peel his shirt off him while his eyes take me in; every inch of me as if he can't get enough. His arms flex each time he enters me and his breathing picks up as he pushes himself deeper inside me. I lean my head against the wall, moaning, with each thrust.

My body becomes heated as the steam fills the shower, causing my head to become a clouded haze. Nothing else can be processed but the moment at hand. Between the water splashing against our bodies and the slow rhythm, I'm becoming hypnotized by him. It's a cruel pleasure. He's teasing me; ruining me. I can't concentrate on anything; only the sensation that is building in my body each time he pushes inside me.

He presses his lips to my neck while picking up speed and pushing harder and deeper as if he can't get enough of me. "You feel so fucking good, Aspen. This feels good." He places a hand behind my head and pulls it to him so it presses against his fore-head; our lips barely brushing. "I'm about to go soon. I can't hold it in any longer. I need you to come, baby."

He presses his body weight against mine and starts thrusting into me hard and deep while swirling his thumb over my clit.

I feel myself shaking in his arms and moaning as I get close to climax. It feels so good that I have to scream. I do too. The pleasure is too much for me to bear internally. I fucking scream and grab onto the shower head almost pulling it off. I feel my release as I clamp down around his thick dick and squeeze my legs around his waist.

His reaction is to speed up and go even faster. He's ready to go now and for some reason I want to experience this in its fullest.

"I'm on birth control," I say out of breath.

He pauses for a second, presses his lips against mine and then fucks me so hard that I bite down onto his tongue. I suck it and he moans just before he pushes as deep as he can go and I feel him release his load inside me.

He holds me up against the wall, our lips twining as we both fight for air. Neither one of us speak. We don't need to. We just bask in our release, enjoying this moment of peace.

After a few moments, he gently sets me down, steps out of his briefs and we shower together with him cleaning me. With him touching me all over it's so hard to not want him back inside of me.

I can see it all over him too as he takes in my body with a look; as if he's ready to back me against the wall and own me. This want is too great for me.

He leans over my shoulder and runs his lips up my neck, stopping just below my ear. "I want you to come for a ride with me after we shower. I have things I want to tell you."

I nod my head and close my eyes as he attends to me.

I'm not used to this kind of treatment. I mean from anyone. Is this the way he always was before his life fell apart? Is this the person he has been fighting so hard to hide?

If so . . . then I'm in deep trouble.

CHAPTER FIFTEEN
Slade

I FEEL AS IF A fucking weight has been lifted from my shoulders. I've been fighting for so long, using every bit of strength I had to keep this shit inside; to not feel the guilt and pain of losing Helena and our baby. It's been almost three years since the accident. It's time I realize the pain will always be there. It's either learn to live or don't live at all. A part of me for the last week has been wanting to live. So, I think I'll hold onto that and go with it.

I'm just throwing on my shirt, when the bedroom door opens and Cale steps inside. He looks a hot mess as if he didn't sleep for shit. Not a pretty sight.

"Dude. What the fuck was all that noise a bit ago? You had some chick fucking screaming like mad in the shower. It woke my ass up and probably woke Aspen up. It's too early for this shit."

I raise an eyebrow at him while slipping on my Chucks and

fastening my belt. "It *was* Aspen. Don't worry, man. She's perfectly fucking fine. Trust me."

He takes a step back and scrunches his forehead up. "Whoa, man. What the fuck do you mean it was Aspen?" He takes quick steps in my direction and stops right in front of me. "That has to be a fucking joke. I know you fucked her the other night. It never happens twice with you. Are you fucking with me?"

I place my hand on his shoulder and squeeze. "Nah, man. I'm not fucking with you." I smile and slap him on the back, almost making him fall forward. "I'm taking her for a ride on my motorcycle and chilling for a bit before work." I walk toward the door and stop to look back at him. "It's a nice fucking day out. I don't want to be cooped up inside."

"What. The. Fuck." He gives me a shocked ass look and runs his hands over his face really fast as if trying to wake himself up. "I must need to go back to sleep. I think I'm hearing things now."

"Definitely not hearing things. Now get the fuck out of my room, mother fucker." I nod my head and laugh as he walks past me, keeping his eyes on me the whole time. He's looking at me as if he's waiting on something. I don't have time for this shit. "What the hell is wrong with you?"

"Nothing. I'm just trying to wrap my head around this shit. Not only did Aspen *let* you fuck her more than once, but you *wanted* to."

"All right, man. Well I don't have time to stand here while you try to wrap your big head around this shit. I have to be at the club in three hours." I walk past him and make my way down the stairs.

Right as I reach for my keys, Aspen steps out of Cale's room, wearing a pair of faded jeans, a white tank top and some old Chucks.

All right. My kind of girl.

I grab her by the waist, pull her to me and suck her bottom lip into my mouth. She seems a little surprised at first, but eventually wraps her hands in the back of my hair and moans as I rub my hands up her sides.

I release her lip and look her up and down, taking all her raw sexiness in. "Shit, you're so fucking sexy." I press my lips against hers while backing her up against the door and cupping her ass in my hands. Right now, I just can't keep my hands off of her. "Fuck, just one taste and I can't get enough. I want fucking more of you."

"Wow. I definitely was not expecting this shit. This is way fucked up and unnatural. For the both of you."

Aspen pulls her mouth away at the sound of Cale's voice and clears her throat. She nervously looks me in the eyes and maneuvers her way out of my hold. "Umm . . . I'll be back in a bit. Slade is just taking me on a ride."

Cale lifts an eyebrow and leans against the couch. "You mean another one? Isn't two enough?"

"Ha. Very funny, smartass." Aspen shoots him an icy glare before reaching for the door handle and pushing me out of the way so she can walk outside.

I turn back to Cale and nod my head at him. "All right, man. We're out. By the way, you can stop worrying about her. I know what the fuck I'm doing."

He crosses his arms over his chest and stares at the door with a sullen expression. "Maybe it's not her I'm worried about." He turns and walks away without another word.

All fucking right . . .

When I get outside, Aspen is leaning against my motorcycle while staring down at her phone as if waiting on something. She shoves her phone in her pocket and smiles when she notices me watching her.

"You ready? Where are we going?" She's looking at me as if she doesn't know how to act around me. I don't blame her. Right now, I'm probably confusing the shit out of her. She knows my fucking rules. She knows I broke those fucking rules . . . and for her. I wouldn't know how to react either.

I walk over to my bike, grab my helmet and slip it on her head. There is something about a girl on the back of a motorcycle in jeans and a tank that is extremely sexy . . . or maybe it's just her on the back of the motorcycle. Once the strap is fastened, I straddle my bike and grab her arm, pulling her on behind me. "Hold on tight."

She wraps her arms around my waist and snuggles up close behind me. The unexplainable feeling I have with her against me doesn't go unnoticed before I fire up the engine and take off.

We ride for about an hour until we finally pull up at the same spot I took her a few days ago. The memory of her soaking wet in more ways than one instantly floods the banks of my memory. The reminder of what happened here last time already has my dick fucking hard and ready for more. I'd always wanted to pleasure a woman out in the rain. I can't deny it was one of the hottest things I've ever done. Not to mention, I was a little surprised she let it happen. That only turned me on more.

Fuck me. Now during a summer rain, I'll never be the same.

I help Aspen off my bike. As I get off, I take notice of the bulge underneath my jeans and adjust the enlarged area of my crotch. My cock is so hard right now that my jeans are almost not loose enough to contain it. I see Aspen looking down at my dick and swallowing as I push it down. She wants me again and it gets me so fucking hot just knowing that I have her ready for more so soon.

"Get over here, babe."

She seems hesitant at first, but walks over to stand in front of me. Her eyes are studying mine and she looks curious. I want to know what the hell this woman is thinking. What the hell, curiosity wins out. "Ask."

"I want to know more about your life, Slade. Why do you have all those suits in your closest? Please don't tell me they're costumes for work because I know that's not true. I saw the pictures of you wearing them. You looked . . . different. Nothing like you do today."

My eyes study her face. She's really serious about this. She wants to know about me. It may sound a little fucked up, but she's the first woman to ask me anything personal about my life. All that the other women wanted was a good fuck and they knew they would get it from me. I grew used to it; got comfortable and became accustomed to it. It became my escape; my addiction. It may make me sound like shit, but when you basically fuck for a living you get used to it; crave it and then it gets hard to stop.

For some reason I want to tell her. I want her to know more about me. "All right. I'll tell you." I pick her up by the hips and set her down so she's straddling the back of my bike just like the last time we were here. I just hope she's ready for this because it's a long fucking story and one I don't usually tell.

"I used to be a lawyer." She gives me a shocked look by widening her eyes, but stays quiet. I know, it's quite a fucking shocker from looking at the man you see today. "I worked for my father's Law Firm. It wasn't what I wanted to do. It was what I was expected to do. I didn't have a passion for it; although, I was one of the best. Everyone wanted me to handle their cases because they knew they wouldn't get any better. I was a damn good lawyer. I just didn't like it. I worked very hard; too hard. It got boring as shit and fast."

I grab her legs and yank her to me so her legs are wrapped around my waist and my hands are locked behind her back. "After the accident, I shut myself off from the world. I didn't leave my house for about a month straight. When that month was up, I couldn't force myself to go back to that life. No matter how hard

VICTORIA ASHLEY

my father pushed me, I just pushed back. I couldn't fucking do it anymore. I was tired of living life the way he wanted me to. There was only one option; to quit."

"A few months later, after draining the money I had in my savings account and not doing shit but eating, showering and sleeping, Cale asked me to come out to a party at *Walk Of Shame*. I hadn't been out of the house pretty much at all since the accident, so I agreed to go out and try to get my mind off things. Cale was dancing that night along with Hemy and somehow the women kept mistaking me for one of the dancers. They couldn't keep their hands off me. I hadn't felt anything in a long time and that night, I had such a rush that I was on some kind of high. It was the first feeling I had since the accident. I grew addicted to the rush and depended on it. It was my normalcy, so I took a job at the club and became roommates with Cale a few months later. I've just barely been getting by. First it was the dancing and the sex, then it became the tattoos and the pain I got from them. It kept me feeling something; made me feel more alive. When that didn't help me anymore, I moved on and it became the drinking. The alcohol was enough to numb it. It has gotten me by . . . until now. I want more though. I just don't know if I can have it; if I deserve it."

She scoots closer to me and reaches out to cup my face in her hands. I find myself reaching up to place my hands over hers as I look into her eyes. It feels nice. "Thanks for sharing that with me. I know how hard this must be for you. I also know that you don't open up very often. It means a lot to me." She leans in, hesitates, but then presses her lips against mine.

She gets ready to pull away, but I tangle my hands in the back of her hair and pull her as close to me as I can. The feeling I have right now is unexplainable. It's so fucking good that I could just kiss her all night and not give a damn about anything else. I haven't talked to anyone about my past and with her, she makes it feel so

142

natural; so damn easy. It's like she's the medicine I've needed all along; the way to cope.

The feel of her in my arms and the taste of her in my mouth makes me feel . . . at ease. Just a little bit of peace finally; not enough to kill the pain, but enough to give me a little hope.

I pick her up off my bike and wrap her legs around my waist while kissing her long and hard. I want her to know that she's only making me want her more each and every day. At first, it was just a sexual attraction; the need to have something that I couldn't, but it's become more to me than just that. She's different than the other girls. She's more than just a fuck. She's addictive, but the right kind of addiction. I have a very addictive personality and she may be the thing I need to feed it.

A few minutes pass before she pulls away from the kiss and places her forehead against mine. We look into each other's eyes and I run my finger over her cheek.

"What," she asks. "Tell me what you're thinking."

"I'm thinking about how beautiful you are and the way you make me want more than what I have."

She sucks in a deep breath and turns her head away from me. Right before she turned away, I caught a look in her eyes that made my chest ache. There's something she's not telling me. I can tell.

"We should get going, Slade. You have to be at work soon. Okay?" She forces a smile and taps my chest so I know to set her back down to her feet.

When her feet hit the ground, she goes straight for my motorcycle and slips my helmet on. She's ready to get away from me. I don't like that feeling. Not one fucking bit.

I stalk over to her, pull her into my arms and make her look me in the eyes. "Tell me something about yourself that I don't know. I don't know shit about your life back at home."

She swallows hard and tries turning her face away, but I don't let her. I need to be able to read her eyes when she talks. "I work at a hair salon. I've been there for four years. I love it. Doing hair makes me happy. I just turned twenty three a few months ago and I have a cat named Puma. He's black and white and a pain in the ass, but I love him. I hate seafood. I eat ranch sauce on everything and have a passion for reading. I'm not much for the party life and would rather curl up with someone that cares about me and watch a movie instead of going out." She pauses to look down at my lips before looking back up. "There's not much else to tell."

I release her face and we both just stand here in silence. Something feels a little off about the way she's acting. Maybe it's just me. I don't blame her for not wanting to get close to me; especially, not knowing my intentions. I don't even know them myself. This is all new to me.

"Okay." I turn and walk to my bike, unsatisfied. "Let's go."

SARAH HAS BEEN GIVING ME weird looks all fucking day. I'm not really sure what's on her mind, but it's starting to get on my damn nerves.

"Say it," I mutter.

She sets her towel down on the bar and begins wiping it off. "Say what?"

I look up from putting the glasses in the cooler and study her face. She definitely has something on her mind. She knows I don't like playing these games. I'm not a fucking mind reader. "You have something you want to say. Since when do you hold back?"

Shaking her head, she turns away and starts working faster at wiping down the bar. "Okay, then." She drops her towel, leans against the bar and smiles. "You broke your fucking rules." Pushing away from the counter, she walks over to me and kneels down next to me. "Someone finally broke you. I'm in total awe of this woman. She's a goddess. I'm definitely jealous, Slade."

Grunting, I slam down the glass in my hand and stand up before rubbing my hands over my face. "Fucking, Cale." I reach for her arm and pull her up to her feet. "I swear he gossips just like a fucking chick."

She quickly grabs for a beer and places it in front of one of her customers before rushing back over to me. "He called me this morning to see if I wanted to get off work early; said he needed some extra cash. He got on the subject of Aspen and it came out. He's just as shocked as I am. Believe me."

"Yeah. Well, you're not the only ones. Don't even ask me to explain it because I can't. I wouldn't even if I knew how so back off." I lean against the register and watch as a few girls look at me from across the bar, smiling to each other. They're both looking desperate; watching my every move as if their lives depend on it. I'm sure it won't be long before they approach me and try to pull me into the back. I've had it happen more than once while working. It used to get me all worked up. Right now, I'm not even feeling it.

"Do you need to take a break?" Sarah stands next to me and eyes the two girls before nudging me. "I can handle the bar. I don't need you."

"Nah." I push away from the register and start checking the bottles of liquor to see if any need to be replaced. I need anything to keep me busy. "Not this time."

"Wow. Two surprises in one day," she says teasingly while walking back over to clean the bar. "I don't know how to take all this in."

"Yeah, well I can be full of fucking surprises. Trust me."

"Oh yeah. Well, here's another one. Look who's here."

I turn behind me to see that Aspen and her friend have just walked in.

Fuck me. She is fucking beautiful.

Aspen's eyes stay focused on me the whole time that her and Kayla make their way up to the bar. They both stop in front of Sarah and order a couple drinks. I see her trying hard not to look at me. I can tell it's a tough struggle for her.

After the way we left things earlier, I'm not sure how the fuck to feel about her being here. I don't get the way she was acting. I opened up to her and it feels as if she's trying to keep me out.

Fuck that. I don't need that right now.

Seconds later, Cale comes walking in and I focus my attention on him. Just the asshole I need to speak with.

The girls have taken their drinks and are heading over to one of the empty couches. Now would be a good time to give Cale a piece of my fucking mind.

I wait for him to step behind the bar before I get straight to the fucking point. "You have a big fucking mouth."

He looks at me and then over to Sarah. "You can take off if you want. I've got it from here. I'm sure you don't want to deal with this side of Slade."

Sarah nods her head and grabs for her things. "Yeah, I'll be more than happy to get the hell out of here." She starts walking away, but then stops to look back at us. "I already closed out my tickets. You boys have fun now; just not too much without me." She winks and takes off in a hurry, waving back at Aspen and Kayla.

"My bad, man. I didn't think you'd get pissed about it. You've never been secretive about your sex life before. It just sort of came out. It's a big deal. I still can't believe it."

"Yeah well, it's a big deal for me too so let's just drop it."

"All right." He looks over at Aspen and Kayla. "You do realize she'll be leaving soon, right?"

"Yeah. So?"

"She probably won't be coming back for a long ass time. There must be something special about her for you to let her get to you the way she has for this past week. Are you sure you're willing to let her go?"

I take in a deep breath and release it. I look up to see Aspen laughing at something some moron is saying to her. I feel my stomach drop as I watch her having a good time with him. "Yeah. It's not my place to have her stay. There's nothing going on between us. She'll be gone tomorrow and things will go back to normal."

"Really," Cale asks. "Is that why you're breathing heavy right now and your fists are clenched at your sides?" He studies me from the side. He's good as fuck at reading me. "You want to rip that guy's head off right now; especially, now that he keeps getting closer to her as if he's going to take her home. You're about to freak the fuck out. Admit it."

Fucking shit, he's right.

I jump over the bar, walk up beside her and nod at the douche in front of her. He looks a bit nervous all of a sudden. Yeah, well he should be. "What's up?" I step in between them, pull her to me by the back of her neck and press my lips against hers, immediately wrapping my hands in the back of her hair.

I kiss her hard; spreading her lips open with my tongue before picking her up and wrapping her legs around my waist. From the corner of my eye, I see the asshole has gotten the hint and has stepped away.

Smart move, mother fucker.

She moans softly before pulling her lips away from mine and running her tongue over them. She seems a bit shaken up by my bold move. "Umm . . . wow," she breathes. "I mean. What are you doing?"

"Kissing you. Isn't it pretty fucking obvious?" I pull her face close to mine before running my lips up her neck and stopping at her ear. "You like my lips kissing yours, sucking them and owning them. Just remember that."

I set her down and walk away. I'm heated.

Cale watches me as I make my way past the bar and outside. I need a fucking cigarette right now. The thought of that guy even trying to take her home has my blood boiling. I need to relax before I break something. I'm not used to this kind of jealousy.

Inhaling the cigarette in record time, I make my way back inside and try my best to focus on anything but . . . her. I never once thought a woman could be such a fucking distraction. All I can do is think about taking her in the back and fucking her; making her scream my fucking name. It's like my body can't get enough of her. I just have to touch her and taste her. She's in for it tonight. As soon as I get her ass home, she's mine.

It's been three hours since Aspen and Cale have gotten here and it's almost time for me to get the fuck out of here. I don't care what Cale says, she is leaving with me. She doesn't need to hang out here all night while he works. Her friend Kayla left about an hour ago; said she had to leave for work. So, Aspen has been going back and forth between hanging out at the bar with me and Cale and talking to some girls she met while getting a drink earlier.

By the way she keeps looking at me, I can tell she's just as ready to get out of here as I am.

"You taking off soon?" Cale's voice causes me to look up from wiping down the bar.

"Yeah." I toss the towel in the bucket and walk over to the register to see what tabs I need to close out still. "As soon as I close out these two tabs."

I look up just in time to see Aspen waving the girls off that she's been hanging out with. She laughs at something one of the girls says and then starts making her way over to us.

Just as she's about to walk up in front of me, some guy calls her name, stopping her in her tracks.

"Aspen." The guy has light brown hair, styled in the front and is wearing a black button down shirt with dark jeans. He's about two inches shorter than me and almost as thick in build, but is clean cut.

There is something about the look on her face that I don't like. She seems surprised and not happy at all.

She turns around slowly and rubs her hands down the side of her skirt. "Jay. What are you doing here?"

Jay as she called him, walks over to her and wraps his arms around her waist, pulling her body against his.

Without thinking, I take a step forward, about to kill this asshole for putting his hand all over her, but Cale stops me.

"Get the fuck off me, Cale." I push his hand away, but he just pushes my chest harder. "Back the fuck up. That asshole is all over her."

Cale takes a long, deep breath and then exhales. "Yeah well, that asshole is her boyfriend."

What the fuck . . .

CHAPTER SIXTEEN
Aspen

THIS CANNOT BE HAPPENING RIGHT now . . .

Jay leans in and presses his lips against mine while lifting me in the air. Without thinking, I press my hands to his chest and push away from the kiss. This is so unlike me, but he doesn't even take notice. "Damn, baby," he moans, while looking down at my breasts and setting me back down to my feet. "You're looking sexy today. It kind of makes me regret this last week."

Kind of? Asshole!

I hear something break from behind the bar before I hear Cale calling out Slade's name. When I look behind me, Slade is leaning over the register, gripping the counter, all of his veins popping out as his muscles flex. He looks like he's about to kill someone. I cringe at the thought of Slade being pissed off at me. I have no idea how I'm going to explain this all to him. It's not what it looks like; not exactly.

Jay looks over at the bar and shakes his head before slipping his hands up my skirt and cupping my ass. I instantly grab his hands and yank them away. I don't like the idea of him touching me sexually in public. When it comes from him it makes me feel dirty; always has.

"Jay. I thought you weren't coming until tomorrow. Why are you here today?" My heart races at the idea of leaving so quickly. I don't know why, but I don't feel ready; not one bit. "Why today?"

Jay flashes me his perfectly charming smile and grabs my chin, causing me to look into his brown eyes. They seem so dull compared to Slade's. "I'm here to hang out with a few of my boys. They're going out for a few drinks here soon. Figured I would come a day early and have a little fun of my own here in Chicago. Now that I see how incredibly sexy you look, I think I'll swing by later tonight, pick you up and bring you home."

"I . . . you should've at least told me. Called or sent a text. Something. What if I had plans?" I can't help my eyes from landing back on Slade. They can't seem to focus on anything but.

Jay laughs, bringing my attention back to him. It's not just a laugh, it's one of those laughs he does when he's making fun of me. I've grown to hate it. He can be such a prick at times. "What is the fun in that? You know I'm a surprise kind of guy and you have plans? I doubt it. Don't be stupid, Aspen. You know you never have plans that doesn't include me and that's the way it will stay." He leans in and gives me a quick kiss before backing away. "I gotta go. The guys will be meeting up soon. It's a good thing I remembered where you said Cale worked at. I love surprising you. I'll text you in a bit for the address. Be ready when I get there."

He backs away while laughing as if he still can't get over the idea that I may have plans. It makes me want to scream. I hate when he makes me feel this way. Once he gets to the door, he turns around and heads outside without another word. Good thing for him. I don't even know what to say or think right now.

I look down at the ground and take a few deep breaths, in an attempt to calm my racing nerves. I can't even look up right now. I know how bad this must look to Slade and I'm not sure he'll even give me the chance to explain. It's why I got so nervous earlier when he was spilling his guts out to me. I just don't know what to do. I shouldn't have pushed for him to open up to me. It's a bit hypocritical when I can't even return the favor. I shouldn't have let it get this far.

I stand here, not making an attempt to move until I see Slade's shoes come into view. I hold my breath waiting for what's to come next as I look up at him.

His expression is hard and cold; eyes so intense that it steals my breath away. "Outside. Now." His voice seethes anger and could cuts like a knife.

I watch as he walks away and yanks the door open before stepping outside. I feel as if I can't move. Why do I feel so fucking guilty? Slade is the one that pushed me to this point and he just wanted me for sex; nothing more. He used me. I play tug of war with the confusion in my mind, *but . . . then why?* Why do I feel like total shit right now?

I gather myself and start heading for the door. Cale tries stopping me, but I hold my arm out to show him that I'm doing this. I need a chance to explain myself. I can't stand the thought of leaving with Slade hating me. It's just too much and would eat at me forever.

When I step outside, I look around but don't see Slade anywhere. I catch a movement in my peripheral vision and he steps around from the back of the building with a cigarette in his mouth. He's pacing back and forth, not even bothering to look up at me. I can see him shaking as he pulls the cigarette from his mouth and blows the smoke through his lips quickly. He's really worked up over this and it somewhat surprises me.

He stares off into the distance for a few minutes, before finally walking toward his truck and nods for me to follow.

I take small steps while going over a speech, trying to think of the best way to explain Jay. It's not an easy thing for me to talk about. Once I get next to his truck, he backs me up against it and places his hands on either sides of me so his hands are pressed against his truck door.

He leans in close to my face; so close I can feel the warmth of his breath kissing my lips. "You have a fucking boyfriend?" His jaw steels as he looks me in the eyes. They hold nothing but pure rage. "This whole fucking time you've had a boyfriend and you couldn't have fucking said something." He slams his hands against the truck before punching it. "I opened up to you. I let you in and told you things I haven't talked about in years. I don't like cheaters. It's one thing that I hate. I know what I do isn't much better, but at least I'm always honest first. Fuck, Aspen!"

I take a deep breath and slowly exhale. I feel like bursting out in tears right now, but I won't let it happen. I won't. "It's not exactly what you think, Slade. You know nothing about what I've been through over the years with that man. You have no right to accuse me of being a shitty person without even listening to what I have to say."

"What? What do you have to say? That you just needed to get away for a bit and clear your fucking head and then I came along and you decided to just let me fuck you knowing that your boyfriend would never find out. Did you think you could just go back to living your happy fucking life with him? Is that it?"

I feel the anger building up inside as he looks at me accusingly. I didn't want this. I didn't ask for this. I will not be judged without him even having proper cause.

I push his chest to try to give us some distance, but he doesn't move. "Fuck you, Slade. Fuck you!" I push him again, but decide to give up. He isn't budging. "It was him that didn't want me. You want to know why I'm here. I'll tell you why. It's because *he* decided he needed to fuck other women for a while. *He* needed a little space before he could give me his full attention. He expected me to be the good little girlfriend while he was back home fucking who knows what. I was supposed to be here just clearing my head and trying to deal with what I had to do to keep him mine. Then, you fucking came along and I caved into you. I broke my own rules for you. I said I wasn't going to stoop to his level because I loved him too much, but you just had to come along and make me want you; Mr. Irresistible."

I give him another shove and this time he lets me push him away enough for me to escape him. I can't look him in the eye right now. I feel too low; the only thing that makes me this way. "We've been together for five years. I was afraid of losing him. I was prepared to do anything I could to prove to him that my love for him was strong enough to handle anything. It killed me to know that I wasn't enough for him; that he needed other women to satisfy him."

Clenching his jaw, he punches the truck and leans against it. "So you were just going to let him go around fucking everyone and then come back to you like nothing ever happened?"

"Yeah, well. If you must know, I knew how he was to begin with and I let myself fall for him anyways. He was the kind of guy always out to find the next best *fuck;* staying out late at night and not coming home sometimes. All the lies. The fucking lies." I stop to wipe a tear off as it falls down my cheek.

I hate letting people see me breakdown. I hate showing what Jay does to me. "All I wanted was for a chance to make that change. I thought if I did this . . . that . . . that he would finally just be mine;

that he would love me with everything in him just as I have loved him all along. I thought that I could be enough for once."

It's silent for a few seconds before once again, I am pushed up against his truck with his body blocking me in. He wraps his hands in the back of my hair and pulls my face close to his so our lips are almost touching. "If he doesn't see that you're enough, then he isn't fucking worth it. He's fucking blind. You deserve better." He pauses and his eyes lock with mine. "Tell me you're not going back with him."

"Yes," I whisper. "I have to."

He presses his body against mine and his arms flex as his grip on my hair tightens. "No you don't. Fuck him. He doesn't deserve you. You deserve someone better than him . . . better than the both of us, but I'm fucking stingy."

He runs his hands through my hair and brushes his lips against mine. "Stay here, Aspen." His breath softly caresses my lips as his breathing picks up. "Don't leave with him. Let me give you a reason to stay."

I sigh against his lips, fighting myself. "It's not that easy. I can't just throw five years away. We have a lot of history. We live together. He was my first. I can't just walk away."

"How do you feel about me," he growls.

"It was fun, Slade," I manage to whisper.

Pushing me harder against his truck, he leans into my ear. "That wasn't the fucking question. Fuck!"

Feeling trapped, I slap him across the face. I don't know why. I'm just so fucking scared to answer this question; scared of knowing the answer. He always finds a way to push me.

"You like that? Did it fucking feel good?" He presses his erection against me, causing me to moan against his lips. "Harder, dammit."

Completely lost in the moment, I slap him as hard as I can

across the face. It feels good to let my frustration out. Not to mention the fact that his dick flexes from my hit. This man turns me on like no other man can. I'm completely breathless; lost to him.

Without even giving me a second to register his reaction, he picks me up and wraps my legs around his waist. "Here is your reason to stay."

His hand works fast to pull out his erection before he slips my panties to the side and pushes himself deep inside me. He stops for a moment before rocking his hips back and forth and slamming his lips against mine. My legs tighten around him as my whole body shakes from the feel of him filling me; stretching me.

"Let me make you feel this way every day." He pushes in deeper before slowly pulling it out and lifting my hands above my head. I'm so turned on right now that I could care less if someone catches us. "Does he makes you feel this way? Does he fuck you as good as I do?"

I shake my head, but don't answer him. I can't. I can't speak.

"Say it. I want to hear you fucking say it." He leans in against my mouth while rolling his hips in and out, giving me pleasure so intense I feel as if I can't even breathe. I'm overwhelmed by this man; completely stunned. "Say it, babe."

"No," I moan out as he lifts me with his hips and starts moving a little faster. Our bodies are so close that there is no space between us. We're both desperate for this moment; our last. "No one has." I lean my head over his shoulder and dig my nails into his back as he works his hips on me.

"Then stay," he whispers. "Give me a chance to change."

I shake my head, but he presses his lips against mine, claiming my mouth with his. Once again, this man completely owns me. At this moment, I am almost willing to give him everything; not just my body, but my heart.

With one arm wrapped behind my head, he grips my hip with

the other while fucking me hard; rolling his hips and slamming hard into me. He can't handle taking it slow at the moment and to be honest, neither can I.

"Slade," I moan out, as my body bounces with each thrust of his strong hips. "Fuck . . ." I grip his hair in my hands and scream out as I feel my orgasm building. The consistent thrusts of his hips and the way he pushes me against the truck with each deep shove, has me ready to explode. "I'm about to come . . . oh shit." I feel myself clamp around his dick and this only causes his movement to pick up.

I can feel the truck start to move from behind me as he puts all of his anger and frustration into fucking me. His grip on my neck tightens before he moans out and I feel his dick throb as he releases himself inside me. Breathing heavily, we both relax into each other with our eyes locked. I can't turn away from the beauty of this man in front of me; I don't want to.

Shit. Why does having him cum inside me turn me on and make me want him even more? I'm so confused.

It's silent with him still inside me as he leans in once more and presses his lips to mine. They're soft and sweet, making me want more of them. I always want more. He's like an addiction. Everything about him just calls out for me; my body needing him to survive. He's an addiction I'll have to break. I have no choice. Too bad, I know guys like him will never change. Jay didn't. I won't start over with another man that's just like Jay.

When he pulls away from the kiss, he looks me in the eyes and sighs. He can see my guilt written all over me. He could probably even taste it in our kiss. "You're still leaving, aren't you?"

I nod and turn my head away. I can't do this right now.

"Fucking shit."

He pulls out of me and gently sets me back down to my feet while pulling his jeans back up. "I don't blame you for not trusting me," he says stiffly. "I don't even trust myself. I don't know how the fuck I feel. All I know is that with you . . . I feel something and I don't want to give that up." He looks away before opening the door for me to get in. "I guess I'll have to. Me wanting to change isn't good enough and I fucking get that, but I can't make any promises. I won't make one that I know I can't keep."

I feel a burning sensation in my chest and it becomes hard to breathe. It's taking everything in me not to cry right now. As wrong as it was, we both needed that one last time. It's unfortunate that it felt even better than the last two. I will forever be fucked after leaving here. Slade isn't someone you can easily forget about. I already feel that; the pain is too strong to ignore.

I HAVEN'T SPOKEN TO SLADE since we got back to the house a couple of hours ago. I decided to lock myself up in Cale's room and hide. I can't face him at the moment, because seeing him will only make me want to change my mind about going. I can't stay though. He'll only hurt me more than Jay has. Jay made a promise to me this time. I have to believe for the sake of our relationship that he means it. I've held on for five years, it has to be worth something.

Right . . .

I'm sitting here on Cale's bed with my suitcase next to me, staring up at the ceiling, when my phone goes off. My hand shakes as I go to reach for it because I know my time is up. I'm not ready yet. A big part of me is holding me back and telling me to stay.

The look in Slade's eyes was almost enough to convince me he wanted me. I could see the struggle within himself while he was asking me to stay. Asking a girl to stay with him is not something he's used to. I think we both know that it wouldn't last. I couldn't commit myself to the pain of losing a man as great as him. I already feel attached and I barely know him. I can't even imagine how I could feel in a few months. I would fall hard and fast . . . right on my face.

I have to go. Home is where I need to be.

I already know that Jay is outside because I hear a car door slam. He's most likely opening the trunk for my luggage. I just hope Slade didn't hear it, because I can't face seeing the hurt in his eyes. He didn't speak to me the whole way back to the house. It killed me. I just need to slip out of here unnoticed. I can't let my heart break anymore tonight.

I grab my suitcase, stand up and drag it over to the door. When I open the door, I look around but don't see Slade anywhere. I should be happy.

Right?

I find myself standing here for a moment, not wanting to move. I feel stuck. I allow myself a few moments of pity, suck it up and make my way outside. The first thing I notice is that Slade's motorcycle is gone. Not sure how I missed him leaving, but he's gone and the ache in my chest returns. I'll probably never see him again. The thought kills me.

Why does it hurt so much? Why do I wish he was here so I could see him one last time?

Jay stands next to the trunk, but doesn't make a move to help me as I drag my suitcase across the ground. Usually, this wouldn't bother me because I'm used to him being this way, but right now, it bothers me. It bothers me a lot. Slade may be all tough and closed off, but he would help me without a second thought. I know that and I love that about him. He's more than what he shows the world. There's a really great side to him that I love and want more of.

Dammit, this is so hard.

I feel numb and closed off as I step up beside Jay and look at him. I thought I would be happy for this moment . . . but I'm not. I'm fucking miserable right now. Seeing him is doing nothing but making me angry. The feeling of wanting to kiss him has now been replaced with wanting to punch him. Unlike Slade, he wouldn't get off on it.

Fucking Slade. Why can't I stop thinking about him?

I stop and look around as if I expect Slade to just pull up on his bike, jump off and kiss me; save me from this possible mistake. The thought gives me the ultimate rush like it did when he kissed me in the bar with the assumption that guy was trying to pick me up. I loved that. It made me feel sexy and wanted. Something I've never really felt with Jay.

What the hell is wrong with me?

"Come on," he says while looking down at his phone impatiently. "I have to be to work early and it's a long drive."

I let out a soft breath and struggle with tossing my suitcase into the back. He doesn't even notice. He's too busy on his damn phone. I really feel a lot of hate for him right now; enough to almost stay.

I get ready to say something, but he looks up and smiles. It's the sweet smile that I fell in love with. "Missed you, gorgeous."

I feel a little bit of my anger fade, but not enough. "I missed you too," I say while shutting the trunk and walking over to get inside the car. I feel like shit because to be honest with myself, I don't mean it; not one bit of me.

I just hope I'm not making the biggest mistake of my life

CHAPTER SEVENTEEN
Slade

TWO WEEKS LATER . . .

IT'S BEEN TWO WEEKS SINCE Aspen left and I still feel like the biggest ass for not fighting harder for her to stay. The one thing that made my life worth a shit I let slip through my fingers. I couldn't even face her. Instead, I left. I couldn't stand to stick around while she packed her shit to leave. I fucking left and rode for hours just thinking back on my life and all the fucked up things I have done over the past couple of years. It took her for me to realize that I'm not proud of what I've become; not one fucking bit. In the end I may not have her, but she has helped me in more ways than she knows and I will always be thankful for that.

I owe her a lot for finally waking me up and I still think about taking my ass to Rockford and showing her how much I have changed, but I know it would be pointless. She made up her mind. I don't blame her for not wanting to give her heart to an asshole like me. I meant what I said when I told her she deserves better than me. We both knew that. That's why she left. She did what she had to do to protect her heart. She could probably see that things would turn out disastrous. She chose to stay far away from me; choosing to walk away when I couldn't.

It's a Friday night at *Walk of Shame* and I'm working the bar with Sarah. Hemy and Cale are working on training some new kid, Stone, or some shit. The kid looks like he's having a fucking blast; probably fresh out of school and dying to get his unexperienced cock wet. He's like the old version of me: dark, dirty and out for a good fuck. Well, this kid is in for the ride of his life here.

"You okay, Slade?"

I lean against the bar next to Sarah and nudge her with my shoulder. "Don't I look it," I ask teasingly. "You've been asking me that practically every fucking day. You're starting to sound like a damn broken record."

She lets out a little laugh and squeezes my arm. "It's fucking weird," she says.

"What?"

"Not having you out there. How am I supposed to get used to this shit? You not taking down every woman in your path or slamming back shots and getting naked. It's a big fucking change. Are you sure you're okay? Have you talked to-"

"Don't even bring her up, Sarah." I take a deep breath and slowly exhale. "I'm cool, okay. It's just going to take a little while to get used to the changes. You can't expect me to do this forever. I just need a change of scenery."

She nods as I walk away to help a young woman waving me over with a flirtatious smile. She's beautiful; long brown hair, big blue eyes and a body you just want to taste and fuck. You would think she would be enough to tempt me back into my old ways, but no. Surprisingly, she does nothing for me. I'm not sure how the fuck to feel about that. All I know . . . is that I'm feeling for the first time in years. It's a scary feeling, but I think I'm going to go along for the ride; I have to.

"What can I get you," I ask while leaning over the bar.

The brunette looks at me long and hard while eyeing me up and down. She almost looks as if she's ready to strip down right here and jump my shit. She's desperate and it's actually turning me off. I kind of liked having to work for it.

"Whatever you're willing to give." She smiles before leaning in and running her tongue over her lips. "You're Slade, right? I've heard *a lot* of things about you."

I stand here slightly amused, watching as she tries desperately to make herself seem willing and available.

"I've had a rough couple days and am looking for someone to take my mind off things. I've heard you're the man to do the job." Her eyes rake over my body as she tugs on the top of her dress, exposing more of her firm breasts to me. "I've heard you're the best."

Clearing my throat, I turn my head and point across the room to Hemy. I wait for her eyes to follow. "I'm good . . . but go take your offer to my buddy over there. He'll be sure to fuck you nice and thoroughly. He'll even throw in a friend to take you up the ass while he's deep inside you, making you scream." She looks curious and a little excited. "If you're looking for a night to remember then Hemy will give you just that. He fucks like a rock star and he's dirty as shit. He'll give you anything you want. He holds nothing back in the sack."

The brunette looks me up and down before fixing the top of her dress and nodding her head. "He'll do just fine. It's a shame you're not up for the task, though. I had my tastes set on something . . . specific."

"It *is* a fucking shame." I pour her a shot of Vodka and slide it across the bar. "You're a little too late, but the shot's on me, sweetheart."

I walk away and take a deep breath; a little pissed at myself for not even being the slightest bit turned on by her offer. A couple weeks ago, I would have taken her right here in front of Sarah and then let Sarah suck her taste off my cock.

Damn. This girl really did something to me.

Sarah rushes over to me and shoves my shoulder before slapping me with a towel. "Are you serious? I would have even fucked that one. Are you sure you're not sick?"

"Sarah. Leave his ass alone."

I look up to see Cale step behind the bar, wiping down his sweaty chest with his shirt.

"How's the new kid doing?"

Cale smirks while grabbing for a bottle of water. "I'm almost positive you two fuckers are related." He opens the water and pours some over his face. "Are you sure Stone isn't your long lost fucking brother? He's a slightly smaller version of you, but with shorter hair and less tattoos. It's a little fucking scary. It's a lot like what you looked like when you were a suit."

"Good. Then he can make up for your slack like I did."

Cale punches my arm before pouring the rest of the water over his head. "She's still eating at you, isn't she?"

I ignore his question. "Have you heard from her yet?"

He shakes his head. "Nah, man. I haven't heard shit."

To be honest, I'm still a little pissed off at Cale for not telling me Aspen had a boyfriend the whole time. That asshole knew we were fucking and he couldn't even warn me? What happened to the bro code? I find that a little fucked up and he knows that.

"Dude, stop looking at me like that. I told you it wasn't my place to say shit. They were sort of on a break and plus you usually only fuck them one time and move on. I didn't know you would fall for her."

My jaw clenches from his words. I don't like hearing that shit out loud. Even though she's been on my mind constantly since she left, it really pisses me off that she has this effect on me. "Yeah, well neither did I."

"Sorry, man." Cale slaps my shoulder and starts backing away. "I'm sure she'll come back as soon as that asshole hurts her again."

The thought of that asshole even touching her makes me want to rip his fucking throat out. The thought of him hurting her, makes me want to kill him. She deserves to be treated like a fucking queen. She deserves to know that she's wanted. That's why I didn't fight harder for her to stay. I was afraid I would never be able to give her that.

Seeing the person that I've become, I have begun to believe that maybe I could have been what she needs after all. Maybe a part of me knew and I was afraid I would fall too far and then fuck up and she would leave me. If she were here now, I know I would do everything in my power to make her mine. She makes me want to be a better man; makes me want to be the old me.

Once upon a time I actually cared about my image and the way I looked from another's perspective. I would have never been caught dead working in a place like this, fucking every hot female with a wet pussy waiting between her legs and drinking myself into my grave. I actually wanted to love and to be loved. I had it before but lost it and myself, but she makes me long to be that person again. She made me realize that sometimes you have to peel back the layers to discover who someone really is. Otherwise, you may miss a remarkable person.

IT'S ALMOST CLOSING TIME AND the only ones left in the bar besides me, Cale and Sarah is a small group of females that can't keep their eyes off me or Cale. I recognize one of the girls, because I fucked her in the back a couple months ago. Her eyes haven't left me once since the crowd died down. It's starting to get a little on the creepy side.

"Dude, that chick is all up on your shit hardcore." Cale leans over the bar and starts wiping it down. "Are you sure you're not down? We can make a great fucking time out of this."

I look from Cale, over to the tatted up redhead whose eyes are practically fucking me. I'm definitely not down. I just don't feel the need. "I'm good. They're all yours, bro."

All I want to do is get my ass out of here. It's been a long ass day and I'm exhausted. The last thing I want to do is deal with some horny ass chick trying to get on my cock.

Just when I think the girls are finally going to get up and leave, I hear the door open and the sound of heels pounding on the marble flooring. The first thing I think is that another girl is joining the group of women that have been waiting impatiently for me and Cale to get off.

"We're closed," I say without looking up."

"I'm sorry. I was hoping to get here sooner."

My heart stops at the sound of her voice and my breath catches in my throat. I feel every muscle in my body tense as I bring my eyes up to see the woman that has been haunting me for the last few weeks. She's standing there in a little green dress with those sexy strappy heels that I love on her.

Holy shit, she steals my breath away.

She smiles shyly when her eyes lock with mine. She looks

nervous. "I can wait outside," she says while pointing to the door. "It's not a big deal."

I get ready to respond, but Cale jumps up from the ground and hops over the bar to stop her before I can. "Holy shit! What are you doing back?"

Aspen looks at me for a second longer before turning her attention to Cale as he reaches in for a hug and shakes her back and forth. "Did you miss me that much," she asks out of breath as Cale squeezes her half to death and then releases her.

"You know it." He takes a step back and I can't help but to watch them. Everything in me wants to jump over that bar and kiss her, but I'm trying my best to hold back. "So, what the hell are you doing here? Are you staying with us again?"

My heart speeds up just at the thought of her being under the same roof as us; a chance for me to show her that I've changed; a chance to let her fall for me.

"No," she says. "I'm actually here because well . . . I moved here."

Holy fucking shit. It's suddenly hard to breathe.

"I just couldn't stay with Jay anymore. As soon as we got back home I told him it was over. I started looking around for a new job and packed up all my shit." She stops to smile at Cale. "I found a job here in a salon and decided I wanted to be back home. I've missed it here and there's nothing left for me back in Rockford. Riley is moving back in a couple months, anyway."

Cale looks paler than a fucking ghost, but I ignore his reaction and focus on Aspen. I can't help the excitement that rushes through me. Every part of me is screaming to fucking kiss her and make her mine while I can. I can't hold back. I need to do this. If I don't, someone else will.

Fuck it!

I jump over the bar, grab her face and slam my lips against

hers, tasting her with desperation. The feel of her lips give me a fucking rush and I know that after this I won't be able to go on without having her as mine. I need her and I'm going to show her she needs me too.

When we're both short of breath, she pulls away and her eyes search mine. She looks scared and lost. The feeling makes my chest ache. I don't want to do that to her.

She just stares, breathing heavily, with her body trembling. Then without a word, she turns and rushes for the door. "Wait. Don't fucking run away again."

I step up behind her and grab her arm right as she's reaching for the door. She yanks it out of my grip and takes a step back as I take a step forward. It seems to be our little game. "Why? Why should I wait?"

I don't hesitate to tell her the truth this time and I don't give a shit that everyone is staring at us as if we're some kind of fucking soap opera. This time, I'm not letting her get away; I can't. "Because I love it when you touch me. It makes me feel as if I'm breathing; makes me feel . . . alive."

Her breathing picks up as I run my lips over her neck and brush her hair over her shoulder. "You make me want to be a better man. I want to take care of you. I want to make you feel wanted like you deserve." I stop to kiss her neck before gently tugging her hair to the side. "I may not be perfect all the fucking time. I'm far from it, but you make me want to be as close to it as I can be. Give me a chance to make you feel good; feel wanted. I want you to be mine. I want to be the one you snuggle with and watch a movie with at night. I want to be the one you stay home with because you don't like to go out. I don't like fucking cats, but I'll love them because you love them."

"I don't know," she whispers. "I'm scared. I can't handle being crushed by you. It will only fucking destroy me, Slade."

"I am too. Trust me. This feeling is new to me. You've done something to me and I can't stop fucking thinking about you. You've fucking ruined me. I'm not giving you up so easily."

Her lips part and it takes everything in me to not press my lips against them again and make her mine. I want her so bad, but I want her to want me just as much. I can't force her to want me this time. It will never work that way.

"You really can't stop thinking about me?" I nod my head and run my thumb over her lip. "What about all the other women, Slade? I can't be with a man like that again. I just can't." She looks around the room at the group of women watching us. She looks upset by them and a bit jealous. I don't like that look on her. "I didn't mean for my presence to distract you from your job. I just wanted to let you know you'd be seeing me around more. I didn't come looking for this."

I cup her face in my hands and step closer to her to show her I don't give a fuck about those women. "I haven't been with any other women since you. The closest I got to having sex with a woman was before you left and I was still being a horny, heartless dick. I was confused and not ready for change. I won't lie to you about that. I'll never lie to you. I haven't had sex or have even wanted to since you fucking left me that night. That's a big fucking deal for me."

A tear falls down her cheek, but she tries to hide it before I can see it. She's too late. I catch her face and rub the tear away with my thumb. She seems a bit surprised and torn. I don't blame her. I was a major dick and I don't deserve her trust. "I don't understand why, Slade. You can have anyone that you want. I do mean anyone and everyone."

"But I want you. I know I've been an asshole and I'm sorry. I don't even know how I let things go so far and let myself become an asshole . . . but when you fall it happens all too fast." I step closer to her so that my lips are brushing hers. "All I'm asking is for you to give me a chance. We can take things slow. The last thing I want to do is hurt you. I can't stop thinking about you, Aspen. No one has been able to make me feel the way you do. No one has been able to make me feel at all."

She tilts her head up and rubs her lips against mine, but doesn't kiss me. "I don't know. I'm not sure it's a good idea."

"How do you feel about me?" I tilt her face up so she can look me in the eyes. The eyes always give the heart away. "Tell me how you feel. I don't want a bullshit answer this time. I'm standing here in front of everyone asking you if you feel the same way I do. Tell me the truth."

Her eyes search mine and I can see her walls break down a bit. She cares for me, but just how much? Is it enough? I can only hope. "I haven't stopped thinking about you since the first time I laid eyes on you. I knew then that I wouldn't be able to forget you. I was right. I was hoping that I'd be able to go the whole week and force myself to hate you. It didn't happen. Every day, I fell further for you." She reaches up and wraps her hands in my hair and gently tugs on it. "Then you opened up to me and I fell even more. It was unstoppable and I knew I was screwed in the best way possible. I wanted to know more. I wanted to help ease your pain. I wanted to cure you."

I pull her face to mine and suck in her bottom lip before releasing it. "You did fucking cure me. Now give me a chance to cure you. If I fuck up you can punish me." I smirk and she lightly taps my cheek. "I mean it."

Her eyes search mine for a second and I leave them open for her. I want her to read them; to see how I truly feel and that I meant every word that I said. "We'll take things slow," she asks. "At my pace?"

"At your pace." I smile as I bite her lip and press my body

against hers. "Except for in the bedroom."

She laughs and again, it's the most beautiful sound in the fucking world. Especially when it's because of me. I never want to forget that sound. "I think I can handle that," she whispers. "Just don't hurt me, please. I can't handle it."

"I won't do that. If I hurt you I will only be hurting myself more." I gently suck her bottom lip into my mouth before kissing her. She kisses me back with a desperation that says she's missed me as much as I've missed her before pulling away and placing her forehead to mine.

"Maybe you should stay at my house tonight. You know, come help me unpack."

"All right, guys," Cale jumps in between us and places his hand on my chest. "This is getting too fucking mushy. Slade, are you running a fucking fever?"

"Fuck you, Cale." I push him out of the way and grab my woman, throwing her over my shoulder. She giggles and slaps my ass. I like it. "Have fun closing up the bar. I'm fucking out."

Before Cale or Sarah can respond, I'm out the fucking door. I smack Aspen's perfect little ass, causing her to bite me as I head for the white Jeep that she points to.

Looks like I have a lot to prove before Aspen will completely trust me and give herself to me fully. I'm willing to give it my all. She deserves better than what she's had and that's what I'll be working to be. She's opened my eyes and I'm not going to fucking let them close again. I'm tired of not living and just getting by day by day, trying my best to feel less dead.

I have no idea where this will take me and if it will work out, but it's worth fighting for. That's the only thing I know at the moment.

I'm going to show this woman that I can be her man and more; show her and myself that I'm still human . . .

WALK OF SHAME #2

VICTORIA ASHLEY

PROLOGUE
Hemy

I FEEL A HAND ON my shoulder pushing and shaking me, causing me to groan and scratch my head. I'm so fucked up that I can barely even move. To be honest, this could just be my mind screwing with me again, so I choose to ignore it.

"Dude. Hemy. Get the hell up. Wake up, bro."

I make an attempt to open my eyes, but all they do is end up rolling into the back of my head and closing. I'm in the middle of my drug-induced coma, fucked out of my mind. My eyes are so heavy that I don't even bother trying to open them again. All I want to do is sleep, to not have to think. My mind is a fog, no clues as to where it's been or what it's done in the past twenty-four hours; my synthetic nirvana.

"It's time for you to get out, man. Take Rachel and go. I got shit to do." The voice echoes through my ears, not sticking to my mind for shit except for one word.

All it takes is Rachel's name for my mind to register what the hell is going on and for me to sober up enough to move. I knew I shouldn't have come here last night. All I wanted was a quick release from my hell for ten minutes. I didn't expect to get as trashed as I did, but then again I never do until it's too late.

Sitting straight up I open my eyes and shake my head, as if that's going to take me out of the state I'm in. The room starts spinning around me, so I lean forward with my head in my hands and squeeze my eyes shut. I need to come down, but my mind is still off in the land of the thoroughly fucked up.

"Dude . . . I told you to take it easy last night, but you were unstoppable as usual."

My brain finally starts to process and I open my eyes again to see my good friend, Mitch, standing above me with my shirt in his hands. He looks both pissed off and sorry for me at the same damn time.

He throws my shirt at my face and it ends up landing on my lap, which I just now realize is covered with Rachel's face buried in the middle. Rachel groans and digs her face into my hard on, but doesn't wake up.

Damn.

In one quick movement I push Rachel out of my lap and jump to my feet. "Ah, fuck." I rub my hands over my face and step away from the bed. "What is this shit?"

Rachel opens her eyes and smiles seductively while reaching for my pant leg. I shake her hand off and push it away. "What's wrong, baby? You seemed to be into me last night. Did I do something wrong?" She pokes her bottom lip out in a pout.

Pointing my finger in her face I take a deep breath and exhale, trying to keep my anger in check. "The fuck I was. You know damn well I don't want shit to do with you." I grab for my shirt and start backing away. "I'll deal with your ass later. I told you this shit had to stop. I have to go."

I rush through the house with Mitch trailing closely at my heels. As soon as I push my way outside, I stop and take a few deep breaths in an attempt to gather myself from the shit storm I just walked out of. My head is spinning even faster now, and I have no idea how I'm going to get my ass home in this condition. I can barely even stand up straight.

"I have some bad news, bro." Mitch's voice is soft and full of regret coming from beside me.

I don't like the sound of this. I lean against the brick wall of the house and rub my hands over my face as fast as I can. "Just say it, man."

Mitch leans against the wall beside me. He hesitates for a short moment, meaning he doesn't want to say what it is he has to tell me. "Onyx came over looking for you this morning. I tried telling her that you weren't here, but man, she isn't stupid."

I turn around and pound my fist into the brick wall as hard as I can, repetitively, angry with my damn self. The crackling of bone against the wall tells me how much pressure I'm exerting behind each swing. The drugs swarming through my bloodstream numbs my mind from the pain I would be experiencing otherwise. "What did she see," I ask through gritted teeth. "Why didn't you wake me up? Fuck, I could have explained everything."

"I tried waking your ass up. You were too fucked up. She walked in the bedroom and saw you shirtless with Rachel laying across your lap. She just stood there motionless for a while before turning around and walking out. She seemed pretty calm, man. I don't know. I tried explaining, but she just kept walking, mumbling something about eternal heartache."

I let out a huff and glide my fingers through my sweaty hair. "How the hell did Rachel get in there with me? When I went to that room last night I was alone. I didn't do shit with her. I never once touched her." My jaw steels as I picture Rachel's scheming hands on me. This isn't the first time she has pulled this shit.

"I don't know, dude. I just went in there this morning to make sure your ass was still *breathing* and there she was, half naked, and sleeping on your lap. I didn't know what the hell happened, so I just left you two alone." He throws his arms up to show me he doesn't really want to get involved. "I'm sorry, man. I think your time with Onyx is up. Everyone has a breaking point, a moment when they throw in the towel and walk away. You've screwed things up way too many times. You need to get your shit together before you end up dead and alone."

I stand here and let his words sink in as he pushes away from the wall and walks away, ending the conversation. I'm at a loss for words. I know I'm nothing but a big fuck up. I've always been worthless. Even my parents thought so.

Giving my body a few more minutes to wake up and get with the program, I just stand here with my eyes closed, gripping the wall in front of me. I can feel the blood starting to ooze out of the torn skin, running down my fingers, but only because of the wetness and not the pain. I'm still numb from the pain, I always am. It's what I spend all of my time chasing, and the reason I'm in this situation. How the hell am I going to explain this shit to Onyx? She'll probably be gone by the time I get there.

Dammit, I fucked up . . .

THIRTY MINUTES LATER I PULL up in front of my apartment and hop off my motorcycle. It took me that *long* to be able to somewhat function normally. Even from the street I can see a couple of her suitcases on the porch, telling me what a damn screw up I am.

I stand here watching Onyx as she throws another bag out onto the porch, not even bothering to look my direction. It's really happening. She's really leaving and I am too fucked up to even fight for her. I am barely holding the bile down that is rising in my throat. Even I think I'm a loser at the moment. How am I supposed to convince her otherwise?

Setting my helmet down on my seat, I sprint over to the porch and reach for her arm just as she sets down another bag. "It wasn't what it looked like. Let me explain."

Her scorching green eyes meet my amber ones and I feel my heart drop to my stomach. There is nothing left in her look but hatred and pain, and it hurts even more knowing where it came from. I did this to her and I've been doing it for the last six years.

"It doesn't matter, Hemy," she mutters. "You don't think I know you didn't sleep with that tramp? I know it . . . but the question is how much did she enjoy getting off on you while you were drunk, high, and passed out? How do you expect me to feel about all of this, huh? The thought of her touching you makes me want to puke. Her hands groping your body, touching your hair; being places mine should be. I can't do it anymore, I can't continue to stay in the shadows, tormenting myself mentally over you. I just can't."

I swallow and place my hand on her chin, stepping closer to her. I see her eyes dart down to my lips before she pulls her face away and takes a step back. "Don't," she whispers. "Just. Don't. Please, let me go."

It hurts having her push me away. Not being able to touch my woman is the worst pain ever, but I don't blame her. "I have no excuse. I'm a mess. I know that. I'm trying to get by the only way I know how, which is to forget sometimes."

"Well, I can't take it anymore. I just can't deal with it. I gave it everything I had, and now there is nothing left to give. Every day that I'm with you I die a little more inside; lose a little more hope. I understand that you had a messed up childhood. I understand that your shitty parents left you. You were a young child, alone, and scared out in the world; I get that, and I can't tell you that your sister is still out there, or that she is even still alive. I can't take that all back, but what I can do is show you that love exists, that I'm always here for you. I have tried. I really have, but I can only take so much, Hemy. I understand your reasoning behind your behavior, but at the end of the day . . . I should be your only." Her voice is broken and it kills me.

She breaks down in tears while moving further away from me as if being close hurts too much. I have the urge to run my hands though her strawberry curls and hold her close, but I don't. I can't. I don't deserve to. "You're a lost cause, Hemy. I can't force you to change. You can't and won't. I'm only eighteen, dammit . . . and you're only nineteen. This is all too much to handle. We're too young for this shit. Can't you see that?"

"I can change. I just need time. My head is not in a good place and I'm not strong enough to move on just yet. Do you know how hard it is to wake up every morning with these memories?" I point to my head, my hand shaking. "The places I have been. The people I have seen. The things I saw my parents do to Sage. It's a gaping wound on my brain. Now I don't even know where the hell she is! She was only nine at the time. I was supposed to protect her. I'm trying my best here, okay?"

"I'm sorry," she whispers. "I tried to help you. I tried, but I can't continue to immerse myself into this filth and heartache. You may not have touched her this time, but what about next time? What extent will you go to in order to get your way of forgetting, huh? I have to get out of here before I lose myself." Her eyes meet mine and her bottom lip quivers. "I've already lost *you,* because you were never fully there to begin with. I have known you for six years; for six years, Hemy, and you have only gotten worse. Don't turn into your parents. Don't let them win."

I turn away from her, no longer able to look at the disappointment in her eyes. It hurts too damn much. "Can you just give me one more chance? I promise I would never hurt you on purpose. The things you've seen in the past were beyond my control. I may have flirted a little when I was high out of my mind, but I have never taken another woman to bed."

"From what you know of, Hemy," she bites out in a clipped tone. "We don't know that for sure and I'm not sticking around to find out. I have to go. I *need* to go. You've hurt me too many times and I feel as if I can't breathe anymore. It. Hurts. So. Much."

She turns around and heads for the door, but then stops. "I just have one question. Have you ever loved me?"

Her words linger in the air as I try to force myself to speak. I want to say yes, but the truth is, I'm not sure I know what love truly is. "Onyx, I-"

"No. No. No. I don't want to hear any excuses. I get it." She grips the doorframe, but doesn't turn to face me. "Tell me you love me, Hemy. Give me some kind of hope, because I've lost it all."

My heart speeds up and it becomes hard to breathe. I'm not worth it and we both know it. She said it earlier when she said I was a lost cause. "I'm sorry," is all I can manage to get out. Someone of my caliber doesn't know how to love. It isn't in my genetic makeup. As bad as I want to keep her here, she deserves so much better. But I'm selfish when it comes to her.

Without turning back she lets out a soft cry and covers her mouth. "Don't bother contacting me, Hemy. I'm moving away from Chicago and I have already changed my number. There's nothing more to be said between the two of us."

"Don't say that," I whisper. "I can't fucking lose you too."

"It's too late. You already have." She bends down and reaches for one of her bags, and that's when I notice her brother outside tossing her bags into his trunk. "My family has already been instructed not to tell you where I'm going. You won't be able to change their minds, so don't try. Goodbye, Hemy. It was fun while it lasted, right?" She laughs sardonically. "Have a nice life."

I fall against the back wall while letting her harsh words sink in. My hands reach up to cover my face and my heart feels as if it's been ripped from my chest; I'm no longer breathing.

The longer I stand here without her the more it hurts; the more I feel like dying. *What the hell am I doing?*

"No, wait!" I run to the door and open it, but I'm too late. She's already gone. I quickly search for my phone, but of course I am so damn stupid that I must have lost it last night.

I turn around and reach for the closest thing to me, slamming it down next to my feet before punching a hole through the wall. What's a few more breaks or scratches going to hurt? Maybe the physical pain in my hands will take away from the pain that is now throbbing in my chest. Trying to catch my breath, I fall against the wall behind me and drag my back down it until I'm on the floor burying my hands in the thickness of my hair.

So this is what love truly feels like . . . and losing it hurts like a bitch.

CHAPTER ONE
Hemy

FOUR YEARS LATER . . .

THE AIR AROUND ME SMELLS of booze, sex, and drugs, my usual Saturday night scene. At one point I lived for these wild nights that consist of bodies upon bodies of people just looking to let loose, get fucked up, and fucked hard without the harsh judgments of society. It became my life; my very reason to breathe . . . until it *fucked* my life up. Then it became my ruin.

I'm leaning against the wall, casually chillin' in the shadows while slamming back a bottle of Whiskey. Lurking in the darkness is the person I've become. I've been at it for the last hour. This party is piled high with willing pussy and roaming hands, yet I've let my thoughts pull me under and drown me in my own fucked up world of mistakes and regret. Tonight, I may need a bit of a challenge to get me off. I'm going to need it rough, deep and fast.

While slamming back another drink of Whiskey my eyes stray over to a petite brunette; Nico's new girl. I met Nico a few years ago at one of these parties while I was high out of my mind. We partied together and we slowly became friends. I like him because he's just as fucked up and twisted as I am.

Nico's girl is slowly swaying her hips to a seductive song while rubbing her ass all over his dick. Her eyes are glued to me, eyeing me up and down like a siren luring her next victim. Fucking perfect. I like the seductress types, because they usually like the rough and rowdy sex that I require. The more she dances the more erotic her moves become. She's working it well, because I feel my feet moving in her direction, not thinking of anything but giving her what she wants. It's a nice distraction.

Nico's lost in his own little world, grinding himself on her backside, but he stops to tilt back a drink of beer and takes notice of me approaching. He watches me with satisfaction; his eyes say it all. A cocky smirk takes over his lips as he gives me a head nod and steps aside. He knows exactly what's coming, and he welcomes it. "Hey, man." He gives me a fist pound before practically pushing his woman into my arms. "Take care of Peyton for me. I know you'll treat her right, man." Most men don't want to share once they've claimed a pussy, but Nico thrives on it. I told you he is just as fucked up as I am.

I grab his girl by the hip and pull her flush against my body. Grinding my hips in rhythm of the music, I press her against the wall and brush my tongue over her lips, causing her to moan out and wrap her arms around me. Our bodies press into each other's as I lean in to whisper in her ear. "You've been watching me all night." I press my body a little closer to hers and tug her hair a little. "Are you sure you can handle me once you get me? I'm not so sure Nico has told you about me. I don't fuck like a boy I fuck like a man. I like it wild, wet, rough, and rowdy. If you want a lover this is your chance to back out. "

She sucks in her bottom lip before turning to Nico who is now standing right next to us with a smile on his face. "So this is Hemy, huh?" She gives me a look of approval before letting out a growl and leaning over to bite Nico's lip. "I can definitely get down with this, baby. Are you sure?"

Nico nods while tilting back another drink of beer.

Don't ask me why, but Nico has this weird shit of getting off to me fucking his girls. It's like it turns him on to know that I've been inside them. It could always be that he just enjoys the show. Either way, I'm not complaining.

I slide one hand up her skirt to grip her tight little ass while running my lips up her neck. "You want me to take you upstairs and fuck you? I bet you're already wet for me." She nods her head and plays with the top button of my shirt while biting her lip with need. "Has Nico told you the filthy things I do, because I'm not one to take it easy? Once I'm inside you, it's deep and hard. There's no in between, sweetheart."

She reaches up to grip my hair as Nico pushes behind her with his body and wraps one of her legs around my waist. He grips her thigh and bites her neck. The way that he's grinding his hips is causing her pussy to rub against my erection, which makes me want to fuck right here in this crowded room; it wouldn't be the first time. "This is so hot right now," she breathes. "I'm ready for this." She lets out a satisfied moan and leans her head back and turns it to the side so that Nico can crush his lips against hers.

Ignoring everyone around us, I lace my hand in the back of her hair and run my tongue over her neck as she grinds into me while kissing Nico. I pull away from her neck and run my tongue over my bottom lip. "Are you sure you can handle me giving your girl a good fuck, Nico? I have some pent up shit to get out. I'm not playing it fucking nice tonight."

"Mmm." He releases the lock their lips have been in, and nods his head. Grasping the top of her head, he pulls downward, revealing her neck closer to his lips for access. "I need this shit tonight. We both want it and you know damn well that you do too," he says with a cocked eyebrow. "Don't back out on me, Hemy."

I smirk as Nico runs his tongue along her jugular and steps back, pushing his hair out of his face. "You know I'm down. Just giving your ass a warning."

With force, I grip Peyton's thighs and pick her up to wrap her legs around my hips. Immediately, she locks them around my waist. The lust in her eyes is thick. No matter the girl, they all have a wild side waiting to be released.

I turn back to Nico while gripping Peyton's ass and sliding one hand under her short dress. There is nothing but a thin string between her pussy and my fingers. I can feel her wetness coating me as she moves back and forth, swaying her hips against me. "You ready to watch Peyton's pretty little pussy get fucked?"

Nico watches me as I push my way through the crowd with his girl plastered to my front. He usually gives me time alone first before he joins in. It's a little routine that he has developed since we started this.

Sucking on Peyton's bottom lip I make my way up the stairs and to the nearest empty room. Turning the knob with my free hand I push the door open with my knee and toss her down onto the bed in front of us.

With her hands gripping the blanket, she spreads out on her back, her eyes locked with mine. Her breathing is out of control with need. "I've never done anything like this before." She runs her tongue over her lips and backs up against the headboard. "I want to. I do. I'm a little nervous though."

Yanking my shirt over my head I walk over to the foot of

the bed and grip her thighs while crawling onto the bed above her. Her eyes widen as they take in my build. "Don't be nervous. I want to fuck you and he wants to see it. There's no shame in that." Gripping her thighs tighter, I spread her legs wide for me and pull her up to meet my hips with a smirk. "I hope you like it long and deep, because that's all I can give you."

Before she can respond I have her dress above her head, ripping it away from her body. My eyes trail over her toned form, admiring it for a moment. "Damn, girl." I pull her up, so that she's straddling my lap as I grind my cock against her swollen clit. Her underwear are already moist, just the way I expect them to be.

Her hands reach out to grip my hair as she rocks back and forth, enjoying the feel of my body against hers. "You're so sexy," she whispers. "I can see why Nico gets off to this shit. It's a little different, but it's the hottest thing I've ever done."

Sitting up on my knees, I arch her back and run my lips over her stomach, stopping at her breasts. "Oh yeah? You like this?" Reaching behind her with one hand, I grip the thin fabric of her bra and rip it open. Her eyes watch me with need as I run my other hand up her stomach before pushing her bra out of the way.

My lips come down to meet her right nipple, gently at first, before I tug on it with my teeth. They are puckered, revealing just how turned on she is. A moan escapes her lips as she rocks her hips into me again, causing me to run my tongue over her soft flesh and growl. "Hemy," she breathes, "I want your cock inside me."

I strain my eyes to look up at her, but keep her nipple in my mouth, sucking the pebble gently and then hard, as I slide my hand down the front of her thong. I glide my finger up and down her wetness before burying it deep inside her tight little pussy.

Her breathing picks up as her hands dive into my long hair, tugging and tangling with deep pants. "Oohhh, that feels so good. Don't stop." Her eyes close as I run my tongue along her smooth body, moving from one breast to the other, all while working my finger deep inside her. I can feel her wetness start to drip down my hand as her body starts to shake in my arms.

"Not yet," I demand. "Save it for Nico." I slow my movement, knowing that at any second Nico will be arriving. She's too preoccupied to take notice, but I hear the footsteps down the hallway getting closer with each passing second. I want him to watch her come under my touch. It's pleasurable for all of us. He likes being the audience and I like being the actor; she gets a good fuck out of it. Everyone wins.

I tilt my head to the side and smirk as Nico steps into the room. *Perfect timing.* Grinding my hard cock underneath her body, I shove another finger inside her and start fucking her hard and fast while biting on her nipple.

"Shit! Oh fuck! That's it, right there . . . . yeah." Her screams come out with a moan as her orgasm takes over, her body clenching my fingers upon her release. "Hemy," she breathes. "Don't stop. I need more." I always did favor a vocal woman in the bedroom, one that tells me exactly what she wants.

I grab her face and turn it to face Nico. Her breathing picks up as he leans against the door watching us. She's starting to feel the high that Nico gets a rush on. It's easier to digest when you realize it's no different than watching a porno, only in real life. Then it doesn't seem so twisted to the outside looking in.

"Take a seat, Nico." I run my tongue up Peyton's lips while pulling my finger out of her pussy. "Things are just heating up. I hope you're ready."

Without waiting for a response I grip her panties in my hands and quickly pull them down her slender legs. I toss them toward Nico and see them land on the arm of the chair he is now sitting in.

Peyton takes turns looking between me and Nico while

breathing heavily. She wants to be sure he's watching, silently awaiting his approval to continue. The thought of knowing he's there turns her on. It turns me on.

Standing up from the bed, I pull her by her ankles, aligning her ass with the edge of the bed. I grab both of Peyton's hands and place them on my belt as she sits up. "Take it off. Everything."

Her hands work fast to undo my belt before she goes for my button and zipper. Within five seconds, my jeans are being pushed down my thighs and I'm quickly kicking them out of the way.

"Have you ever had a pierced cock inside of you before?" She shakes her head as her eyes look downward toward my erection. "Good. Take my briefs off, Peyton. Show Nico how hard I am for you."

She glances over at Nico before biting her bottom lip and slowly pulling my briefs down. My cock springs free from the material, getting a small gasp from Peyton. I can't tell if she's excited or terrified by its size, not to mention the two steel bars pierced through it. This girl is in for something she never saw coming.

"You like my cock, Peyton?" She nods her head. "Taste it. Rub your sweet little tongue over it. Bite it, suck it, and make it yours." I tangle my fingers into the back of her hair while pushing her head down to my cock. The thought of her boyfriend watching her take in my thick cock only makes me harder; making me want to fuck her mouth even faster and deeper.

Her tongue darts out to swirl around the head of my cock before she suctions the top of it into her mouth. She has to open her mouth extra wide to take in its thickness.

I turn to the side and grip her hair harder while giving Nico a view of me fucking his woman's mouth. His eyes meet mine for a brief second before moving down to my length that is barely even half way in Peyton's mouth. I thrust in and out, grinding my hips while pulling on her hair. I can see Nico's cock grow hard through his jeans as he takes in a deep breath and exhales.

"Touch it," I demand. "Pull out your cock and stroke it while I fuck her mouth. Pretend her lips are on *your* dick, sucking it, licking it, and making it come. Show her how good it makes you feel."

His eyes darken with desire as he shoves his hand down the front of his jeans and starts stroking himself with a loud moan. He's slowly working himself up to join.

"Peyton," I whisper. "Stand up."

She runs her hand up and down my shaft a few more times before pulling her mouth away and doing what she's told. Her tongue runs over her mouth, tasting me on her lips before she looks behind me at Nico.

"Grab my hair and hold the fuck on," I growl, "And you better fucking watch, Nico."

Her hands reach out and grip my hair as I lift her up so that she is sitting spread eagle on top of my shoulders, her pussy in my face. I walk over to the wall next to Nico and press Peyton's back against it, hard. I want to be sure he can see *everything* I'm about to do to her body. I look up at her. "Hold on tight and don't let go."

Once she has a good grip on my hair, I spread her pussy lips and run the tip of my tongue over her clit. I feel her body tremble from my touch, so I softly suck it into my mouth while shoving a finger inside of her, fucking her soft and slow to loosen her up for what's to fill her later.

From the corner of my eye, I see Nico undo the button of his jeans before leaning back in his chair and gripping his hair. "That's so damn hot. Yeah. Finger fuck her tight little pussy."

I devour her pussy even harder as I reach up with one hand and grip her breast in my hand, squeezing it until I hear her moan out. Her moans turn to screams as I suck her clit harder into my mouth in rotation with running my tongue up and down her wetness and moving my finger in and out in perfect rhythm.

I hear the sound of Nico's zipper before I see his cock break free from his boxers from my peripheral vision. He's stroking his cock with one hand while gripping the arm of the chair with his other. He's so turned on that he doesn't know what to do with himself. He can't even sit still. I don't blame him. Seeing me fuck Peyton with my tongue has to be a damn hot sight. I know I'm good at pleasuring anyone I get my hands on; eating pussy is my specialty.

I look up at Peyton while circling my tongue over her swollen clit. "You ready to come again? Then, when you're done, I'll bury my cock deep inside of you."

She leans her head back and tries to keep her leg from shaking. Her thighs are practically squeezing my head off, but I keep spreading them wide so Nico can see my tongue on her soft pink flesh.

"Yes." She nods her head while moaning. "Yes. This feels so good. So good."

I smile against her pussy before pulling away from the wall and kneeling on my knees, setting her down on the plush carpet close to where Nico is sitting with his cock in his hand. "Turn over and get on your knees." I rest on my knees and stroke my hard cock while waiting for her to get positioned. "Such a hot little pussy, Nico. Thanks for letting me get a taste."

I run my hand down the seam of her spine and down the crack of her ass until I reach her wet pussy. Spreading her wide, I bend forward until my tongue is aligned over her pussy, plunging it inward. I fuck her with my tongue and run the thumb of my free hand over the puckered hole above, causing her to tense; the reaction I was looking for. I like a little anal play from time to time, and the girls love the sensation mixed with filling their pussy.

Her hands grip the carpet as she moans out. "I'm about to come. I'm so close." I speed up, shoving my tongue deeper while

VICTORIA ASHLEY

messaging the opening to her ass above. "Yes! Right there. Ahhhh!"

Her body trembles beneath me and I have to catch her to keep her from falling over. I can hear Nico's breathing pick up as his strokes become longer and faster, desperate for more action than he's getting. He wants to get off so bad, but he's fighting it.

Slapping Peyton's ass, I reach beside me in the pocket of my jeans and pull out a condom. I rip it open with my teeth before rolling it over my dick and adjusting it over my piercings. "You ready for me to fuck you hard?" Peyton nods. "You want to see Nico get off on us? I'll make sure you both come; show him how good your pussy is."

"Mmm . . . yes. Please. Just put it in me." She reaches behind her and grips my dick while licking her lips. "It's so big. Will the piercings hurt?"

I lean my head back and moan as she works the head of my dick up and down her folds. Reflexively, she is backing her ass up closer to me. "Fuck me. It won't be the piercings that hurt. Trust me. That's the last thing you should worry about."

Pushing her head down, she frees me from her hold and places both hands flat on the floor. I position my dick at her entrance before shoving it in with one swift movement, slamming against her with force. Her hands grip the carpet as she screams out in pleasure. I still for a second, letting her adjust to my size before pulling it out and ramming back into her a second time. With each hit against her wall, she inches forward slightly, screaming out in a pleasure filled pain. I pick up my speed while yanking back on her hair to keep her still.

"Stroke your cock faster," I demand. "Get yourself off for her."

Nico looks at me with hard eyes. He spits in his open hand and closes it around his dick to give it the effect of her wet pussy, and continues stroking it hard and fast. "Fuck. Her. Harder." He

194

starts moaning and thrusting his hips up and down, fucking his hand. "Shit. This has me so damn hard," he moans.

Smirking, I grab a breast in each hand for leverage to make each thrust harder and deeper. I bend forward and grind my cock each time it disappears inside her completely. Slowly pulling back, I ram it hard at the same time I bite her shoulder. She screams out and a throaty groan sounds out from Nico. "You want a fucking taste? Huh?" I look over at him while slowing my movement down. "Take your jeans off and get down here on your knees."

Nico lets out a long puff before nodding his head and squeezing his eyes shut. "Hell yes." He stands and drops his jeans down to the ground before stepping out of them and yanking his shirt over his head. He's in good shape, but not even close to my build. Still, he's a damn good catch for the ladies.

I pull out of Peyton, but continue to fuck her with my finger, one finger at first, and then two. She's so wet it's oozing out of her pussy. She's still enjoying it. I pull my hand free from her body. "Lay on your back, baby, and spread your legs wide for us."

Peyton does as she's told, baring her clean shaven pussy to us. Nico is now on his knees next to me, eyeing her wet, glistening body as if he's never seen her this way before.

"Good. Now I want you to watch this, Peyton. You want to see how bad he wants you?" She nods her head and looks over at Nico, who is watching her with want in his eyes. "That's my girl." I stand up and grip the back of Nico's head, which gets an instant reaction from Peyton. I like reaction. It's what gets me off. "Does it make you hot to see two men together?"

She lets out something between a moan and a growl, letting us both know what she wants.

Nico runs his tongue over his lips while watching her squirm. His eyes land on Peyton as she reaches down to pull my hand over to her pussy, running it through her folds. He watches the both of us play with her, until finally, he leans in and presses his lips against mine, tasting her sweetness on my tongue. I can feel his body reacting to mine. His body wants what it wants. No judgment here. To me, a kiss is just a kiss. I can partake in the activity without associating it with the gender of who is on the other side. Like I said, it's reaction that gets me off.

Gripping his hair with one hand, I suck his tongue into my mouth before releasing it and pulling away. He's breathing heavily while looking down at my finger buried inside of Peyton. "You like that, Peyton? Huh? You want to see more?"

She nods her head and grabs a breast in each hand, pinching her hardened nipples. She looks him in the eyes, moaning, as she lowers one hand to her clit and begins to rub it as she speaks. "Suck his dick for me, baby." She runs her tongue over her lips. "Do this for me and I'll do anything you ever ask. I promise."

Nico's nostrils flare as he looks down and takes in my size. This is a line we have never crossed, but fuck it. The way I'm feeling at the moment, I could care less whose mouth is around my dick. If it gets her off, then it gets me off.

He hesitates for a moment, looking between the two of us, before leaning down and taking my cock in his mouth. He's gentle at first, clearly uncomfortable, and barely moving until he starts to get the hang of it.

I push my cock further into his mouth as I look down to see Peyton finger fucking herself while she watches him suck my dick. It's evident that she is turned on by this just as much as he is. Her pace increases in speed to match his the faster that Nico takes me.

"She tastes good doesn't she?" I push my dick in further and pull on his hair, causing him to choke a little. "Suck it harder, Nico. You have to get her off by sucking my dick. I don't want to come. I want her to come. Make her come."

He stops for a second to moan before taking it out on me.

He takes my dick so hard and fast that it's almost better than most girls I've had. I'm fucking impressed. "You see how much he wants you, Peyton? You see what he's willing to do to get you off? Rub yourself faster, fuck yourself harder, picturing your fingers being his dick." My filthy words coaching her, has her screaming and moaning from another orgasm.

I pull out of Nico's mouth and start stroking my cock. Peyton is crossing her legs from the aftermath of her self-induced orgasm, still playing with her breasts and licking her lips for more. "Get down on all fours. I want you to take my cock in your mouth this time." Hers eyes meet mine as she gets positioned in front of me. She plays with my cock piercings before taking it deep into her mouth and reaching down to play with her pussy. "Get behind her, Nico. Show her how turned on this shit has you."

Gipping her by the hips, Nico gets behind her and slips inside her. He lets out a little moan as he squeezes her ass and slowly starts moving in and out. "Oh shit! Yeah, baby. Suck his dick faster. Take it deep."

I wrap Peyton's hair around my fist and start thrusting my hips faster as her speed picks up. "Fuck yeah, baby. Take it at the back of your throat. I'm about to blow." I feel my orgasm building, so I pull out of Peyton's mouth, yank my condom off, and aim for her mouth.

She opens wide, taking my cock into her mouth, and swallowing every last drop like a pro. I reach over and grab the back of Nico's head, causing him to speed up. The sight of me busting my load in Peyton's mouth pushes him over the edge, and within seconds he is shaking in his own orgasm.

He pushes himself deep, burying his cum as deep as he can. "Holy shit! What the fuck! That feels so damn good." He stills for a second and pulls out before pulling Peyton's body up so that her back is pressed against his chest. He lays one arm across her breasts, cupping the farthest one and runs the opposite hand down her stomach until it's cupping her mound.

She leans her head back and I grab the back of Nico's head, pushing his mouth against hers. He almost pulls back from the taste of me in her mouth, but I reach out and grab his hand, pushing his finger into her wet pussy. She begins grinding her bare ass against him, causing him to go stiff instantly. This is enough to get him going again.

He kisses her harder and deeper while moaning, ready for another round. He watches as Peyton breaks the kiss, lies on her back, and spreads her legs wide before him. I grab his shaft and begin stroking as he watches her. "You see your cum running out of her pussy, Nico?" I increase speed, making him hard as a rock. He nods. "She can hold more . . ."

After a few more strokes, I rub Nico's cock over Peyton's wet little pussy, aligning it with the opening, causing them both to moan out. "Fill her, fuck her, and don't stop until she's filled to max capacity with your cum."

I back away from the two of them as he follows my command. I reach for a damn cigarette and enjoy the show before me. I deserve one after this shit. I should feel some kind of pride for getting them both off and for knowing that they both came here looking for it. But I still feel empty.

There's my screwed up and twisted. This is the person I've become, the life I live . . .

CHAPTER TWO

Hemy

I'M STANDING IN CALE'S KITCHEN waiting on the idiot to gather his shit when Slade walks in wearing his damn suit. I'm never going to get used to this sight. I'm used to him taking clothes off not putting them on. The sleeves to his white button down are rolled up to the elbows, exposing his tattoos, and even I have to admit he looks sort of badass. It makes me want to buy some suits just to strip out of them. That would be a for sure way to pull pussy, not that I have a problem in that area, but it seems women have some sort of fantasy for men in suits. I may just raid his closet later for a trial run.

"Dude." I grip his shoulder and shake him as he reaches in the fridge to pull out a beer. "Since when the hell do you drink beer?"

He smirks while leaning against the fridge and unbuttoning his shirt with one hand. "I told you, man. I'm done with that hard shit. I don't need it anymore." He takes a swig of his beer. "I can't be all shitfaced when I have a woman to please and a job to do. I'm not fucking shit up."

Wish I would have been that smart.

"Good shit. Where is that sexy little mama anyways? I'm sure she's missing me by now." I wink and grab his beer out of his hand. I get ready to take a drink, but he swats my dick, causing me to groan out as he steals his beer back.

"My bad, mother fucker," he says with a grin. "And hell no. She doesn't miss you. Trust me. I keep my woman well above satisfied. Why do you think we never leave the bedroom?" He gives me a cocky grin.

"It would be better if I joined. You can't deny it," I tease, causing him to tense up. "She's already touched my-"

"Umm. What are you boys doing in here?"

We both look over to see Aspen leaning against the door wearing one of Slade's t-shirts. She smiles at me before turning her attention to Slade and practically growling.

Slade tilts back his beer before shoving it into my chest and walking over to stand in front of Aspen. He presses his body against hers and kisses her neck before picking her up and wrapping her legs around his waist.

"Mmm . . . damn baby. You've been here waiting for me?" Aspen nods her head while biting her bottom lip. "I've been thinking about your sexy ass all day. I need a taste of my woman."

She pulls Slade's bottom lip into her mouth, causing him to growl. "I want to see you strip out of that sexy suit, baby. You know, I still can't get used to seeing you in it, but it's *so, so, so* sexy." I watch as she trails her tongue along his jaw up to the lobe of his ear.

"Oh yeah. Keep on talking like that and I'll take you right here."

Pushing down on my erection, I lean against the counter and eye them both up. "Hell yes. Just don't get mad if I jerk off to you guys fucking. I'll do my best not to join." I pause as they both look over at me. "Unless you want me to. I don't mind getting you both off. My cock is irresistible, so don't complain if you get addicted."

"Fuck off, Hemy." Slade calls over his shoulder as he starts walking away with Aspen. "Save your dick for the private party tonight. I'm sure you'll be using it a lot."

Aspen smiles at me from over Slade's shoulder and I bite my bottom lip as I point at my cock in question. She laughs and shakes her head as I tilt back the bottle of beer.

Aspen and I have a little playful side, but Slade has gotten used to it. He knows I would never really fuck with his woman. Back before, I thought nothing of it, because Slade treated women just as I do now. Nothing but a good fuck to pass the time and get my head off of shit. Things are different now. Slade is a changed man. He's been seeing Aspen for a month now. I've never seen him so damn happy in my life. He even started taking on some cases against drunk drivers or some shit and has completely stopped stripping. He's working hard toward a happy life for them. Aspen is his Onyx. At least he's smart enough to keep her.

Cale passes the happy couple in question and pops into the kitchen. "I'm ready, man. I wanted to wear a uniform or some shit to make it more exciting tonight, but I don't have shit in my closet." Cale runs his hand through his hair while in thought. "I'm tired of just stripping out of my jeans and t-shirt. It's getting boring. Same shit different day."

"Is that right?" I think for a second while finishing off the last of the beer in my hand, before tossing the empty bottle in the trash. "Follow me. I'm sure Slade won't mind if we borrow a couple of his suits. I bet we'll look like fucking studs. If there was a way to wear an invisible sign that said guaranteed mind-blowing orgasm here, this would be it." We rush up the steps to Slade's room.

When I get to his door I hear something fall over and crash to the floor. This fucker really doesn't waste any time. I knock once on the door before pushing the door open and stepping inside.

Oh damn . . .

Slade has Aspen leaned over his dresser with her hands gripping onto the sides. Her upper half is completely bare and pressed against the wood. He has each of his hands locked onto her hips, lifting her feet off the floor, and pounding into her from behind. He notices me walk in through the reflection in the mirror, so he pounds into her one last time and then stops to yell at us.

"Seriously, fuckers? Go ahead, just come on in and enjoy the show! Have some damn respect for Aspen at least. Shit."

I raise my brows at the both of them and walk over to Slade's closet. "I'm offended," I say placing my palm over my heart. "You know damn good and well that I respect your woman. She is one fine piece of ass and she knows it," I tease and wink at her, now staring back at me in the mirror.

She smiles back at my grin, knowing it just revs his engine up more. I knew the girl had a little kinky side buried beneath that shy exterior. I'd be willing to bet she'd let me watch if he would. "Carry on as if we're not even here. Give us a few minutes and we'll be gone. We need to borrow a couple of suits for tonight." I peek over my shoulder and take in the sight of Slade moving in closer to her, as if he's trying to hide what isn't even visible. "Don't keep your lady waiting, Slade." Giving him hell is so much fun, because he's so protective of her.

"You're a real pain in the ass sometimes. You know that?" Aspen growls out trying to feign anger, but I hear the laughter in her tone she is trying to keep hidden. She has to have a sense of humor to deal with me, because I just don't give a shit. "At least

Cale is decent enough to peek in from the hallway. Yeah, I see you out there."

Slade lets out a frustrated growl before standing Aspen up from the dresser and covering her nipples with the length of his arm as well as cupping her mound with the opposite hand. He walks them over together to grab Aspen a sheet to cover up with. "Just pick out your damn suits and get the hell out of here. Take them all. I don't care. Just hurry the hell up. I'm putting a lock on my door tomorrow."

Cale steps into the room and laughs. "The dresser? Really?" Slade is wrapping the sheet around her and pulls out when she is covered enough we can't see her.

Slade lights up a cigarette and leans against the dresser with his cock bared for all to see. "Just because I wear a damn suit now doesn't mean shit. What's the fun in sex if you aren't breaking shit and putting holes in the wall? Just hurry up."

"Seriously, dumbass," I jump in. "You would know that if you would actually put your dick in someone. It's fun. Give it a try sometime."

"I plan to, dick. Now let's get these damn suits and go before we're late." Cale shoves me into the closet and reaches for the first suit. "And women don't seem to complain when I use my tongue." He sticks his tongue out and starts waving it around.

"Gross," Aspen calls out. "I don't want to hear that, Cale."

I reach for a slick black suit and toss it over my shoulder. "Alright, man. Let's get the hell out of here.

WE ARRIVE AT THE PARTY and I kill the engine while pumping myself up. It's not very often that we do parties outside of the club, but one of the girls is turning twenty-one and wanted a big blow out. To be honest, I would rather do a house party anyways. More freedom to please the women.

I see the headlights to Stone's Jeep pull up behind us and he quickly jumps out dressed all fly in his own suit. I tug on the sleeve of the white button down before reaching for the black jacket and pulling it on. It's a little tight, but I still look damn good. Cale is wearing a black suit too except his button down is more of a silver color or some shit, maybe gray, hell I don't know. It's cool though. He still looks good.

"You boys better be on your shit tonight," I say while stepping out of my truck. "Especially you, rookie." I point to Stone and shove his shoulder. "Nice fucking suit, man."

He pulls down the front of his suit as if he's all fancy and smirks. "I know." He starts grinding his hips while messing with his buttons. "Once I start grinding, this suit won't even matter." He puts one leg up against his Jeep and starts swaying his hips in a slow motion. "Oh yeah. I'm working my shit tonight."

"Take it easy, lady killer," Cale says with a smirk. "Look." He nods his head toward the small white house and lifts an eyebrow. "The ladies are spying on us."

I tilt my head to the side to take a look. At least six girls are shoved up to the window, watching us with open mouths while fanning themselves off. They're going to need a lot more than a hand to cool them off once we get inside.

I walk over to the door with Cale and Stone trailing closely at my heels. I don't even bother to knock. I just push the door open and step inside. A fast rhythm is playing over the speakers, so I start grinding my body to the music while pulling my tie off and wrapping it around the birthday girl.

She lets out a nervous laugh while checking me out and fixing her tiara. "Oh my . . . yes." She takes a step back and I take a step forward, still grinding my hips. "Best birthday gift ever," she exclaims in a slight slur.

I wrap my hand around to grab the back of her neck before grinding my body against the front of hers and placing her hands on my chest. I don't really pay much attention to the other two, but I assume they are doing something similar from all the screaming that is piercing my ears right now.

Backing the girl up, I walk over to the stereo and change the song. A slow, seductive song comes over the speaker causing my rhythm to become slow and hypnotic. The girl's hands roam my body as I thrust my hips back and forth, close enough for my cock to hit against her stomach. I'm not wearing any briefs, allowing it to hang free. She feels it hardened against her and starts screaming in excitement.

"Oh my god!" She covers her mouth to hide her excitement as I push her against a wall and wrap one of her legs around my waist. "Is this really happening?" She squeals. "This is the best birthday ever. Thank you!"

One of the girls responds from behind me. "Anytime, Jade. Just relax and enjoy. This night is yours."

Her voice sounds a bit familiar, but in the heat of the moment I don't even bother trying to put it together. With both hands I rip my shirt open and watch the girl's eyes widen as she takes in my sculpted body thrusting in her face.

I can feel her wetness on my stomach, because she is wearing a short dress with only her panties between us, so I turn us around until she is sitting on top of a table. I run my hand across it to knock a few things out of the way before pulling my shirt and jacket completely off and throwing it aside.

I hear a few girls scream, so I look over to see Stone already down to a pair of white briefs. He has some girl in a chair and is grinding his dick in her face.

"Holy shit! Take it off! I can feel it on my face," the girl screams. "Oh my God, it's so hard."

"Bite it," another girl screams. "Take me next!" I ignore all the noise behind me and focus on the birthday girl. She's sexy with long red hair and big blue eyes. The dress she is wearing is now pushed up above her hips and she is looking at me as if she's ready to fuck. This drives me wild, especially with everyone watching.

"Just so you know, I'll let the birthday girl touch." I lean into her ear and whisper, "Anything you want."

Her breathing picks up as she looks over my shoulder and then back at me. "I like the sound of that." She smiles and bites her bottom lip. "Dance for me. I've always loved a man in a suit."

I pull her by her thighs so that her body is hanging slightly off the table. I wrap my hands into the back of her hair and press my cock against her heat, while grinding my hips. "Touch me," I whisper. "I'll even let you taste it."

Her hand reaches down in between us as she strokes my cock through the fabric. Her eyes widen as she takes in the size and piercings. "Oh. My. God." She licks her lips and closes her eyes as she strokes it faster. "I'm so damn horny. It's my birthday, you know." She leans in to my neck and kisses it. "No one will mind if I have a little fun. No judging tonight."

"Is that right," I ask. "I can take you right here if you want. I'm here for entertainment and it's what I do best. I'll fuck you here, in front of your friends, and put on a good fucking show."

Reaching down with one hand I undo my pants and pull them slightly down my hips so the tip of my cock is showing. I move my hips into her and start swaying fast as the song picks up in beat. She's leaning into me, moaning, until her eyes land on the tattoo on my side. She eyes it for a few seconds before speaking. "Onyx," she whispers. "Holy shit!" She looks behind me and around for a few seconds before smiling and fingering for someone to come join us. "Look at this. One of the strippers has your name tattooed on him. That is crazy. I don't know anyone else by that name."

I turn beside me to see a woman with platinum blonde curls, tattoos, and piercing green eyes. The whole world crashes around me. It's not just any woman. It's her. It's Onyx. My Onyx. Except . . . she's different now. She's even sexier than I remember and she looks as if she's just seen a fucking ghost. I can't breathe for a moment as I take her in, trying to decide if this is really happening. It's been four years, four fucking years. She is the most beautiful woman, still, to this day.

Her eyes meet mine and her whole body stiffens, but she doesn't speak. Her eyes just take me in as if trying to figure out how I look so different.

Well, damn! I am trying to figure out the same. When did she get all of those damn tattoos and color her hair? She looks wild and dangerous. I love it.

She's stunning, hypnotic, and addicting . . . and I want her.

Four years I have wondered where she's at and here she is right in my damn face.

CHAPTER THREE

Onyx

MY HEART HAS LITERALLY JUST stopped in my chest. *Four years.* I have gone four years avoiding the very man that is standing next to me with his dick practically hanging out of his pants. And of course, it's for another woman. I guess some things never change.

Hemy. My Hemy?

No matter how hard I want to deny it, my traitorous heart gives me away. This man still makes my heart beat wild in my chest and steals my breath away with just one look into those amber eyes. This is going to be hard. Really hard.

It takes every bit of strength in me to pull my eyes away from his gaze. He's looking at me as if he wants to wrap his hands in my hair and pull me into his arms. The pain in his eyes is so intense that it causes an ache in my chest. It's the very look he gave me for the six years we had known each other. What started out as a friendship, turned into something passionate, wild and painful. Very painful. I really tried healing him. I did. But a person can only take so much before they lose control themselves.

I take a step back to compose myself before bringing my eyes down to Hemy's side where sure enough, Onyx is tattooed in big black fancy letters. I feel my throat close up as tears sting my eyes. I won't do this here. I won't show my weakness. I'm different now. I've changed. I'm no longer that weak woman that just let everything slide. I'm much stronger now and no one will break me down again and let me lose myself. Not even . . . him.

"Onyx," Jade squeaks. "Do you see this?" She runs her hand over Hemy's skin causing instant jealousy that I quickly push away. I won't let myself feel. I can't.

I bring my eyes up to meet hers and put on my mask; my game face. "Yup. That is definitely my name. How strange is that?"

Hemy has finally come out of his frozen state and is now staring at me, looking me up and down. I look different. A lot different. But . . . I'm not the only one.

Holy hell!

He runs his hands through his long hair and takes a step away from Jade. His hair is much longer than I remember. It's sexier, making me want to run my hands through it myself. "Onyx," he says in a painful whisper. "What the fuck?" He goes to reach for my chin, but I move away too fast for him to even make contact. "You're back and you couldn't even tell me."

I watch as he rubs his hands over his face in frustration. Of course I didn't tell him. He ruined me. Paralyzed my heart and soul. I wanted to live with him but the truth was, I was doing anything but. I was far from living. I was surviving and he was barely even doing that.

"I'm not doing this, Hemy." I turn to walk away but he grabs my arm to stop me. My heart skips a beat from his touch. "Let go," I snap. "I don't owe you anything. I told you I was leaving and I did. I had to. This is not the time or place." I give him a quick once over, taking in his thick build, tattoos and piercings before yanking my arm from his reach and turning away. "Just do what you're getting paid to do."

Why the hell does he have to look so damn delicious? Even better than before. Not good. Not good at all.

"I'm sorry, Onyx. I had no idea." Jade jumps down from the table and fixes her tiara. "I'll grab another one of the guys. It's not a big deal. You two umm . . . I'm going."

I grab her arm right before she walks away. "No. You won't. *He* is getting paid good money for tonight and he better damn well deliver. I'll be upstairs if you need me."

"Onyx, wait!"

I hold my hand out in front of me and start backing away. "Don't! Just please let my girls enjoy the night. That is all I ask. What we had was in the past. It doesn't matter now." I bite my tongue and walk away as fast as my heels will allow me. I can't let him talk. I can't let myself fall back into him.

I take the stairs two at a time and rush into the bathroom without looking back. As soon as the door closes, my back is pressed against it and I'm falling to the ground with the door supporting me. My hands grip my necklace as I fight to catch my breath. The necklace that Hemy gave me eight years ago. The only piece of him I took with me.

I'm not ready for this yet. I thought it would be different seeing him again. I thought I would be over us. I'm not. I'm so far from it. The truth is, if I hadn't run away when I did, then I would be wrapped up in his arms, clutching him instead of this damn necklace. I came back too soon.

Why do I do this to myself? Why am I still doing it?

Four years of not seeing his face or hearing his soothing voice has been damn near torture. Not a day went by that I didn't wonder where he was or what he was doing. The other problem was, I had to wonder who he was doing. I couldn't allow that to bring me down so I found other things to occupy my time. I can almost see why he did what he did. Almost.

After a few minutes, I calm down enough to push myself back up to my feet. I need to just suck it up. I can't let him see the effect he still has on me. That will only allow him to hurt me again. I won't let that happen.

"Okay. You can do this," I whisper. "He's part of the past. He's part of the past." I try to convince myself but I suck at it. "Dammit."

I stand up tall and take a deep breath before exhaling and pulling the bathroom door open. What I see in front of me causes my breath to be taken away . . . again.

Hemy is standing there still shirtless, just staring at the door as if he had been waiting for it to open.

"Onyx," Hemy whispers. His eyes are soft and caring as they meet mine. Something in them looks different but I can't tell what that means just yet. It's like he's looking at me with different eyes than before. It makes me want to believe he's clean but I know that's almost impossible. "We need to talk about us."

"Hemy," I breathe in frustration. I run my hands through my hair and close my eyes. "There is nothing to talk about. There hasn't been an *us* in a very long time."

I try to step around Hemy, but he places one arm against the wall, blocking me in. "There is an us. There always has been and you know it." He stops and brings his eyes down to my lips. He licks his own and slides his free hand in the back of my hair. "I've missed you, Onyx. I've tried for the last four years to find you but your family are stubborn assholes. I've ended up at their doorstep once a month for the last four years. They're definitely dedicated. I give them that."

Hemy admitting he tried for years to find me shakes something loose inside me that I thought was long lost, but I must remain strong.

I suck in a breath as his body presses against mine. "Hemy." I place my hand to his firm chest to block him from getting any closer. "Please," I plead. "Don't do this to me. It's only going to get you hurt. I don't want to hurt you. Don't make me do it." My eyes land on his lip ring as he bites it. *Damn! I want to bite it too.*

He takes a step back and untangles his hand from my hair before placing it against the wall so I'm completely blocked in. "You already have. You are right now, dammit. I can't believe you didn't tell me you were back. We were friends before we dated and you decided to throw that away as well. You left! You actually fucking left! "

I try to concentrate on what he's saying but him being so close is making it nearly impossible. I can't think straight. Especially when I have a clear view of my name going down his side. It's not only there, but it's huge. It's definitely there for show.

"When did you get my name on you?" I ask while staring at his naked torso. "Why? Why would you do that?"

He drops his arms and takes a step back. "I got it a year after you left. Why? I got it because I couldn't get over you. And I'm still not."

My mouth opens but I can't speak. If I do then it will put me right where I don't want to be. So instead, I just walk away.

"Onyx." I keep going. "Fuck!"

I hear something crash as I walk down the stairs as calmly as I can and try to ignore the fact that Hemy is still into me. All I have to do is make it through this stupid party and then I'll just pretend I never saw him. Pretend that seeing him doesn't still take the breath straight from my lungs.

"There you are." Ash appears at the bottom of the staircase looking up at me. *Shit. Not good.* She brushes her brown curls behind her ear. "Why did you run off? The party is just starting. These boys are so sexy. You need a dance from Stone."

I reach for Ash's arm and pull her around the corner just as Hemy starts walking down the steps. Today is definitely not the day for all this shit to happen. It's too soon and I can't be sure that Hemy has changed. I need to think of something fast.

I press Ash against the wall and force a smile. "Hey. I'm sorry. I was talking to Roman and he needs you to go into work. I would but I really have to be somewhere." I brush her hair behind her ear and try to calm myself. "Is that okay? Would you mind going in? It's Jade's birthday and I-"

"Onyx," she cuts in. "Of course I will go in. I could use the money anyways. No worries. I'll leave now."

She goes to walk away, but I grab her arm to stop her. "Thank you. I owe you."

She flashes me her perfectly sweet smile. "You've already done enough for me. I'll catch you later at home."

I nod my head and lean against the wall as she walks outside. *How the hell am I going to do this? I don't know if I can.*

Hemy appears around the corner with a frustrated scowl on his face. He looks around for a few seconds before his eyes find me. And when they do, they go soft for just a brief moment. "Don't run away again. I can't do this shit, Onyx."

My eyes rake over his gorgeous, toned body before I pull my eyes away and walk toward the door. "I have to go. Just please go take care of Jade. Tell her I had to run out."

I pull the door open and start heading for my Harley. I pull the ponytail holder from my wrist and wrap my hair in it before straddling my bike.

Of course that stubborn ass can't listen and I feel his presence behind me once again. Hemy walks over with wide eyes as I grip the handle and start the engine. "You drive a motorcycle," he says in disbelief. His eyes take in my ride before it finally dawns on him. "Is that my old Harley? You had it fixed up?"

I toss my helmet on and kick the stand up with my foot. "*I* fixed it."

"Since when do you know how to work on motorcycles?"

I give him a stern look and rev the engine. "I learned from the best." I rev the engine again and force a smile, fighting back my emotions. "Actually, I've learned a lot from the best."

His jaw grinds as he watches me drive away. I don't look back. I just drive, needing to escape.

Crap! Crap! Crap!

CHAPTER FOUR

Hemy

ONYX HASN'T LEFT MY MIND once since last night, not that I tried very hard to forget her. After she rode off on my old motorcycle, all I wanted to do was chase after her. I fought so hard not to jump into my truck and chase her down. I know she needs time. I'm trying to respect that, but it's been four damn years already. How much more time could she possibly need?

I stood outside for a good twenty minutes, just staring out at nowhere, until Cale came outside looking for me. Without a word, I followed him inside and went back to work. Nothing about it felt right. All I could think was that I was doing something wrong. How can I feel that way when we aren't even together? She practically hates me, yet I feel bad for stripping for other women. Now isn't that some shit.

"How's that engine coming along?"

VICTORIA ASHLEY

I look up when Mitch snaps me out of my thoughts. He's standing on the right side of me, chewing on a sandwich. He's shirtless and equally as dirty and greasy as I am.

"Good. It's all good." I toss down my dirty rag and grab for my t-shirt. "I'm going to head out so I can shower before work. I'll finish this later."

Mitch looks between me and the red mustang I've been working on since eight this morning. He doesn't look happy. He knows something is up, but it's too soon for me to tell him. I don't feel like getting into it just yet. "What's up with you? You've been at this shit for the last eleven hours and now you're about to head out to *Walk Of Shame*? Don't you think you need a break? If I had known you worked tonight then I would have kicked your ass out of my shop a long time ago."

"It's nothing, man." I throw my shirt on and reach in my pocket for a cigarette. "I just wanted to get this shit done. This Mustang has been in the shop since last week and it's not even ready to go yet. I'm sure the owner is ready for his ride back." I brush the loose strand of hair out of my face that has fallen out from the rubber band before lighting my cigarette. "I'll be back after work to finish it."

"Nah, I don't think so. Not tonight. You can finish it in the morning." Mitch takes the last bite of his sandwich before shutting the hood. "This car is off limits until you come back *after* you've gotten some sleep. I hope whatever is bothering you isn't going to make you want to-"

"It's not. Shit, Mitch." I take a long drag of my cigarette and grind my jaw. "I'm done with that shit. You don't need to worry about it." I grip Mitch's shoulder before giving it a shove and walking backwards. "I'm outta here. I'll see your ass bright and early."

"Alright, man. Sorry. Just looking out for ya." He tosses his dirty rag at me and starts walking over to help some scrawny little dude with glasses. "See ya."

"Yup," I mumble, while blowing out smoke. "See ya."

I ARRIVE AT *WALK OF Shame* early and with three shots of Jack and one shot of Patron in my system. The last thing I need to do is let thoughts of Onyx ruin my damn night. I've been doing this shit for too long to care about what someone else might think. Who gives a shit if I strip for the pleasure of women? Onyx left a long time ago. I shouldn't feel guilty. This is me now.

When I walk in, I instantly spot Sara behind the bar. She smiles, but then gives me an *oh shit* look before reaching for a shot glass. "Jack?" She doesn't even wait for me to answer before filling up the shot glass and sliding it in front of me.

I take it and quickly toss it back with a moan. I slam the empty glass down and look around the bar. "It's slow as shit in here."

She smiles. "Because you just got here." She reaches for a glass and mixes a drink for one of her regulars. "They'll start piling in soon. I had at least ten girls ask me if you were working tonight. I told them you'd be in later ready to shake your damn dick. Damn vultures." She hands her regular his drink and then returns to me. "You look like shit by the way."

"Thanks for noticing," I scowl. I scoot my empty glass in front of her. "One more, Sara. You owe me now."

"Damn you, Hemy. I swear you boys have issues. Cale is the only one that doesn't drink his dick swinging life away." She gives me a curious look and gets ready to speak.

"Just do it, dammit."

She rolls her eyes and pours another shot.

The last thing I need is her prying into my business. This is something I need to deal with on my own.

After I tilt back my fifth shot of Jack for the night, I swallow back my pride, stand up, and look back at Sara. "Give me a bottle of whipped cream." Sara reaches in the fridge, tosses it to me, and I catch it and walk away.

I stand in the doorway of the back room for a few minutes pushing my thoughts away, until a slow seductive song plays over the speakers. Without thinking, my body starts moving to the rhythm of the music.

I run my hands down the front of my body while grinding my hips to the beat. My jeans are sitting low on my waist and my button down shirt is rolled up at the sleeves, halfway undone. The girls take notice and instantly start screaming while waving their money around.

Stopping at the first round table I set the bottle of whipped cream down, grab the closest girl's chair, and spin her around to face me. Her eyes go wide as I straddle her lap and grab the whipped cream off the table.

I start grinding my hips to the music, pushing my erection into her as I grab her hands and place them on my chest. "Undo my shirt. Slowly."

She starts doing as told. I tilt my head back and spray whipped cream into my mouth. Reaching beside me, I grab for the sexy brunette close by and run my whipped cream covered tongue across her soft lips, slowly and teasingly. I love teasing these women. It's the perfect distraction.

When I pull away I see the brunette run her tongue over her mouth, licking off every last drop of cream. She sits back in her chair and watches me with hooded eyes, no doubt wanting to taste more.

Noticing that my shirt is now undone and hanging completely open, I yank my shirt off and wrap one of my hands in the back of the blondes hair with one hand, while squirting whipped cream all the way down my chest, stopping at the top of my jeans.

I grind my hips against her one more time before standing up and reaching for the brunette's hand, pulling her to her feet. "On your knees," I command.

She gets down on her knees and all the women start screaming random things.

"Take it off, Hemy!"

"Grab his dick, Katy."

I block out the noise and smirk down at her. "Take my pants off."

Looking up into my eyes, she reaches for my jeans and slowly starts undoing them.

"Faster," someone screams.

That must motivate her, because she yanks my zipper down and rips my jeans down the top of my muscular thighs. I place my hand on her head and push it against the thin fabric of my white briefs.

After rolling my hips a few times, I pull away from her and smear a huge amount of whipped cream down the length of my hard cock. "You ready to get dirty?"

She nods her head as I rub my finger over the fullness of her lips, getting a feel for what's going to be wrapped around my cock. "Lick it off. All of it, from the dirtiest place first."

Running her tongue over her lips, she grabs my waist and leans in to press her tongue against my pelvis, rolling it in the trail of whipped cream. Her eyes watch mine as she slowly lowers her mouth, running her tongue down my defined abs and over my cock.

I wrap my hands in her hair and close my eyes as I slowly rock my hips into her face. I feel her teeth softly nibble my piercings and I yank her head back before stroking my hand over my cock and stepping away from her.

Ignoring the screaming women, I make my way over to the couch, and grab for the chick in a small black dress and heels that is standing up waving money at me.

Gripping her ass, I wrap her legs around my waist and start grinding my hips to the music. I move, slow and deep as if fucking her. She arches her back and wraps her hands in her own hair before sticking a wad of cash in the front of my briefs and moaning out.

I pull her back up and thrust into her one more time before setting her back down to her feet.

Just as I'm about to head over to the next table, I catch a glimpse of a woman with platinum blonde hair and tattoos. I stop dead in my tracks, my heart racing as I watch her, until she turns around to face me.

As soon as I realize it's not Onyx, my heart rate slows down and I let out a breath of frustration. A part of me wishes it were her.

"Fuck!"

I run my hands through my hair and just stand there. The screaming doesn't die down as they wait for me to continue my rounds.

A part of me doesn't want to. I knew this shit would happen. I told myself I wouldn't let myself think about her anymore. Yeah, well great fucking job.

"Hemy. Dude!"

I snap out of it enough to see Stone approaching. He grips my shoulder and pushes my chest. "What the hell is up, man? You're just standing here. You've been acting funny since last night."

I push his hand away and grind my jaw. "Nothing. I just needed a second." I pause and exhale, hating myself for what I'm about to do. "I have to go."

"What the hell? What do you mean?"

I grab for my jeans and start heading for the door. "I have somewhere I have to go. It's important. I need you to take over my room."

Stone gives me a confused look, but doesn't question me further. "Sure. Yeah. Go then."

I walk through the bar, past Sara who gives me a confused look, and outside over to my truck. I quickly hop inside and shove my keys into the ignition while tossing my jeans into the passenger seat. As stupid as I know I'm being, I know it's smarter than just letting her walk away again. I refuse to let her disappear from my life now that I've found her. There's always been something about her that draws me in, holding me to her. It's a curse as much as a craving.

I start the engine and pull out onto the dark street. Without a second thought, I head toward the house I saw her at last night. I don't give a shit what anyone thinks. I'm going to find out where she's at and I'm going to make her mine. Her and I both know that we are meant to be together. The hard part is making her see that, making her see the new me.

After about ten minutes, I find myself pulling up in front of the small white house. I kill the engine, grab for my jeans, and hop out to put them on.

Just as I'm buttoning them, the front door opens and two girls walk out. I notice one of them right away: Jade.

She gives me a curious look before smiling and walking over to me.

"Look who's back," she says teasingly. "You come back for your tie?"

I lean against my truck and look over her shoulder at the door. "It's not what I forgot, it's who," I say firmly. "Where can I find Onyx?"

Jade quickly turns away and starts heading for the little black car that is sitting in the driveway. "I don't know," she calls over her shoulder. "I'll let her know you're looking for her."

I quickly catch up to her and grab her arm. "Tell me." I walk over to stand in front of her. I look into her eyes so she knows how important this is to me. "I need to know where she is. Can you just tell me where to find her?"

She lets out a breath of frustration before looking over at the other girl who nods at her. She turns back to me and rolls her eyes. "Follow us. She's at work and we're heading there now. I'm going to get in deep shit for this," she mumbles.

"Thank you, Jade." I don't waste any time jogging over to my truck and jumping inside. I've waited too damn long for this shit and she's going to listen to what I have to say.

I follow the little black car for what seems like forever. In reality it was probably a whole fifteen minutes. Still, fifteen minutes too long, and now I'm anxious as shit.

When we pull up in front of the huge black building, I sit there wondering if this is some kind of joke. There's no way that the Onyx I knew would work at a place like this.

I sit here for a few minutes until I see Jade and the other girl get out of the car. Jade looks over at me and waves her arm for me to follow. "You coming or what?"

I take a deep breath to calm myself before getting out of my truck and slamming the door behind me. Every part of me wants to scream and break something. The idea of her working here makes me sick to my stomach. "Vixens Club," I growl to myself while staring up at the neon sign.

She's a damn Vixen? A stripper . . . like me. Well fuck me.

CHAPTER FIVE

Onyx

"OKAY, GIRLS, JUST REMEMBER TO have fun. This is free night. You are welcome to roam as you wish. Just remember the rule: no touching unless you put their hands there. You know what to do if someone breaks the rule. I'm sure there's no need for me to go over it again."

I get a few head nods from the girls and a hell yeah from Ash.

I stand up from straddling my chair and walk in front of it, facing my group of girls. The first shift of the night is almost done, and I made sure that all of my girls work together all night. I always stress their safety on free nights. I don't like the idea of not being able to keep my eye on them individually. There are quite a few creeps that come in here and I would hate to have to break a heel off in a few of their asses. That's why I have "the talk" with my girls once a week.

"Alright, ladies. Let's get ready to make some cash then." I smile and head over to my makeup station as the other girls head over to the floor.

I've been hiding in the back for the last twenty minutes. I'm not really sure why, but my game seems to be a bit off tonight. I keep telling myself it has nothing to do with Hemy. The truth is, I'm not very convinced. I could never convince myself of anything when it came to him. I went to sleep with him on my mind and woke up with him on my mind. I guess not much has changed over the years.

"Shit. Stop thinking, Onyx." I rub my hands over my face and take a deep breath. "He'll only hurt you again. Don't do this to yourself. You finally got rid of that pathetic little girl that was nothing but a doormat for him."

I curse to myself when I feel a hand grip my shoulder. I have no idea who it is or how much of my rambling they have heard, but I suddenly feel really nervous. I'm not ready to explain Hemy to anyone. I'm not sure I'll ever be.

"What's going on, Onyx?" Jade takes a seat at the makeup table next to mine and starts digging through her makeup bag. "Something's been bothering you since last night. You can talk to me . . ."

"I'm fine." I force a smile and look at myself in the mirror. My blonde curls are wild tonight and my makeup is a little too dark on the eyes. I look a lot different than I did four years ago. I can't even imagine what Hemy must have thought when he saw me at the party last night. He seemed a little shocked, but couldn't seem to keep his eyes off of me. It made my heart race, making it hard for me to think straight.

I let out a little laugh and stand up, fixing my black lingerie. It's barely covering anything, yet it makes me feel more confident and alive than I have felt in years. "You know I just get a little stressed on free nights. I worry about you girls roaming around where I can't see you all. That's all."

Jade gives me a look as if she wants to say something. She almost looks nervous. She opens her mouth a few times and then shakes it off before starting in on her makeup. "Yeah. I know," she says softly. "We do fine though. You taught us all well. Stop worrying so much."

I stand here for a few seconds before I realize that Lily isn't here yet, or that I've seen. The girls usually show up together since they're roommates. "Where's Lily?"

Jade nervously clears her throat while walking over to the closet to grab her outfit. "She's here. She'll be back in a minute. She's, ah . . . showing someone around."

"Alright," I say softly. She's definitely acting a bit strange right now and I'm not so sure that I like it. "I'll see you out there."

"Sounds good. See you in a few."

After walking through the door, it takes my eyes a couple minutes to adjust to the dim lighting. The music is playing loud and the room is filled with a light fog so I can barely make out Ash and the other girls dancing at tables for the overly eager dirtballs.

I barely get ten feet into the room before I am called over to a table. Although I'm still feeling a bit off, I shake it off and walk over with a seductive smile.

"Hey, boys," I say sweetly.

"Mmm . . . very nice." One of the three men holds up a handful of cash as I lean over and grab his tie, winding it up in my hand. I hear him let out a little moan, so I wrap it tighter and pull myself to him, straddling his chair.

"So you like it rough, big boy?" I yank his hair back and starting moving my hips to the music, grinding myself against his erection.

He bites his bottom lip and gets ready to place his hand on my ass, but I yank his hair as hard as I can, causing him to growl.

"Damn, you're rough, baby," he says with a hint of laughter. "I would love to see the things you do in bed."

"That won't be happening," a deep, rough voice growls behind me.

My heart instantly drops to my stomach as soon as the words leave his lips. It doesn't take me having to look behind me to know who it is. I've heard that voice a million times before and I'll never forget it. The only difference is, now it has a deeper edge to it.

"Excuse me," the guy below me bites out. He lets out a sarcastic laugh and places a possessive arm around my waist. "She's in my lap. Wait your turn. *If* it ever comes."

With my left hand, I choke him with his tie while yanking his head back with my right. "Don't ever touch me again."

The guy starts choking and I look back at Hemy to see his fists balled at his sides. I don't need him to protect me. He has a history of fighting and that's the last thing that I need him doing right now. He would kill this guy. This douchebag is nowhere even close to Hemy's huge build.

"Don't even think about it, Hemy." I push away from the guy and he starts fighting for air and pulling at his tie. "What the hell are you doing here?"

"Crazy, bitch," the guy chokes out through breaths.

Hemy looks down at the guy with a hard look, so I place my hand across his chest and push him away.

He takes in a deep breath and exhales, his jaw steeled. I can tell he's fighting really hard right now to keep his control. "I could ask you the same," he growls. "This place isn't you."

"Ha!" I walk away from him, but he keeps following at my heels. "Like you have room to talk. You're a male stripper. Do I need to remind you of that?"

He grabs my arm to stop me from walking. "Yeah, and I'm a piece of shit. That is the difference." He turns me around to face him and backs me up against the wall with his arms and body blocking me in. "You are too good for a place like this. What the hell, Onyx? You could get hurt here. I would fucking kill someone for hurting you. Do you get that?"

I find an empty room in the back and push him into it. Then I turn away and fight to calm my breathing.

Neither of us speak for a few minutes.

"What are you doing here, Hemy? How did you . . ." I stop as I put the pieces together. "Damn you, Jade," I whisper.

I feel the warmth of Hemy's body as he steps up behind me. A part of me wants to lean into him, but the rational part of me moves away. "I can't stop thinking about you, Onyx. You've been on my mind every day for ten years." He wraps an arm around my waist and presses his body against mine. It feels good. So damn good. "Don't tell me I haven't been on yours," he whispers, leaning into my ear. "Tell me I've been on your mind." He pushes my hair behind my ear before brushing his lip piercing up my neck. "Say it."

I let out an unwanted moan as my eyes close to his touch. The feel is so familiar, yet it feels so much better than before. My body is reacting in a way it hasn't reacted to anyone but him. It's unstoppable. "Yes," I admit while finally pulling away and spinning around. "You have. What do you expect? You hurt me. You broke my heart, dammit."

He lets out a frustrated groan and runs a hand through his short beard. *That sexy beard.* I can't help but to imagine it rubbing against my naked flesh. Everything about Hemy is sexier than I remember. He's taller, thicker, full of tattoos and has long, thick, hair that I want to pull. Not to mention those piercings. It makes me wonder where else he might be pierced. He always was the wild one.

"I'm not the same person I was back then." My eyes land on

his bare chest as he takes a step toward me. "I'm different now."

"Oh yeah?" I swallow as I reach out to trace his tattoo with my fingers before pulling away. "How so?"

He wraps his hands into the back of my hair and presses me against the wall with his body flush against mine. "I would give my last breath to be with you." He looks into my eyes with an intensity that makes my knees go weak. "I will stop at nothing to make you mine, Onyx. I'm not letting you run away from me again, from us. You can hurt me all you want. You could stomp on me till I'm no longer breathing and it wouldn't make a difference. I'm. Not. Going. Anywhere."

Inside, I am going crazy. I can't think straight and my body feels like giving out on me. I can't give myself away though. As much as I wish I could, Hemy can never be trusted.

"Hemy," I say firmly. "Don't start something you're not going to like. I'm not letting myself get crushed by you again. Things are different now. You're not the only one that has changed. Do you get what you put me through?" I place my hands on his chest and push him away. "How many girls had their hands on you, how many nights I cried myself to sleep not knowing if you were even alive."

"I'll be with you every fucking night. You'll never have to worry about that shit again." He pounds his fist into the wall before placing both hands against it. "I'll wake up next to you and fall asleep holding you for the rest of my fucking life. Nothing else matters anymore. I've learned to let go and move on."

I suck in a burst of air and cover my face. Those are the words I longed to hear for so long in the past and they never came. Hearing those words makes my heart feel as if it's about to burst out of my chest. The ache is so strong that I have to grip my chest.

"Onyx!" Roman pokes his head into the door and looks between me and Hemy. "What are you doing? I've been looking for you." He gives me a concerned look. "Is he giving you problems?"

Hemy turns away from the wall and pops his neck. "Who the fuck are you?"

I hold my hand out and place it on Hemy's chest. "He's my boss," I snap. I turn to face Roman. "No, and he was just leaving."

Roman looks Hemy up and down one last time before turning back to me. "You have a private dance waiting in room six. Don't keep them waiting too long."

I nod my head and give Hemy a dirty look. "Okay. I'm almost done."

Hemy watches with dark eyes as Roman walks away. He looks like he's ready to kill someone. "A private dance?"

I give him a little push toward the door. "Yes. You need to go."

He walks out the door and starts looking around at the room numbers.

"What are you doing," I bite out. "The exit is that way." I point over to the exit sign, but he ignores me and starts heading for room six. "Are you kidding me?" I follow behind him and we both stop in front of the door.

"It's my turn to see you dance." He turns to me and flashes a cocky grin. "You want to dance for me, baby?" He leans in and kisses my neck. "Because I'm not going anywhere."

"No." I lightly tug his hair back, causing him to growl. "The point of a private dance is for it to be private, Hemy. There's no way my client is going to be okay with you joining."

"Oh yeah," he says. "I wouldn't be so sure about that." He yanks the door open and walks inside. His eyes set on the handsome guy with blonde hair wearing a business suit, holding a bottle of beer to his lips. He pulls out three hundred dollar bills and slaps it down in front of him. "I'm paying for the second dance." Then he pulls back a chair and sets it so he's sitting on the side of the client, but facing him. "You have a problem with that?"

The business guy looks at Hemy, a little intimidated and then down at the pile of money in front of him. "No, man. Not at all," he slurs. "Enjoy the show."

Now pissed, I slam the door behind me and yank Hemy's head back by his hair before whispering, "Just remember you did this to yourself." I push his head forward and walk over to the man in the suit.

I grab his beer from out of his hand and toss it across the room. I'm pissed. Not only at Hemy, but at this drunken idiot for agreeing to let him watch. I lift my leg, placing my heel next to him on the couch. I dig it into the leather while grabbing him by the tie and yanking his head to my breasts.

I squat so that I'm closer to his waist. I start to sway my hips to the slow rhythm while running my hands through his hair and rubbing my breasts over his lips.

I allow myself to get lost in the music playing over the speakers, doing this for a few minutes before releasing his tie, and pulling his head back by his hair. I look down at his lap and smirk. "Someone's already hard for me." Opening the top of my black bustier, I straddle his lap and start grinding myself against his erection.

The guy starts moaning while looking down at my breasts and licking his lips. "Oh yeah, baby. Keep rubbing against my dick."

I don't usually talk much with the men in private dances, but having Hemy in the room somehow makes me want to have a little fun. After all those years of me sitting by, while women touched and enjoyed him, why not give him a little taste?

"Mmm . . . you like that, big boy?" I rip his shirt open and grab onto it while arching my back and rolling my front against his. "It's so big and hard for me."

I grind my hips faster while moaning out and biting my bottom lip. I place my hands on my hips and roll with the beat of the music, popping my ass with each one. I trail my hands upward and continue the slow hypnotic motion of the dance. I stop briefly when I reach my breasts that are peeking out of my top. I can feel his eyes on me, both of them. I close my eyes and continue my path upward until I reach my long blonde hair.

The heels of my black leather knee-high boots are pressed into the leather of the sofa. I keep my balance steady as I grind against his cock. My eyes remain closed. I fist through my hair, messing it, as I seduce him with my movements.

I sit up and tease him in reverse, running my hands down my breasts, down my stomach and in between my ass and his hard on, while looking over at Hemy.

His eyes go hard as he reaches down to adjust his cock. Seeing him hard gets me even more excited. It actually has me turned on. Our eyes lock as I grasp Mr. Professional's cock in my hand and start rubbing myself faster while stroking it through the fabric.

The guy starts moaning and gripping onto the couch as his cock starts throbbing in my hand.

I stand up and turn back around with my pussy in his face as he comes in his fancy slacks.

"Oh fuck," he moans while rubbing his hands over his face. "That was fast."

I look at Hemy and smirk. "That was fast."

Hemy runs his hand over his cock, but looks pissed. I can tell he wants to get off too. Hemy's not as easy as this guy was. He needs more. "Now, it's time for round two."

"Are you sure you can handle round two?"

A rumble comes from Hemy's chest. "If I can handle losing you, I can handle anything."

Now my focus is all on wanting Hemy to come for me. As bad as it sounds, I need this. I'm wound so tight right now, and that's all I need to push me over the edge.

I pick up the three hundred dollar bills and hand them to the messy guy that couldn't hold his shit. "Leave," I say. "You should probably go clean up."

My eyes meet Hemy's and they stay there as the man quickly leaves us alone.

"Lock the door," I demand. Hemy follows him and locks the door with a smirk before he walks over to stand in front of me. "No touching," I state. "Just yourself."

Hemy grabs me by the hips and sets me on top of the table before walking away and taking a seat on the other side of the couch. The clean side.

His eyes watch me with heated desire as I open the rest of my bustier and pull it open. My hands reach up to rub my pierced nipples, causing Hemy to growl and adjust his cock.

"Mmm . . . you like that?" I run my hands in between my breasts until they reach the top of my panties. "I want you to come for me, Hemy. I miss seeing you lose it over me."

He watches me as I drop down on my knees and spread my legs apart. I slowly slide my hand down the front of my panties and run my finger up and down my wetness before sliding a finger inside. "Mmm . . . I'm so wet for you." I push in and out. "Can you hear it, Hemy? Remember how much you loved the sound of me being wet for you?"

"Fuck yes." He undoes his jeans before pulling down the zipper. "Fuck yourself faster and rub your nipple with your other hand." I do as he says while moaning out. "That's it, baby. Do it for me."

I position myself so that I'm sitting on my ass with my legs spread eagle in front of his face. I want to be sure he gets a good view. Then, I pull my panties to the side and bare my wet, throbbing, pussy to him.

"That's it, Onyx." He pulls his cock out of his jeans and I

instantly notice the piercings. It has me so turned on that I have to stop all movement in fear of getting off too soon. He notices me eyeing his cock and grins. "Imagine these steel bars deep inside you as I pound into you. You know I like it deep, baby." His hand starts stroking his cock and I instantly notice the bead of pre-cum that drips off the head and onto his hand.

I bring my hand down to touch myself again and move at the same rhythm Hemy is, as he strokes himself. His eyes never stray away from my fingers shoving themselves deep inside me.

I've needed this for a long time. Ever since leaving Hemy, reaching orgasm has become almost close to impossible. Just watching him get off as I get myself off is enough to make me want to explode.

He starts stroking harder and faster while sucking on his lip ring. "I'm about to blow, baby. I wish it were inside of you."

His words set me off and I find myself shaking from the most intense orgasm I have had in years. A few seconds later, Hemy is blowing his load into his free hand, moaning out my name.

We both look at each other while coming down from our temporary high.

He reaches for a clean towel and wipes his hand off. "We still need to talk."

I cover myself back up and close my eyes. "I don't have time right now. I'm working."

Right as I'm about to close my legs, his eyes meet the inside of my right thigh.

He jumps out of his chair and grips my thigh to hold it open. "What the fuck is that?" He spreads my legs wide open and runs his hand over my tattoo while breathing heavily. "You got my name tattooed on you?"

I never meant for him to see that. It was for my own private reasons. The lettering is so small that you can barely even make out what it says unless you look extra close. "Not now, Hemy. I'm not getting into this."

He growls as I push his hands away and force my legs closed. "That was my favorite spot. I would kiss you there almost every night before bed. Is that why you did it?"

I'm not answering that. This was a horrible idea but I needed to get off.

"I don't have time for this." I climb off the table and walk toward the door with speed. I get ready to open it, but get stopped by Hemy's voice.

"Come to my work when you have time." He walks past me and stops to look back at me with hurt eyes. "I'll always make time for you. I won't break anymore promises."

I stand there and watch him as he walks away. He knows damn well that he has me hanging on again. The question is . . . how tightly?

Well that went well . . .

CHAPTER SIX

Hemy

IF ONYX THOUGHT FOR ONE minute I was going to back off she really doesn't remember how persistent I was when it came to her. Now that I've gotten another glimpse at what's been mine all along, there is nothing that can stop me from claiming her as mine again. I'm a lot stronger than I was back then. My head is a lot clearer. I know what I can't live without and without a doubt that is her.

Knowing that she has my name permanently inked on her skin is fucking with me so bad that I can't even think straight. She can get my name tattooed on her body, but she acts as if she doesn't want shit to do with me. It has my chest aching at just the thought.

"A fucking tattoo, man," I mumble while looking back up at Cale. "My name branding the inside of her perfect little thigh. Do you know how bad that screws with my head?"

He watches me as I take a long drag of my cigarette and slowly exhale. "I guess you both had it a lot deeper than you thought, man. She obviously loved you and missed you or else she wouldn't have gotten it. Plus, no other guy wants to see that shit, so I doubt she's seriously dated anyone since you. Think back to when you got yours. What made you do it?"

I take another drag while running my hand through my hair. I don't even need to think about this one. "I missed her so damn bad that the thought of her made it hard to breathe. It still does, man. It's been four damn years and I feel exactly the same about her. It kills me to think about all the time we have missed out on. No other girl compares to her, never will. They are simply temporary fill ins for what I wish I still had." I toss my cigarette and pull both hands through my hair in frustration. "I'm getting her back, man. I don't care what it takes."

Cale nods his head in understanding and grips my shoulder. "Make sure she sees that. It may hurt a shit ton getting there, but it will be worth it in the end. All she has to do is see that." He watches me as I toss my cigarette down and rub my hand down my short beard. "It's all good, man. You need to relax a bit. Give it some time. You remember that stupid shit saying we used to hear as adolescents? The one that goes, if you love something set it free and if it comes back it was meant to be?"

I look up; my interest slightly peeked. "Well, she's back isn't she? Time, man. Just give it time."

"Yeah. Sure," I mutter. "Time . . . because four years isn't enough damn time." I walk past Cale and into my garage, shoving my head back under the hood of his truck.

It's been five days since I have seen Onyx and I'm starting to go insane. My patience is wearing thin and I'm not sure how much longer I can wait before I show back up at *Vixens* and take her my damn self. I'm doing my best not to push her away again. It's a lot harder than I expected, so I'm spending my time trying to occupy myself anyway I can.

I'm lost in my own little messed up world, doing my best to concentrate on Cale's truck, when I hear a set of heels pounding up the driveway.

"Holy shit," Cale mumbles. "If you are Onyx then I can see why my guy is so screwed up in the head right now."

I toss down my wrench and grip the edge of the hood, trying my best to keep my cool. The thought of Onyx possibly being here gets my heart pounding. I try my hardest not to get my hopes up, but knowing that she has no clue where I even live is making it slightly difficult. It could be one of numerous girls that I have brought here in the past, but what if it's her? That means she premeditated coming here and had to find out from someone else how to get here.

"So, you've heard of me?" Onyx's voice comes out cool and calm, causing my grip on the hood to tighten. "Hemy."

I release the hood and turn around to face her, leaning my back against the truck. I look her over in her short black shorts and white tank top. I can't help but to admire her stunning beauty. She always did take my breath away, even before the dark side took her, but I can't deny it looks damn sexy on her.

Her legs are long, slender and well sculpted, making those shorts look as if they were made just for her. Perfection. They're hard not to stare at, and her hair that was once a strawberry blonde is now a platinum blonde, her curls falling just below her tight little ass. The sight of her is enough to take any man's breath away.

"I'm guessing you paid Mitch a visit?" She nods her head. "Yeah. Figures he wouldn't tell me."

I tilt my head to Cale before reaching in my pocket for my keys. I toss them to him and he quickly catches them. "What's this for, man?"

"Take my truck. Come back after work and I'll have yours ready." I give him an impatient look as he just stands there staring. "Any day now."

Cale looks at Onyx while backing away with a smirk. "Take it easy on the guy." He winks before turning away and jogging to my truck.

Onyx walks over and stops right in front of me. Her eyes search mine for a moment before she pulls them away. "I need to ask you something and I need you to be-"

"Yeah," I answer, already knowing what her question is going to be. It's the one thing she wanted the whole time we had been together. "I'm clean. For three years now."

She looks back up and her eyes soften for a brief moment before she puts her guard back up. "How do I know you're telling the truth? That kind of life isn't easy to give up."

I take a step closer and lean down close to her face. Our lips are so close to touching that it takes all my strength to not kiss her. "I may have been a piece of shit, but did I ever lie to you?"

Hurt flashes in her eyes before she quickly shakes it off. "I don't know," she whispers. "Do you even know?"

A pain aches in my chest, knowing what she means. I was so damn messed up most of the time that I don't even remember a lot of shit that happened. "I would like to believe that I know." I wrap my hands in the back of her hair liked I used to in the past. Her eyes close as I start to massage my fingers through it. "I've missed this."

I press my body against hers, causing her to let out a small moan. "I can't think when you touch me like this, Hemy. You should stop. Now," she says breathless.

"I can't think when I *look* at you. I never could." I turn us around and back her into the garage and against Cale's truck. I can tell how much my body against hers is breaking her willpower, and

I can't help but to use it to my advantage. I press my leg between her thighs and grind into her. "You feel good in my arms, baby. You see how good this feels?"

"Hemy. I didn't come here for this."

"Answer me," I breathe. "We've always been honest with each other. Don't change that now."

She lets out a small breath and tangles her fingers in the back of my hair. "Yes," she moans. "Physically it feels great. Emotionally, it terrifies me. I'm not letting you in, Hemy. I've learned my lesson."

I run my hands down her back before cupping her ass in my hands and running my lips up her neck. "Oh, but I want in. Deep." I suck her earlobe into my mouth before whispering, "You remember what it feels like to have me inside you? The way you moaned out my name and pulled my hair. That mix between pain and intense pleasure. It can be even better now."

Her head tilts back as she falls into my touch. I can hear her breathing pick up as I squeeze her ass tighter. "Don't make me think about sex. It brings back bad memories." She grips onto the hood with one hand as I kiss her neck. "Questions. The fear of you being with other women. All those hands groping you. How am I supposed to get over that? Maybe I want a little fun of my own."

My body stiffens from her words. As much as I hate it, she's right; because of my fuck up she had to live in fear of me being touched by other women. The thought makes me sick now. I need to somehow make it up to her. "What do you need? I'll fucking do anything for you."

"Do you realize how many women I had to see touch you while you were passed out? Every time I close my eyes I picture someone's hand down your pants. Their hands on my man. That image does a lot of damage. You'll never get that until you have to deal with it yourself. I just can't. I can't be with you like that again,

Hemy. Ever."

Her grip tightens on my hair as I wrap mine in the back of hers and lean my forehead against hers. "I can arrange that," I grumble. "I'd have to fight my hardest not to kill someone, but I get where you're coming from. I would do it. I would watch it even though the thought kills me."

She looks at me in shock and laughs in disbelief. "Are you joking?" I shake my head and her face becomes serious. "And what if I want a threesome? Would you do it? With another man?"

I brush her hair over her shoulder and kiss her neck, then her chin. "If it involves me touching you or tasting you . . . then yes. I will do anything you tell me to. Even that."

She pushes away from me and turns around. "Shit, Hemy. I was joking." She grips the top of her hair and tilts her head back. "Why did you have to say that? You're supposed to make it easy to not want you in that way. I'm not supposed to want to touch you, but I do. No man turns me on like you can and it drives me mad."

I don't want to hear about other men. I just want her anyway I can. "Stay with me tonight." I know her answer will be no, but I try anyway. "You don't have to let me in emotionally; not yet at least. Just let me take care of your needs."

"Hemy," she warns. "I have to work tonight, and that's a horrible idea. Do you realize what kind of shit that will start?"

"Yes," I admit. "Why do you think I asked?"

"Dammit, Hemy. I have to go." She takes off walking down the driveway as fast as she can on her tall heels. "Bye."

Without a second thought, I jog down the driveway, grab her by the waist, and turn her around to face me. "Not yet. There's something I've been waiting four years to do." I grip the back of her head and slam my lips against hers, running my tongue over the seam of her lips for access.

All of my breath leaves my body as she opens up and kisses

me back, her arms snaking around my neck. It feels like the past four years disappearing between us and it feels like we are back in the past. My tongue desperately seeks hers, sucking it into my mouth as I back her up against a little blue car and cup her face in my hands.

Pressing my body against hers, I tug on her bottom lip before releasing it. Both of us stand here panting while looking into each other's eyes. I can barely catch my breath.

Standing here, looking in her eyes, I realize the distance between us still remains and I have a lot of work to do in order to close the gap. But I'm willing and in it for the long haul.

"I never want to hear bye come out of your mouth again. I'll be waiting for you. I've waited for four years. Don't think I will give up now."

I turn and walk away before she can say anything. I don't want her to. I want her to think about the last thing said between us. It gives me more confidence that she will show up at my doorstep tonight.

I hear a car door slam behind me, but I refuse to turn around. I never want to have to see her driving away from me again.

Within a few seconds, she starts the car and I hear it pull away. I walk over and stand in front of Cale's truck for a few minutes before walking inside and grabbing my phone.

I dial Nico's number and wait for him to answer.

"Yo. What's up, bro?"

I grind my jaw and take a deep breath. "I need you to do me a favor. Tonight."

Damn. I can't believe I'm doing this . . .

I PULL MY HARLEY INTO the back of *Walk Of Shame* and kill

the engine. I haven't stopped thinking about my plans for tonight since Onyx drove away from my house. It's had me on edge all damn day.

I'm here to ease my mind a bit. Not to get plastered, but to douse the anger that is building inside at the thought of another man touching Onyx. I want to protect her, but at the same time . . . I want her back. I want to take care of her needs and ease her mind.

It may hurt like a bitch, but I deserve it. I hurt her far worse than I can ever imagine. I was her weakness. I broke down her walls while keeping mine up. I was too broken to let her in. I had lost everyone that I loved in life and I was afraid of letting myself love anyone else. I was afraid that if I lost one more person that it would push me over the edge. The day she walked out my door was the day I realized I had loved her all along. Made me realize I wasn't as damaged as I thought.

This is her payback. I need to feel her hurt, drown in my own pain and suffering. I'll do whatever it takes and you better believe I won't back down.

I see Stone as soon as I walk through the door. He nods to me with a wink while grabbing some chicks head and grinding his cock against her face.

I nod back and go to find Cale at the bar. It's a Tuesday night; it's one of our slowest days.

"What's up, man."

Cale slides a glass in front of the girl across from him before cashing her out and slipping the change into his tip jar.

"Not shit." He smiles, flashing his deep set of dimples. "Just enjoying this relaxing night. I sometimes forget how nice it can be to just bartend. No screaming girls in my damn ear. You know?"

"I hear ya." I pull out my wad of cash and throw him a ten. "Give me a beer."

Cale reaches below him in the fridge and slams a beer down

in front of me. "You look like you need one. Things didn't go well with your girl?"

I give him a hard look and grind my jaw, trying to keep my cool. "Depends on what the hell you consider good." I tilt back my beer and look up at him. "Let's just say I arranged a little fun for her tonight and it has me a little on edge." I run my hand through my hair and tilt my head back. "I deserve it though. I have no right to be mad."

"Ouch. You just have to think of it this way. At least she wants you there for her *fun*. She could want to do whatever that is without you. It's a step, my man."

I nod my head while slamming back more of my beer. I sit here in silence for a moment and try my best to think of the positive shit this could lead to. "I suppose your ass is right. If it's one step closer to making her mine again then I'll do it and show her how far I'm willing to go for her this time."

Cale jumps up to sit on the bar and slaps my shoulder. "Right on. You know no woman can resist the Hemy charm."

I tilt my head up and give him a dirty look. "She left me, asshole. It obviously doesn't work on her."

"Yeah. And that's why you have to show her the new Hemy charm. Has any other woman been able to resist you?"

I shake my head while finishing off my beer.

"Exactly!" He jumps down from the bar and fetches me another beer. "She'll come around. Now drink that and get the hell out of here. I have shit to do."

He backs away with a smile while giving me the middle finger with both hands before turning around and helping another customer.

I'm going to please my woman and make her mine again. I don't care how . . .

CHAPTER SEVEN

Onyx

I'VE BEEN OFF WORK FOR the last hour, trying to get my head straight. I spent the whole night lost in thoughts of Hemy, and trying to decide what I should do. He hurt me. He hurt me numerous times and the visions I have of him playing in my head are like a poison. They're draining me bit me bit, making it hard to even function.

We weren't supposed to meet up like this. I was supposed to have more time to prepare. I was hoping he wouldn't recognize me at first and that I would have more time to feel him out, to see if he has changed. I have something to tell him. This is something that will change his life forever, but I need to know that he is clean, and the only way to do so is to spend time with him.

I have no idea how I'm going to be able to hang out with him without wanting him. That's why I have to be careful. I have to do whatever I can to keep him at a distance, and to keep my heart safe. The kiss that he surprised me with still has my heart beating wild and my legs trembling. It was all too familiar and reminded me of what I've been missing.

"You can do this," I whisper while looking into the mirror. "You'll just go there and feel him out." I grip the sink and close my eyes.

I need to do this. The only problem is, I have no idea what he has planned. Hemy is wild. If he thinks I want a threesome with him and another man, he'll find a way to make it happen. He has a way of getting anything that he wants. He's better at this than I am. That's why I have to push back and not give him the alone time he needs to win me back. If he wants me physically, the only way I'll be safe is by making him share me. Once he gets me alone, he wins.

I open my eyes and take a deep breath as the bathroom door pushes open to Ash peeking in. Her dark curls fall over her shoulders when she smiles. "Hey," she whispers.

I force a smile and choke back my emotions. I know I'm doing the right thing. "Hey, sweetie," I reply. "You do good on tips tonight," I ask as a distraction.

She pushes the door open and leans against the frame. "I did great on tips." She looks me over and frowns. I guess the distraction didn't work. "What's been up with you tonight? You've been acting strange. Is everything alright?"

Not really. Not yet. "I'm good," I lie. "I'm just feeling a little off tonight." I push away from the sink and turn to walk toward the door. "There's an old friend of mine that I haven't seen in a while. It's just bringing back a lot of old memories."

She smiles in understanding and nods her head. "Memories are the last thing I want to think about. Hopefully yours are a lot better than mine."

I run my hands over my dress to dry my sweaty hands. If only she knew. "Some are good." I smile. "I'm heading out for a while. I'll be back."

She takes a step back, allowing me to walk through the door. "Onyx." I stop and turn around. "Will I get to meet this old friend?"

I swallow and nod my head. "Someday."

I turn and walk to the door as fast as I can.

I hope I'm strong enough to do this . . .

NICO ARRIVED ABOUT AN HOUR ago. Of course he is always down to do whatever I ask. It's been that way since the day I met him. It's nice having someone you can rely on.

"You want another beer, man?"

I tilt my head to look at Nico. He's standing by the fridge, dressed up in a black button down and dark jeans with his light hair styled back. He can hold his own when it comes to physical attributes. Getting girls is never a problem for him. I have no doubt that he won't please Onyx. The thought kills me, but I won't let it win and bring me down. I will smolder it on contact. She needs this. I need to give it to her, so maybe we can move on from the past. People like to say not to get even, but it's the only way to lay things to rest.

"Nah. I'm good."

My heart jumps to my throat when I see a car pull up in front of the house. I knew she would show. The question was when. It's already past three a.m. Not that it matters. She's here and that's what counts. It just gives me the confirmation that a part of her still wants me. Whether it's just physical, emotional, or both, I will find out soon enough. Time. Just a little more time.

A light knock sounds at the door, causing Nico to set his beer down and lift his eyebrows. "She's here, man."

"Yeah," I whisper to myself. "Let her in. Just remember what I said. Don't push the limits," I say firmly.

I walk to the bathroom and close the door behind me. This is going to be a lot harder than I thought. I'm already fighting the urge to crush Nico for touching her. I never was one for sharing. That's what makes it even harder knowing that she felt like she had to. Being sober makes it easy to feel what she must have, and brings it all forth to the light. I hate myself for always keeping her in the dark.

I take a deep breath and slowly exhale as I hear their voices in the distance. I can't make out what they're saying, but I can hear the tone in Nico's voice. He's getting himself ready and easing her in for what's to come.

"Fuck." I hit the sink before leaning into it and resting my head against the mirror. "Don't be a pussy. This is for her. She deserves this," I tell myself. I need to get this over with, and fast. No putting it off. It's time to get straight to the meaning of this visit and show her I'm willing to fight for her this time. No pussying out.

Pushing the door open, I walk through the hall to meet them in the living room. Onyx instantly spots me and freezes in her tracks. She looks stunning in her little black dress and heels. It's enough to take my breath away. The ink on her skin only adds to it, giving her a sexier edge now, which is my kind of woman; although, my kind has always only been her, and always will be.

She clears her throat and looks between Nico and me. She looks slightly nervous, but quickly shakes it off. "Well, I'm here, Hemy." She runs her fingers across the wall while making her way over to the couch, seductively. She looks over her shoulder at me. "Are you sure you can handle this?" The girl I knew four years ago is forever gone. I need to keep reminding myself. We are on a different game level now.

I swallow back my anger and focus all my energy on pleasing her. I just need to remember that she needs this to move on from the world of hurt I bestowed on her. She needs me to feel what she felt. "I can handle a lot of shit. Pleasing you is one." I nod my head toward Nico. "This is Nico. He's yours to do with as you please."

"Nico." She smiles while leaning against the back of the couch. "I like that name. Come here, big guy."

Nico looks at me in hesitation before I motion for him to go. The faster, the better, cause after this is done, she's staying with me. I don't care what it takes. She'll sleep in *my* bed and wake up in *my* bed.

Already knowing the plan, Nico walks over to stand in front of Onyx. He wraps one arm around her waist while fisting her hair and kissing her neck.

Onyx lets out a little moan as her eyes connect with mine. I hold her stare and bite my bottom lip as I nod my head for her to go on. I'm not surprised that she's a tad hesitant.

Grabbing onto the top of Nico's shirt, Onyx pulls him into her, causing them both to fall over onto the couch. His lips instantly seek hers as he buries himself between her legs and squeezes her bare thigh.

I walk over to the leather chair and take a seat in front of them. As much as I hate the thought of someone touching her, I can't help my cock from getting hard. The plan is to watch him touch her, taste her, and arouse her for a while before I join. It's how Nico always does it with me. Sitting here now, in his seat, I'm not sure how he does it.

"Take her dress off," I command.

Nico pulls away from the kiss and they stand, before he grabs the bottom of her short, tight, dress and eases it up her body, then pulls it over her head. "Fuck me," he growls out as he takes in her body.

I sit here, my eyes roaming over her tight little body as I grab my cock and rub it through the fabric. "Don't be shy, Onyx. This is what you wanted." I bite my bottom lip in anger. "Take his clothes off. Show me how it feels to be the viewer, witnessing the ultimate betrayal from someone you trust. Hurt me like I hurt you. My heart is yours to stomp on."

She looks at me, clearly struggling on the inside. I can tell she wants to see me suffer as much as she did, but a part of her hates having to hurt me. I have to push her more, or else she may just walk away for good. I can't live with that option.

"Remember those hands on my body, Onyx. Do you still visualize all of those girls touching me while I was high out of my fucking mind? How did that make you feel? Make me feel exactly how you felt."

Full of heated anger, she rips the front of Nico's shirt open and rubs her hands over his defined chest and abs with an animalistic growl.

"That's it, baby. Let it all out. Do this for you . . . do this for us." I grip the arm of the chair, biting back my anger as she goes for his jeans and tugs them off with force. He's standing there in only his briefs now.

"Touch her, Nico," I bite out. "Give her what she needs. Bend her over the couch and lick her pussy. You better fucking lick it good too."

Knowing I'm a pro at eating Onyx's pussy makes me smile to myself. There is no way she will enjoy it as much as when it's my tongue pleasuring her. Knowing that I'm here watching her will only make her realize that it can be me. All she has to do is ask.

Nico smirks while gripping Onyx's hips and pushing her down so that her hands are buried in the couch and her ass is up in the air. He squats, slowly pulling her panties down along the way, baring her pussy to both of us. My cock jumps at the sight and I have to fight the urge to run my tongue up it.

I watch as Nico positions on his knees, grips her firm ass, and runs his tongue up her slick folds. I glance down at Onyx's face to see her not looking the least bit impressed. It makes me smile on the inside, although, the bigger part of me wants to yank Nico away from her. She's supposed to be mine and mine alone, but I fucked that up.

Nico gets into it, shoving his tongue deep, pulling it in and out while pulling his briefs down and stroking his cock behind her. A little moan escapes from Onyx's mouth, but nothing compared to when I pleasured her.

"Hemy," she moans out. "I need you to get naked. Take those clothes off before I scream." She twists her neck to look at me in anticipation.

Smirking, I slowly unbutton my white shirt before ripping the last few buttons off and tossing my shirt aside. I stand and pull my belt through the loops, the leather sounding along the way. I unbutton my jeans, sliding down the zipper, slowly and teasingly.

Her eyes stay focused on me as I slowly pull my jeans down my body and step out of them. I'm not wearing any briefs, so I'm now standing here completely nude and hard, baring my whole body to her. I hear her suck in a breath as her eyes look me over, taking in every inch of my flesh, but mostly my hard as steel cock that gives away the effect she has on me.

Walking over to the couch, I stand beside her face, but at eye level. Her eyes follow her peripheral vision until she is staring directly at my rock hard cock before her. She licks her lips and moans as she takes me in. She always did like it rough.

"Damn, Hemy," she breathes. "I can't believe you're going through with this without killing someone. It fucking hurts, doesn't it? It killed me, Hemy. How the hell are you standing there and not choking someone?"

I grind my jaw, keeping in my anger. "Other people might not understand why I am willing to do this or why you would enjoy it, but fuck them. They never understood us in the first place and we have always been anything but normal," I whisper. "I'm doing this for you."

I stroke my cock close to her face as Nico devours her pussy from behind. "You like this, baby?" I step closer and rub the tip of my dick against her lips, causing her to tremble. "Remember how much you loved sucking my cock?"

She nods her head and lets out a little moan so I stroke it faster. I see her eyes zoned in on my piercings, letting me know she's imagining what it feels like to have them inside her. She won't be waiting for long. She'll be asking soon enough. I can see it in her eyes – all hooded.

I rub the tip of my cock across her eager lips again, but this time she opens them and slowly takes my length in, moaning out as it hits the back of her throat. Looking up at me, she swirls her tongue around my shaft and slowly trails it up toward the head, focusing on the piercings. I allow her to enjoy the taste of me for a few more seconds before pulling out, causing her to groan. That should be enough to make her want more.

Nico, still stroking his cock, slaps her ass before shoving a finger inside her pussy and moving in and out while moaning in pleasure. "You want my cock," he questions. "I can fuck you good for Hemy. You want that?"

Onyx looks up into my eyes before whispering, "No. I want yours, Hemy. I want you to fuck me while he watches. You're the only one that has been able to fuck me right. God, those piercings are so hot. What are you trying to do to me?"

Now that's what I like to hear. We always did have a good time and I can't help but to gloat at the fact that no man has ever been able to pleasure her like me. I also love that she mentioned the piercings. I knew she would love them.

"Back up, Nico," I command. "Stroke your cock for her while I fuck her. Don't come until she says so."

Nico stands up with his cock in his hand before walking over and taking a seat in the chair in front of the couch. This is exactly what we were both hoping for. Nico likes to watch as I put on a show. Having Onyx as the show is not what I hoped, but if it helps her move on, then I have to do it.

Walking behind Onyx, I push her face into the cushion and hold both of her legs up, gripping her thighs. This makes it easier to pound into her sweet little pussy from behind. Fuck, how I have missed the feeling of being deep inside her.

She may want me to go down on her first, but I'll save that for a different day since that's her favorite thing. I'm going to make this rough and deep to remind her of our wild sex life. That will only make her crave more and keep coming back until I can make love to her and make her mine again.

"No condom with me anymore, baby. I'm claiming this pussy as mine. I want to feel all of you as I pound into you." I grip onto the back of her hair with one hand and pull back. "Is this pussy mine?"

She moans out and her grip on the couch tightens. "Yes. Just fuck me. Stop with the teasing. You know we've both been waiting a long time for this."

"I know," I say firmly. "Now you're going to remember what it's like to have a real man inside you. Fuck all the boys in between. This is the real thing."

I adjust my cock at her entrance and gently slide into her while wrapping my arm around her neck. I bury it deep with one thrust, causing her to moan out and dig her nails into my arm. "Oh shit!

It's so deep," she moans. "Hemy! I want to feel those piercings as you pound me. Fuck me like you used to. Please!"

Fuck! She feels so good . . . so warm and wet for me. I've never been inside her like this before and I can't help but to dwell on the fact that she didn't resist. She has to have been wanting me for as long as I have wanted her. We're both desperate for each other's touch but that's not going to be enough to stop her from guarding her heart.

"You miss screaming my name, don't you?" She nods her head as I pull her neck back. "You want to scream it for Nico?" I slap her ass and grip her thigh tighter. "This is just a taste of what you've been missing over the years. Hold on tight, baby."

I pull out and pound back into her with force while holding one leg up and gripping her neck with my other hand. "Oh God," she cries out. "Yes . . ."

"Scream my name and I'll give it to you harder. I'll make both you and Nico come at the same time. As soon as you tell him to go, you're both done for."

I pound into her with deep, fast movements, causing her to scream out my name. Being inside of her has me on a temporary high. This is better than any high I used to get in the past. This is the ultimate high. She's all I need.

I continue to thrust into her, stretching her tight little pussy to accommodate my huge size. She cries and screams with each thrust, causing Nico to stroke his cock faster.

Releasing her neck, I reach below us and rub my finger over her swollen clit while pulling her hair and pushing as deep as I can go, swaying my hips in and out in a fast rhythm.

Her screams become louder as I bite into her shoulder and moan out with her. I wish I could give her more right now, but this is what I need to do to keep her coming back and wanting more. I'll do whatever it takes. That's a fucking promise.

Holding her against my body, I swing her around so that her hands are on the floor and I'm holding her legs up as I continue to bury myself deep. I'm fucking her in a handstand, her fingers digging into the black carpet as she screams out. It feels so good from this angle. There is no doubt in my mind that she's about to come for me.

"Now, Nico," she cries out. "Fucking come! Please!"

Her head tilts to the side to watch as Nico strokes his cock a few more times before he's moaning out and shooting his cum into his palm.

Right before he's done, I pound into her one last time causing her body to convulse as she throbs around my dick, bringing me to climax along with her. I shoot my cum deep inside her tight little pussy before pulling out, flipping her around and slamming my lips against hers.

Her lips instantly react to mine as she tangles her fingers in my hair while panting and still shaking from her release. I always did love the feel of her panting in my mouth after she came. That hasn't changed. I love it just as much.

Fisting her hair, I place my forehead against hers and rub my hand up her back. "Stay with me tonight. I want you in my bed."

She gets ready to shake her head, but I pull her closer to me and pull her bottom lip into my mouth. She always loved that in the past. "I won't take no for an answer. Just for tonight. Let me run you a bubble bath and take care of you. You need to see me for who I am now."

She lets out a little breath before relaxing in my arms. She's silent for a few moments, lost in thought, before looking up at me. "Just for tonight, Hemy. After this, I have to be careful. This is it. I have no choice. This is pushing it. I should say no."

I look over at Nico as he stands up to get dressed. "Thanks, man. You can go now."

Nico smiles while wiping his hand off on his shirt and balling it up. "Not a problem, man." He grabs for his shoes. "I hope you two work shit out. That was some hot shit."

I turn my head away from Nico to look into Onyx's eyes. I want to see her reaction to his words. What I find is not good. She looks terrified. Being close to me scares the shit out of her. I need to change this.

And fast . . .

CHAPTER EIGHT
Onyx

I CAN'T BELIEVE I JUST let that happen. What was I thinking? Now, I'm really confused. I thought making Hemy watch me with another man would make me feel good. It didn't. It hurt. It made me feel sick to my stomach. I had to stop things before they got too far. The truth is, all I wanted was Hemy.

As much shit as Hemy put me through in the past, hurting him only hurts me more. How am I supposed to do this? How am I supposed to ever get over all the pain and suffering he put me through? I can never *be* with Hemy. All he does is hurt people. That's exactly why I need to see if he has changed before I tell him what I know. I have to be 100% positive first. I won't let him hurt anyone else like he hurt me.

I'm sitting on the couch wrapped up in Hemy's shirt when he walks out from the bathroom and runs his hand through his hair.

It reminds me of how good it felt to run my hands through it and I can't help the butterflies in my stomach that are fluttering freely. "Hey," he says in a low, flat tone.

"Hey," I say back in the same voice level, not really sure what to do next. This feels so strange. Being with him again brings me back to the past, making me feel as if we were never apart.

"Come here." He reaches above him and grips the molding above him on the door. I can't help but to notice all of his muscles flex as his grip tightens. It's so damn sexy. "Take my shirt off. I need to see all of you. Never cover up around me."

He always did hate it when I wore clothes after sex. He said he couldn't sleep afterwards unless he had my naked body pressed against his. I learned very quickly to stop getting dressed after sex, because it was pointless. If I did he would just remove them himself. Sometimes when he was out at night, I would even lie in bed naked hoping it would help me sleep better. It never did.

Standing up, I grab the bottom of his shirt and pull it over my head. I stand here in place, watching his eyes scan over my body, before walking over to stand in front of him. I want him now that I've had another taste and I hate myself for feeling this way. I'm only going to get hurt. I was devastated for far too long, and I'm finally in control of my emotions, or I was.

Biting his bottom lip, he reaches out and cups my face in his hands. His eyes meet mine, causing my heart to speed up. They look clear again. A spark of hope shoots through my body, making me want to believe it's not a coincidence that he's been clean the last few times I have seen him. I want to believe he is telling me the truth.

He must notice me focusing on his eyes, because his lips turn up into a slight smile before he tilts my chin up and looks directly into my eyes. "I wasn't lying when I said I was clean. I will never lie to you. That's a promise I made ten years ago and I'll never break it."

"Hemy . . . I-"

"I know," he breathes, cutting me off before I can finish. "It's not that simple. If you just give me the chance I will show you." He swallows hard while tracing my bottom lip with his thumb. "I will *never* hurt you again. That is a fucking promise, baby. The day you walked away changed my perspective dramatically."

Before I can respond, Hemy scoops me up in his arms and carries me into the bathroom. He steps into the huge bathtub filled with bubbles and sits down, pulling me into his lap. I instantly rest my head back on his shoulder and sigh in contentment. He's never done this with me before. I'm going to soak this feeling up while I can, before I have to put my guard back up.

I should be keeping my distance, but maybe letting him in for one night won't be so bad. I mean, how much can really happen? It's just one night.

I close my eyes as I feel Hemy wrap his arms around me, underneath my breasts. His touch is so gentle, yet possessive; as if he's telling me I am his and his alone. The thought causes my heart to pound in my chest. The thought of being his gives me a feeling of warmth and safety, even though being with him in the past was anything but that.

"I'll take care of you if you let me," he breathes into my ear. "I may have only been rough in the past, but I promise you I can be gentle with you too. Things are different . . . I'm different. If you give me another chance to love you, I promise I will make you the happiest woman in the world. I don't need other women, Onyx. None of them are you. None of them took care of me when I was a broken boy, scared, and alone in the world. None of them took me in and held me at night after my parents left me and I lost Sage. That was the most devastating time in my life. Only you were there. Not even my foster parents cared for me. They let me do as

I pleased and never gave a shit, but you did."

He takes a deep breath and squeezes me tighter, resting his chin on my shoulder. His hair brushes over my neck, causing me to shiver in his strong arms. I want to give into him, but I can't. *Damn, this feels so good; too good.* "I'm sorry I couldn't be there for you like you were for me. I just . . . I had to numb myself from the world. I had a constant storm of fucked up memories in my head that consumed me. I can't change the past, but I can promise you better for the future."

I can't help the tear that runs down my face. I still remember Hemy as the broken boy I met ten years ago. He was roaming down the alley behind my house with a group of older boys – all troublemakers. He stopped when he saw me and I couldn't help but to smile at him. He was the cutest boy I had ever seen and when he smiled back, a warm feeling enveloped me. After that day, I sat behind my house for at least a week waiting for him to walk by again. When he did, he walked over to me and I instantly wrapped him in a hug, surprising him. There was something about him that made me feel like he needed some tender care. I was right. He needed that and much more. After that, we were inseparable.

I let the tear roll down my cheek, being sure that it drips away from Hemy. I don't want him to know he's sparking some deep emotions inside of me. I have to be strong.

"Hemy," I whisper.

"Yeah." He pulls my hair back and holds it in a ponytail.

"I don't want to talk about us. Can we just enjoy this bubble bath without me having to hurt you? Please, I don't want to hurt you."

Letting out a small breath, he shifts so he can reach beside him and light the few candles that surround the tub. When his arms release me, a part of me feels dead inside. The feeling scares the shit out of me. I haven't even spent much time with him and

I'm already dreading not being in his arms.

After lighting the candles, he grips my hips and turns me around so that I'm straddling his lap. I grip his shoulders and push away from him as he tangles his hands in my hair. "Hemy," I warn. "I need to be careful."

"There is no being careful when it comes to me," he says confidently. "I'm yours. I always have been. Nothing will ever change that."

His hands tighten in my hair and he grinds below me, digging his semi hard erection between my legs. The feel of the steel bars, poking me, make me want to jump on his cock and go for a ride – a Hemy ride.

I wrap my legs around his waist and close my eyes as he brushes his lips over my neck and shoulder. Being with him this way feels better than anything I have felt in years. I need a distraction, something to steer my thoughts in another direction.

"Do you still wonder about your sister," I ask, stopping his kisses. "Are you still looking for her?"

I feel his body tense below me before his arms wrap around my waist and pull me closer to him. "Every fucking day. It seems no one in Wisconsin is named Sage. Wisconsin was the last place I saw her before I was adopted and my foster parents moved me here to Chicago. I still check in, hoping that maybe she will pop up. No fucking luck. I have even checked anywhere within a few hours of Wisconsin and nothing. My parents were pieces of shits and did this on purpose. They left us in different places, Onyx. They dropped me off an hour away from home and then took off with Sage. I know they dropped her off too. Then they ran. No one has seen them since. They were miserable and wanted to be sure we would be too."

I take in a gulp of air at the reminder of how Hemy was left alone at such a young age. He lost his whole family; they never even cared to begin with. Sage was the only one he truly had and he couldn't even protect her from his parents' harm.

"Do you think you would know Sage if you saw her? I mean how would you know it was her? It's been ten years and she was so young."

His eyes go hard as his jaw ticks. He has so many bad memories that I hate even asking this.

"I may not recognize her right away, but I would know if I saw the back of her neck."

I reach behind his head and wrap my fingers in his hair for comfort. "From when your father burnt her with that pan?"

"Fuck!"

I jump away from his loud outburst, but he grabs me and pulls me back to him.

"I'm sorry." He grinds his jaw and closes his eyes. "Yes. That happened like two years before I lost her. We were all in the kitchen, waiting for my mother to finish the last bit of dinner. Sage was crying. She was hungry, because we hadn't eaten in over two days. I tried to comfort her, but she just kept crying and saying *Ty, I'm hungry* over and over again. Back then I didn't go by Hemy. My father hated my mother for naming me that. He made me go by my middle name." He stops and shakes his head. "Anyways. My father got tired of her crying so he picked her up by her arm and dragged her across the kitchen and over to the stove. He grabbed for the pan my mom was cooking on and held it against the back of her neck, smiling as she screamed out in pain.

"When I ran over to help her, my dad took the pan and swung it at my face, hitting me, and causing me to fall back and hit my head on the corner of the counter. I blacked out, and all I remember is waking up to Sage crying and sitting next to me on the kitchen floor while my parents were at the table eating without us. The pan left an odd shaped scar on the back of her neck. I'll always remember that mark."

I turn my head away and swipe at the tears as they begin to fall down my face. The thought of Hemy hurting kills me. All of a sudden, all I want to do is go to bed and get the night over with. I can't think anymore. I want to hold him while I sleep – one last time. Just this one night.

Hemy notices me crying and instantly reaches out to dry my tears. "Don't cry for my past. It only made me stronger. I may not have been strong four years ago, but I promise you now, that I will be the strongest man you know. Taking care of you is what will make me strong; protecting what I love the most in life."

My heart takes on an odd rhythm as I watch his face. All I see is truth in his words. He's never told anyone that he loves them, except Sage and although he didn't exactly come out and say it, it's the closest thing to it for him. It makes me want to hold onto him and never let him go.

I clear my throat and pull his hands away from my face. "It's getting really late and I'm tired. Can we just go to bed now?"

He looks my face over before smiling and rubbing under my eyes one last time. "Yeah. Let me put you to bed. It's late as shit."

He stands up and gets out of the tub. Reaching for a towel, he turns around and reaches for my hand to help me out of the water, before draping the towel over my shoulders. I stand here and watch as he blows the candles out and drains the water out of the tub.

"Next time we're in that tub, I'll be making love to you."

He grabs my hand and pulls me through the house, his body dripping wet as he guides us to his bedroom. Without turning on the light, he gets into his bed and tugs on the towel, pulling me down next to him.

"Lose this," he whispers while unwrapping me from the towel. "You know I can't sleep unless I'm wrapped up in your naked body."

I sit on my knees, naked, as Hemy takes me all in. Then, he pulls me down so that I'm lying down next to him. He leans over and presses his lips against mine, soft at first, before going rough and deep, causing us both to moan into each other's mouths. He kisses me for a few seconds longer, before moving down in between my legs, spreading them apart and kissing his name that is tattooed on the inside of my thigh.

My heart melts at the familiar feel, making it harder to fight my emotions.

"Goodnight, baby," he whispers, while lying back down and pulling me close to him.

I close my eyes and cuddle in next to him, feeling his naked body flush against mine. Man, it feels so, so good; too good.

"Goodnight," I whisper as his grip on me tightens.

Guarding my heart is going to be a lot harder than expected . . .

CHAPTER NINE

Hemy

I WAKE UP TO AN empty bed; the sheets smell of Jasmine and Vanilla. I always did love the scent of her hair. It always relaxed me, making me feel . . . alive. I've missed that scent almost as much as I have missed her.

Getting her to stay last night was a long shot; having her here in the morning was the impossible. I knew that from the beginning, but I learned to live with the idea and flowed with it. I just hope our night was enough to have an effect on her. If not, then I have a shit ton of work ahead of me.

Grumbling, I sit up and bury my hands in my hair. Having her next to me felt a lot better than I remembered. How can I ever live without that feeling now? She has ruined me. With her; I feel at peace. I feel like a real person. There is no way I'm giving up this fight, as much as I know she wants me to. A real man never gives up on his woman; he would die for her . . . and I would.

Sitting here; I feel empty. I don't have to work tonight so I need to find a way to keep my mind busy before I drive myself insane with thoughts of her.

"Shit! I need to do something."

I stand up, still naked and smelling of her. It instantly arouses me and I need a release. I make my way to the bathroom and run a cold shower; my thoughts stray back to her and the smooth curves of her body.

The ice cold water should be helping with my hard on, but it's not. It's so fucking hard, it's beginning to hurt. The only way to get rid of it, is to release the pressure. Placing one hand against the shower wall, I grip my cock, close my eyes and stroke it to the images of Onyx in my head.

Picking up speed; it doesn't take long before I'm busting my load into the water, it washing down the drain.

I stand under the frigid water for a few more minutes before quickly washing up, turning off the water and reaching for a towel. The doorbell rings, just as I finish wrapping the towel around my waist.

A spark of hope surges through me at the idea that it could be Onyx. Although the rational part of me already knows that it isn't. She said so herself that she needed to keep safe. The more she's with me; she's in danger of falling for me again and getting hurt. At least in her eyes; she thinks I'll hurt her. I don't blame her for being afraid.

Securing the towel, I make my way to the living room, crack open the shade and look out. I almost feel like punching something when I realize that it's only Stone outside. What the fuck could he want?

I yank the door open and give him a hard look. I can't really be mad at him, but I can't help but to be disappointed that I was right about it not being Onyx.

"What the hell are you doing here?" I growl while pushing my wet hair away from my face.

He smirks and slaps my shoulder, walking past me and into the house. "Nice to see you too, guy." He jumps over the couch and takes a seat. "Dude, this couch smells like sex."

Slamming the door shut, I walk over to stand behind the couch. "Yeah. Your hand is in my dried up cum right now. Now what the fuck do you want?"

My attitude doesn't even phase Stone. He's so used to my mood swings that he just brushes it off. He knows I mean no harm. That's one thing I like about this kid. He may only be twenty-one and a little inexperienced, but he's a pretty decent dude and doesn't take stupid shit to heart.

Lifting an eyebrow, he shrugs off my outburst. "Let's go out tonight. It's Cale's night to work. I have a place in mind that I want to go to but I need a partner." He pauses for a second to turn on the TV. *Sure, make yourself at home.* "There's a girl I want to see. I met her at that house we danced at last week. Her name is Ash. She's sexy as all hell but I'm trying to play it cool. I know she wants me, but I'm not giving this dick up that easy."

I think about it for a second and then I realize that this Ash girl probably works with Onyx. She might not like me showing up at her work again, but I don't give a shit. I will show up there every night until she gives me a second chance. That's how stubborn I am.

"Where?" I take my towel off and run it through my hair. "I might be down."

Stone turns around to look at me right as I wrap the towel back around my waist. "*Vixens Club,* man. I heard from one of the other girls that she works there. I've been thinking about going to see her for a while. You down?"

"Yeah," I say stiffly. "I'm down. Meet me back here around nine."

Standing up, Stone gives me a fist pound and heads for the door. "Alright, bro. I'm out."

"Cool."

I watch as Stone walks outside, forgetting to shut the door behind him. "Idiot," I mutter before walking over to shut it.

I stand here in thinking mode for a moment. This may make me sound like a pussy, but I want to be sure to look sexy as hell for her tonight. I'm going to dress this body of steel up for her and she won't be able to resist. I'm making it my mission to make her mine again.

WHEN NINE O'CLOCK ROLLS AROUND, I'm standing outside my house waiting on Stone to show up. I'm dressed in my favorite white button down, the sleeves rolled up to the elbows and the top few buttons undone, displaying my tats. I threw on a pair of dark fitted jeans that show off my muscular thighs, black boots and my hair is pulled back out of my face. Hell, I even trimmed my beard a bit to be sure it looks sexy for her.

Stone rolls up in his Jeep and whistles when I walk over and jump in the passenger seat. "Damn, dude. You trying to give the ladies a walking orgasm? You look studdish tonight." He reaches over and grabs the top of my collar, tugging slightly. "Damn, guy. I need to borrow that shirt sometime."

Shutting the door, I smirk slightly. "Come on, man. Stop creaming yourself over my clothes and let's go. No woman is going to want your ass if you walk in with nut stains."

"Fuck yeah, they would. Once I bust out my moves; the ladies can never resist." Stone lets out a satisfied laugh while grinding in his seat and pulling back out in the street and taking off. "No worries here."

We drive in silence for a few minutes, me lost in my own thoughts, trying to decide my best move for tonight before Stone interrupts me.

"You dressing up for someone? You never did tell me why you ran out of *Walk Of Shame* that night." He glances over at me and I grind my jaw at the thought of that night. I still can't get over what I found that night; her being in that place, rubbing all over that filth. She's too good for that shit. "I'm guessing it's for some fine ass girl. I've never seen your ass try before. Usually the grungy Hemy look is enough, my man."

"Yeah, man, not this time. Trust me," I reply. "It's for *the* girl. Not just any fucking girl. And she works with this Ash chick so don't make a fool out of yourself around me. I need to prove to her that I'm a different person. I'm taking it easy on shots and all that hard shit. Got it?"

Nodding his head, he pulls up to *Vixens Club*, parks the Jeep and kills the engine. "Sure thing, man. I've been there once. Good luck is all I can say. Once a woman sees all your fuck ups, it's hard for them to see you for the good. That shit stays with them forever."

My jaw ticks from his words as I stare up at the neon sign in deep thought. It just reminds me that there's a huge chance that Onyx will never forgive me for all the shit I put her through. Doesn't matter. It won't stop me from trying.

"Come on, man. Let's go."

I jump out of the Jeep and slam the door behind me, with Stone hopping out right after. I didn't mean to close it to the point of almost breaking it, but I can't seem to control the negative thoughts swarming through my head. The thought of not having her as mine makes me want to slam my fist through something.

"Take it easy, dude." Stone flares his nostrils while looking his

Jeep over for any damage. "Don't take it out on my shit. Save it for the assholes in the bar."

"My bad," I growl. "I'll buy you a new one if I fucked it up. Let's just get this over with."

We reach the door and some guy made of muscles with a bald, shiny head and long beard about six foot five comes over and asks for Stone's ID. He gets ready to ask for mine but after getting a glimpse of my face, decides against it and just waves us past.

"Seriously, dude?" Stone complains. "Is it because of my handsome baby face?" He rubs his hand over his face as if he's all smooth and shit.

I give his dumb ass a push as the bouncer gives him a blank look while crossing his arms. "Real men have beards. Grow one," I say annoyed.

After getting past the bouncer, we quickly order a couple drinks and take a seat in the far back. The club is fairly busy to-night and the thought of having all these creeps' eyes on my girl is driving me mad.

I know she hasn't danced yet because the bartender said there are a couple more girls before her. I don't really care to watch the show. Onyx is the only one I came to see. Until then, I'm invisible in the background.

Sipping back a Gin and Tonic, Stone pulls out his wallet and sets it on the table. "This club is pretty damn nice. A hell of a lot nicer than ours." He runs his hand over the table in front of us while admiring it. "Black glass tables, red suede chairs and look at that stage. That's a sweet ass stage. I wonder if they'll let me dance here. You know," he smirks confidently, "To help bring them some more cash in."

I tilt back my beer and block Stone out. I haven't been this fucking nervous since before I hit fucking puberty. All I can think about is thrashing all the men in this room. I saw the way that piece of shit handled her last time I was here and it makes my blood boil that I didn't kick the shit out of him.

I take a look around the room, taking in all the assholes waving money around and screaming out like pigs. This must be the image Onyx has of me in her mind. I'm just like every one of these assholes. Until I can change that; that's what she sees.

Taking a long swig of my beer, almost finishing it off, I slam it down on the table and look over at Stone. He's too zoned in on the entertainment on stage to even notice me standing up. "I'll be back."

Walking away with a quickness, I make my way back over to the bar and call for the bartender to come over. The beautiful blonde that helped us when we walked in, lifts her eyebrows and adjusts her tiny top while walking my way.

"Can I help you with something," she looks me up and down while playfully biting her lip, "big guy? You're looking awfully sexy to be here alone."

I ignore her sorry attempt to get my interest and pull out my wallet, prepared to make this shit happen my way tonight. "How much would it cost to get one of the girls to dance for me in a private room instead of on stage?"

The girl looks me up and down while leaning over the counter and reaching for my collar. "Why would you want to pay for one of these girls to dance for you when you can get *any* girl for free?"

"How much?" I growl out, pulling away from her touch. She gives me a confused look. "If you don't know then ask your manager. I need to know and quickly."

She takes a step back, her cheeks turning slightly pink with embarrassment. She clears her throat. "Umm. Well, we don't get that happening very often. If they're set to dance on stage then they usually can't do private dances until they're through. It's all on a schedule to fill the time."

Aggravation takes over as another girl enters the stage, swaying her hips wearing next to nothing. Onyx is next and I don't have time for games. I'll pay whatever the hell they want. I could care less about the money.

"Tell your boss I'll pay three grand to have Onyx dance for me in private. I'm sure he wouldn't mind the extra cash. Just make it happen."

The girl holds up her finger before walking over to the phone and making a call. She comes back a minute later and points down the hall. "The room all the way to the back. It's our biggest room and it gives you some privacy in case you don't want to be seen by the dancer. Roman said he'll make it happen. I'll give Onyx the message."

I turn to walk away, but stop before taking a step. "Do me a favor and don't describe me to her."

She nods in understanding so I turn and walk away.

Hope she still likes surprises . . .

CHAPTER TEN

Onyx

HALF ASLEEP, I FIGHT TO stay awake while finishing up my makeup. As much as I don't want to be here tonight, I'm up next on stage and I really don't have much of a choice. A huge part of me wanted to call in tonight, but the other part of me knows I can't let my emotions get in the way of earning my bill money. Still, I'm just so . . . exhausted.

I crawled out of Hemy's bed around eight this morning and left while he was too deep in sleep to take notice. I knew I had to get out of there before he woke, or else he would've somehow talked me into spending the whole day with him. I couldn't let that happen. The more he brings up the past and shows me how different he is, the more I want to give in and trust him. It's too soon for that.

After I got back to my own bed, I thought I would be able

to get some rest, but I couldn't shut my mind off enough to fall back asleep. I ended up spending most of the day cleaning a house that was already clean and watching stupid TV shows, hoping they would wear me down enough to sleep. No luck there.

Tossing down my eyeliner, I look over to see if Ash is dressed and ready to go. She's up for her set on stage after me. I met Ash about a year ago, before I moved back home. We hit it off really fast and after she explained how she was tired of her dull life and her parents smothering her, I thought maybe it would be nice to bring her home with me and let her live a little.

I really had no idea what the hell I was going to do for a job, but then an old friend of mine told me about *Vixens* needing a couple dancers. I mentioned it to Ash and in her rebellious state she was down for it, and ready to have a little fun. Plus, knowing that I was going to be so close to Hemy kind of made me want to rebel a bit myself. I needed a hard exterior to make me seem less vulnerable. It worked for a while.

"You still like this job, Ash?" I ask, now questioning my decision to bring her here.

Smiling, she sets down her red lipstick and uncrosses her legs. "Yeah, for now. It's not a bad place. Plus, the money is way better than working some dead end waitressing job." She shrugs. "Might as well have a bit of fun while I'm still young."

I return her smile and then look beside us as the door opens and Kylie rushes in. She gives me a not so pleasant look and rolls her eyes. "There's been a change of plans. You're not going to be dancing on stage tonight."

Standing up, I place my hands on my hips and give her an equally disgusted look. Kylie usually seems to be friendly, but right now, I feel like slapping that smug look off her pretty little face.

"And why the hell is that?"

Mumbling under her breath, she tosses me a wad of cash and

I reach out, barely catching it. "I can't believe Roman agreed to this, *but* someone paid a shit ton of money to have you do a private dance instead. Roman told me to give you a grand to do it." She turns and starts heading back for the door. "The sexy asshole is waiting in room ten. You probably shouldn't keep him waiting. Damn asshole," she mutters and leaves the room.

I hold up the wad of cash and bite my bottom lip in thought. I feel a rush at the thought that Hemy could very well be that sexy asshole waiting on me. The problem with that is I wouldn't expect him to pay a ton of money for me to dance for him when he knows he can practically get anything he wants. He always did . . . until I left him.

Just as quickly as I let the thought consume me, I push it away and take a deep breath. I guess if anything, it's still better than being on stage. I still can't get used to dancing for a room full of men. I seem to do better one on one. Plus, it's easier to stay in command when you only have one asshole to deal with.

Handing the cash to Ash, I force a smile. "Mind putting that away for us? Looks like I have a sexy asshole waiting for a show."

We both laugh as I start backing away.

"Seems like a pretty generous asshole at least." She lifts a brow and waves the cash. "Tell him thanks from the both of us. I'll be lucky to make half that on stage."

GATHERING MY THOUGHTS, I TAKE my time walking to room ten. If this asshole was desperate enough to pay the amount of money this had to have cost, then he's desperate enough that he'll wait and still enjoy it when I get there.

Walking past the main room, I see it's almost filled to capacity now. The music is loud, the men are loud, and the flashing lights make it harder to concentrate on what's on stage. I guess the strobe effects and beat of the music make it more exciting for the men, and to make them feel they have to fight in order to see the half naked girls swaying before them. It keeps them around longer, wanting to see more. That's what Roman thinks, at least. I think it's annoying as shit.

I make it down the hall and stop directly in front of the door, labeled with the number ten, staring for a moment before pushing the door open and stepping inside. I close the door behind me and try not to pay attention to who is in the room.

Room ten is the biggest private room we have. It's used for rich clients that want to remain discrete and don't want their faces shown to the public. Off in the back of the room, there's a huge leather chair for the client to relax in, and a light switch, giving them the option of showing their face or not. Lucky for me, this client wants to be kept a secret. It makes it easier to dance when I don't have to look into the creepy eyes that are glued to my every move. It's hard to be sexy when you feel so damn gross sometimes, as if the filth is sticking to you just by being in the room.

Pushing all thoughts aside, I walk past the darkened corner, taking long, smooth steps, and swaying my hips on my way up to the stage. The music is already playing a slow, sexy song; perfect for getting aroused to.

Standing with my back against the pole, I bring one arm back to wrap around it, and slowly lowering my body down the pole, while rubbing my other hand down the center of my body, over the white lace. Once I get close to the ground, I spread my knees apart and lower my hand some more, biting my bottom lip, seductively.

I sway my hips to the rhythm of the music, releasing the pole, and wrapping my hands in my hair, tugging as I make my way back up the pole in a stance. I make sure to look in the direction of the darkened corner to verify to the client I'm indeed dancing for his pleasure and his alone. This usually helps me get additional tips on top of what I already get for doing the private dance.

Slowly turning around, I wrap one leg around the pole and arch my back, swinging my wild hair around, before gripping the pole and spinning around it. I spin around a few times, moving seductively to the music, before releasing the pole, walking to the edge of the small stage, and reaching for the ribbon that's holding my corset together.

Pretending as if I'm looking directly in the mysterious guy's eyes, I lower myself to the surface of the stage, down to my ass, and spread my legs wide apart, revealing the sheer lace that's in between. I slightly tug the ribbon, opening my top a little more, and rolling my hips up and down with my back pressed against the stage.

I'm lost in my own little world, hoping to get this guy off, when all of a sudden I feel two hands grip my thighs and pull me to the edge of the stage. Out of instinct, I swing one leg up and wrap it around the guy's neck, squeezing.

I expect for whoever it is to let go of my thighs and apologize, but to my surprise, I get a growl and a bite on the inside of my thigh.

I recognize the growl right away, and I can't help the reaction that my body gets from it. My heart jumps to my throat and my whole body trembles with pleasure.

Another soft bite causes me to open my eyes to the sight of Hemy standing there, his hair pulled back, and his deep amber eyes set on me. His grip on my thighs tightens as I release his neck and lean my head back with my hands in my hair.

"Fucking shit, Hemy," I bite out. "You scared the shit out of me. What are you doing here? I told you-"

"Shhh . . ." he whispers against my thigh. "Don't talk. I'm not here for that. I'm here to taste my pussy and remind you of what is mine."

Before I can think of a response, my panties are pushed aside and Hemy moans out while running his thick finger over my slick folds. My body instantly reacts to his touch, causing me to moan out and bite my lip.

"You miss my mouth owning your pussy? It craves my tongue, doesn't it, baby?" He runs a hand down my thigh while shoving a finger deep inside me, causing me to grip the stage. "Tell me how bad you want me to taste you," he demands.

I look up at him, now getting a bit angry at him for making me admit it first. He's doing this to see how badly I want him. It makes me want to slap him and then ride the shit out of him. He always had that effect on me.

"Maybe I don't want you to," I whisper, looking up to meet his stare. "Maybe someone else has already claimed what was once yours." I can't resist but to push him back. One of us is bound to cave first.

Pulling my body up higher, he softly blows on my swollen clit while pushing his finger in and out. "You'll always be mine, Onyx." He squeezes my thigh and rubs his bottom lip up my heat, causing me to moan out silently. "This pussy . . . will always be mine. I claimed it six years ago when I made you my girl, and nothing has changed since."

He runs his lip up my pussy again, teasing me with his lip ring. I'm fighting so hard to resist, but I can't help it. Seeing Hemy dressed up, makes me want to have an orgasm right on the spot. *Feeling* his mouth on me almost has me exploding beneath him.

I thrust my hips upward, silently begging for him to lick me. He laughs against my throbbing clit before reaching up with one hand and grabbing my left breast. His dominance has me on the verge of explosion and I want to feel this to its full extent.

"I want to feel your tongue on me so damn bad," I blurt out, thrusting my hips again to meet his mouth. "Remind me of how good it feels. Now."

With a cocky smile, Hemy grips my ass with both hands and pulls my hips up to meet his face. Looking at me with pure heated desire, he runs his tongue, slowly and teasingly, up my wetness, causing me to shake uncontrollably in his arms.

He rubs circles around my clit with his tongue, before trailing it back down my folds and pushing it into my entrance. This causes me to wrap my legs around his head and squeeze. I can't seem to get him close enough and he knows this. He knows my weakness and is using it against me to get me where he wants me. It's working and I hate him for it.

The better it feels the angrier I seem to get, until finally, I growl out and pull away from him. At least, I try to. He catches my legs and pulls me off stage so that I'm straddling his narrow hips. With a smile, he walks us both up the stairs and up to the stage.

He stops in front of the pole, turns my back toward it, and presses me against it, breathing in my ear. "Hold on tight." With little effort, he lifts me up, causing me to reach behind me and grip onto the pole at a higher level. Before I can wonder what he's doing, he rests my thighs on his shoulders, grips my waist, and buries his face in my pussy.

His tongue works like magic, owning my pussy just like in the past. My whole body trembles from the heat of his mouth and the feel of his tongue tasting me, slowly and teasingly.

He reaches up with one hand and rubs his thumb over my clit, while working his tongue, rough and fast, speeding up to get me off. My grip on the pole tightens as he shoves his tongue back inside just in time for me to come.

I shake on his shoulders for a few seconds, high off the release of my orgasm. It feels so damn good I can almost cry in relief. Releasing the pole, he pulls me away from it and slowly lowers me down his body, kissing me in different places along the way. It doesn't take much for him to lower me back down to my feet and press his body into mine.

Looking into my eyes, he cups my face and runs his tongue over his lips in satisfaction. "I want you back at my place tonight." I shake my head, but he stops me by pressing his lips against mine, claiming my lips as his. The kiss is rough and possessive, and I can't help but to get turned on again.

After a few moments pass, he pulls away from the kiss and turns to walk away without another word. My whole body screams for me to run after him, but I can't. I'm stuck in place, trying to figure out how I let him take control of me again.

Screw this. I'm letting him know that he doesn't control me. He hasn't in a long time. He has no say whether or not I go to his place and stay with him. He lost that say years ago.

Making sure that I'm covered, I rush out of the room and walk down the dark hallway. I stop when I get to the main room and look around in search of him. It doesn't take long to point him out. With Hemy looking as sexy as he is tonight, it's hard to miss him.

He's standing next to a table with another guy. I recognize him from Jade's party. He's one of the three strippers that danced that night. I recognize the black hair and tattoos. Realizing that he must be here to watch one of the girls, my gut tells me to get Hemy out of here.

He might assume I'm giving into him, but I'm really just trying to preserve my secret a bit longer. He *seems* different, but I'm still scared.

Clearing my head and coming down from my temporary high, I walk over to the table, stopping in between him and the other guy. I place my hand on Hemy's chest and can't help the moan that slips out of my mouth. Just touching him has me all worked up.

"Wait for me outside. I'll go grab my things and meet you by your truck."

Biting his bottom lip, he grabs both of my hands and runs them up his chest, before pulling them up to wrap around his neck. He presses his body flush with mine and gives me a hooded look. "I don't have my truck. We'll take my motorcycle."

I smile at the memory of when the bike was his. After a while, he gave up on it and got a new one. I couldn't leave without it, because it brought back too many memories. I needed it as my safety net. I needed it to fall back on when I missed him too much, so after I packed my things and left that night, I sent my brother to pick up it up from storage. I made it mine with the memories of him.

"You mean my bike?" Smirking, I turn around in his arms and walk away, making him release me. If I know Hemy still, he'll be outside as soon as I'm out of sight.

After quickly grabbing my things and changing, I make my way outside to see Hemy leaning against my bike. Seeing him standing in front of it causes my heart to clench in pain. It brings back too many memories of us as teens, me holding on tightly as he learned how to ride it. It didn't take long and I always trusted him to keep me safe; a part of me still does.

He sees me approaching and walks over, placing the helmet on my head. "Give me the keys," he orders.

I think about it for a second and almost consider making him ride on the back, but that would just look too weird to even enjoy. Hemy is definitely too dominant for that. Alpha male is what he'll always be. Shit, it's such a turn on.

I toss him the keys without a fight, pull my helmet on, and put my backpack on. My black boots dig into the gravel as I hop on the back and watch as Hemy jumps on the front.

I don't know how much more of this I can take while guarding my heart. *I need to figure something out and fast . . .*

CHAPTER ELEVEN

Hemy

THE FEEL OF HER ARMS wrapped around my waist brings me back to the past. After I learned how to ride this motorcycle for the first time, she spent almost every day on the back of it, the two of us just riding to forget. Those are some of my happiest memories.

I can tell she's thinking about it too, because she hasn't said a word since we left the club, and not to mention that her arms are practically squeezing the life out of me. She always did that unintentionally in the past when she was deep in thought, and man does it feel good. This is exactly what I was hoping for. If I want another chance with her, then I'll have to remind her of the good stuff.

Riding past my block, I make a turn down the street that leads to Mitch's shop. Mitch's family has owned *Greenler's Mechanics* his whole life. Onyx and I spent a lot of time in it, playing and fooling around, when I was working on my motorcycle or showing off my mechanic skills to get her worked up. She always did have a thing for a dirty, hardworking man. I'm sure that hasn't changed much. At least, I can only hope.

Onyx doesn't bother looking up until we are already pulling up to the shop and parking. I can tell from her lack of smartass remarks. That, and I can feel her chin resting against my back. I don't think it's intentional, but I would dare say a word at the risk of her moving it. I feel her grip loosen as she lets out a little surprised breath. "Seriously, Hemy?" She releases my waist as I kill the engine. "Why would you bring me here? I thought we were going to your place."

Not bothering to respond, I help her off the bike and watch as she walks up to the building and stands there in silence. She probably hasn't even thought about this place in over four years. Bringing her here is sure to get the memories flowing in. It has to. I'm counting on it. Hell, I'm having a hard time just being here with her. I could do it alone over the years, but having her here makes my chest ache. It always will until she's mine again.

Grinding my jaw and pushing back my emotions, I grab Onyx's hand and pull her along with me as I walk around to the back and pull out my key. I've been meaning to work on my Harley for a while now, but I've been so damn busy working on other projects for Mitch that I haven't been able to touch it. It's about time I get my baby running good.

I push the door open and flip on the light. I feel Onyx's hand squeeze mine, and then she lets go and steps inside. "I haven't thought about this place in years, Hemy." She looks around, her face void of emotions. "It looks exactly the same." She cracks a smile. "As a matter of fact, I think you guys are still working on the same vehicles too."

I let my own smile take over as I watch her laugh at her own joke. Damn, her laugh is just as beautiful as ever. I never could get enough of that sound.

I step up beside her and nudge her with my shoulder. She looks up at me. "I love that sound," I say softly.

She looks around as if listening for something. "What sound?"

"When you laugh," I say honestly. Her smile fades as I look down into her eyes and then walk away.

I keep on walking, making my way to the back where my motorcycle is parked. It doesn't take but a few seconds before Onyx is standing right behind me. She's so close that I can feel the warmth from her body. I can sense her eyes studying me as I stand here.

"Why are we here?" she finally asks.

"I need to work on my bike. Why else would we be here?"

"It's like midnight. Don't you ever sleep?"

"Not anymore. I told you, I can't sleep for shit without you naked and next to me." I walk away, unbuttoning my shirt, before pulling it off and setting it on the closest car.

I kneel down in front of my Harley and reach for my tools. Onyx watches me in silence for a few seconds before she drops her bag down beside her and takes a seat on the hood of the car next to her. "I've kind of missed this, you know." She pauses and waits for me to respond, but I don't. I want her to keep going. "You working on your bike here and me watching. Us laughing and talking. I miss you like that."

I continue to work on my bike, not looking back at Onyx. "You always made it hard to get any work done. Your smell alone was enough to arouse me, but when you would undress behind me, sitting on a car . . ." My words trail off and I smirk to myself, knowing by the sound of her breathing that she's reliving the memories.

"What," she breathes. "Don't stop there, Hemy."

"All I could think about was burying myself deep between

those thighs." I stand up, drop my tools, and walk over to stand between her legs. Placing my hands on her thighs, I trail my hands up them. "*My* thighs. All I wanted to do was to own your little pussy and release myself so deep inside you that I would ruin you for anyone else."

Her breathing picks up as I spread her legs and step between them. "Mmm . . . and I wanted you deep inside me. I never could watch you getting dirty without wanting you to get me dirty. Funny how that works." She leans forward and runs her tongue over my mouth, her tongue lingering on my ring before sucking my lip along with it into her mouth. "You were so damn sexy working on your bike that my clothes practically fell off. That look you made when concentrating on your work. Oh shit, I'll never forget that look."

I tangle my fingers in the back of her hair and look down at her with a serious look of concentration, imitating what she just described. It's not all just an act. I'm taking my time and concentrating on every last inch of her beauty. I bite my lip as she closes her eyes and breathes in. I know I have her. "This one," I question, stepping in closer to press my erection between her thighs.

Her body jerks from below me as I grind my hips a little. "Oh God, yes." She opens her eyes and takes in my face, her eyes filled with lust. "That one, exactly. Why are you doing this, Hemy? You knew this would happen if you brought me here. We can't keep doing this. I can't let myself fall in love with you again."

"You falling back in love with me is the *only* thing I want." Gripping her hair tighter, I crush my lips against hers, owning her lips, breath, and taste. Everything that she is right now is mine and I intend on keeping it this way. I'm taking this moment and owning it.

Her lips instantly part, allowing me entrance just like in the past. Everything about this moment brings me back to four years ago, and it only makes me want her more. Pulling back, I breathe against her lips, my hands still tangled in her hair. "You taste so damn good, baby." I bring one hand down and rub my thumb over her cheek before trailing down and over her bottom lip. "Seeing you up on the hood of this car makes me want to take you right here." I kiss her neck and make my way up to her ear, stopping to whisper. "Do you want that, baby? Huh? You want to remember what it was like, me taking you here, me all dirty and sweaty?"

"No," she whispers, pushing on my chest. "That's the last reminder I need, Hemy."

Grabbing her chin, I force her to look up into my eyes. I can tell by her heavy breathing and fidgeting that she's lying. She always did have a hard time hiding her feelings from me. "Dammit, Onyx. Don't lie to me. Tell. Me. The. Truth."

She nods her head, her breathing picking up as she reaches up to let my hair down. She looks lost in thought for a moment before she speaks. "You have no idea how sexy your hair is. Every time I look at you, all I can think about is gripping onto it as you make love to me."

My heart beats wildly in my chest, but then sinks to my stomach as she turns her head away in shame. She does that when she says something she didn't mean to. Every part of me wants her to mean those damn words. I may not have made love to her in the past, but things have changed. I've changed. I'm willing to give her anything she wants.

I pull her face back to mine and bring my lips down to hover over hers, our heavy breathing mingling together. "If you give me a chance," I bring my eyes up to meet hers," I'll make love to you. I'm capable of more than you think now, Onyx."

She stares at me for a second, not saying a word, before a small smile creeps over her face. "Well, not tonight." She grips my hair and pulls on it roughly. "Tonight, I want you to fuck me like you did four years ago." She yanks my hair harder before releasing it. "Show me the old Hemy. *My* Hemy."

Her words set me off and before she can register what I'm doing, I have her back pressed against the hood of the car and her pants in my hands, yanking them down her legs. Kissing the inside of her thigh, I pull her boots off and toss them, before tossing her tight little jeans next to them.

I spread her legs further and kiss my way up to her stomach while reaching for her white tank top. "Fuck, Onyx." I love the way she looks laying across the hood of a car. I nibble my lip ring while pulling her shirt above her head and reaching behind her to release her bra. I take a few seconds to admire her body before gripping her thong in my hand and pulling her body into mine. Nothing is standing in the way of being inside her now but my jeans and her tiny lace thong. It's exactly like it was when we first fell in love. It's just too bad she never knew it.

Twisting her panties in my hand, I rip them off, the white lace coming untied with little effort. Onyx lets out a moan and arches her back as I lace one arm beneath her and bite down into her shoulder. "Oh God, Hemy," she pants. "Hurry up and get those jeans off."

Smiling against her neck, I work on taking off my jeans with one hand, while reaching down with my other to rub circles over her swollen clit. "Mmm . . . you're so wet for me, baby." I slide my jeans down my legs and let them drop, before spinning Onyx around and slamming her down onto the hood, grabbing the back of her hair.

"Spread your legs, baby." I lean down next to her ear and growl as she bites my arm. "Show me how bad you've missed me inside you."

She bites me harder, causing me to squeeze her left ass cheek before slapping it. She cries out with pleasure as I slap it one more time before gripping her ass with both hands and spreading her cheeks. "It's so damn beautiful," I whisper, while running a finger up her slick folds. "Hold on, baby. I'm about to take you for a ride."

Gripping my cock, I align it with her opening, rubbing the head of it over her slickness, teasing her with my piercings before shoving it deep inside with a moan. Holding onto her hips, I pound into her hard and fast, causing her to grab onto the hood and scream. The faster I go, the more she begs for me to go harder.

Grinding my hips, I yank her hair back with one hand, pushing hard and deep. I want her to still be able to feel me inside her after we're through. I want her to know she's mine and mine alone. I may have shared her once, but that'll never happen again.

She sticks her ass up higher, gripping onto my hand as I thrust into her. I'm already as deep as I can go and she still wants me deeper. We never could get enough of each other, even when it hurt her.

A few thrusts later, I feel her clenching around my cock, so I give her one hard thrust before yanking her neck to the side and pressing my lips against hers, right as she moans out. I wait for her to stop shaking before I pull out and spin her around to face me.

I crush my lips back against hers, both of us breathing heavy, as I pick her up and walk until we're pressed against the wall in our favorite corner. It was where we went to fuck when Mitch's ass wouldn't leave for the night. Even though he could still hear us, it kept us hidden pretty well in the shadows. The risk of getting caught made it more of a rush.

Pulling away from her lips, I wrap my hand around her throat and push myself inside her, causing her to shake in my arms. "Remember this spot, baby?" I pull her bottom lip into my mouth and bite into as I start thrusting hard and fast, pushing her up the wall with each movement.

I reach down and grab her hands, binding them in one hand, and raising them above her head. Both of us are breathing heavy, me holding her hands above her head while holding her up with my opposite arm supporting her waist.

"Hemy!" She pulls back on my hair as I push into her one last time, feeling my orgasm build before I release myself deep inside her.

We stand here, me holding her and her holding onto me as we fight to catch our breath. Lowering her back to her feet, I tangle my fingers in her hair and press my forehead against hers. "I fucking love you," I breathe out. "I love you so much that it hurts."

Sucking in a breath of shock, she places both her hands on my chest and shoves me away. "Damn you, Hemy!" Rushing over to her clothes, she struggles to get dressed while muttering under her breath and holding back tears.

I don't blame her for her reaction. I hurt her beyond words, and me dropping the L word like this was probably the last thing she expected . . . but I don't give a shit. I love her and she needs to know, no matter how much she hates me. I missed my chance the first time. It won't happen again. I'll never lose her again because I couldn't tell her how I felt.

I feel my heart shattering in my chest as she throws on her boots and reaches for her bag. As much as I know she needs to go, I don't want her to. She heads for the door, but then stops to turn around and throw something. Whatever it was hits the wall before she buries her face in her hands and shakes her head.

"Do you even know what pain feels like, Hemy?" Her jaw clenches as I stare at her. "Well, do you? Do you even feel pain?"

"Oh, I feel it alright. That burning sensation deep down inside that feels as if my heart is dying, being crushed." I look up from the ground and right into her eyes. "I felt it the minute you walked out my damn door."

She stands there, unable to say anything, before turning around and walking out the door, slamming it closed behind her. I have no one to blame but myself. I did this to her . . . to us.

It just means I need to work harder to show her the new me.

CHAPTER TWELVE
Hemy

IT'S BEEN FOUR DAYS SINCE I've seen Onyx and it's taking everything in me not to go to *Vixens'* and claim her as mine. As much as it hurts, she needs time. Me forcing her to admit her feelings isn't going to do shit but make it worse on my part. I can't have that.

Taking a drag of my cigarette, I tilt my head back up to look at Slade. He's puffing on his own cigarette while texting Aspen. "You love her, man?"

Slade gives me a hard look before shoving his phone in his pocket and taking one last drag of his cigarette before tossing it. "With everything in me," he says with confidence. "There's not a thing I wouldn't do for that woman."

I can't believe I'm even doing this right now. Going to Slade for advice was the last thing I thought I'd ever do. "What would you do if you hurt her so bad in the past that she was afraid to open up and let you back in? What if you told her you loved her for the first time and she walked away?"

Taking a step closer to me, he grips my shoulder and smirks. "My guy's in love. This must be one badass chick." He shoves my shoulder before placing me in a headlock and rubbing the top of my head. "You've been holding out on me, my man."

I take one last drag of my cigarette as he releases my neck. "Yeah, she's badass. She's my first and only love, man. I fucked up bad and I'm paying for it now." I toss my cigarette and take a deep breath before quickly releasing it. "I'm trying to be patient, man. It's been four days and I haven't heard shit." I steel my jaw while leaning into the building and digging my fingers into it. "How much time should I give her?"

Without hesitation, he answers, "You know me, man. When I want something I go after it, sometimes a little too hard. If it's love, then you need to let her know that you're not going anywhere. Let her know you want her without pushing her away. You get me?"

I nod my head, getting what he means. I can still let her know I'm not going anywhere without being too pushy. My shift is almost over for the night, so as soon as I'm out, I'm going straight to *Vixens'*.

"Hemy."

We both look over at the sound of Sarah's voice. "The group dance is up next. You better hurry and get your fine ass in there." She smiles at Slade before shoving his shoulder. "Your woman is at the bar waiting on you. You better hurry before someone else snags her sexy ass up."

Oh boy. She just had to go there.

Without hesitation, Slade stalks off, rushing inside to his woman. He knows damn well he has nothing to worry about with Aspen, but he's still so damn protective. He reminds me a lot of myself. When we find that special woman, we'll do anything for her. I just wish I wasn't too late.

"Thanks, Sarah."

"Yeah, yeah. Just hurry your ass up," she teases.

IF THERE'S ANYTHING THAT I hate, it's doing a stupid dance routine on stage. It involves costumes and all of us men putting a dance together. It makes us all feel like fucking idiots. That's why we only set up a dance routine once a month. It's the one thing that some of the women travel to see. It's the biggest night of every month, packed to maximum capacity.

Adjusting my tie, I laugh at Stone as he jumps up on a table and thrusts his hips while gripping onto his hat and tilting it down, over his face. "Man, I'm such a stud in a suit."

"Is that right, asshole?" Cale asks.

"Um . . . fuck yeah," Stone replies while jumping down from the table. "Don't get mad when I get all the tips. I have this routine down pat, bros."

"Alright, *stud*." I slap the back of his head before reaching for my black hat and putting it on, tilting it a bit to the side. "This is the biggest crowd you'll see for a while, so you better show them Slade's not around anymore. A lot of them come just for that motherfucker."

"I'm the new Slade," he says with a smirk. "These women will leave screaming Stone. You feel me?" He gives both Cale and I the middle finger before jogging up the steps to the back of the stage.

This kid really has no idea what he's getting into right now. Some of these women still even scare my ass with all that shrieking.

The stage is dark when we line up next to our chairs. I can hear the screaming of hundreds of women as soon as the music starts playing. This used to get me hard at one point. Undressing for all these horny women. Now, I don't feel shit. I just want to get this over with.

Out of instinct, my body instantly reacts to the music when the lights flicker on, lighting up the stage. Placing one foot on the chair, I grab the top of my head and grind my hips to the music, the other two doing the same.

I thrust my hips slow and seductively as if I were fucking someone with deep passion. This causes the girls close by to lean over the stage and start waving a handful of cash while others toss some onto the stage.

I reach up with one hand and loosen my tie, swinging one leg over the chair to straddle it, rocking my hips a few times just before grabbing the chair and lifting it up to place at the end of the stage.

I look out into the crowd and motion with my finger for the closest girl to come up on stage. With little effort, I grab onto her arm and pull her up next to me.

Swaying my hips to the slow rhythm, I pull the knot of my tie until it transforms back into a straight piece of fabric. Grabbing each end, I slide it around her waist and pull her body up against mine, transferring the ends of the tie in one hand. I lean into her neck and grip my hat with one hand while grinding against her, causing her to scream out with excitement.

Out of the corner of my eye, I see Cale and Stone doing the exact same thing. For as little as we actually practice, we're completely in sync with each other. I have to admit we don't look half bad for not putting much effort into the routine.

Walking her backwards, I guide her down into the chair before dropping my tie and ripping the buttons off of my black button down. I grab the girl's hand and place it on my chest while standing above her lap and dancing against her.

The girl's hand goes to reach for my dick, but I grab it,

stopping her before she can get there. The thought of another woman touching me there right now is not sitting well with me. It actually pisses me off.

Pushing back my anger, I tilt her chair back until I'm standing over her face, grinding my hips above her while holding the top of the chair up with one hand. My dick is directly in front of her face and all I can think about is Onyx doing something similar with some random dude in her club.

Jealousy courses through me, but I do my best to keep it in check and make it through the dance. The routine is almost over. Only one more thing left to do.

Pulling the chair back up on all fours, I run my hands down my bare chest before undoing my pants and placing the girl's hands on my waistline, allowing her to undress me. She pushes them down my legs without hesitation, leaving me standing here in my short boxer briefs, the women all screaming at us practically naked.

Picking her up and placing her to lie on her back on the stage, I slide across the floor, on my knees, while thrusting my hips until I'm above her face again. I place both hands on the ground in front of me and thrust in a fast motion, brushing against her in the face with my package.

She reaches up and grabs my ass until I'm done and moving down her body, pretending to lick her body on the way down. Once I reach the bottom, I help her to her feet and smile as she shoves a handful of cash in the front of my briefs.

We do a few more short dances, filling the time, until finally the night is almost over and we're heading back stage to get dressed.

I TAKE A SEAT AND look around, swallowing the realization

that none of these girls even come close to comparing to Onyx. This place isn't good enough anymore. Onyx is sexy, strong, passionate, and doesn't take shit from anyone. She has always been that way . . . except when it came to me.

I reach over to the table next to me and grab for my beer. I hold it against my lips for a few seconds before pulling it away and setting it down, pissed off at my damn self for thinking. "Fuck me."

"Hello, sexy," a soft voice says from beside me.

Without looking over, I nod my head and reach for my beer again. I really don't feel like being messed with at the moment. "I'm done working for the night," I say stiffly.

"Even better." I feel the couch dip next to me, so I look over to see a sexy brunette. It's the same one that licked the whipped cream off my body that night I left to go find Onyx. She smiles victoriously as if she's been waiting for the exact moment to get me alone. "It looks like you could use some company."

She reaches over and slides her hand up my leg, gripping my thigh just below my dick. I look down at her slender hand and grab it right before she reaches for my package. "I don't want company." I set her hand on her own lap and stand up while taking a sip of my beer. "I'm good being alone."

Leaning forward, she pokes out her chest while running a finger over her half empty glass. Her lips curl up into a smile as she takes a sip and scoots closer to the edge. "I think you just need to release some tension." She licks her lips. "I'm sure I could help you with that."

"I said I'm good." I go to turn around and stop as I almost bump into someone. Not just anyone . . . Onyx.

Her nostrils flare as she stares me in the eyes, not saying a word. I can't even move. I'm frozen in place from her stare, so I just stare back, waiting for her to speak.

"Here's your chance, Hemy." She looks between me and the brunette. "Here's your chance to speak. That is, if you're not too busy."

"Hey!" The brunette sets her drink down on the table next to her and sits straight up as if ready for a fight. "Can't you see he's busy, bitch?"

Onyx runs her tongue over her top teeth before placing the heel of her boot into the girl's chest and shoving her backwards, then leaning down toward her face. "I'd watch who you call a bitch. Got it, sweetheart." She pulls her foot away and leans into her ear. "Keep your dirty little mouth away from my man or you'll be eating my heel for a late night snack."

"Fuck me. That's hot." I set my beer down and watch as Onyx turns around to face me. "Your man, huh?"

"Shit!" She walks away from me while mumbling some shit under her breath.

I quickly catch up to her and grab her by the waist to stop her. "Where are you going?" I spin her around and brush a curl out of her face. "Come to my house with me."

"No." She places her hands on my chest and pushes me away as I pull her into me. "Dammit, Hemy. See what you do to me?" She lets out a breath of frustration and turns away for a second. "I didn't mean to call you that. It just sort of came out."

"It sounded damn good coming out too," I admit. "Come to my house so we can talk. I'm not taking no for an answer anymore."

"No, Hemy. We can talk here. We never talk in private and you know it."

I pull my eyes away from hers and look around to see that a lot of people have stopped to stare at us, including Sarah and one of our other bartenders, Amanda. I flex my jaw at them and they both turn away to resume minding their own business.

"Let's go," I say firmly. "We're going to my house."

"Onyx! What are you doing here?"

I look beside us to see a pretty girl with dark curls standing next to Stone. The look that crosses Onyx's face as she takes her in surprises me. She looks sick, as if she's about to pass out.

"Um . . . Ash. What are you doing here? I thought you were still at work?"

Ash looks between me and Onyx and forces a small smile. "Is this your friend?" She looks me over as if she's trying to figure something out. "The one you said I might meet someday?"

Onyx looks between the two of us, her face pained before she reaches for my arm. "Yeah, but now is not a very good time. I'm suddenly feeling like shit."

Ash steps up beside Onyx and grabs for her purse. "I can take you home. I have my car outside and-"

"No," she cuts in. "You just got here. I'll be fine." She turns to face me and her eyes lock with mine. The pain in her expression confuses me. "Let's go to your house. I think we have a lot to talk about."

"Alright." I take one more look at Stone and Ash before following Onyx through the crowd and outside. As soon as Onyx gets outside, she pukes.

This could be a messy night . . .

CHAPTER THIRTEEN

Hemy

AFTER ONYX CALMED DOWN AND the puking stopped, I took off my shirt and wiped her face off before helping her into my truck. As tough as she thinks she is now, I know she still needs a little taking care of. She deserves it and I want her to know that. I would take care of her for the rest of my damn life if she would just let me.

Onyx lets out a heavy breath beside me. "I can't do this, Hemy. I can't fucking do this. Stop the car."

Pulling the truck over, I grip the steering wheel before slamming my fist into it. I can't stand those words coming from her mouth. I wish she would stop trying to keep me out. "Dammit, Onyx!" I lean back in my seat and rub my hands over my face in frustration. "I've been trying to show you that I'm a different person. Can't you fucking see that? All you want to do is keep me out and push me away."

It's silent for a moment as I stare at the side of her face, taking her in. She looks so pained that it breaks my damn heart. I wish she would just fucking talk and put me out of my misery.

"Hemy," she breathes, breaking the silence. "I know you're trying to prove that you've changed and you can give me what I wanted back then, but you don't understand. You broke me . . . shattered me. I'm not the same girl I was, and I don't think I can love you that way again. You need to let me go. I refuse to go through that again."

Grinding my jaw, I try my best to hide my anger. "You won't even give me the chance, Onyx! I know you're not the same girl and I'm not the same guy. We are different, but that isn't a bad thing. We still belong together like we always have and always will . . ."

She holds her hand up to stop my words before tugging on her hair in frustration. "You know how easy it would be for me to give in and believe you, right? You and I, it's never been easy and I can't go down that path with you, Hemy. Please, leave me alone. Maybe we can be friends someday, but I can't handle this now."

"I can't just be your friend. I'll always want more with you, and you know you feel the same damn way."

She must be done listening to me, because she goes for the door handle and quickly pushes it open. "I'm just going to walk home, and please, don't come after me."

Before I can say anything, she hops out of the truck and slams the door behind her. She takes off walking as if she's trying to get as far away from me as she can. The thought crushes me and I feel as if I can't breathe. I want to be pissed at her for being scared, but I can't. It's my own damn doing and I need to fix this. I knew going in that there was a possibility she wouldn't take me back, but it isn't in me to give up, not this time.

Following her actions, I jump out of the truck and take off

after her. I catch up to her quickly, grabbing her arm, and spinning her around to face me. She looks up at me with pained green eyes, before turning away. It's as if looking at me kills her.

"Don't walk away from me when all I've been trying to do is show you how much you mean to me." Wrapping my hands in the back of her hair, I pull her closer to me and force her to look into my eyes. "I fucking love you. Do you know how hard that is for me to say to anyone? Sage is the only other person I have ever said that to and she's fucking gone. You two are the only ones I've ever loved and I lost you both. I want us back. I can't stand to be without you."

"And you don't think I've lost the one person I ever loved? Huh?" She shoves my chest, but I don't budge an inch, which pisses her off more. "Dammit, Hemy!" She shoves me again, but I only hold her tighter, letting her know I'm not going anywhere. I'm not giving up and walking away like she did. Fuck that. I refuse. "I don't love you anymore, okay! I don't want to go back and try again. I won't let history repeat itself. There is no starting over, there is no us, and there never will be. So. Let. Me. Go."

I close my eyes and take a deep breath to calm myself. Her words sting like hell, but I don't believe her for one second. Her eyes give away the truth and that's enough to keep me going. She never was a good liar.

I drug her down into my dark, tormented world of demons and hate, slowly killing her day by day, making it hard for her to breathe. I shook the angel in her and now she's pulling me into her dark, twisted world of hate and revenge, fighting to keep me out, and forcing me to hate her. Well . . . hating her is the last thing I have in store.

"I don't believe you," I say through clenched teeth.

Picking her up, I throw her over my shoulder and hold her up by her ass. She instantly starts struggling against me as I walk her back to my truck.

"Damn you, Hemy! Why are you so hard headed?"

I open the door and shove her inside, being careful not to hurt her. She may want to play games, but I'm going to play harder by showing her the man she fell in love with.

I lean in the window and rub my hands through her hair, causing her to look up at me with a pained expression. She always loved it when I did this in the past. It calmed her down. "You can damn me all you want, but the last thing I'm doing is letting you go again."

Without a word, she swallows and looks away from me. I push back my emotions and walk over to my side of the truck to climb inside. It's time to take her home with me, where she belongs.

She's not leaving until she sees how much I love her . . .

I HATE DOING THIS. I hate trying to push him away when all I really want to do is hold him close and bury my face into his chest. It hurts more than anyone could ever imagine, lying to everyone, even yourself. It's something I have to do now. At first it was just to guard my heart, but now . . . it's because I know he's going to hate me after I tell him what I've been keeping from him for a while now. Why let myself get close and let him in when he'll be hating me soon anyways? I did it for a good reason. I had to.

Hearing him say *I love you* breaks me down, making me want to run into his arms and scream that I love him back, and that I never stopped. Shit, all that will do is guarantee for me to be crushed again. It broke my heart to lie to him and tell him I don't love him anymore. I hate it. I hate it.

Hemy doesn't waste any time driving off, heading in the direction of his street. I can see the fight in him this time. He's different: stronger, sober, and determined, all the things that I hoped for in the beginning. Now . . . it will be me to fuck things up.

I keep my face toward the window for the rest of the ride, fighting my hardest not to cry. I have been strong for four years and I refuse to let anyone see me cry now, especially Hemy. As long as I pretend that I don't have feelings, the safer from him I will be.

When we arrive at his house, Hemy turns to me and reaches out his arm. It's so inviting, making me want to crawl over to him and give into everything I'm fighting. "Come here," he whispers.

I look at him, but don't say a word. I can't or I'll cry.

"I. Said. Come. Here." Reaching over, he pulls me into his lap so that my knees are positioned on the outside of his thighs. "Don't be afraid of me." He wraps both hands in the back of my hair and looks me in the eyes. My heart skips a beat at the warmth of his touch. "I love you more than anything in this world. I would give my life to make you happy. Please, don't be afraid of me. It kills me."

Feeling a tear form in my eye, I try to turn away, but Hemy grabs my face to stop me, his jaw clenching as he watches me.

"Let me see you," he breathes. "I need to see that you still love me. You may not want to say it . . . but I see it. Just let me see it."

I let the tear fall freely down my face, followed by a few more that I can't seem to hold back. Hemy reaches up to wipe my tears away and that's when I lose it. My whole body shakes as I let it all go. All the pain and hurt I have been keeping inside since the day I walked out his door comes raging out.

My face is flooded with tears now. I can barely see Hemy through the mess, but I can feel him squeezing me closer, telling me to let it all out. A part of me feels relieved.

"You're so beautiful," he whispers, while pressing his forehead against mine. "I promise to show you that you're the most beautiful woman in the world to me. Do you understand?"

"Hemy," I cry out. "I need to tell you something. I-"

"Do. You. Understand?" I nod my head, while trying to catch my breath. "I don't want to talk about your doubts or anything bad tonight. I just want to be with you. Can you do that for me? Please."

Taking a deep breath, I swallow and wrap my arms around his neck, pulling him as close to me as I can. I love this man so much. He's my world and has been for ten years. This feeling I have right now, in his arms, him holding me as close as he can, is the best feeling in the world and I never want to lose it again.

I feel Hemy plant a few kisses on the top of my head before he reaches for the door and pushes in open.

"Hemy," I cry.

He places both hands on my face and looks at me with questioning eyes.

"I really have something important to tell you tomorrow. This can't wait much longer," I say nervously. "You might just hate me forever after I tell you. I'm so scared."

A small smile crosses his face before he playfully sucks in his lip ring and rubs his thumb under my eye. "Nothing could ever keep me from loving my world and you've been that for the last ten years." He helps me out of his lap and out of the truck before hopping out himself. "Let's go."

Once inside, Hemy runs a bubble bath and lights the candles while I brush my teeth, watching him in the mirror. I still can't get enough of him. I see him approaching me from behind, before I feel his arms wrap around me. I can feel the warmth of his breath kissing my neck.

I lean my neck back and moan as he teases me with his lip ring, running it up my neck and stopping under my ear. "Take your clothes off."

Turning around in his arms, I reach for the bottom of my dress and slowly lift it over my head, with Hemy's strong hands trailing up my skin behind it. His touch gives me instant goose bumps, hardening my nipples, and making my flesh tingle.

Nothing turns me on more than being naked for this man. The way he handles my body is beautiful and breathtaking. He may have a rough exterior, but once he lets you in, he's the best lover you could possibly have; although, this is the gentlest I have ever seen him. It only makes me love him more.

I toss my dress aside. Hemy reaches behind me with one hand and unclasps my bra, before kissing his way down my stomach while pushing down my panties and tossing them aside after I step out of them.

He's standing before me in just his briefs, his muscles flexing as he looks me over. "Undress me, Onyx. This body is yours and yours alone. You'll never have to worry again. I promise."

His words cause me to clench at just the thought of all of this beauty being mine. I hate sharing, especially when it comes to him. I never wanted to, but back then I didn't seem to have a choice.

Getting on my knees, I grip the top of his briefs in my hands and slowly peel them down his muscular body, watching as his cock springs free. Damn, those piercings get me every time. I didn't think it was possible for Hemy to get any more beautiful, but somehow, he has. Everything about his body: his muscles, his tattoos, his piercings, even the way he moves leaves me breathless.

Once I toss his briefs aside, Hemy lifts me up and wraps my legs around his waist, me latching on as he holds me. "Remember what I said to you the last time we were in this tub?"

I nod my head and bite my bottom lip as Hemy steps into the tub and slowly lowers us into the water with me straddling his lap. I have to admit, there is nothing I want more than to have Hemy make love to me. I've wanted it for as long as I can remember and as scared as I am, I need this. I need it so bad.

Gently gripping my waist, he lifts me up before slowly setting me down on his erection, his lips pressed against my neck. We both moan as he eases into me, pushing inside of me as deep as he can fit. Our bodies are plastered together, the both of us holding on for dear life, and it feels so damn good, too good.

Kissing my neck, he whispers, "I love you." He pushes into me while bringing me down to meet his thrust, before whispering again, sending chills up my spine. "Let me hear you say it, Onyx."

He pushes in deeper and wraps me in his arms as tightly as he can. I hold on for dear life, wrapping my legs and arms around him, unable to get close enough. My love for this man is so strong right now that I can barely breathe. I can't hide it anymore. It hurts too damn much.

"I love you, Hemy." He quickens his thrusts, causing me to moan out and grip his hair. "I've never stopped. I can't. I love you so damn much."

He smiles against my lips before crushing his lips against mine and making love to me. Not the rough, crazy sex that I'm used to with him. No, him holding me tenderly and thrusting into me, our bodies both working as one. It's the most intimate moment I have ever shared with Hemy, and it breaks my heart to know that it will probably never happen again.

Tomorrow, I'm going to tear his world apart . . . and mine.

CHAPTER FOURTEEN
Hemy

WAKING UP TO ONYX IN my bed is the best thing that has happened to me in four years. Seeing her here, naked, and wrapped up in my arms is almost enough to make me forget all the bad shit in the world. Almost . . . but not quite. There is still something that's holding me down and as much as I still try to hide the pain, it's always there threatening to surface. I just hope she understands that and tries to be patient. I've grown a lot since four years ago, but I will never be one hundred percent whole.

    She stirs in my arms, gripping me tighter as I kiss her on the top of the head. I've been awake for the last hour, but haven't wanted to move in fear of waking her. I'm afraid of what's to come today. She said she had something important to tell me. I have to be honest, it makes me wonder if maybe she has a child with some-one that she is afraid to tell me about. I can't stand the thought of that. It kills me.

When I look back down at Onyx, she's looking up at me with a small smile. It makes my heart burst with happiness. Damn, I love this woman. That smile is the best thing to ever happen to me.

"Morning," she whispers. "What time is it?"

I grip a handful of her hair and lean down to crush my lips against hers. She lets out a small moan before smiling against my lips. "It's noon," I respond. "I wanted to let you sleep."

She sits up with a yawn before reaching for her phone. "Crap! I should probably text Ash and let her know that I'm okay. She's probably wondering why I didn't come home last night."

Kissing her one more time, I stand up and reach for my briefs. "Alright. I'll go make us breakfast." I turn back to look at her and smile as she throws on one of my shirts. "Damn, you're sexy as hell in my shirt."

She places her hand on her hip and bites her bottom lip. "You can show me after breakfast."

"Fuck yeah," I growl, while backing away from her and turning into the hallway. Shit, that woman is going to be the death of me.

Opening the fridge, I pull out the eggs and bacon, setting them on the counter. Just as I'm about to reach in the cabinet for some pans, the front door opens. That could only be one person: fucking Stone.

"Don't you fucking knock, asswipe?" I grab out the pans and set them on the stove. This idiot is just lucky that I'm in a good mood for once.

A few seconds later, Stone appears in the kitchen followed by Ash. My eyes linger on her for a moment as she gives me a worried look. There's something about the look in her eyes that seems oddly familiar.

"Is Onyx with you? I haven't heard from her since last night and I didn't know who to ask," she questions while looking around the kitchen. "I called Stone and he said she might be here. Is she?"

Pulling my eyes away, I rub my hands over my face really fast and point down the hall just as Onyx appears.

"Okay, I sent her a text . . ." She looks up to see us all standing in the kitchen and freezes. Her eyes linger over to Ash and she turns ghostly white, all the color draining from her face. "Ash! What are you doing here?"

Ash walks past me and over to Onyx. "What the hell? I was worried sick about you. I'm here to make sure that you're okay."

Onyx leans her head back before turning to face the other direction and breathing heavily. "Shit! I can't do this anymore. I'm so sorry, guys. I'm so damn sorry."

My chest aches from her words. I don't understand why she's so worried about Ash coming here and why the hell she's apologizing to us. I walk towards the girls. "Talk, Onyx. What the hell is-"

I look up and my eyes meet the back of Ash's neck. My whole fucking world comes crashing down in front of me. I have to turn the other way and clench my hands together to keep from breaking something. "Fuck!" I crouch down and grip my hair in anger. This can't be happening. Please tell me Onyx has not been keeping this shit from me. "Onyx. What the fuck? You better start talking and now!"

She's hesitant for a moment, the whole room in a thick silence.

"Ash. I have something to tell you," she whispers. "I have something to tell both you and Hemy. "

Taking a few deep breaths, I stand back up and turn around to face Onyx. I want to see her when she fucking crushes me and turns my world upside down. "Say it," I growl out. "Fucking say it, dammit."

She turns her head away as a tear rolls down her cheek. "God, this is so hard. I never meant to hurt anyone. I just wanted to keep you safe, Ash. Please understand that. I didn't want you to get hurt like I did. I didn't want to get your hopes up and then have your world crushed." She pauses as Ash gives her a confused look. "Back when I met you in that coffee shop in Wisconsin and I saw that scar on the back of your neck . . . I had an idea of who you were."

Ash's eyes widen and her nostrils flare as she rubs a hand over the back of her neck. "What are you saying, Onyx? I don't like where this is going . . ."

Onyx looks over to face the both of us, her face wet with fresh tears. I always hated that look. It fucking hurts. "As soon as you told me you were adopted, I knew you were Hemy's sister. I knew you were Sage. I'm so damn sorry. You're probably going to hate me forever but I did it for a good reason. It's just too bad it's going to hurt us all in the end. Shit," she cries.

Ash lets out a soft breath before turning to face me. Her eyes look pained as she takes me in and shakes her head. My heart fucking hurts as I watch her; my baby sister and she's standing right in front of me.

"That makes no sense. My brother's name was Tyler. His name wasn't Hemy." She looks up at my hair. "And his hair was lighter." She swallows and looks into my eyes. "Those eyes . . ." She turns away. "Why are you messing with me? Why are you trying to hurt me? Please stop this."

Out of instinct, I step up beside Sage and touch her scar just like I used to when we were kids. Her bottom lip quivers just like in the past and she sucks in a burst of air. It's taking everything in me right now not to break down into tears. I've searched for ten years; ten fucking years, and now here she is, but on top of it Onyx knew and kept it from me. How could she keep something like this from me? Fuck!

"It's the truth, Sage. Shit, I can't believe this is happening." I pause to catch my breath and pull my hand away. "She's telling the truth. You were too young to remember, but I went by my middle name when we were growing up. Dad hated mom for naming me Hemy so everyone started calling me Tyler. It's the only thing you knew me by. That piece of shit. Fuck!" I turn around and punch the wall. "I couldn't fucking find you. I've searched for ten years. I'm so sorry." My voice cracks as I attempt to keep my composure. It's proving to be harder than I thought and all I want to do is ruin my parents and then break down.

Sage lets out a strangled cry before falling down to her knees and covering her face. "This can't be happening. I don't . . ." She sucks in a breath. "I don't know what to say. I've wondered about you my whole life." She shakes her head and cries harder. "Tyler . . ."

Falling down on my knees next to her, I pull her into my arms and press her face into my shoulder as she cries. Holding her next to me makes me want to bawl like a baby, but I fight it. It's so damn hard. I let a few tears fall as the anger and relief floods through me. I'm relieved to have Sage in my life, but angry as hell that Onyx would do this to me when she knows how badly I've been hurting.

I look up to the sound of Stone's voice. "Holy shit. I'm going to go and give you all some time. I don't need to be here for this. Sorry, man."

I nod my head and pull Sage closer as she wraps her arms around me, her whole body in a shaking mess. "I'm never letting you out of my damn sight again." She lets out something between a cry and a laugh and I can't help but to smile. "I mean that, Sage. Not a day has gone by that I haven't thought about you. I love you so damn much." Her grip on me tightens, but she doesn't say a word. She doesn't have to. It may take her a while to remember me as much as I remember her and that's okay. I'll give her as much time as she needs, but she's not leaving Chicago. Her home is with me, like it should have been over ten years ago.

After what seems like a lifetime, Sage pulls away and looks at my face. She lets one last tear roll down her face before reaching for my hair. "This hair," she says with a laugh. "I think my big brother needs a haircut."

I let out a small laugh and help her up to her feet. I still can't believe she is here and standing in my damn house. The feeling is so surreal.

We both stand here for a moment, taking each other in with smiles before turning to find Onyx pacing around the living room. She's biting her nails and shaking as the tears pour out.

As much as I want to hold her and tell her that it's okay, it really isn't. She just made the worst mistake of her life and it's going to take a while for me to get over this. It doesn't matter what her reasoning is. She hurt me, knowing that she was, and in the worst way possible.

"I'm sorry. I'm so sorry. That's all I can say. You don't think I wanted to tell you? I did. Trust me, I did." Onyx walks over to us and looks between the both of us. "I love you both so much," she cries. "I never meant to hurt anyone, but you have to understand that Hemy is a different person than the one I knew years ago. I couldn't put you through what I had to go through. That's all I can say. I was going to tell you as soon as I knew things were different for real this time." She sucks in a breath and walks past us. "I'm sorry."

"I don't know what to fucking say," I seethe. "I trusted you."

She swallows hard and fights back more tears. "I'm going, just please don't hate me. I can't survive knowing you hate me."

Exhaling, I watch as Onyx walks down the hall and disappears into my bedroom. I'm so fucking mad right now that if I open my mouth again I will probably say something I will regret forever.

So . . . I just watch as she walks away . . . again.

CHAPTER FIFTEEN

Hemy

IT'S BEEN THREE WEEKS SINCE I found out Ash was really Sage and I watched as Onyx walked out of my life again. Not a second has gone by that I haven't thought of her and missed the shit out of her. I have wanted to call her so many times and tell her I forgive her and I understand why she did it, but the pain is still too fresh. As far as I know, she has known about Sage for over a year, over a fucking year. How am I just supposed to forget about that?

A part of me knows that she didn't find me right away because she was scared of getting hurt again and didn't know if she'd be able to handle being around me without losing control, but it hurts like hell. I could have had Sage back in my life that whole damn time. I just can't get over that as much as I want to.

Everything has changed in the last few weeks and besides not having Onyx in my life, things have been good. Sage has been staying with me and I spend most of my time at Mitch's shop instead of at the club. I've told the boys I will stay on for two days a week until they can find someone else to take over. After that, I will stay and bartend. I guess I'm pulling a Slade.

It didn't take long for me and Sage to get comfortable with each other again and we have actually been spending a lot of time together talking about our childhood; only the good stuff though, I'm not reminding her of the all the fucked up shit our parents did to us. She doesn't deserve that and I won't put her through it.

I've been pacing around my living room with a beer in hand for the last three hours, trying to drown out the damn noise in my head. Nothing has been working. "Shit!"

I'm just pulling out another beer when I hear the front door open, so I pull out three beers instead. Sage and Stone have been spending a lot of time together and I need to keep my eye on that slick motherfucker. I won't hesitate to hand him his ass.

"Yo!" Stone calls out while stepping into the kitchen, instantly spotting the three bottles of beer with a grin. "This is why I love you so damn much, man. Always looking out when a brother is thirsty."

I slap him upside the back of the head as he reaches for a beer and pops the top. "Where's Sage?"

He lets out a sigh and quickly takes a drink of his beer. He's hesitant for a moment before he replies. "With Onyx. They've been talking a lot. She's meeting me here in twenty." He takes another drink of beer before setting it down and focusing his attention on me. "That girl loves you, man. I know what she did hurt you, but you have to look at it from her point of view too, man."

I take a gulp of my beer and clench my jaw. "Keep talking." Maybe I need this.

"Alright then. The truth hurts, but . . . from what I've heard, you had a lot of fucking issues. You were never really here." He points to his head and looks me in the eyes. "You can't expect her to risk hurting someone she cares about by bringing them into your sick fucked up world. I know you're not like that anymore, but for someone that experienced it every day for ten years, it's a little harder to convince. You ripped that girl's heart out and stomped on it and she still brought your sister back in hopes that you would be able to meet her one day. She just wanted to make sure the time was right for all of you; not just her, or you, but all three of you. You can't be mad at that, man. That's a good ass woman."

I close my eyes and run my hands through my hair, lost in thought. He's fucking right and hearing someone say it out loud really opens my eyes. She was there for me every fucking time I needed someone.

"You don't have to fucking tell me. She's the best woman I've ever known." I pause to let out a sigh. "I'll never forget that shit."

She's always done what she felt was best. This isn't any different. If I would have gotten Sage back while I was high out of my mind and always fucked up, then I would have probably lost her for good, just like everyone else; her and Onyx. Maybe I can't blame Onyx for being as cautious as she was. Maybe, I should be blaming myself and thanking Onyx. I always was the one to fuck shit up. Still am.

"I fucked up real bad, man. I'm not proud of the things I did one bit. I had a lot of shit I was dealing with and I couldn't handle it without getting out of my head." I open my eyes and grip onto the counter, realizing that I'm the one that fucked up once again. "I need to go find her. Fuck, I can't live without her. I've loved her since the day she attacked me in the alley with a hug. I fell in love with that girl and it took me what seems like an eternity to figure that out. It might be too late now. Fuck me!"

Gripping my shoulder, Stone nods his head in understanding. "Better late than never, asshole," he says jokingly. "Never *too late,* not when you have the kind of love you two have. I have heard it all, man. Now, I'm no mushy pussy or anything, but it's real, bro. Even I can see that."

Shaking off Stone's grip, I pace around the kitchen, trying to get my thoughts in check. I really can't fuck this shit up again. At some point I'm going to be out of chances. No one gives an unlimited supply. I need to let things go and chase after what makes me happy. That has always been her. Always will be.

"I need to go." I rush past Stone and through the living room, slipping on my leather jacket. "Tell me where she lives."

He hesitates.

"Now dammit!"

"Uhh . . ." He closes his eyes in thought for a moment. "1623 Spring Drive." I open the door and get ready to walk out. "Dude, you want me to go with?" he asks.

I turn back around. "Nah. I need to do this alone." I give him a nod. "Thanks, man." Then, I turn around and rush out the door, jumping in my truck.

I'm about two blocks away from Onyx's street when it starts pouring outside. It's coming down so hard that it's making it hard to see out the window. "Fuck! Please be here." I pull up in front of the house and jump out, leaving my truck running. I don't want to waste anymore time being away from her. I can't do it.

I run up to the porch and reach for the handle, but it's locked, so I knock loudly, hoping that Onyx will answer. If it were unlocked then she wouldn't have much of a choice.

A few seconds later the door opens to Sage. She steps out, holding her car keys. "Hey. What are you doing here?" She sounds a little panicked as she looks around. "I'm sorry-"

"It's fine," I cut her off. I don't have time for this right now. "Where is she?"

She shuts the door behind her and holds her hand up in an

unsuccessful attempt to block the rain. "I don't know. We were talking and then she just took off on her motorcycle like twenty minutes ago. She seemed upset and in a hurry."

Dammit! I hope she's not caught out in this downpour.

"Fuck!" I punch the porch railing and fist my hair. "I'm going to find her. Where would she be at?"

"I don't know. Maybe at *Vixens'*. She didn't say . . . or maybe at Jade's."

"Alright. I have to go." I grab her head and quickly kiss her on the forehead. "Love you."

"Love you too, Hemy," she screams after me as I run over to my truck and hop in.

Riding around, I start to panic at the thought of Onyx out riding in this weather. Two wheels on slick roadways doesn't mix. I would never forgive myself if something happened to her.

I pull up to *Vixens'* and drive around the whole parking lot in search of my old motorcycle. My heart sinks when I don't spot it anywhere. "Dammit, Onyx! Fuck, you better be at Jade's."

The rain doesn't let up any as I pull back out onto the street and head over to Jade's house. I pull up in front of the house that changed my damn life. If it weren't for Jade's birthday party then who knows when I would have seen Onyx again.

I notice immediately when I pull up that the motorcycle is nowhere to be seen, but I jump out anyway and run through the rain to the door. I knock as hard as I can, losing every bit of patience I have left.

As soon as the door swings open, I rush inside and look around. "Is Onyx here?"

Jade gives me a confused look. "No. What the hell is going on?" She watches me as I run my hand down the front of my face, wiping the rain off. "I haven't talked to her all day."

"Shit!" Without saying another word, I rush back outside and to my truck. Reaching in my pocket, I search for my phone, but come up empty. I must have left it on the kitchen counter at home. "Of fucking course!" I slam my fist into the horn before gripping the steering wheel and letting out an agitated breath. There's only one last place to check and this is a long shot.

Back when we dated, she would surprise me by showing up at Mitch's shop when I was working. She always loved watching me work and I loved having her watch. It was our place. We both made a lot of memories there.

Taking a chance, I head over toward Mitch's shop, looking around for signs of her out on the street, but come up empty. It's already past nine so the shop is closed. Mitch would have left at least an hour ago. That's another reason I have a feeling she's not there either, but I refuse to go home until I look.

When I pull up to the shop, I quickly park and jump out. I look around me, but don't see the bike anywhere. Jogging, I turn around the corner of the building and freeze when I see Onyx standing there in the rain, leaning against the building. She's soaked and more beautiful than if she were dolled up to perfection. The air gets sucked from my lungs at the sight of her and for this moment, I feel more alive than I have in years.

She pushes away from the building and looks at me. "I've been waiting for you," she whispers. One sentence and my heart feels like it's about to burst at the seam.

Well, she'll never have to wait again. That is a promise. . .

CHAPTER SIXTEEN

Onyx

KEEPING SAGE FROM HEMY WAS the hardest thing I've ever had to do. I just wish he would understand that I did it for Sage, because I love her like a sister myself and was only thinking of her best interests. I could never hurt her in any way. As much as I love Hemy, I had to think of Sage too. Hemy may hate me forever, but I did what I felt I had to do, even though I knew it would end up with him hating me in the end.

I just hope he'll give me a chance to explain, because I don't want to leave here without him. I never want to be without him again. I've lived day after day without him, years on end, and I can't do it anymore.

I've been here for the last half hour or so thinking about us; thinking of all the time we have missed out on and it hurts my heart so bad knowing that I left him and let him down. It kills me.

I was scared and young back then. I didn't know what else to do but remove myself from the situation. I should have stuck around and tried to get him help, but I was just a kid trying to deal with something bigger than myself.

I walk closer to Hemy as he stands there in shock and relief, just looking me over as if he can't believe that I'm here. "I was hoping you would come here. I'm so sorry. I wish I could take back what I did, but I can't. You hate me and I don't blame you."

Stepping closer to me, Hemy runs his hands through my wet hair before pressing his forehead to mine, something he always did. "You're wrong," he whispers. "What if I told you I could never hate you, no matter what you do? What if I told you I have loved you since day one, but was too afraid to say it?"

I look up into his eyes and cup his face in my hands. Looking at him makes it hard for me to breathe. The pain I put him through kills me. "How could you even say that, Hemy?" I can't hold my emotions back anymore. Being here in his embrace makes me lose all composure. The tears rush out as I wrap one arm around his neck and hold on for dear life. "I hurt you. I walked out on you when you needed me the most. I never stopped loving you. I thought about you every day and not one day went by that I didn't fear for your life. I was so damn scared."

"I know," he breathes. He rubs both his thumbs under my eyes, wiping the smeared mascara, before cupping my face and hovering his lips above mine. "I was a fool for the way I acted and I should have done the right thing by you. I should have been the one to let you go. I hurt you so damn bad and I'll never forgive myself for what I put you through. You did the right thing. You had to for the both of us, because I was too weak. Watching you walk out of my life and waking up alone is what woke me up. I realized that you were more important than the drugs. No high is better than the high I experience when I'm with you. I'm a different person and I have you to thank for it. Don't ever question what you had to do. Do you hear me?"

His warm breath kisses my lips as he presses his body closer to mine and waits for me to nod. "Hemy," I manage to get out. "I love you so damn much. I'll never-"

Hemy crushes his lips against mine, cutting me off. My body feels weak in his arms as he pulls me as close as possible, kissing me with so much passion that the tears start falling for a whole different reason. I love this man with all my heart and after all that we have been though, I know he feels the same way.

Pulling away from the kiss, Hemy searches my eyes before kissing my tears. "I love you more than life itself. I promise to never hurt you again. All I want is to be with you. I've never wanted anything else besides having Sage back in my life. I have Sage now," he pauses to give me a deep look, his eyes glassing over, "Let me have you. That's all I ask. I need both my girls."

Looking into his eyes makes me weak in the knees. There is so much promise behind them that I know being with him would be different this time. I'm just not sure I can get over me hurting him and Sage. It's myself that I'm angry with now, not him. I'm mad at myself for leaving.

"Are you sure you want me," I ask, my heart pounding.

He kisses me softly before pulling away and smiling. "More than life itself."

We both stand here in the rain just looking each other in the eyes before Hemy sucks in his lip ring and smirks. "Stay here with me tonight. Do you remember those nights?"

I let out a little laugh and nod my head. "How could I forget, Hemy? I can't even count how many people's trucks we had sex in the back of."

"Twenty three," Hemy says with a grin.

I slap his arm. "You kept count?"

He laughs and picks me up, throwing me over his shoulder. "Fuck yeah. Those were twenty-three of the best nights of my life." He bites down into my ass, making me squirm as he pulls out a key and unlocks the door. "I counted a lot of our good memories. Now, tonight will be number one that I undress you out of those wet clothes, put you in my shirt and take care of my future wife. Promise me you'll be mine, forever. Say it. Let me hear you say it."

All the breath leaves my lungs hearing those words leave his lips. I want to cry, but I don't. All I want to do is be close to Hemy and let him back in. No holding back this time.

"I'm yours. Forever," I whisper."

"I've been waiting four years to hear those words," he breathes as he walks us through the dark garage, pulls down the back of a truck bed and carefully sets me down.

He doesn't hesitate undressing himself from his jacket and shirt before pulling off my wet clothes and replacing them with his dry shirt.

He holds me close to him, whispering in my ear and rubbing the back of my head. Here, right now. I feel safe. I feel loved. This is the feeling I want for the rest of my life and can't live without.

It's him and it always has been. Tonight I'm making a promise to never let him go again.

The rest of my life starts tonight . . .

CHAPTER SEVENTEEN

Hemy

THREE WEEKS LATER . . .

WE'RE ALL SITTING AROUND IN *Fortune* – a normal bar, eating dinner and having a few drinks. The whole crew is here: Slade, Aspen, Cale, Stone, Sage, Onyx and myself. It's the first time we have all gotten together since me and Onyx worked things out. I have to admit it feels good.

It took a bit of convincing, but I finally got Onyx to move in with me. I knew she would eventually cave in. The only downfall to that is that it left Sage needing a new roommate. As you can guess, Stone was quick to jump to fill that spot. I'm still keeping my eyes on that slick fucker, but he's grown on me. Plus, he seems to be crazy about her and she deserves someone to treat her the way she should have been all along.

"Dude!" I feel something hit me upside the back of my head. I pull away from kissing Onyx to look over my shoulder. Slade flicks a chicken wing at me. "Stop that shit. You're making me want to take Aspen home and fuck her. My cock does not appreciate you right now." Aspen elbows him in the side and laughs. "What?" he questions with a laugh.

"You and your dirty mouth." Aspen grins.

Slade throws his hands up. "My bad." He bends down and kisses her neck before biting it. "You can just punish me later."

"Alright, dicks," Cale says annoyed. "You all can stop your shit now. You're making me sick. I'm trying to eat."

"Shut up and go get your dick sucked, pussy," I say teasingly, causing Cale to toss a fry at my head. What's with the fucking flying food?

Onyx grips my thigh from under the table, causing me to instantly go hard. She always does it, letting me know what she wants. She knows exactly what she's doing to me and as soon as I get her alone, she's getting . . . fucked, and hard.

Aspen smiles over at Cale before taking a sip of her beer. "So . . . Riley gets home next week."

Cale turns white in the face, but quickly tries to shake it off. "Yeah? That's nice," he says, nonchalantly. "Next week, already?"

Aspen laughs and sets her beer down. "Already? It's been like six years since she moved away to Mexico."

I can't even believe how pale and nervous Cale looks. He definitely has it bad for this Riley chick. Maybe he'll man up and finally give his dick up. I knew he was holding back for a reason.

I take a bite of my steak and notice Stone getting a little cozy with my sister at the end of the table. I get ready to say something, but Onyx leans into my ear, distracting me.

"I love you, baby." She places her hand on mine and I smile down at the diamond on her left finger. Knowing that I placed it there makes me the happiest man on earth.

When I proposed to her in the hot tub last week, I about died when she broke down in tears and screamed, *yes*. I'll never forget that feeling for the rest of my life. I'm not going to lie I shed a few tears myself. What can I say? I've waited for a lifetime to have her back in my arms and I'm never letting go. She's my everything. I love her and I love this new life with her. I can't be any happier.

I bite my lip when I realize Onyx distracted me on purpose. I know this now by her little fit of laughter. She saw me eyeing Stone and Sage down. She's good. Too damn good.

When I go to focus my attention on Sage and Stone again; Sage is gone and Stone is chatting with Aspen. That lucky fucker.

I feel a small arm wrap around my neck, distracting me, before Sage rests her head on the top of mine and laughs. "Stop being such a big brother." She squeezes my neck and both girls laugh as Onyx pinches my cheek. "I love you, but seriously . . . don't make me kick your ass. I know what I'm doing with Stone. Okay?"

I look over at Stone and see the look in his eyes as he focuses his attention on Sage as if she's the only woman in the room. I have to respect that. That's the same way I look at Onyx. I need to give Sage the space she needs. I keep forgetting she's a grown woman now.

"Okay," I mumble. "I trust you." She kisses my head and rushes over to sit in Stone's lap, wrapping her arms around his neck. I guess they make a nice couple.

Looking around me; I realize this is the happiest I have ever been in my life. This is where I belong. Where we all belong. This is my family. Family isn't always bound by blood. It's so much more than that. This is it, and it's what I've been missing all along.

I'm ready to spend the rest of my life making my family and future wife happy. This is my ending . . .

WALK OF SHAME #3

VICTORIA ASHLEY

PROLOGUE

Cale

SIX YEARS AGO . . .

GRABBING RILEY BY THE WAIST I fall backward, pulling her into the freezing water with me. I feel her stiffen in my arms and squeal as the frigid water surrounds us, numbing our skin, as we slowly sink to the bottom with me still holding onto her. She's leaving for Mexico tomorrow and this might be our last moment together. The thought causes my chest to ache as I pull her even closer while we break through the water's surface, both of us fighting for air, and our bodies frozen.

She sucks in a deep breath before releasing it and screaming, "CALE!" Turning around in my arms, she presses her hands against my chest and shoves me, while trying to keep her teeth from chattering. "The water is free . . . eezing."

Her body is shaking violently from the cold, so I use this as an excuse to keep her warm. I've had feelings for Riley for as long as

I can remember, but timing has never seemed to be on our side. If I can't have her . . . then I'll wait. She means more to me than any woman ever could, and I have a plan to show her that—a promise that I made to myself. I just don't know how to tell her I want her without ruining our friendship, but I'll show her when the time is right.

Placing one arm behind her head, I pull her body against my chest and then wrap both of her legs around my waist as I back up against the wall of the pool to support her. "I've got you, Rile." I brush her wet, brown hair out of her face and smile as I reach out and touch her quivering bottom lip. I have to admit, she's so damn adorable while freezing her ass off. I should feel bad for torturing her, but I don't. Not really. I know she loves me teasing her. "If you don't stop shaking that lip . . . I'm going to bite it."

I see a hint of a smile, before she punches my chest and laughs. "You can be such a dick sometimes, Cale."

"I know," I admit. "That's why you love me so much, Riley Raines."

All laughter and playfulness seems to stop as our eyes meet. It looks as if she wants to say something, but stops right as her mouth opens to speak. Her face looks guilty and I hate it. I hate that look.

"What, Riley?" I pull her chin up as she looks away. "Say it," I whisper. "You know you can tell me anything."

She closes her eyes for a moment before shaking her head and biting her bottom lip. She looks hurt, but I have a feeling she won't give me the info I'm seeking. "It's nothing," she says softly. "It's just that . . . I'm going to miss you. That's all." She forces a smile and tugs on the ends of my hair playfully. "Don't look so sad, you big stud you. You'll do fine without me and forget about me in no time." She turns her head, hiding her eyes from my view.

"Not true. Don't *ever* say that." My heart is beating so damn hard against her chest that I'm surprised she hasn't asked me if I'm about to have some kind of freak attack. She's the only girl that makes my heart race like this and hearing those words out of her mouth causes it to ache like nothing else. How can she not realize how much I'm truly going to miss the shit out of her? "It's kind of hard not to be sad."

I make my best pouty face, trying to make her feel bad. This face always seems to work on her. "I have to wait for you to come home, all alone, so I can give you my virginity."

She looks stunned for a moment before she bursts out in laughter and squirms her way out of my arms. Her laugh is so damn beautiful. "You jerk. You almost made me feel bad for you for a minute . . . and we both know you're not a virgin. Stop kidding around." She attempts to pull herself out of the pool, but I grab her waist, stopping her.

"Where are you going?"

She looks down at me, water dripping down her beautiful curvy body. I want so much to just take her right here and give her all of me, but time is not on my side at the moment; it never seems to be when it comes to Riley. "It's getting late. I told my mom I'd be home early so I can finish packing."

"Stay," I whisper, pulling her back into the pool with me. My hands cup her face and I pull her so close that our lips are almost touching. "Don't leave me here."

"What?" She shakes her head and kisses me on the cheek, her lips lingering for a moment. "I can't. My grandma needs me. I have to go, Cale. I have no choice."

I watch as she gets out of the pool and grabs for my dry shirt, snuggling against it to keep warm, before pulling it over her head. I can't be sure, but it looks as if she sniffed it. I love that.

"I'm keeping this by the way." She smiles with a sad look in her eyes. "I'll be back. I promise. Time will fly by. Just watch." Her voice comes out sad and hesitant, because she and I both know that's not true. Time will definitely be a bitch while she's gone, and I'm sure it's going to feel like a lifetime without seeing her smile or hearing her beautiful laugh.

I nod my head and turn away from her as she starts walking away. I can't stand to watch her walk out of my life. It hurts more now that it's actually happening, especially knowing that there's nothing I can do to stop it, but . . . I need her to know one thing before she leaves. One thing that I hope will mean something to her in the future.

"I *am* still a virgin by the way," I say, wanting her to know I wasn't lying about that. I would never lie to Riley. I can't.

I hear her stop walking before I hear a small, but painful laugh. "Yeah, me too," she says. She whispers something afterwards but I miss it, too scared to look her way. I hear her footsteps in the grass as she starts walking again and it hurts so damn bad that I can't breathe.

By the time I get the courage to turn around she's gone . . . out of my life and soon she'll be out of Chicago. She's the one and only girl I have ever loved and I never even got the chance to tell her.

Life can be a bitch . . .

CHAPTER ONE

Cale

PRESENT DAY . . .

WALK OF SHAME IS FULL of people partying and getting wasted beyond sense, but really, I just can't seem to get my head into being here.

My mind has been on one thing and one thing only: Riley. Ever since Aspen blurted out that Riley would be home soon, my mind has been stuck on her. I've been replaying our last moment together, before she left, and it almost feels as if it were yesterday. The ache is still there, weighing on my chest.

We haven't spoken in over two years now, and even I know that I'm not over her. I'm not sure that I ever will be, and knowing that she's coming home reminds me of the promise I kept to myself six years ago, when I was still just a stupid teen.

We kept in contact for the first four years, talking on the phone at least once a week, late into the night, until she mentioned that she'd met someone that was interested in her. It hurt like hell, but knowing that she wouldn't be back home for a while I realized that I needed to let her live while she was there. There was no way I was going to hold her back by breaking down like a pussy and telling her how much I loved her. Asking her to wait for me as I have planned on waiting for her would be selfish.

Eventually, the calls slowed down until we were at the point that we barely talked but once every few months. Then . . . they ended all together. I think it was necessary in order for us both to go on with our lives, because every time we talked I could hear the ache and longing in her voice. I had to make it easier for *her* to live in hopes that it would make it easier for me.

Knowing that she'll be back any day now, possibly even now, has me unable to function properly.

I've been holding back from fucking other women, only giving them oral pleasure, because to me she's more important than just a meaningless lay. I thought that after we stopped calling each other every week that I would just forget about my promise to wait, but I never did. It's always been in the back of mind, fucking with me and making it impossible for me to take a woman to bed and give myself to her. I want her to find peace in knowing that when my cock enters her that she's the only woman I've been inside of and that I plan on pleasuring her over and over again until she can no longer handle me. I won't be able to stop and I sure as hell don't have any plans to.

Standing up straight, I run my hands through my hair while letting out a frustrated breath, bringing myself back to reality. I'm not much of a drinker, but right now . . . I feel like downing a fifth of whiskey.

Trying to get my head back into my performance, I twist both of my arms into the chain hanging above my head and thrust to the slow rhythm, while letting my unbuttoned jeans fall lower and lower with each movement. The screaming of the crowd causes me to put on a fake smirk and get into the moment as much as I will get, enough to at least finish my last performance of the night.

I'm close to the edge of the stage. Girls are reaching out to grope me as I give them a show. I can feel the sweat rolling down my body, dripping onto the marble stage at my feet as I continue pretending that I'm fucking every single girl in this room.

That's what they all want. That's *all* they ever want. These girls are here because they want to feel as if I want them, so . . . that's what I make them believe. As fucked up as it sounds, it sends them home happy. That's what matters here at *Walk Of Shame*.

"Right here! Cale!"

I open my eyes and bring them down to meet the brunette below me that is eagerly waving a wad of cash above her head. Releasing the chains, I walk to the edge of the stage, grab onto the back of her head, and grind my crotch into her face before thrusting repeatedly. In no time my jeans are on the floor and I'm standing in nothing but my white, very see through, boxer briefs.

I grind slow and hard, making her reach around and shove her cash into the back of my boxer briefs, just above my ass crack. I feel her hands exploring my ass, so I reach behind me and discretely pull them away before jumping off the stage.

The screaming of the women gets significantly louder as soon as my feet hit the main level. It's almost the end of my performance, and tonight I'm ending it with a little something special.

Making my way through the crowd I stop in front of the redhead that is hopefully going to help clear my head later. Straddling her lap, I sway my hips while running her hands up my bare chest, before pushing them down my body and stopping at the waist of my briefs.

I hear a little gasp escape her lips as I release her hands, letting her explore while I grind on her as if I were fucking her deep and hard; very deep and hard.

Smirking, I stand up from her chair before turning the other way and doing a quick handstand so that my cock is in her face. I begin to thrust my hips, swaying them around in a circle as the music speeds up, ending my performance.

All the women go wild as I grind my hips one more time and end it with a thrust to her face, before maneuvering my way back to my feet. Looking down at the ground, I focus on catching my breath, noticing all the cash surrounding me. Even with my head fucked up and lost somewhere else, my body still knows exactly what to do.

Walking away, I head over toward the back room to change, as Kash, the new kid, cleans up my stash of money. He showed up about a week ago asking for a job, so Lynx, the new owner, decided to make him our grunt for a few weeks first just to mess with him.

I'm standing here naked, just pulling a fresh pair of jeans on when I hear Kash step into the room and slap the pile of bills onto the table.

"Holy shit, bro." He slaps the money down a few more times and grins as I button my jeans and throw my white tee on. "Those girls are fucking insane. I've never seen such horny women in my life. This is a damn dream job. I swear my cock got grabbed at least five times just now."

Grabbing my tip money from Kash I grin and slap five twenties down into the palm of his hand. He hasn't seen shit yet. "Yeah, well you better be prepared to work that stage next week, rookie. You gotta learn to shake that cock of yours first. You've got some major shoes to fill."

He nods his head while stuffing the cash into his back pocket.

"I already know how to work it, bro. No worries."

"Alright, man." I slap his back. "I'm getting out of here. I'll see ya later."

"See ya," I hear him say right as I push my way back out into the crowd of women. It only takes me a few seconds to spot the sexy little redhead from earlier. She's watching me as if she's been waiting for me to come back out.

The cute little brunette that I was grinding on earlier is with her, sipping on her drink as they both eye fuck me all the way up to the bar.

Sara shakes her head and slides a draft beer across the bar top. "Damn Cale. I don't think I've ever seen you work it like that on the stage." She wipes her forehead off and waves her hand as if slinging sweat off of it. "So good tonight, baby."

I give her a half smile and reach for the frosty glass. "I have a lot on my mind tonight. I guess I was zoning out." I tip back the glass and let the refreshing liquid cool me off. I'm still sweaty from the show and all of my clothes are practically plastered to my wet body, irritating me.

"Yeah, well . . ." she tilts her head toward the right. "Those two girls definitely liked what you had going on tonight. It looks like they're about ready to rape you before you even get a chance to finish that beer off, babe." She rolls her eyes and dries off a glass. "Lucky dick. Those bitches are hot."

A few second later I feel a hand on each of my shoulders, before the brunette appears on my right and the redhead on my left. I don't even bother looking at them as I speak. "Ladies." I guzzle back my beer and toss down some cash for Sara. "Later, Sara."

Sara just waves me off as she gets called over by a small group of women. Shoving my wallet back into my jeans, I turn and walk through the crowded bar, not surprised to hear the sound of heels clicking against the floor behind me.

Yes, I could definitely use a very long blowjob right now, but to be honest, I could also do without. These two women, even combined, could never measure up to the woman that I have waited six long years for. I'm not saying that I'd turn them down, just saying that maybe I won't be seeking out tonight.

As soon as I step outside and head for my truck, I hear one of the girls call my name, stopping me. Leaning against my truck, I exhale and look up, while dangling my keys around my finger.

The redhead pushes her hand against my chest as the brunette leans in and whispers in my ear, "Let us take care of you, Cale." She runs the tip of her tongue over my earlobe before speaking again. "Just relax and enjoy."

Leaning my head back, I close my eyes and take in a small breath as my jeans get pulled to my knees, and then I feel two small hands grip around my ready cock.

A pair of soft lips wrap around my head as a hand runs up and down my shaft, and I know right away that both women are sharing right now. I'm not selfish. It's big enough for the both of them and maybe right now . . . this distraction . . . is what I need, so I let them both take turns sucking me off right here in the parking lot until I blow my load all over both of their mouths.

Licking the remainder of cum off my dick, the redhead stands up and places her arms around my neck. "Let us take you home where we can show you a *real* good time. I promise you that it will be worth it."

"More than worth it," the brunette chimes in.

That offer would usually have any man falling to his knees and drooling, but not me. I've gone twenty-four years without it and I'm pretty damn sure I can go another few weeks.

Trying my best not to be an ass, I take turns pressing my lips to both of their temples, before saying goodnight and hopping in my truck.

Once I pull up at the house, I realize that having my dick sucked hasn't done shit to clear my head. Riley Raines is coming home and I know without a single doubt that she's going to ruin me.

CHAPTER TWO

Riley

I'M SO NERVOUS RIGHT NOW. I've only been back in Chicago for two days and in about two seconds I'm starting my new job here at *Sensual Touches*, the massage parlor that I applied for online a few weeks ago.

No one knows that I'm back yet. I made sure to tell Aspen not to tell anyone until I'm ready. The only people that know are my family, and I plan on keeping it that way for a couple of weeks until things settle down and I can relax a bit. My heart is still hurting and my head is spinning out of control at the fact that Tyler and I are no longer a couple and that I have to get familiar with my surroundings again. When I made plans to move back home Tyler decided at the last minute that he didn't think he'd be up for the move . . . so he stayed behind.

I care about Tyler, but Chicago is where my heart is. Not to mention . . . it's where *he* is: Cale Kinley. As much as I've tried to convince myself seeing him again won't stir some crazy emotions inside of me, I know with everything in me that's not true. I'm not sure that I can handle seeing him while in this emotional state.

Shaking my head, I run my hands down my black, skinny jeans, wiping the sweat from my palms as I approach the door to the massage parlor. "It's no big deal, Riley. You've done this a million times before . . . just not here. You have magic fucking hands." I convince myself before stepping inside.

As soon as I enter the building I'm greeted by a woman that looks to be in her early twenties, with long, purple hair. She plasters on a smile and stands up from her chair, looking impatient. "Please tell me you're Riley Raines. Hailey hasn't shown up yet and we have two clients waiting. I need to get these two satisfied and hitting the road."

I nod my head as the nerves flow through me, causing butterflies to fill my stomach. "That's me," I say with a fake confidence that I definitely don't feel at the moment. "Is there anything you need from me before I start?" I open my purse and start digging for my ID and paperwork. "Here's my–."

"No time for that, sweetness. Myles will deal with that when he gets in later. I don't get paid enough for that." She gives me an impatient look and starts shoving me down the hall. "I need you in room three. That's your room." She takes a deep breath and bites her bottom lip. "You're going to enjoy this one. *Please* put your hands all over him since I can't. Hailey is going to be one pissed off bitch, but this will teach her a lesson for showing up late." She lets out a satisfied laugh while spinning on her heels. "Hurry. I can smell the skank coming now."

Lifting my eyebrows, I smile small and push open the door to room three, almost unable to breathe from the nerves. Without paying any attention to the waiting client, I quickly observe the room to find a chart hanging next to the door. I grab it quickly to prepare for his needs.

While searching for my supplies, I introduce myself, trying not to draw attention that I have no clue where anything is. "Sorry for the wait. My name is Riley and I'll be taking care of you today. Hailey is running a little behind and this is my first day here, so please be a little patient while I get everything ready."

Looking around the dimly lit room, I find the stereo and turn it on, letting the relaxing sounds fill the space to hide my erratic breathing as I try to stay calm. I've been at the same place for three years, and being somewhere new, with new clients, is a bit nerve-wracking; especially when you're getting rushed around by some chick with purple hair and tattoos that looks as if she wants to choke someone today.

After securing my apron filled with my lotions and oils, I turn to the table and my heart starts pounding like crazy in my chest as I see a body, barely covered by a small towel, just waiting to be touched by me. I swallow hard while letting my eyes roam over the stiff muscles of the tanned back on display. The top of the client's ass peeks out of the towel, displaying the roundest, firmest ass I have ever seen before . . . and the dimples in his back are making it hard for me to gain some much-needed confidence.

Doing a silly little shake in an attempt to shake my nerves off, I squirt some oil in my hands and slowly run my hands up the bottom of his back, being sure to make it feel as insanely good as I possibly can.

The feel of his muscled back beneath my fingers and the deep, undeniably sexy moan that escapes his throat almost has me turned on as I start to go lower, until I'm right above his ass.

"Go lower," the deep voice whispers. "Take the towel off."

I almost deny his request, when I remember that *Sensual*

Touches is clothing optional. That's the *one* thing that almost kept me from applying, but comparing the pay that you get here versus the other options, I knew what my choice had to be.

"This is new to me," I whisper, before speaking up. "Let me know if you get uncomfortable and I'll replace it before you flip over on your back."

"That won't be an issue," he says huskily.

Keeping my moan to myself, I lower my hands down to his ass, removing the towel little by little as I continue to get lower. As soon as my hands reach the bottom of his ass, I remove the towel completely and hold back the gasp that fights to escape me.

Holy hotness . . .

Remembering that this was per his request, and that it's fully professional to be doing this here at *Sensual Touches,* I grip the back of his upper thighs and massage it while rubbing my thumbs over the bottom of his tight ass, enjoying every single moment of it.

In fact, I'm enjoying it so much that I almost feel guilty. Tyler and I have been broken up for less than a week, and here I am enjoying myself as I rub on another man's ass, listening closely for each moan that he will grace my ears with.

After spending a good, long, fifteen minutes on his ass itself, I focus my attention on the rest of his muscular body, mentally preparing myself for the rest of his gloriousness that I'll be seeing in the *flesh* as soon as I finish up on his backside.

Now I understand why that Hailey chick is going to be pissed off. Massaging this stud has to be the best part of her job here. How can you *not* enjoy this?

Pulling my hands away, I turn away to give him some privacy. "I'm ready for you to flip over, sir. Please let me know when you're ready."

"I'm always ready for you, Rile."

Fighting to catch my breath, I place my hand to my heart and slowly turn around to see that the naked stud whose ass I have been ogling over this whole time is Cale. Cale Kinley. My Cale Kinley, the one person that I've been so worried about seeing again and now here he is, naked and in front of me.

"Cale," I whisper. "Holy shit. I don't . . . I don't know what to say. Wow. It's you. I . . ."

Sitting up, he smiles and grabs my hand, pulling me closer to him as if it were old times again. "Get the hell over here, woman." Pulling me into his arms, he hugs me tightly against him, while running his nose up the side of my neck. "I've missed you so fucking bad, girl."

Feeling overwhelmed, my eyes water a little bit as I hold him as tightly as I can. A smile spreads across my face as we pull apart and check each other out. Luckily, he didn't ruin me completely and decided to cover his junk up. "You look just like you did the last time I saw you, except a hell of a lot stronger and even hotter. Holy hell, you have grown up, Cale. I didn't even recognize your voice. My Cale is a man now."

He grabs me by the hip and squeezes. "Yeah . . . I guess you can say I've grown quite a bit." He flexes his jaw as he checks me out, completely taking me all in. His striking green eyes almost melt me on the spot as I watch them. "All of me."

I find myself swallowing hard and slightly sweating as I try to figure out what exactly he could mean by *all of him*. I think I know the answer to that and I have to admit that it has me turned on completely.

"You look fucking beautiful, Riley." He bites his bottom lip and releases his grip on my hip, letting his hands brush over my ass, before he grips my upper thighs. "So damn beautiful."

Without even thinking, I reach out and grip the blonde hair at the back of his neck. He wears it slightly shorter than he did six years ago, but still sexy as can be.

"I see you're still the same smooth talker," I say with laughter. "Good to know."

He grips my thighs tighter, pulling me closer to him. "And you're still the most beautiful woman I've ever laid eyes on."

Feeling myself come undone under his intense stare, I release his hair and reach for his hands, pulling them away from my thighs. "I've missed you, Cale." I watch him with a smile as his eyes follow my movements to my hands. I squirt a handful of oil into my palm.

His eyes take on a darkened look and he grabs my hands, placing them to his chest, and holding them there. "Why didn't you tell me you were back already?" He rubs his thumbs over my wrists, looking me dead in the eyes. "When did you get home?"

Letting out a small breath, I shake my head and begin rubbing my hands over his body while pushing him backward until he's lying flat on his back. "Only two days, Cale." I suck in a breath and try to hide the small moan as my hands explore every hard ridge of his chest and abs, attempting to continue his massage. God, this is torture right now. This is the kind of body that you only see in the damn movies. "I just wanted a week or so to get settled in first. No one knows that I'm back except for my family. You were going to be the next to know. I promise."

He smiles up at me and I can't help but to notice the way my heart skips a beat. That smile—seeing it right now is a painful reminder of what I've been missing for the past six years. The ache in my chest almost causes me to lose my composure, wondering what all I've missed while being away.

The only thing I've heard over the years is that he works at a bar. I don't even know if he has a girlfriend. For some reason, I just couldn't allow myself to know that bit of information, so I made Aspen promise to never tell me. Well . . . more like I threatened to choke the life out of her through the phone.

Now standing here, touching him and seeing his beautiful

smile, I can't help but want to know. Is he going home tonight to make love to some woman while she gets to put her hands on the places that I'm touching now? I don't want to know!

"Have dinner with me tonight."

A smile spreads over my face, unexpectedly from his request. It's so big that my face hurts, but I try my best to hide it so I don't look like a desperate loser. "Are you cooking me dinner, Chef Cale? If so, then I hope it's better than what I tasted the last time you attempted to cook for us," I tease, even though I'd eat dirt if it made him happy.

"Of course," he says confidently. "And it will definitely taste damn good. I promise you that the only things I'll put in your mouth are the things that I know will satisfy you completely and ruin you for anything else."

I swallow hard and try not to take that comment sexually, even though my body is definitely taking it *that* way. "Alright." I agree. "I'm trusting you with my mouth, so you better not disappoint."

He lifts his eyebrows and I can't help but to notice him harden beneath the towel, but I play it off as if I hadn't noticed. "You have no idea, Riley. You should be careful what you trust me with." Sitting up, he leans in and kisses me on the side of the mouth, his lips lingering for a few seconds too long. "I have an early shift at the bar today, but I'll get your number and address from Aspen."

"Alright." I smile. "I'll be here until six, but I'm free after that."

Nodding his head, Cale jumps up from the table, allowing his towel to drop as he reaches for his clothes to get dressed. I somehow manage to turn away before I get to see what I've been longing to see since we were in high school. Damn, I really hate myself right now.

I hear a small chuckle from Cale before I feel his hands wrap around my waist and his lips press against my neck from behind. "Gotta go, baby. Be ready for me tonight."

Next thing I know, Cale is out the door, and I'm standing here fighting to catch my breath. "Baby . . ." I say softly. I have to admit I like being called that by Cale. That's definitely new.

Being back is going to be a bigger challenge than I thought . . .

CHAPTER THREE

Cale

THERE'S ONE MORE HOUR BEFORE my shift ends and I'm feeling so restless that I can barely pay attention to the drinks being ordered. Hemy and I are working the bar while Stone is busy with the girls on the floor. I have to admit that the dude has skills.

I wasn't sure if he'd be able to fill Slade's shoes, but I'm pretty damn impressed at how crazy and out there he is with his abilities.

I look away from the crowd of crazy women, when I'm caught off guard with an elbow as it jabs me in the ribs. "What the shit?"

Turning beside me, I look up to see Hemy glaring at me. "What the fuck are you doing, staring off and shit? I'm working my dick off over here."

Ignoring his ass, I quickly snap out of it and focus on the steady flow of drinks that keep getting requested, trying my hardest to not think about Riley and how fucking fantastic it felt having her hands on my body. Truthfully, I wanted them *all* over, but I don't think she's ready for that quite yet, so I'm doing my best to respect her and take things slow. Well, as slowly as I can.

As soon as I get a free moment, I pull my phone out and send Slade a quick text, asking him to get Riley's number from Aspen. At first Slade texts back with a big FUCK YOU, before he sends another message about five minutes later, telling me he had to wrestle with Aspen to get her phone and that I owe his ass.

He's just lucky that he's my guy and that I know how much of an ass he is and still tolerate him. I have to admit that he's gotten about eighty percent better since meeting Aspen, so really, I owe *her*.

Leaning against the register, I send Riley a text, ignoring the screaming crowd for a moment. There's no way she's getting out of spending the night with me. I don't care if I have to throw her over my shoulder and handcuff her to me for the night. I've missed the shit out of her and tonight . . . she's mine.

> Me: *Hey, baby. Where am I picking you up tonight? I hope you save room for dinner and dessert, because I'm ready to work magic with my hands . . .*

My phone vibrates a few minutes later, causing me to turn away from the girl chatting my ear off at the bar. She's still talking as I read Riley's message.

> Riley: *Magic, huh? So you're that good? ;) Don't even answer that. I'll be the judge of that later. Pick me up at my mom's around seven. I'll be ready and waiting . . .*

Damn girl . . . She has no idea what she's just started.

I adjust my cock and hope my boner will quickly go down. The last thing I need is something to set these women off. I barely make it through a shift as it is without getting attacked with a set of tits in my face. I don't need anything slowing me down tonight.

"Are you free tonight?" Biting my bottom lip, I shove my phone in my pocket and shake my head at the girl in front of me, before letting her down as easily as I can.

"Sorry, beautiful, but I'm taken for the night." I slide a free drink across the bar as a look of disappointment takes over her face. "The drink is on me."

She smiles small and reaches for the drink, not doing much to hide her sour face. "Just let me know when you're free." With that, she turns and walks away, swaying her hips in the process. I know without a doubt that she's trying to lure me in, but that shit isn't working on me, especially when the woman that I've waited six years for is within my reach.

She's about to finally see how much I truly want her . . .

CALE WILL BE OUTSIDE ANY minute, and for some reason that thought has me extremely nervous and sweaty. Why am I so nervous when this is the guy that I spent most of my teen years with? He's still the same guy, except . . . he's drop dead gorgeous and every inch of his body is covered in hard muscle that I want nothing more than to explore with my tongue.

This new desire stirs me up, making it hard for me to act normal and pretend that I don't crave to be with him. It seemed a lot easier six years ago when I saw him almost every day, but after being away from him for so long, seeing him just brings back all of my old feelings on top of the ache that I felt when I could no longer spend my days with him.

I shake my head. "Doesn't matter, Riley," I whisper. "Just act normal." I rub my sweaty palms down the side of my black dress and take in a deep, calming breath. "He's still the same sweet Cale that wants nothing more than to be friends. Just friends . . ."

I hear a noise in the hallway that causes me to look up and walk toward my bedroom door. My parents went out to dinner after I told them that I had plans, so I've been here alone for the last thirty minutes.

"Aspen," I call out. "Is that you? I'm in my old bedroom."

I hurry into the hallway and slam into a hard body, almost causing me to stumble backward, but Cale catches me with a grin. His arm tightens around my waist as his smile broadens. "You look hot, Rile." He leans in and kisses me on the forehead, before pulling me straight up and back on my feet. "You ready to go?"

I tug on the end of my skirt, pulling it down, and then smile, as Cale looks me over with wide eyes, whistling softly. "I've missed you, Cale. You seriously have no idea." I laugh as he grabs my arm and spins me around as if checking me out. It's something he used to do to me when he would first see me for the day. I know he's doing it now to make me feel comfortable and I love him for it. It reminds me of how strong our friendship was and why I adored him so much.

"Let's go." He nods his head and places his hand on the small of my back, guiding me through the house. "I have dinner in the oven."

I step outside and watch him as he locks the door and closes it behind him. "Oh really?" I smile big at the thought of Cale cooking. I thought he was only kidding. "You're really cooking us dinner?"

He wraps his arm around my waist and pulls me against him as we walk to his truck. "Hell yes I am. I owe you after all those times you cooked for me while we were hanging out at your house. At my house, I will always cook you dinner, especially if it keeps you coming back for more." He winks and helps me into his truck.

He refuses to tell me what's for dinner on the way over to his house, even though I made it a point to ask him every few minutes, just to see if he'd cave. I almost forgot just how strong Cale's will-power is. He's pretty set once he makes his mind up. He's always been the strongest person that I know and I admire him for that, even though it sometimes has the power to annoy the shit out of me.

He jogs over and helps me out of his truck once we pull up to his house. "You'll be spending a lot of time here, Rile, so I hope you like it just as much as I do." I laugh and he raises a brow in question. "What? You don't believe me?"

"What makes you think that I'll like you as much as I used to?"

He pushes the door open and pushes up behind me, guiding my body with his into the house. His lips brush my ear. "I have a pretty good feeling," he whispers. "You'll like me even more . . ."

Walking around me, he throws his keys onto the kitchen island and walks over to the oven with a confidence that makes me melt. "Make yourself at home, because you're spending the night. We're having a movie night and I'll take you home before eight in the morning to change for work."

This time, I'm the one lifting my brows. "How do you know what time I work tomorrow, *Cale?*"

He opens the oven and pulls a pan out, setting it on the stove. "Because I asked on my way out. You didn't think that I would be making all my future appointments without booking with you, did you? You're the only woman that I'll be getting a massage by from now on. I promise that."

I swallow hard and try to keep my nerves from jumping all over the place. He has no idea what his words are doing to me. He may not be trying, but they're definitely making me extremely *hot.*

I take a seat at the table when Cale refuses to let me help with anything, and within ten minutes the table is covered with food: baked chicken alfredo, breadsticks, salad, wine for myself, and beer for Cale.

Looking at all of the food makes my mouth water in anticipation. Cale cooked all of this knowing damn well that it's my favorite meal. I'll definitely owe him for this later and I'm positive he won't forget to collect. It's a good thing that I know practically all of his likes and dislikes. At least . . . I used to.

We don't talk much until we've both eaten a good amount and we're both on the verge of being stuffed. Cale must notice me slowing down, so he leans back in his chair and smiles up at me.

"So talk to me, Rile." He takes a swig of his beer and looks at me, ready to listen.

I take another huge bite of noodles, before licking my lips and smiling up at him. "About what?" I breathe out, feeling like I'm about to pop from overeating. "About how damn delicious this food is? Holy crap, Cale. This is so good. I'm very impressed."

He bites his bottom lip and leans in closer to me. "Told you I'd only put tasty things in your mouth." He shakes his head with a slight smile as my face undoubtedly turns beet red. "But I want to know about you. What's been going on? Where's the boyfriend? Why are you at your parents' house? That kind of stuff."

I take a huge drink of my wine and reach for the bottle to refill it. "We broke up before I left. It's a long story that I don't feel like talking about right now. I'm only staying with my parents until I can find my own place. Aspen offered to let me stay there, but I don't want to intrude on her and Slade." I take another drink and pretend to be unaffected. "I'm sure that I'll find a place soon and being back in Chicago will feel like home again. It will just take some time."

He looks me in the eyes for what feels like an eternity before he speaks. "Come stay with me."

I smile at his offer. "Thanks, but I don't know about that, Cale. My parents don't mind me staying there for a while. We haven't seen each other in six years and I don't want things to be awkward."

I stand up and get ready to clean up my mess, but Cale stops me and tells me to leave it on the table. "I'm not worried about that mess right now. What I'm worried about is spending time with you and there's no way in hell that things could *ever* be awkward between us. I don't care if it's been twenty years, we're still Rile and Cale and I always have the time and room for that in my life." He pulls me up from my chair and grabs my glass of wine. "Pick out a movie and I'll be there in a few minutes."

"Are you sure you don't–."

"Hell no, Rile. I invited you here for dinner. There's no way I'm allowing you to clean up." He pulls me by the back of the neck, until our faces are almost touching. "Now go to my room and find a pair of my boxer briefs and a shirt. I'll meet you on the couch."

I close my eyes and nod as his smell surrounds me. He smells so damn good that I just want to snuggle into him and run my nose all along his chest and neck. "Okay," I say softly.

Without warning, he releases my neck and walks over to the table to start cleaning up. I watch him for a second to try and imagine what it would be like living here with Cale. Seeing him every morning when I wake up and every night before bed. I have a feeling there's no way I could handle that without wanting more. Plus, it would kill me to see him bring other girls home. Cale truly has no idea how much I care about him and I'm hoping to keep it that way.

After slipping into some of Cale's clothes, I take a seat on the floor and search through his DVDs. I instantly spot a new comedy that I've been wanting to see, so I pop it into the PS4 and curl up on the corner of the couch to wait for Cale.

A few minutes later I hear Cale approaching, so I look up. Without a care in the world he yanks his shirt over his head before stepping out of his jeans, making my heart race with every movement that he makes.

He smiles at me when he notices me watching him. "I've been waiting to get out of these clothes all fucking day." With his abs flexing, he walks toward the couch and takes a seat, practically pulling me into his lap. He reaches for the blanket on the back of the couch and drapes it over us before pressing play with the controller. "You comfortable," he questions.

Yes . . . and no.

He isn't hard, but feeling his dick pressed against my ass definitely steals my breath for a brief second. There were so many times in the past that I wanted to feel him against me, but was too afraid to get close to him, so I always found ways to avoid contact with his junk. There's no way I would have been able to withstand begging him to take me, and right now . . . I'm fighting that urge.

"I'm fine." I lie. "Just let me know if you want me to move and I will."

He pulls me tighter against him and smiles into my neck. "I haven't seen you in six years. There's no way in hell that I'm letting you move away from me."

My heart beats faster from his words and I have to admit to myself that those are the exact words I wanted to hear. Being with him feels like old times and I'm happy to see that Cale wants me around just as much as in the past. I was scared things would be different . . .

I just hope that I can keep my feelings under control before I mess up everything we've had over the last ten years.

CHAPTER FOUR
Cale

RILEY FELL ASLEEP IN MY arms over two hours ago, but I haven't had the heart to move her so that I can get comfortable. She's sleeping like a damn baby, as if she's completely exhausted and hasn't slept in days. I can't even imagine how much of an effect this huge change must me taking on her both physically and emotionally.

Everything has changed dramatically for her in the last week. Her grandmother has gone off to a nursing home, she's packed up all of her things to move from the home she has known for the last six years, and on top of that has just gotten out of a relationship that I'm guessing was not by *her* choice.

I'll sit here all night if she's content and at home for the first time since she's left Mexico. She loves her parents, but there's no way she will be able to be herself there without having them on her ass constantly, making her feel as if she's a kid again; not to mention that she has to feel lonely there without someone she's close to. That's why my offer for her to stay here will always stand.

I feel her stir in my arms before she looks up at me with tired eyes and attempts to sit up. I pull her back into me and smile down at her as she begins to speak. "How long have I been sleeping?" She asks tiredly. "Sorry if I drooled on you."

I give her a small smile as she wipes her mouth. There's a wet circle of drool on my chest, but I could care less. "You're all good, Rile. Nothing that I haven't dealt with before from you." I help her stand up before I get to my own feet. "You dozed off a couple hours ago. I figured you needed the rest so I didn't want to wake you."

"Cale." She smiles at me gratefully and pulls me in for a tight hug. "You've always been so selfless when it comes to our friendship. I think I've missed that the most about you."

I smile against her neck. "Now why don't you go crawl into my bed and fall back to sleep. I'll take the couch for the night."

She pulls away from me and looks as if she wants to say something, but doesn't. She just turns away and starts heading for my bedroom, before stopping at the door and turning back around. "Night, Cale."

I turn off the lamp and strip out of my boxers, while holding the blanket against me. "Goodnight, Rile. I'll wake you up in the morning."

Her eyes linger down to my hand that is holding the blanket, before she nervously turns away and disappears into my bedroom.

I might have forgotten to mention the little fact that I *always* sleep naked. It was a struggle for me when Aspen and Slade were staying here, but as soon as they left I went back to my nudist ways.

If Riley agrees to stay here, then she's going to see me naked whether it's me running around the house or me on top of her, burying myself between those thighs of hers. I just hope that she's ready for me.

I've been more than ready for her . . .

THE ALARM ON MY PHONE woke me up at seven, not that I really slept much anyways. Having Riley sleeping in my bed kind of prevented that. I kept thinking about crawling into bed with her, but decided that it's probably too soon. There's no way I would've been able to lie next to her without wanting to pleasure her and make her scream until she fell asleep in my arms from exhaustion, so I spent most of the night fighting with my damn dick.

I quietly slip into my boxers and prepare a quick breakfast before waking Riley up. There's no way I'm sending her to work on an empty stomach.

I walk into my room to see Riley curled up in my bed, holding my spare pillow against her body for comfort. Every part of my body aches to be that comfort. It's probably been a while since she's slept alone, and seeing her having to use a pillow makes me want to show her what my body could do for her.

She looks so damn beautiful and peaceful, lying there in my clothes and bed, that I feel bad for having to wake her so early. A part of me just wants to crawl into my bed with her and say fuck everything else. Fuck *Sensual Touches* and fuck *Walk Of Shame*. I want Cale and Riley time and you better believe that I will be getting it as soon as I get off work tonight.

Just as I'm about to lean in and brush her beautiful, brown hair out of her face, she opens her eyes as if she can sense I'm next to her.

She stretches and smiles up at me, looking sweet and innocent.

It makes me wonder just how innocent her sexy little body really is; although, I have a feeling that it hasn't been as innocent over the last six years as I'd hoped. "Morning." Sitting up, she looks around as if trying to figure out what time it is. "Did I over sleep? Shit!" She changes position in a panic, tossing the pillow aside.

"Hell no, Rile. I wouldn't let that happen. I got you." I reach for her hand and help her up to her feet. "Come eat so that I can take you home to shower and get ready for work."

She stops walking and gives me a funny look. "You cooked us breakfast?"

I give her a light slap on the ass to get her moving again. "No." I laugh as her eyes light up at the food on the kitchen island. "I made *you* breakfast. I hardly eat in the morning. Plus, it's early as hell, Rile. I'm never up this early." I lean against the fridge and cross my arms as she pulls out a stool and takes a seat. "I'm going back to sleep as soon as I drop you off. I have to work later tonight."

She holds up a pancake, before slapping it down onto her plate. "Thank you. You really didn't have to do all of this. I could have stopped for a quick sandwich on the way to work. That's what I usually do."

I shake my head. "You're in my house; therefore, I feed you. Now eat up."

It's silent for a few minutes while she eats, before she finally speaks up, breaking the comfortable silence. I bring a glass of orange juice to my lips. "You work at the bar tonight? Bartending, right?"

I choke a little on my orange juice, realizing that I haven't mentioned the small fact that I'm a fucking male stripper. The last time we had talked I was mostly bartending. I didn't think the stripping part was going to last.

I set my orange juice down and walk over to grab her empty

plate, bringing it to the sink. "Why don't you go and change real fast and we'll talk on the way to your parents'."

She nods her head and sets her empty glass into the sink. "Good idea. I'm running out of time and I can't afford to lose this job if I want to find my own place soon."

I quickly dress and we both end up meeting by the front door in less than five minutes. Opening it for her, I lock the door before closing it behind us.

It feels so strange being outside at this time in the morning. It's so quiet and peaceful. I have to admit, I sort of like being up right now, and having Riley by my side makes it that much more enjoyable.

After helping her into my truck, I jog over to the driver side, mentally preparing myself for the bomb drop. I just hope that she can handle it without thinking any less of me. I never really cared what anybody thought about it until . . . *now*. She's always known me as the *sweet* Cale. I'm definitely far from her sweet Cale today, especially with my body.

She smiles and faces me as I pull out of the driveway and onto the road. "So . . . tell me about your job, Cale. I want to know what you've been up to. I want all the details."

I grip the steering wheel and grind my jaw, preparing for her reaction. There's really no way of sugarcoating this. I just have to come out and say it and hope that she accepts it. "I'm stripping tonight."

She lets out a small laugh as if she thinks I'm joking. "Stop playing around, Cale." She grabs my knee and squeezes it. "Really, tell me."

I stop at a red light and look over at her. I give her a serious look to show her that I'm not joking. "I've been stripping at *Walk Of Shame* for a while now. I only bartend a couple of nights a week now."

"Green light," she says quickly.

I turn away from her to pay attention to the road, just waiting for her to say something else. I want to know what she truly thinks about me now. I always want nothing but the truth from her and I always know that she'll give it to me straight.

"That's actually pretty cool. I bet you make a lot of money," she says, as if it's no big deal. "If you have the body, then hey . . . show it off. I can't imagine anyone complaining." She smiles at me and I feel a flood of relief wash through me.

"I haven't had any complaints yet."

She laughs. "Well obviously, Cale. You have the body of a God." She gives me a look that makes me want to rip her clothes off and fuck her right here. "I've always wanted to go and see male strippers. I've just never had the opportunity."

I lift an eyebrow. "You going to come and watch me one night then?"

She gently bites her bottom lip. "We'll see."

I pull into her parents' driveway and lean in to give her a kiss on the cheek. "I'll come pick you up when I get off work tonight. We still have *a lot* of time to make up for, and until then you're mine."

She huffs and glances at the house, looking as if she already wants to run away. "I'll be here, waiting. I'm off by four and I've been thinking about swinging by to see Aspen for a bit."

"Sounds good, Rile. Tell Aspen that she needs to come and see me soon. It's been too long."

"Will do." She smiles one more time before hopping out of the truck and walking away, stopping to smile back at me, before disappearing into the house.

Damn, this is going to be a long day.

CHAPTER FIVE

Riley

I'M JUST GATHERING UP MY things to leave work for the day when Hailey stops me by poking her head out of her door.

"Hey. Are you leaving?"

I nod my head and look down at the keys in my hand. "Yeah, I'm heading out right now. What's up?"

She gives me a sweet smile, obviously trying to butter me up for something. "I'm running a little behind and I have a client that's been waiting for like twenty minutes. Kylie has been on my ass and I can't handle her shit right now. Can you please take care of them so I can finish up?" She nods her head toward her door and whispers, "This suit pays a lot of money and he's not ready to leave yet. So?"

I look down at my phone in my hand to see that Aspen has

finally responded to my message. Holding up my finger to Hailey, I quickly check the message to see that Aspen won't be home until at least five thirty. I really have nothing better to do anyways.

"Yeah, I can do it. I'll tell Kylie to send them to my room."

Hailey flashes me a half smile, before disappearing back into her room.

"Yeah, you're welcome," I mutter to myself.

I walk down the hall to find Kylie at her desk. She looks up from twisting her purple hair around her finger and waves me over when she hears me coming. "You better hurry up and get out of here before that skank cons you into staying longer."

I let out a frustrated breath and lean against the desk. "Too late. Send her client to my room."

"Seriously?" She questions. "You're that easy, huh?" She grins while reaching for the phone. "I had a feeling that was going to happen so I didn't tell Hailey who her client was. You just keep getting lucky, sweets. I'll call and tell him to come back in."

"Alright," I say while walking away. "Send him on back to my room."

I'm in my room for about three minutes before the door opens up and a handsome guy dressed to impress walks in. He smiles at me before reaching out to shake my hand. "Lynx," he offers. His blue eyes meet mine and capture them.

I smile back at him as he begins to look me up and down. "Riley," I say back. "I'll be taking care of you today. I hope you don't mind."

He offers my hand a little squeeze before releasing it. "I don't mind at all." He reaches for the top button of his black button-down and starts to undo it. "Mind if I get undressed?" He lifts a brow, waiting for my response.

I shake my head, embarrassed, and reach for the door handle. "Oh sorry. Not at all. I'll give you a few minutes."

I quickly escape to the hall and give Lynx a few minutes to get undressed and comfortable before I knock on the door in warning and push it open.

Lynx is laying on his stomach, dressed in a tight little pair of black boxer briefs clinging to his small, muscular ass.

"Oh thank goodness," I whisper to myself, glad that he didn't decide to get naked like Cale did. I'm not sure I'd be able to handle that at the moment. Cale had me about to explode from touching his body and I have to admit that I'm still worked up and sexually frustrated.

"What was that," he asks.

I smile down at him as he twists his neck to look at me. "Oh nothing. Sorry." I take a second to take in his body and can't help but compare him to Cale. This man is undoubtedly sexy with his dark, messy hair, and muscular, lean build, yet . . . he doesn't even compare to Cale.

My heart skips a beat at the thought of Cale and it's that moment that I realize I miss him already. I've been trying all day not to think about last night and the fact that I fell asleep in his arms, but seeing this gorgeous man and realizing that he *still* doesn't come close to Cale and the effect his body has on me, makes me realize just how much I truly want Cale. I guess six years hasn't done shit to make my heart forget him. It's pretty sad that I just got out of a two-year relationship, yet it's *Cale* that's on my mind. He's always had that power over me.

ASPEN HAS BEEN TALKING ABOUT her job at the salon and other random things for the last hour, but I haven't been able to stop thinking about Cale and the fact that he's at the bar stripping right now. I didn't really think about it much earlier, but knowing that he's there now, taking his clothes off for tons of women that are probably pawing at his body, has me kind of jealous. I hate that they are there and I'm not. I really *want* to go and see what it's like.

"Let's go to *Walk Of Shame*," I blurt out, cutting Aspen off.

Aspen leans back on the couch and smiles as if she's a bit surprised by my request. "Oh boy. I don't think you can handle it." She shakes her head. "As a matter of fact . . . I *know* you can't handle it. You don't even know the things those boys do with their bodies."

Excitement surges through me at the thought of watching Cale move his body, and now I'm anxious to hurry and get there. "I can handle it. That's where you met Slade, right? If you can survive there, then I'm pretty damn sure I can too."

"Yeah," she says with a laugh. "It was a bumpy ride, that's for damn sure." She stands up from the couch when she hears the shower water turn off. "You should go by yourself. I think I'm going to be busy for the next couple of hours."

Standing up, I give her a surprised look as she starts ushering me toward the door. "How damn rude. You're just going to kick your big sister out like that?"

We both look over to the hallway when Slade appears dripping wet, his waist wrapped in a small towel that leaves little to the imagination.

"Damn," we both say in unison.

Aspen gives me a little shove as Slade smiles at us and runs a hand through his wet hair. "Hell yes I am. You have somewhere to be and I have someone to do. Goodbye."

I wave goodbye to Slade as Aspen shoves me outside and kisses me on the side of the head. "Love you too," I mumble.

"Love you, sis, but you gotta go right now." She hands me my purse. "Slade says hi and bye and hopes to see you soon. Tell Cale we love him. Buh bye."

I roll my eyes and smile when the door closes in my face. As *rude* as this was . . . I want that. I want to want someone like that and for him to want me just as much. I never felt that with Tyler. Yeah, I loved him and he loved me, but we were never desperate for each other and never just *had* to have each other. What I wouldn't give to have that feeling, and if I were to admit it to myself, I sort of felt that way last night when being in Cale's arms. I felt this want and need to be close to him. Sort of like I do now.

I blow out a breath while walking to my car.

Walk Of Shame . . . here I come.

I get hit with a brick of nerves as soon as I pull into the parking lot of *Walk Of Shame* and see how many cars are occupying the lot. It's packed and finding parking won't be easy.

"Holy shit, these women don't play around," I mutter. Grabbing my wallet, I shove my purse under my seat and hop out of my car, pressing the lock behind me.

Just walking in the door of this place is overwhelming. My ears are instantly assaulted with the sound of screaming women and I can barely concentrate as the guy at the door checks my I.D. I keep my eyes on the crowd of loud and crazy women as the guy places my I.D back in my hand and greets the group of women behind me.

The crowd is pretty much shoulder to shoulder and I can barely see what's happening on the stage. That is until Cale jumps down into the crowd and starts grinding his hips to the music while bending some girl over as if he's fucking her.

He's wearing a short pair of red boxer briefs and his muscular body is covered in sweat as he continues to grind behind her, working her nice and good, before thrusting her away with his dick and dropping to the floor as if he's making love to someone below him. He's working his hips so powerfully and with such a perfect rhythm that it takes my breath away just imagining being below him. Now I know what my sister meant by not being able to handle this place. I'll never be able to look at Cale the same now, and I'm pretty positive that there's no way that man is *still* a virgin. I guess I didn't really expect him to be . . .

Holy. Hotness.

CHAPTER SIX

Cale

I SLOW MY RHYTHM AND close my eyes as I picture Riley below me. These women might be imagining me fucking them, but I'm imagining fucking Riley, nice and slow, and taking care of her every fucking need.

I feel hands grab at me and start tugging on my briefs, trying to get me naked. Someone gets my briefs down far enough in the back that my whole ass is hanging out, so I push myself back to my feet, smile at the ladies, and slowly thrust the air, giving them a view of my bare ass flexing.

Right as I'm pulling my briefs back up I look to the left and set my sights on Riley. She's looking at me with wide eyes, appearing slightly uncomfortable and out of place. My body instantly reacts to seeing her and I have to fight against my erection, knowing that these red boxer briefs will do nada to hide what I'm thinking.

Ignoring all the women around me, I walk toward her, letting her know that I see her. The last thing I want is for Riley to feel as if she doesn't belong when she's here to see me. She's the most important woman in this damn room and I'm about to show her that.

When I approach Riley, I wrap my hands into the back of her hair and bury my face into the softness of her neck, pulling her as close to me as humanly possible.

She's stiff at first, but loosens up and grabs my forearms as I run my lips up her neck, grinding my hips against her. I hear her let out a little gasp as my erection presses against her stomach, and that little sound alone is enough to make me want her even more than ever.

"You came to see me," I whisper against her neck. I grab one of her legs and wrap it around my waist as I dig my hips into her. "You're the most beautiful girl in this room, Riley. I promise you that."

Reaching for her other leg, I pick her up and wrap both of her legs around my waist, thrusting my hips into her, nice and slow as if fucking her. My hands grip her ass and I hold her as close to me as I can, grinding her against me.

I look up just as Stone slides a chair in front of me, giving me exactly what I need as if reading my mind. Being careful with Riley, I set her down on the chair and then straddle her lap, wrapping both of my hands into the back of her hair and forcing her to look into my eyes. I'm unsure of what she's thinking, but now is the time to show her what she could have. All she has to do is give me a clue that she wants it just like I do.

Biting my bottom lip, I reach for both of her hands, lightly lacing mine on the backs of hers, before running them slowly down my chest and abs, ensuring she feels every ridge as I grind into her. I lean into her and moan against her ear, showing her just how turned on I am without her doing anything at all.

Her body shivers and she lets out a small moan as well, confirming what I want to know, and letting me see exactly what my body is doing to her. Pleased, I pick her back up and grip her ass as she wraps her legs around me once again.

She leans her head back, getting lost in the moment as my body stills against hers and the song comes to an end.

We stand here for a few moments, holding each other, until finally she lets go and clears her throat, dropping back to her feet. "Told you I've always wanted to see male strippers." She smiles nervously and brushes her hair out of her face. "You should go. The crowd is waiting."

I press my lips to her forehead and offer her a thankful smile, before turning away from her and finishing up the show.

RILEY IS OUTSIDE WAITING BY my truck when I'm done. She looks up from her phone and smiles when she sees me approaching. "Done shaking your junk for the horny women already?"

I walk up to her and kiss her on the forehead, before pulling away and laughing. "Yeah, my junk is tired from all the shaking. It's Stone's turn now."

She lets out a small laugh. "Well, you were great." Her eyes search mine before she speaks again. "Everyone loved you."

"You haven't seen anything yet, Riley." I lean against my truck, beside her. "How was your day?"

"Good," she responds. "I'm just a bit tired and sore."

I look around the parking lot in search of her car. "Did you drive here or take a taxi?"

She pushes a button on her key ring, making it beep, before holding up her keys. "Drove." She yawns and leans against my truck, looking exhausted. "I was only planning on stopping in for a few minutes, but kinda got sucked in by the action," she teases.

I walk around her and open the passenger door to my truck. "Let's go. We'll get your car tomorrow."

She shakes her head while yawning. "It's fine, Cale. I'll just drive and meet you at your house."

Ignoring her request, I pick her up and set her in my truck, refusing to let her drive in her exhausted condition. "Your car will be fine. You're riding with me."

Smiling, she leans back and buckles her seatbelt. "Yes, master Cale," she quips.

"I like that." I respond with a grin. "Say it again."

Laughing, she smacks my arm and reaches for the door to close it. "Back up before your junk gets stuck in the door."

I bite my bottom lip and back away, watching her in amusement. God, I've missed this woman. Having her here reminds me of why I chose to wait in the first place.

By the time we pull up at my house Riley is practically sleeping in her seat. She slowly straightens and looks out the window while rubbing the back of her neck. "We're here already?" She unbuckles her seatbelt and turns to me as she stretches. "Sorry if I dozed off. I got stuck at work longer than expected. I guess I'm a lot more exhausted than I thought." She rubs her neck again. "And sore. Ouch."

I smile at her and gently touch her bottom lip. "No worries." Hopping out of my truck, I hurry to Riley's side before she has a chance to open the door herself. "You don't have to do shit for the rest of the night. I got you, girl."

She lets out a surprised squeal as I reach in the truck and pick her up, throwing her over my shoulder. "Cale!" She grabs onto my shirt and laughs. "What are you doing?"

I slap her ass and start walking for the door. "Stop squirming.

I told you that you don't have to do shit for the rest of the night. Did you think I was joking?"

She places her hands on my ass and pushes up as I walk through the door and shut it behind us. "Well, I didn't think that included walking." She looks up at me, and smiles after I toss her on my bed. "What . . . are you going to undress me for the night too?"

I lift my eyebrows and look her in the eyes as I crawl onto my bed and hover above her. "Yes," I say firmly. "You've been taking care of people your whole life. Let me take care of you tonight."

She swallows as her eyes meet my lips. "Cale . . . you don't have to take care of me. You don't owe—"

I cut her off by pressing my lips to hers, gently but possessively, letting her know how much I want her. I've waited for far too long to kiss her, and there's no way I'm holding back. Tonight . . . she's going to see just how fucking good my tongue can make her feel.

She lets out a moan and grips my shoulders as I run my tongue across her lips, hinting for her to open up for me.

"Cale . . ." She moans again as I press my hips between her legs. "I don't know if we should do this . . ."

I smile against her lips and whisper, "*We* don't have to do anything." Running my hands down her sides, I kiss my way down her stomach, stopping above her jeans. "Just let *me* take care of you."

Her eyes search mine for a moment, but she doesn't say a word as I work on taking off her jeans. Slowly, I pull them down her legs, kissing the inside of her thighs on the way down, before tossing her jeans aside and gently nibbling her clit through her thin panties.

She squirms and slams her head back while gripping the blanket in anticipation. "Cale," she breathes heavily. "I don't want to mess things up between us. You should stop . . ."

I slowly pull her panties down while looking her in the eyes.

"Don't worry about that. Trust me, Riley. You need this . . . just sit back and enjoy it."

Before she can say anything else, I run my tongue over her clit, before gently sucking it into my mouth. The taste of her against my tongue is almost enough to make me bust my load.

I've wanted to taste Riley for so damn long now. I probably shouldn't be doing this so soon, but I can't help myself. She's just so beautiful and tense. She looks as if she hasn't been pleasured in a long time, and I want her to know how good it can feel to be taken care of, especially by me: her *sweet* Cale.

Riley's hands wrap into my hair as her hips buck upward, begging for more, so that's what I give her.

My tongue explores every last inch of her sweet little pussy, tasting it as if my life depends on it. I work my tongue slow at first, teasing her and making sure that she's left wanting more. Then I speed up, fucking her with my tongue, before slipping my finger into her tight little pussy, pumping in and out as I move back to her clit.

Squeezing her hip, I pull her body closer to me while giving her just a small taste of my skills.

Her grip on my hair tightens as her legs begin to squeeze my face. "Oh God . . . Oh God . . . Cale . . ."

I suck her clit into my mouth, working my tongue and finger fucking her until she's shaking beneath me, her pussy now clenching around my finger. Her muscles tighten so hard that it almost hurts my damn finger.

I look up at her and run my tongue along her folds one more time, before pulling my finger out and sucking her sweet release into my mouth.

Smiling at her new, relaxed state, I crawl above her and press my lips to her forehead. "Goodnight, Riley."

Not wanting to pressure her any more than I have and make

her feel uncomfortable, I help her back into her panties before heading for the door on my way to sleep on the couch.

"Goodnight," she whispers softly. "I . . . uh . . . I'll see you in the morning."

I keep my cool until I shut the door behind me. "Fuck me," I growl out.

One taste. One fucking taste and I'm ready to give her all of me. I want to bury myself between her legs so bad, but I know that moving things too fast will only ruin her.

She's too fresh out of a relationship and too concerned about ruining things between us to be able to take that step. Truthfully, I don't even know if she's going to be able to handle what I just did to her. I took it easy on her tonight. Just wait until she can see how rough I can be.

"Shit . . ." I strip down to the nude and lay on the couch, knowing that I won't be sleeping for shit tonight. My dick won't either.

Closing my eyes, I grab my shaft and slowly stroke it to thoughts of Riley riding my hard cock. I want to feel her take it deep and hard, knowing that she's the first to take it.

My strokes become faster as I think back to the sexy little sounds that Riley made when she came on my tongue. "So fucking hot, Riley."

A few minutes later and I'm busting my load all over my tight abs, wishing that it were inside Riley's tight little pussy instead.

Fuck me . . .

CHAPTER SEVEN
Riley

I'VE BEEN LAYING HERE FOR the last hour, unable to shut my mind off and fall asleep. Guilt has been eating at me, making it impossible to shut my eyes.

I should feel guilty for letting another man touch me so soon. I should feel guilty for kissing another man, and enjoying it, but I don't. No . . . I feel guilty for not feeling guilty and knowing that there is only one reason for that: Cale Kinley.

I know without a doubt that if it had been anyone other than Cale I would feel bad for letting another man touch me. Don't get me wrong; I still love Tyler. I mean . . . we were together for two years, so how could I not. I can't just shut my feelings off. Of course I still care about him, wonder what he's doing and how he's feeling now that I'm gone.

The part I don't understand is why when Cale's lips were on me that not one thought of Tyler crossed my mind, as if he was forgotten. Cale consumed my every thought and need, making me feel . . . alive, and cared for. He made me believe for just a small moment that it's possible to let everything go and let someone else take care of you. I really needed that and he could tell. He's always been able to read me.

Now I'm left with another question: how does he feel about me? I know he loves me as a friend and that he'll do anything for me, but would he really go out of his way to please me sexually if his only feelings toward me were platonic? Knowing that he's a stripper confuses me, because I'm sure he doesn't have a problem with sexual attention, and it makes me believe that he possibly does have real feelings for me. Male strippers are known for their reputations. Considering what they do, it's plausible that they're sexually active with probably about seventy percent of the girls that come and see them, but I hope that's not the case with Cale.

Throwing the blanket from my legs, I quietly get out of bed and walk through the living room on my way to the bathroom. I'm sure to be as quiet as possible, worried that I'll wake Cale up. He's had a long night and the last thing I want to do is take away from his sleep.

On the way back to the bedroom, I find myself wanting to see Cale one more time before falling asleep. For some reason my body aches just to get a glimpse of him.

I quietly make my way over to the couch and peek over it.

"What are you doing, Rile?"

I jump back from the sound of Cale's voice. I wasn't expecting him to be awake.

"I couldn't sleep. I just wanted to make sure you were sleeping."

He tiredly smiles at me and reaches for my arms, pulling me onto the couch with him. "I'll help you fall asleep. Come here." He lifts the blanket so that we're both underneath, before snuggling me to his chest and wrapping his arm around me.

I let out a small gasp when I feel his bare dick against the exposed skin of my belly. "You're naked, Cale?"

He just pulls me closer and starts rubbing his hand through my hair, calming me. "Just close your eyes, Rile. I got you." He kisses the top of my hair. "Go to sleep."

I'M JUST FINISHING UP WITH Lynx when I hear the door open behind me. I got a little behind because Lynx constantly wanted to talk and request that I spend extra time on his upper thighs. Every time I tried moving to the next body part, he kept saying that his muscles were still tense.

Feeling frustrated, I don't even bother turning around. "I'm almost done here. Come back in ten please. I apologize."

I hear the door close behind me, so I automatically suspect that the person left, but when Lynx opens his eyes and smiles past me, I realize that the person is still in the room.

I quickly turn around and get ready to usher the person out when my eyes set on Cale. He smiles at me before turning to Lynx. "No wonder your ass wasn't at the club."

Cale lifts an eyebrow as Lynx sits up and slowly gets dressed. "Yeah, well I was feeling a bit tense and this beautiful lady was helping me relax. What's it to you?"

I see Cale's jaw tense, but he quickly shakes it off and leans against the wall as Lynx finishes dressing.

I look between the two of them, before setting my gaze on Lynx. "So I'm guessing you're a stripper too?"

Lynx gives me a cocky grin, before walking up to Cale and squeezing his shoulder. "Nah . . . I'm the boss man. Right, Cale?"

He winks.

Cale shrugs his shoulders and eyes him carefully as he reaches for the door handle. "When you're actually there," he says stiffly.

Lynx brushes off Cale's coldness and turns back to me. "I'll see you in a couple days, Magic hands." He winks and then disappears out into the hall.

Cale grunts to himself and quickly starts getting undressed as I clean and prepare the bed. "Is he in here a lot, Rile?"

I smooth out the new sheet and look behind me. "He's been in here a couple of times. He's pretty persistent when he wants something. I guess I can see why now."

Cale reaches out and grabs my chin, bringing my eyes up to meet his. "Has he tried anything with you? Tell me right now if he has."

I shake my head. "No, Cale. Nothing besides the extra time that he requests on his upper thighs, but I'm starting to get used to that with this job title." I let out a small laugh, but Cale still seems tense.

"Promise me that you'll let me know if he touches you. I don't like the idea of you two in here alone together. He's got quite the reputation at the club."

I place my hand on his arm and he releases my chin. "Don't worry, Cale. I'll be fine." I point down at the bed. "Now get your ass naked so I can get started." I offer him a lighthearted smile. "I'm starting to see that you do everything naked."

He pulls his jeans down and I turn my head away so he can get out of his boxers. "I'm happier when I'm naked, Rile. What can I say?"

I'm happier when you're naked too . . .

When I turn back around, Cale is laying on his back, looking up at the ceiling. The small towel is doing an even shittier job of hiding his junk than the last time.

Squirting some oil into my hands, I start at Cale's shoulders and slowly work my way down his chest. "You working tonight?"

He lets out a small moan when I reach his lower abdomen. "Yeah . . ." he breathes. "In a few hours actually."

The way that he bites his bottom lip each time my hands get lower on his abdomen makes me want to see what he'll do if I touch him sexually. Would he stop me or let me keep going? I try to push the thought aside, but each time I notice him bite his lip and growl I feel my insides jump.

He seems a little tense after seeing Lynx in here . . . He did do me a little favor last night. I just wouldn't be a very good friend if I let him go to work like that, now would I? I'm going to say no . . .

Taking a deep breath, I round the table without removing my hands to create a better angle, and then slide my hands under the towel, wrapping both of them around his thick dick, slowly stroking up and down, feeling it quickly growing in my hands.

"Oh shit . . . Rile." He bites into his lip again, but harder this time, as he grips my waist. "Fuck . . . my cock is so hard for you."

As his grip on my waist gets tighter, my hands work faster and firmer, being sure to pleasure him just as much as he did me last night. His dick is now so hard and big that I definitely need both hands to take care of him.

My heart is racing, but I don't want to stop. Touching him and knowing that I'm giving him pleasure has me more turned on than I've ever been in my entire life. I've waited a long time to touch him like this . . .

"Fuck yes, Rile . . ." He sits up and bites my shoulder, but not hard enough to hurt me. "Keep going. Ah . . . fuck me, Rile."

I lean my neck back as he runs his lips up the side, moaning all the way up until he stops at my ear. "You feel so fucking good, Rile." He moans. "I bet your pussy would feel even better . . ."

I close my eyes from his words and almost feel as if I'm on the verge of having my own orgasm. Stroking his dick, I find that both of us are now moaning, until finally he releases his load on his stomach, before pulling my bottom lip into his mouth and biting it.

As soon as he moans into my mouth once more, I surprisingly find my own release. I instantly feel embarrassed, shocked that something like that could happen without even being touched.

"Shit, Rile." He lies back on the table and runs his hands through his thick, messy hair. "I love it when you touch me."

He looks over at me and grabs my arm as I take a step back. "What's wrong?" He smiles at me and looks down at my legs that are still slightly shaking. "Did you orgasm, Rile?"

I nod my head, my fingertips instantly going to my mouth to create a diversion, too embarrassed to actually speak.

Cale grabs the towel and wipes himself off, before standing up and grabbing my chin after removing my hand from my mouth, forcing me to look up at him. "Well damn, Rile. That's the hottest thing I've ever heard." He smirks down at me and wets his lips. "Knowing that I can make you come without even touching you . . . is by far the sexiest, most satisfying thing that's ever happened to me. All it does is make me want to bend you over this massage table and fuck you until we both can't walk."

"Cale . . ."

He places his finger to my lips and bends down to whisper in my ear. "As soon as I know that you can handle it . . . you *will* be the first woman to have me inside of her. I promise that . . . Rile. Just wait and see."

I stand here, frozen and unable to think clearly as Cale gathers up his clothes and gets dressed.

He must be able to tell that his words have shaken me up, because the next thing I know I feel his lips on the top of my head, before I hear the door open.

"I'll see you tonight, Rile."

Shaking off my frozen state, I turn to Cale and offer him a small smile. "Yeah . . . I'll see you later . . . um . . . after work."

The door closes behind him and I instantly go into panic mode.

"He did not just say that, Riley." I walk over to the bed and start stripping it down, barely able to even function right. "You're just hearing things. There's no way in hell that Cale is still a virgin . . ."

I have no idea how long I've been standing here, dazed and confused, when my door opens and a woman walks in.

Pulling myself together, I smile at her and introduce myself, before walking out into the hall, giving her time to get ready.

How I'm going to be able to function for the rest of the day is beyond me. I had to have heard him wrong . . .

"Yeah, that's it." I try to convince myself. "I'm tired. He could have said anything."

The woman calls my name, interrupting my thoughts, so I shake off my personal thoughts and prepare to make it through the day, hoping that I'm just going crazy.

Cale . . . a virgin . . . me his first . . . friends . . . we're just friends . . .

CHAPTER EIGHT

Cale

MY SHIFT ENDS IN TWENTY minutes and I can't deny that I'm a little disappointed Riley didn't stop in to see me. I haven't heard from her since I left *Sensual Touches* and it's really starting to bother me.

I guess she wasn't ready to hear that I really did wait for her, and I bet that she doesn't believe me. I wouldn't believe me either if the roles were reversed. A virgin stripper. . . . No fucking way. Impossible right? Well, I'm the fucking exception. She is the reason that I'm the exception.

I look up from the ground when I feel a hand on my shoulder. Stone grins like a fool. "Dude . . . you've been standing there for ten damn minutes now. Just get the hell out of here. You're useless here in that state."

Shaking my head I steel my jaw. "Nah, I'm good. Just get the hell back over to your side, man. I don't want your dick over here."

Stone laughs and starts backing up. "At least I'm actually working my dick, bro. That's more than you can say." Grinning like a fool he gives me the middle finger with both hands, before busting back into a dance.

I get my head back into the game for the last ten minutes, trying my best not to think about Riley and whether or not I fucked things up.

Just as I'm pushing through the crowd of women and getting ready to head into the back room, I spot Riley sitting at the bar talking to Sara.

Sara looks over at me and notices the stupid ass grin on my face, raising her brows as she figures it out. Hell yes it makes me happy as hell to see that Riley is here. I don't give a shit who knows.

Gathering up my shit, I get dressed quickly and snatch my tips from Kash, tossing him a pile of twenties on my way out the door.

I stop dead in my tracks when I notice Lynx at the bar talking Riley up. That dick better learn his place when it comes to my woman. She may not know it yet . . . but she's my girl. I'm going to make that very clear, and real soon.

"Just admit that you came to see me," Lynx says with a confident grin that makes me want to choke the life out of him. "I can definitely put on a show one night if it keeps you coming back."

Riley laughs as if she finds him amusing, but doesn't say anything as I approach them at the bar.

Lynx quickly turns to me as I place a kiss on Riley's head and wrap my arms around her from behind. "I didn't think you'd show up," I whisper next to her ear. I look up at Lynx as I say the next part. "I'm glad that you came to see me. I'm ready when you are."

Riley takes one last sip of her drink and slides it across the bar to Sara. "Thank you for the drink, Sara." She gets ready to reach for cash, but Sara and I both stop her.

I look at Sara. "I'll pay for it."

She shakes her head. "It's on me. A little welcome home present. Well besides what I'm sure you've given her." She winks and walks away.

Lynx stands up at the same time that Riley does. "Well, I guess I'll be seeing you tomorrow," he says stiffly. "Same time as the last." He raises his drink to me and smirks. "You did good tonight, Cale. The women got a good show. *All* of them."

I tense my jaw and bite my tongue. I know damn well what he's doing. "Let's go, Rile." I place my hand on the small of her back and guide her outside, fighting the urge to kick the shit out of that dick.

As soon as we reach my truck, I slam Riley against it and crush my lips against hers, claiming them and letting her know how much I want her. Fuck Lynx. He can't have her, not now or ever.

Seeing another man wanting her only makes me want to take it out on her *sexually* and give her all that I have. I may not end up being her first, but I know damn well that I will be her second and her *last*.

Lifting her leg, I thrust my hips into her and moan against her lips. "I want to be inside you so bad, Rile." I kiss her again, before whispering against her lips. "Let me give myself to you. I want you to be my first. I know you may not believe me, but I would never lie to you. You know that. I've done sexual shit, Rile. Lots of things, but I've never entered a woman. I promise you that."

She moans loudly and grips the back of my hair as I suck her bottom lip into my mouth. "Cale . . ." She moans again as I grind my hips between her legs. "You really waited all this time for me?" I roughly kiss her neck and nod my head, just eager to continue tasting her. "What if I told you that I'm still a virgin? Would you still want to make me your first?"

VICTORIA ASHLEY

Her words cause my heart to beat erratically in my chest and I freeze mid-kiss. "What?" I pull away and run my hands through my hair. "Are you, Rile? Are you still a virgin?"

She nods her head and covers her face. "I just couldn't do it, Cale." She pushes me away so she can get some air. "Every single time that Tyler and I began to get sexually active I would stop him right before he could enter me." She looks up to meet my eyes. "I kept thinking about you and wondering if you really meant what you said about waiting for me. It didn't feel right so I never had sex with him. I only allowed him to touch me sexually. No wonder he didn't want to follow me to Chicago . . ."

"Holy fuck, Rile." I run my hands through my hair and start pacing. "You telling me that you're a virgin makes me want to fuck you right here, right now." I stop pacing and press Riley back against my truck. "But it also makes me feel like it needs to be special for you, and whenever you're ready. My virginity doesn't mean shit to me as long I lose it to you. It could be in the fucking dirt or mud for all I care."

Riley swallows hard, before standing on the tip of her toes and wrapping her arms around my neck. "Is this really happening right now?" She questions. "I thought that us waiting for each other was just some stupid fantasy that I dreamt up. I thought I was being an idiot."

"Hell no, Rile." I lean down and press my lips against hers. "You really have no idea how much I really care about you, do you?"

She shakes her head and bites her bottom lip.

"Well fuck. I'm going to show you." I open the passenger door and point. "Inside. Now."

With her eyes locked on mine, she climbs into my truck and wraps her legs around me as I step in between them. "I've missed you, Cale." She lets out a small breath. "So much. There were times

392

when I almost ran away in the middle of the night and got on a plane. I had tickets each time, but always talked myself out of it, knowing that I couldn't leave grams like that."

I grip the back of her hair and lightly tug. "Me too, baby. But you're here now and I'm going to make up for it." I bite her bottom lip before releasing it. "Let's go."

AS SOON AS WE PULL out of the parking lot I place her hand on my hard cock, letting her know what she's doing to me, before I slide my hand up her dress. Her pussy is so warm and wet, just waiting for me to touch it. I love that . . . my pussy.

We drive in silence as I gently slide my fingers in and out, loosening her up for what's to come when we get home. Knowing that no man has been inside her has me so anxious to sink deep between those beautiful thighs and take her over and over again, all night long. Now that I know how much she wants it too . . . it's happening.

Once we pull up at my house, I pull my fingers out of her pussy and suck them into my mouth, looking her straight in the eyes. She lets out a small moan and grips the seat. "Riley . . . are you sure you want this?" She nods her head. "You do realize that once I fuck you that it will be happening every day and there's no turning back to just being the old Rile and Cale right? I will pleasure you any and every chance that I get and there's no taking it back: giving me your first time."

"Cale . . ." She reaches for the door handle. "I have always wanted you to be my first. I just didn't think it would actually happen. Knowing that it can. . . . I'm not passing that up for anything."

I feel my chest ache at the thought that we had to go so long without each other, waiting for this fucking moment that should have happened six damn years ago. "Good . . . because I wasn't willing to let you."

Jumping out of the truck, I run over to her side and open the door. I lean inside and wrap both of my hands into the back of her hair, before pulling her toward me and kissing her long and hard. I place one hand on her knee and slide it up her leg, shoving a finger inside of her, while biting her bottom lip and tugging.

"Fuck me . . . I can never get enough of kissing you, Rile. I wanted to kiss you so damn bad the night that you left, but I didn't have the balls to mess things up for us. If I would have kissed you then I know I would have given you so much more that night in the pool, and I couldn't make love to you and just let you leave. I knew I had to wait."

She smiles against my lips. "It's a good thing, because if you would have kissed me . . ." She grips my hair. "Especially like this, then there's no way I would have gotten on that plane. Just one kiss was all I needed from you."

I lean in to kiss her again, but stop when her phone goes off. "Ignore it," I whisper.

"I plan to." She pulls me closer between her legs and reaches her hand down in between us to rub my cock.

I throw my head back and grip her hair tighter, so damn turned on by her touch. "Undo my pants, Rile."

Without hesitation she starts to undo my pants, but her phone goes off again, causing us both to freeze.

"Dammit," she mumbles. "I'm sorry. Let me turn it on silent."

I stand patiently as she pulls out her phone and unlocks the screen to silence it. The pained look on her face tells me who it is and the moment shatters on the spot.

She awkwardly clears her throat and turns her phone on vibrate. "Well that kind of kills the moment. I'm so sorry." Her whole mood has changed and now I feel as if comforting her has

CALE

become my priority. Riley has a big heart and I'd be stupid not to know how this moment is affecting her.

I pull her chin up and gently kiss her lips. "It's okay, Rile." I rub my thumb over her bottom lip. "Let's go inside and I'll make us a late night snack before bed. "Sound good?"

She nods her head, ashamed, and runs her hands through my hair. "Thank you, Cale. I just want this moment to be the two of us. I don't want any hint of Tyler in the back of my mind."

I kiss her again, letting her know that I'm okay with it. "You can't just shut your feelings off, Rile; I know that and I don't expect it. This won't be our last opportunity. Trust me."

She smiles as I help her out of my truck and guide her to the front door.

I definitely want her mind to be focused on just me once I'm burying myself between her sweet thighs. It will happen soon.

Just not tonight . . . tonight she knows how much I care about her.

CHAPTER NINE

Riley

IT'S BEEN TWO DAYS SINCE I received those missed calls from Tyler and I respect with everything in me that Cale has given me some space in case I wanted to call him back. I thought long and hard about it, and then decided against it. He broke my heart when he decided just *two* days before we were to leave that he didn't want to be a part of the plans. Why should I call him back? He's the one that didn't care enough. He didn't even come to say goodbye the day that I left.

Cale and I are sitting on his couch watching hilarious prank shows and snacking on popcorn, and right now . . . that's all that matters. He's been able to keep a smile on my face throughout the pain that I thought I'd be feeling when I got home, and he's had my back through everything. I'm here and I'm focused on the now.

Tyler is no longer clouding my thoughts and I want Cale to see that.

Setting the bowl of popcorn aside, I straddle Cale's lap and gently kiss him on the lips. His lips are so soft and delicious that I unconsciously lick them before pulling away. I swear that I could kiss him all day and never grow tired of those lips. I've waited too long to not take advantage now.

"Damn, Rile." Cale squeezes my hips before moving down to my thighs, while running his tongue over his lips. "What are you trying to do to me? Are you trying to get me naked, because it won't take much more of that."

I lean my head back and moan as he buries his face into my neck and roughly kisses it, pushing me down onto his lap. "See what you're doing, Rile? You feel that?" I still can't seem to get over feeling his dick against me. It's so damn big and hard . . . and I want it, every inch of it . . . of Cale. My Cale.

He starts grinding below me, rubbing his hardness between my legs. "Yes," I breathe. "God . . . yes . . ." Just the thought of him being inside me makes me break into a sweat. It still amazes me how turned on I get with Cale. It's overwhelming.

After not feeling him touch me for two days, I feel like I could orgasm just from the feel of his tongue alone. That's how good this man is and I have a feeling that he knows it. He may be a virgin . . . but the rest of his body isn't . . . far from it.

"I want to take you somewhere, Rile." He runs his lips up my neck and stops at my ear. "Will you come with me?"

I swallow hard from his words. He just had to use the word *come*. "Cale . . . it's like two in the morning. Isn't it a bit late to take me somewhere?"

He laughs against my neck and squeezes my hips, lifting me from his lap. "It's never too late, Rile." Standing up, he reaches for my hand and pulls me into his chest. His hands tangle in my hair as he runs his tongue up my lips, tasting me. "Fucking delicious, baby."

Smiling, he walks toward the door, picking up his keys on the way out. I follow behind him, curious to where it is that he wants to take me so late at night. I have no clue where he wants to go, but truthfully I'd go anywhere with Cale. I always did in the past, including late night trips . . . but we were just kids then. Sneaking out late at night was in. We're definitely not kids anymore and don't need to sneak out to hang out.

I'm so anxious when we get into Cale's truck that I can't stop looking out the window, trying to figure out where he's taking me. It takes me a good five minutes to figure it out.

"Cale . . ." I sit up straight and look out the window. "Are you taking me to your old house?"

He smirks and pulls off to the side of the road, killing the engine on his truck. "I thought a late night dip sounded good. You know . . . pick up where we left off six years ago."

I sit still as Cale jumps out of the truck and jogs over to my side, opening my door. "But didn't your parents move out like five years ago?"

Laughing, he reaches into the truck and pulls me out, onto my feet. "Yeah, they did." He shuts the door behind me, and then starts pulling me through the grass, toward the back of his old house.

"What?" I look around me, nervous that someone will see us, possibly resulting in cops. "We can't just swim in some stranger's pool, Cale. What if someone catches us?"

He stops and picks me up, wrapping my legs around his waist. As soon as his lips meet mine, all worries seem to disappear. All that exists is Cale and I. Right now I could care less about the consequences.

Walking through the grass, he somehow manages to keep his

lips on mine until we're both sinking into the deep water.

The water is cold at first, a shocker, but as soon as Cale pulls me into his arms . . . he's all that matters. My body is slightly shivering as he swims us toward the side. It reminds me of the last time we were here: the night that I left.

"Remember this?" Cale questions as he holds me up against the side of the pool.

Biting my bottom lip, I nod my head.

"Good . . ." He slides his hand behind my neck and hovers his lips above mine. They're so close that I can almost taste him. "I'm about to do to you what I wanted to do six years ago."

His lips slam against mine, stealing my breath away. I can barely breathe at the moment as I'm taken back to six years ago. I almost feel as if I'm getting the one moment that we missed out on, the moment that I could only dream about *after* I was gone.

"Are you on the pill, Rile?" His eyes meet mine as he pushes my hair out of my face. "Are you?"

I nod my head and rub my thumb over his sexy bottom lip. All I want to do is suck it into my mouth, so I do. I suck it so hard that he growls.

He leans in and kisses me again, hard and firm as he finds my aching pussy with his free hand. I moan against his lips as two of his fingers enter me. They feel so big, but I relax for him and let him loosen me up.

"So good, Rile." He pulls his fingers out and slides my shorts over to the side. I can feel him messing around between our legs, probably pulling himself free from his black pants. He's not wearing any boxers. That was noticeable as soon as he came out of his bedroom earlier, so it doesn't take long before I feel him poking at my entrance.

I shake in Cale's hold, as he looks me in the eyes. I'm so overwhelmed with emotions that I can't even manage to speak. This man has been my best friend for ten years, and I have spent most of those years dreaming of this very moment.

"I've been waiting so long to be inside you, Rile. Are you sure you want this?" He rubs his thumb over my bottom lip as I nod my head. "Say it for me. Tell me that you want me inside you. I want to hear it from your lips. I've waited too long not to."

I lean my head back and moan as I feel the tip of his dick push against my opening. There's no doubt in my mind that I want this. Not having him inside me right now is torture. "I want it, Cale. I've always expected you to be my first." I lean in and whisper against his mouth, "Make love to me."

With those words, he slowly enters me, inch by inch, him holding me so tightly that I can barely breathe.

"Oh fuck," Cale whispers. "You're so tight, Rile. So fucking tight." He slowly pushes all the way in and stills, practically holding me against the wall with his dick. He's breathing so hard right now, that I can feel his chest hammering against mine.

It hurts, but feels so good to have Cale inside of me that I don't want him to stop. He can't. I dig my nails into his arms, letting him know that I need a minute. "It's so big, Cale." I let out a calming breath. "I need a second. Don't move."

Being sure not to hurt me, he reaches back and tugs his shirt off and over his head, before tossing it into the grass. He grips the edge of the pool with one hand and my waist with the other. "Can I move now?"

I wrap both of my arms around his neck and squeeze, preparing myself for him to move. "Yeah," I whisper. "I think I'm okay now."

Pressing his lips against mine, he slowly pulls out and pushes back in, both of us moaning into each other's mouths.

He does this a few more times, as gentle as he can, before his movements pick up, becoming more steady, until he's consistently

thrusting inside of me, making me feel so damn good that it's surreal. Having Cale inside of me is so overwhelming that I can barely
breathe from the emotions that are taking over me.

Gripping my thigh, he raises it and pushes in hard and deep,
before stopping and grinding his hips. He's so deep that I feel as if
he's about to rip me apart.

"Cale . . ." I dig my nails into his shoulder as he pulls out and
shoves himself in deep again, stopping to kiss me on the lips.

"I want to fuck you so much harder, but I'm holding back,
Rile." He lifts me up with his thrust. "Can you handle it harder?"

Hearing him ask me if I can handle it harder sets me off, and
suddenly all I can think about is him fucking me so hard that I'm
screaming his name. I want him so bad right now. So. Bad.

"Yeah," I say softly. "I can handle it."

"Alright, Rile." He wraps his hands into my hair and tugs.
"Don't be afraid to scream. I don't give a shit who hears us. This is
our moment . . . just the two of us."

I nod my head and almost feel myself come undone when he
digs his teeth into his bottom lip and begins taking me hard and
deep.

All I can hear are the sounds of the water slapping between
our bodies and our heavy moans. Cale works fast, slowing down
once in a while to kiss me and make me feel special . . . and it does.
It's as if he knows exactly what he's doing and he's an expert at
pleasuring women. He's almost too good to be true, and now the
thought of him being inside another woman kills me.

My thoughts cause me to dig my nails into his back roughly,
instigating his movements to pick up and become harder.

"This cock is yours, Rile. No one else has had it. Never fucking
forget that." He pushes into me and stops. He's breathing heavily,
his strong chest moving up and down. "I want to come inside of
you, baby."

"Yes . . . yes." I pull him closer to me and kiss his chest. "I want you to."

Gripping my thigh, he pushes in even deeper and rolls his hips. He does this a few more times until I'm practically screaming and shaking in his arms, about to come.

"Yeah, Rile." He pulls out before pushing in deep. "Come for me, baby. I want to feel you squeeze me."

Leaning my head into his neck, I dig my nails into his back as I feel my orgasm taking over. In that moment, Cale thrusts into me a few more times before I feel the pulsations of him filling me with his own orgasm.

Knowing that no other woman has experienced this with Cale has me on some kind of high. He's inside of *me* right now, holding *me* and kissing *me*. A part of me is selfish and wants to keep Cale to myself. I don't want any other woman to experience this side of Cale.

We're both wet and completely satisfied, holding each other tight . . . in someone else's pool.

I would've never thought of my first time being like this, but it was perfect. This pool is where Cale and I spent most of our time in the summer. This pool is where I imagined giving myself to him numerous times. This pool is the last memory I had of him over the last six years.

Now this pool is where we've given ourselves to each other. It's our pool. Our memory to keep and I'll *never* forget his moment. *Ever.*

I feel Cale smile against my neck, before he kisses it and pulls out of me. "Holy shit." Cupping my face, he kisses me long and hard before resting his forehead to mine. "I want to take you again, right here, right now. Is that bad?"

I let out a small laugh and smile. "No," I say breathless. "It's definitely not bad."

He releases my face and pulls his pants back up. "I have a feeling we should get out of here. You were kind of loud." He smiles and I slap his chest.

"Oh . . . just me?"

He laughs and hops out of the pool, pulling me out behind him. He quickly grabs for his shirt and picks me up, throwing me over his shoulder.

He carries me through the grass and over to his truck, the two of us soaking wet and laughing. Setting me down against his truck, he kisses me one last time before opening the door for me, and giving me a boost inside.

When we arrive back at his house, he lets us both in and immediately undresses me as soon as he closes the door behind us, dropping our soaked clothes to the floor.

After we're both completely naked and standing here, he picks me up, wrapping my legs around his waist before carrying me to his bed.

He crawls in behind me and snuggles up against me, covering us up. He notices me shivering, so he pulls me closer to warm me up, just as he always has. "I got you, Rile. I'll always have you."

I smile to myself and grip his arms, feeling completely satisfied and alive, knowing that he does. *He's always had me . . .*

CHAPTER TEN
Cale

I'VE BEEN LAYING HERE FOR the last three hours thinking about tonight. Being inside of Riley was the best feeling in the damn world, and I know without a doubt that no other woman would have been able to make me feel that way. I've always known that and that's why I waited for her.

Fuck having meaningless sex just to experience a bunch of women and get off. None of that matters and I know damn well that it could never feel as good as having sex with someone you have a personal connection with. When you have that, the pleasure is intensified. You feel *everything*.

Watching Riley sleeping in my arms makes me want to bury myself between her thighs and really take her. She's seen my sweet side. I just hope she can handle my dirty side too, because she's about to experience it real soon. I'll let her sleep it off for tonight, because I'm not going to be selfish with her. Riley doesn't deserve that shit.

Pulling Riley as close as I can, I bury my face into the back of her neck and gently kiss her, wanting to show how deeply I care about her.

"Goodnight, Rile," I whisper.

The real pleasure is about to start . . .

SLADE, HEMY AND STONE ARE sitting around like idiots, looking at me as if I've grown a second dick. If it doesn't stop, then I'm going to nut punch the closest one.

"What are you idiots looking at?" I shove a fry in my mouth, eyebrow raised, as I look around the table.

Slade stands up and walks over, sandwich and all, stopping in front of me. "Stand up."

I stand up.

He smirks. "I want to shake your dick and congratulate it on finally becoming a man."

I shove him backward, making him bump into Hemy. "Fuck you." I reach down and adjust my hard dick. Thoughts of Riley naked have been on my mind all morning, leaving me hard, and there's definitely no hiding it. "Talk all you want, assholes."

Stone gets up and starts fucking the edge of the table like an idiot. "Is this how you did it?" He slows down and acts as if he's about to blow his load.

"How the fuck do you idiots even know my business?"

Hemy nods to Slade. "This asshole told me in a text. Ask him."

Slade shrugs his shoulder while biting into his steak sandwich.

"Aspen, man. Your girl was on the phone with her for a good hour, talking about how *sweet* and *passionate* it was."

The guys start laughing as if it bothers me. Fuck them. I can't help it that I'm good at making love. "Laugh all you want, because I'm going to make that girl feel so fucking good that all of your women will be complaining to each other and talking shit about how all you guys care about are your own dicks. My woman will be completely satisfied. So fuck you."

"Your woman?" Slade asks with a sly grin. "It's like that already?"

"What . . . are you fucking surprised?" I watch as he walks around the table and takes a seat again. "I wouldn't have waited all this time for a woman if she wasn't worth it, man. Riley is more than worth it, and when she's ready . . . yeah . . . she will be *my* woman."

Stone squeezes my shoulder. "I feel ya though, guy. Sage is the one for me. Being inside her–."

"Fuck you," Hemy shouts. "Say another fucking word and see if I don't shove your dick up your ass. That's my sister, fucker."

"Yeah, I am your sister's fucker," Stone says, egging Hemy on. This dick still has some shit to learn, because that's the last thing you want to do.

Cracking his neck, Hemy stands from his chair and starts walking around me to get to Stone, but I put out my arm stopping him. "Dude, chill. All you fuckers chill and eat your damn food. Can't go anywhere with you dicks anymore."

I feel Hemy's chest flex under my arm, so I pull it away and say fuck it. I'm hungry. These two can kill each other all they want.

Stone stands up and smiles as Hemy approaches him, trying to prove he's badass. "Don't hate me, because I might be your brother-in-law someday. It'll be all good. I promise."

"Hey!" We all look away from the table when Sage comes

storming in with Onyx beside her. "Sit down, Hemy! Don't you even think about it."

Hemy gets *the look* from Onyx, so like a good boy he backs off. I don't blame him. Not only does he have a spitfire for a sister, but also his woman is just as wild as her. I don't know how he handles it.

Next thing I know Hemy has his mouth pressed against Onyx's and his hands are groping all of the inappropriate places. I'm pretty sure that's my cue to leave.

Standing up, I pop one last fry into my mouth before tossing some cash on the table. "I'm out. I've gotta go keep my eye on Kash and make sure he can handle his first night on the floor." Walking over, I place a kiss on the side of Onyx and Sage's cheeks, before turning back to the guys. "This kid better not make me work tonight."

I get a, "Get the hell out of here," from Hemy and an "Alright, go fuck off," from Slade, before Stone just waves and grabs his woman.

"What a great group of friends," I mutter to myself. Thank God Riley is back. I don't know how much longer I can handle these assholes.

I'VE BEEN HERE KEEPING MY eye on Kash for the last two hours, and so far I haven't had to save him. I got to give the kid some credit. The women seem to be enjoying themselves.

I have a feeling that he's been watching me a lot, because right now he's got some girl on her knees and he's grinding his dick in her face. The women always seem to love that.

Pulling out my phone, I send Riley a text, hoping that she's not busy. I've been thinking about her all damn day, reminding myself of the moment we shared in the pool. The best damn moment of my life.

Me: How are you doing? Are you at home?

I get a response almost immediately.

Riley: I'm good. I'm not home at the moment.

I stare down at my phone, my stomach sinking from her stiff text. We haven't spoken all day, and I have no idea how she's feeling about last night.

Me: Can I pick you up in an hour?

Riley: No

"Shit." Dropping my phone down onto the couch next to me, I run my hands through my hair. My jaw stiffens as I stand up and get ready to just leave and go find her.

"Because I'm already here."

I turn beside me to see Riley standing there, looking drop dead gorgeous in a little red dress. Her hair is curled and pulled over to her right shoulder, and her lips are slightly tinted pink.

"Fuck me, Rile." I grab her hand and slowly spin her around. "Are you trying to make me take you right here?"

Smiling, she wraps her arms around my neck and steps into my body. "What if I am?"

I slide my hands down her back and stop on her ass, cupping it. "Then you better be ready, because I don't think I can wait another second." I bite her neck, before pulling away. "Especially after seeing you in this dress."

Leaning her head back she laughs. "When did my Cale become so dirty?" Stepping up on her tippy toes, she sucks my bottom lip into her mouth, before releasing it and sliding her hands up the front of my shirt. "I definitely like it. A lot."

"You haven't even begun to see how dirty I can get, but you're definitely pushing me right now." Grabbing her legs, I wrap them around my waist and carry her through the darkened room and to the back corner.

Everyone is too busy paying attention to the new dick that's swinging around on stage than to even notice us. Slamming her up against the wall, I slide her dress up her body. "See the things you make me want to do?" I grind my hips into her and wrap my hand in her hair. "Are you ready for this, Rile?"

She doesn't say anything for a few seconds. She just plays with the ends of my hair and looks me in the eyes. "I've never been more ready for anything, Cale. Trust me."

"Neither have I." Reaching down between us, I work on getting my cock out, while pressing my lips to her neck.

"Hurry, Cale." She tugs on my hair. "I've been thinking about you inside me all day. I need this right now."

Hearing those words set me off. Dropping her feet to the ground, I bend down and yank her panties down her legs, before shoving them in my pocket.

Then, I pick her up and wrap her legs back around my waist, before sliding inside of her. "Oh fuck." We both moan out at the same time.

She's so wet and ready for me that it's hard to not bust my load just from the thought alone. Riley Raines . . . the woman I have wanted for most of my damn life.

I slowly slide in and out, stretching her to accommodate my size, before thrusting into her deep and hard. She lets out a small scream, but muffles it against my chest.

"It's okay, baby." I pull out and thrust into her again, grinding my hips into her as deep as I can. "Let it out. I don't give a shit who hears."

Moaning, she presses her lips to mine as I push into her again.

I push into her harder and harder each time, slamming her against the wall with my thrusts.

"Shit, Cale . . ." She digs her nails into the fabric of my shirt and buries her face into my neck. "Oh my God. Yes . . . faster."

Speeding up, I take her as hard and fast as I can, feeling her pussy squeeze around me, bringing me to my own release.

My cock pulses inside of her, filling her with my cum. Biting her bottom lip, I hold her up with my hips and wrap both of my hands into the back of her hair. "Shit, Riley." Both of our bodies are covered in sweat. This place has never made me sweat so fucking much. "You can't dress like that anymore around me. I can't fucking handle it."

She smiles against my lips. "I was hoping for that."

"Cale, dude, what the fuck are you doing back there? Kash needs you for a minute," Lynx yells from across the room. Lazy motherfucker.

Riley's eyes widen and she throws her hand over her face. "Oh. My. God." She starts struggling to get back to her feet. "I almost forgot where we were."

I kiss her one more time and smile against her lips as I readjust myself. "Dude, I'm coming."

She slaps my chest and playfully covers my mouth. "Shh . . . don't say that."

"Well hurry the fuck up."

I press my forehead to hers. "Wait for me." I pull her bottom lip into my mouth. "Let me go help this dick and then we'll leave. Yeah?"

She nods her head and works on pulling her dress down as far as she can. "I'll wait in your truck so I can be panty-less alone."

I reach into my pocket and pull my keys out, handing them to her. "You won't be panty-less and alone for long. Trust me."

Raising a brow, I back up and start walking, before turning

around to see what the hell Kash needs me for.

The faster I do the faster I can make it back out to my woman . . .

CHAPTER ELEVEN

Riley

HOLY SHIT! I FALL AGAINST Cale's truck and run my hands over my face. "What the hell was that?" I never act this way. Ever. Cale just does something to me that I can't explain. It's insane and so is what we just did. "Wow . . ."

Anyone could've walked back there and caught us. Then what? He could've lost his job. I would've felt like a complete idiot. I definitely need to get a grip before it's too late.

Unlocking his truck door, I jump inside and rest my head against the back of the seat. My pussy is still pulsing from my orgasm and I can't help but to smile. I shouldn't be smiling after what we just did, but I can't help it. Nothing has ever felt so good in my life. Nothing.

Tyler was never able to give me orgasms. He tried multiple

times and I always had to fake them just to make him happy. It always left me feeling like shit and a complete failure afterwards. Not with Cale. With Cale I almost feel like an idiot for having one too soon. Is that a thing? Shit . . . I don't know.

A few minutes later, the driver's side door opens and Cale jumps inside with a look of aggravation. "That dick head."

I look at him and laugh. "What?"

A small smile crosses Cale's face. "He wanted me to teach him a new dance move. He actually stopped in the middle of his performance so he could ask me to teach him a new move." He shakes his head while starting the engine. "That kid needs some serious work if he wants to make it here."

I can't help but to laugh. His face always cracks me up when he's aggravated. I've always found it hard to take him seriously, probably because his aggravation has never been aimed at me. Thank God.

"He seemed to be doing good to me."

Cale sits up straight and grabs my thigh. "Oh yeah." He runs his hand higher up my thigh and stops right below my pussy. "So that's why you were so wet earlier?"

I squirm as he starts tickling me. "No . . ." I say in between laughs. "No . . . stop it!" I slap at his hand until he finally stops and smiles at me.

"I didn't think so," he says confidently. "I was pretty sure it was all me." He winks and I shake my head at him.

"Confident Cale." I reach over and grab his dick, almost making him swerve off the side of the road. "You do something to me."

"Shit, Rile." He grips the steering wheel, fighting hard to keep his eyes on the road. "What did I turn you into?"

I release his dick and lean back into my seat. "A woman that likes to tease you and see you squirm. You've been doing it to me for years and just didn't know it. You and your little touches. You didn't think that I noticed how close you were to my ass and pussy sometimes? I noticed. Very much so."

Cale smirks. "Well you never said anything." He glances over at me. "I wanted to touch you so bad. That was me getting as close as I could with still being able to control myself. It was harder than you think. Trust me."

My stomach does some kind of little happy dance as I remember the old times with Cale. It's crazy how you can want something so bad and then it happens years down the road. It almost feels as if no time has passed at all.

With Cale . . . I feel like we're still teenagers. He's always made me feel younger than I am. Knowing that I can finally touch him has me all worked up and extremely aroused . . . again.

Reaching for his jeans, I slowly undo them. I tilt my head and look up at Cale to see him watching the road with a smirk. "What are you doing?"

I bite my bottom lip as I pull his erection free, running my hand up the length. "I'm just admiring your body." I sit back in my seat and take in the image of him driving with his dick out. "I definitely like this view."

Cale glances over at me. "Oh yeah?" Keeping his eyes on the road, he grips the steering wheel with one hand and his dick with the other. "What about this?"

A small gasp escapes my lips as he slowly begins to stroke himself. "Oh. My. God." I fan myself off and crack the window some more. "Yes. The view is definitely getting better. Keep going." I whisper the last part, completely lost in him.

Leaning his head back, he quickens his strokes, letting out a small growl. "Do you have any idea how many times I have done this to thoughts of you, Rile?"

My heart jumps out of my chest from his words. "No, I don't."

Feeling completely turned on, I spread my legs a little and moan. "Tell me."

He notices me beginning to squirm in my seat so he lets out a small, amused laugh. "Too many fucking times." He slows his strokes for a second, before he releases his dick and grips my thigh, yanking me toward him. "Almost every damn time you left my house." He pushes my dress up, baring my lower half, and runs his fingers through my slick folds. "Did you ever pleasure yourself while thinking of me . . . huh, Rile?"

I press my head back into the seat and grip it as his finger slips inside of me, slowly pumping in and out.

"Did you ever imagine me fucking you in your bed all those times that I slept in your room?" He shoves his finger in deep and stops. "Did you ever imagine me deep inside you, taking you and making you scream all night? Did you," he whispers.

I jump and grip the seat tighter when he finds my spot. "Yes!" I scream. "Yes . . . so many times. I could never sleep," I admit. "I kept imagining how it would feel."

"Stroke me, Rile." We pull up at a stoplight, but Cale is looking at me as if he could care less what others may see. "Touch me like you always wanted to. I. Want. You. To."

I moan out as his fingers pump into me, fast and hard. "Cale . . . oh my God. That feels . . . so . . . good."

"Touch me," he growls out.

Looking around me, I realize just how dark it is and how high up we are in his truck. It gives me the courage that I need. Reaching over, I take him in my hand, stroking him, and imagining that we're the old Cale and Riley. I'm finally able to touch this man and it feels so damn good.

Leaning toward him, I take him in both hands and pump as fast as I can. Cale has me on the verge of orgasm. "Keep going," I moan. "Faster, Cale."

Turning the corner, Cale slams the truck into park and leans into me, fucking me with his fingers as fast and hard as he can, until I'm squirming in my seat, my arousal covering his fingers.

Not even a few seconds later Cale falls apart beneath my touch, releasing himself onto his shirt. "Fuck me, Rile," he says through heavy breaths. "You've got me feeling like a fucking horny teenage boy again."

I burst into laughter in between heavy breaths. "I hope that's not a bad thing."

Shaking his head, he pulls his shirt off and balls it up, before tossing it in the backseat. "Nothing you do to me can ever be bad, babe."

I feel my heart soar as he flashes me his sweet, dimpled smile. He's the most beautiful man in the world and here I am in his truck. I'm finally able to do the things to him that I've wanted to do for most of my life, and I don't plan on stopping anytime soon.

Shifting the truck into drive, Cale reaches over, intertwining his fingers in mine. "I'm happy that you're back."

"Me too," I say with a smile. "Oh . . . I almost forgot." I shift in my seat so that I can face him. "My parents are having a cookout tomorrow and they want you to come. They've been asking about you. Aspen and Slade will be there too. Are you up for it?"

He smiles while pulling into his driveway. "You know I'm in. I haven't had the chance to bug your parents in a long time; too damn long."

I roll my eyes at just how much my mom loved Cale. I swear she had her own little crush on him. "I'm sure my mom won't mind one bit."

He points to his tight chest and abs. "I'm not sure she can handle all this new goodness that I have. Your father might have to keep her contained."

"Someone's a little cocky." I lean in and motion for him to

meet me half way. "Come here."

Smiling, he leans in and reaches his hand behind my neck. Just as he's about to kiss me, I grab his nipple and twist it. "Mmm . . ." he moans. "Are you trying to work me up again?"

Sucking his bottom lip into my mouth, I slap his chest, before letting my hand trail down it. "A little sleep would be nice . . . so . . ." I bite his bottom lip and pull away. "I think I'll go to bed instead."

He gives me a long, serious look, before jumping out of the truck and running over to my side.

Before I can lock it he pulls my door open and reaches inside, tossing me over his shoulder. "You should know better than to tease me, Rile. Haven't you learned anything about me over the years?"

He shuts the door and slaps my ass, before laying me down into the grass and crawling above me.

Looking into his eyes, I tangle my fingers into the back of his hair. "I don't want this to end, Cale."

He swallows and reaches down to brush my hair out of my face. "No one says it has to."

"But . . ." I stop to collect myself. "What if it ruins us? I can't lose you, Cale."

Pushing my thigh up, he presses himself into me and kisses me long and gentle, before pulling away. "I will never let that happen. I'll die before it does."

Rolling over, he pulls me into his chest and we both lay here, looking up at the night sky just like we used to do some nights after a late night swim at his house. It's so calm and relaxing that I almost feel myself falling asleep, but I keep catching myself, not wanting to lose one minute that I have with Cale.

"It's okay if you fall asleep," Cale whispers. "I'll carry you inside."

I shake my head and wrap my fingers in his. "I'm fine . . ." I yawn. "I'm not going to fall asleep."

"That's what you always say," he says softly.

Next thing I know, I'm falling asleep in his arms . . . just like I always did.

Cale has always been my comfort and safety . . .

CHAPTER TWELVE
Riley

"HURRY UP," I MUTTER UNDER my breath while looking up at the clock on the wall. "Ten more minutes. Ten more minutes."

Mr. Peterson attempts to sit up, but I politely push him back down onto the table. "No more flipping over please, Mr. Peterson. We only have ten minutes left of your session."

Relaxing once again, the elderly man places his hands behind his head and lets out a long sigh. "An hour isn't enough time. What you need to do is teach my damn wife how to do that stuff you do with your hands. That's what I need."

I let out an amused laugh while firmly massaging his left calf, being sure to work out the knot as best as I can. "I'll see what I can do, Mr. Peterson." I smile down at him as he struggles to look up at me. "But then you may not need me if I do that."

"Nonsense," he growls. "You're not getting rid of me that easily. I haven't felt this young in ages. My wife . . ."

Mr. Peterson continues to babble on about his wife, but all I can focus on is the fact that Cale will be here any minute to pick me up. It's only been eight hours, but it feels a hell of a lot longer since I've felt his lips on mine, and it's driving me insane.

As much as I would like some alone time with him before the cookout, we're heading straight over to my parents' to please my mom. She's been asking when he's going to come visit her ever since I walked in the damn house a little over a week ago.

My parents haven't seen Cale in over a year, and I know without a doubt that my mom is going to freak out as soon as he walks in the door. I wouldn't be surprised if she attacks him with kisses.

She's always loved Cale, and when I had to leave to help care for my grandmother it seemed as if it hurt her that I had to leave him behind almost as much as it did me. I cried myself to sleep that night, and my mother watched me with wet eyes, telling me that Cale would still be here when I returned. She was right, even though I didn't believe it at the time.

I shake out of my thoughts in just enough time to see that our time is up. *Thank God!*

"Alright, Mr. Peterson. We're out of time."

Grunting, the old man sits up and stretches as I turn on the sink to wash my hands. "Much better," he says in a raspy voice. "My wife might just be a lucky lady tonight, thanks to you."

"Glad I could help," I say, while trying not to let *that* image ruin my day. "So I'll see you the same time next week?"

I get another grunt and a, "Yes," as he stands up, letting his towel fall to the floor. I'm greeted with the sight of his baggy tightie whities, making me instantly turn my head and cover my face. That's definitely not a friendly sight.

"Whoa," I say, taking this as my cue to escape. "I'll just head out and let you finish up. Tell your wife hello for me."

I hear a mutter. "Yeah. Yeah." I quickly dodge out into the hall and shut the door behind me.

"Oh, sweet freedom, how I love you," I say to myself while making my way past Hailey's door and down the short hallway.

As I get closer to the front desk I stop and instantly smile when I notice Cale is waiting inside for me. My heart goes crazy just from the sight of him, and I get this sudden urge to run and jump into his arms. Of course I'm not going to though.

I get ready to start walking, but stop and swallow back my jealousy when I notice Kylie's hand slide across the desk and reach for Cale's arm. From afar it looks as if she's rubbing her fingertips over his muscle.

Cale looks down at her hand on his arm, but doesn't say anything as she leans over the desk in an attempt to get his attention.

Seeing another woman want him in that way feels like getting punched in the gut. Even though he doesn't seem interested, it still gives me a sick feeling in my stomach.

If it's like this here—outside of the strip club—I don't even want to begin to think about what goes on at the club when he's half naked and shaking his goods for drunken, horny women. I've gotten a small glimpse, but I'm sure that's nothing compared to what could happen. I'm not sure what to do with that.

Sucking it up, I walk up beside Cale and get ready to greet him. Without hesitation Cale turns to me and wraps both of his hands into the back of my hair, slamming his lips to mine and pulling me as close as he possibly can.

Talk about taking someone's breath away. His lips assault mine, repeatedly sucking and tasting me in a way that almost feels desperate. He's devouring me. Pulling away, he runs his tongue over his bottom lip before biting it. "Shit, I've been waiting all day to do that."

Kylie looks us both over before rolling her eyes and sitting down in her chair, clearly aware that Cale is not interested now. "Looks like I did someone a favor last week," she says stiffly. "Better you than Hailey, I suppose."

Her words somehow piss me off. He's been my Cale for far longer than this girl even knew he existed. Leaning over the desk, I get ready to say something, but Cale pulls me to him, cutting me off.

"Nah, actually you did me a favor." He slaps the desk, before leaning in and sucking my bottom lip into his mouth. "And it's always been her. Simple as that." With a lift of his eyebrow, he grabs my hand to get me walking. "Ready?"

Trying to fight my grin, I nod my head and wrap my arm around his waist as he starts walking toward the door. "So damn ready."

Just as we're about to walk out the door Hailey appears next to the desk, glaring at Kylie and complaining about something. I hear Cale's name, but choose to ignore it. I don't need anything dragging me down at the moment; especially two girls that I can barely even stand to be around.

After hopping into Cale's truck I reach for my seatbelt and get ready to pull it down, but look up surprised when Cale reaches over me and reclines my seat back as far as it will go.

"What are you doing?" I laugh as he crawls over the seat until he's hovering over me, gripping the seat with his hand to keep balance. I can't help but to notice the way his muscles flex as he stares down at me.

"Something I've always wanted to do in the past." He positions himself between my legs and presses his lips to mine . . . hard; so hard that it almost hurts. "I've always wanted to take you in my truck," he says against my lips.

"Cale . . ." I run my hands up his strong back as he sucks my bottom lip into his mouth, teasing me and turning me on completely. "There's people everywhere," I say with a small moan.

He grips my thigh and smiles against my mouth. "Then let them watch." His lips slam against mine, causing me to moan out as my eyes close. "Fuck, I can't hold back with you, Rile. I've kept my hands off of you for long enough; too damn long. Touching you everywhere is the only thing I can think about anymore."

I start reaching for the back of his shirt, getting completely lost in the moment, but jump when I look beside us to see Slade leaning against the truck, casually just chilling and enjoying the show. "Holy shit," I laugh. "Seriously?"

"What?" Cale stops kissing my neck and looks up. "Fucking idiot," he growls as soon as he sees Slade. With his jaw steeled, he rolls down the window, glaring at Slade the whole time, as if he wants to kill him. "What dude? What are you doing here?"

Slade lifts an eyebrow and uncrosses his arms. "Just enjoying the show, man. Don't stop on my account. I'm curious to see just what I need to teach you. You gotta catch up with the big boys now."

Cale's grip on the seat tightens. "You're an idiot," he growls. "What do you really want?"

Slade shrugs his shoulders and grips the window. "Aspen told me you were stopping to pick up Riley on the way over. I was driving by and noticed your damn truck. The windows looked a little frosted and shit, so I came to hurry your ass up."

Grinning, Cale gives Slade the middle finger while rolling up the window. He leans in and kisses me quickly, breathing heavily against my lips. "Dammit! Let's go before this dude busts a nut outside of my truck. Anything can work him up."

I laugh and roll the window back down as Cale crawls over to his seat and adjusts the crotch of his jeans. "Hey, Slade," I say with a small laugh.

Slade gives me a slick head nod and smiles. "Looking good, Riley." Leaning in the truck, Slade kisses the side of my head while smiling over at Cale. "Both of you hurry your asses up."

Cale starts the engine, gripping the wheel while glaring at Slade. "Don't push it, fucker. We're on the way."

Slade winks and turns on his heels, walking over to his nice new car.

"Remind me to kill Slade later," Cale says while pulling out of the lot.

I can't help but to laugh at the boys for acting so silly. I definitely won't mind this kind of entertainment to get us through dinner. "Sure thing," I say with a smile.

I try to stay cool on the way to my parents' house, but the way Cale is rubbing my leg has me squirming in my seat and gripping the seat. The satisfied smirk on his face only shows me that he's doing this on purpose and enjoying this much more than I am.

"You're enjoying this, aren't you?" I grab his hand and place it on his own lap as he pulls up in front of the house. "It's already going to be hard enough to act normal around my parents, pretending as if nothing is going on. Please don't make it harder." I suck in a breath and attempt to compose myself.

He unbuckles his seatbelt and reaches over to undo mine, hovering his lips above mine. "Who said anything about acting normal?" He brushes his lips over mine, causing my heart to jump out of my chest. "You can touch me, kiss me . . . or fuck me for all I care. There's plenty of rooms to choose from." He whispers the last part before smiling and jumping out of the truck, leaving me wanting him even more.

"Damn you, Cale. You're still a pain in my ass," I say to myself while gripping the door handle and jumping out to catch up with him. "Well, it's definitely going to be easy to talk to my parents now," I tease. "So thanks for that image."

Without bothering to knock Cale opens the screen door and lets himself in, holding the door open for me. My mom is standing in the kitchen mixing some kind of dessert when we walk in. It smells like chocolate. Cale loves chocolate.

"Oooh. Oooh." My mom cleans the chocolate off of her hands hurriedly, and smiles as Cale walks over to her with open arms.

"Did you miss me?" Cale asks while squeezing my mom in a bear hug and shaking her back and forth.

She pulls away and grabs his face, looking him over. Her smile is so big that it looks like her face is going to split open. "You know I did. Look at you," she squeals. "Oh my goodness." She backs away and looks him up and down, taking in his large build. "You have gotten so much bigger since the last time I saw you, Cale, and more handsome too. Oh my. Come here."

She grabs my arm and pulls me next to her, while holding onto Cale's waist. "It's so good seeing you two hanging out again. It makes me feel young again. Isn't this something?"

Rolling my eyes, I kiss my mom on the cheek and laugh. "Yeah . . . yeah. Where's Aspen and Slade?"

My mom releases her grip on both of us and points to the back door. "They're outside with your father."

"It smells so good in here," Cale says before kissing my mom on the cheek. "I've missed your cooking. Don't be surprised if I eat all that dessert you're working on."

My mom blushes while going back to stirring her dessert. "Yeah, well what can I say? That's why I made so much. I learned my lesson eight years ago." She turns to me and winks. "The food is on the grill and should be ready to eat soon. Just hang out for a bit and keep your father company. We all know he doesn't get it very often."

"Alright, Mom. Let me know if you need help."

My mom shakes her head and motions toward the door. "Nope. Just go and enjoy yourselves. Scoot."

Cale places his hand on my lower back and guides me toward the sliding door. "Your ass looks fucking delicious in those shorts," he whispers, before sliding the door open and pulling me outside. "Can't wait to taste you later."

I break into an instant sweat from his words mixed with the heat. As soon as my dad sees us, he waves us over, holding up a beer for Cale. I just need to get away from this man before I melt into a damn puddle at his feet. He's the perfect distraction.

Pulling away from Cale, I rush over to Aspen and sit down in the chair next to her while Cale goes to hang out with my dad and Slade.

My dad stands up as soon as Cale approaches. Handing him a beer, he grips Cale's shoulder and greets him with a smile. I'm actually surprised to see how happy my dad looks to see him. I knew he always liked Cale. He just didn't want to admit how much.

I turn to Aspen. "This is torture," I say in a hurry.

Aspen takes a sip of her pop and looks over at the picnic table where the guys are hanging out. "Tell me about it. I'm bored already. Mom talked our leg off when we walked in the door and dad keeps talking about his work."

I shake my head and look in Cale's direction to see his tight muscles flexing as he grips his beer and laughs along with the guys. "No, I meant Cale. All I want to do is take him up to my old room and jump on him. It's like I can't even be in the same room without touching him. You know?"

Aspen smiles at my comment and lifts a brow as she watches the guys. "I definitely know, sister. Welcome to my world."

We sit here, just watching the boys for a few minutes, before Aspen speaks up, breaking the silence. "So what *are* you and Cale anyway? Are you doing this whole 'friends with benefits' thing? Or what? That could definitely get messy, so be careful."

I let out a frustrated breath and grab for Aspen's pop, taking a quick drink. My mouth suddenly feels extremely dry. "I don't know, Aspen. I care about Cale a lot, you know that, but I really don't know what he wants out of this. I'm worried if I ask him that I'll mess up what we have. I can't have that. We've been friends for too long, so I'm just sitting back and enjoying the ride."

"Literally," Aspen replies.

"Shut up," I say, while punching her in the thigh. "Can you talk any louder?"

"Ouch, asshole." Aspen smiles, taking another sip of her pop. "Nothing to be ashamed of."

We both look up when my father calls us. "Girls. Get over here and eat."

We both grumble to each other before getting up and joining everyone else at the table. I take a spot next to Cale as Aspen takes her place beside Slade.

Dinner passes quickly as my parents talk to Cale about what he's been up to over the years. Leaving out the male stripper part, Cale tells them stories from his bartending experience. Now I'm just hoping they don't look up *Walk Of Shame* and decide to drop in for a quick drink sometime. They are supportive like that and it might be a little awkward to explain.

After all conversation with my parents is done and everything is cleaned up, we decide to head inside for a few drinks and a game of darts. The boys talked shit to each other the whole time during dinner, betting money on who would win. Everyone was pretty surprised when my mother jumped up and threw in some money on Cale. That definitely gave him an extra confidence boost, not that he needed one.

There's fifty bucks on the line, so the boys are getting into a serious mode, trying to intimidate each other while us girls sit back and watch.

My parents are sitting in the next room watching a movie, just enjoying the fact that we're all still here. It's not very often that they have both of their girls home, and they're definitely working to keep us here as long as they can.

I have to admit that we're all having fun, a lot more fun than I expected. It sort of feels like old times, back when Aspen and I lived at home. I like this carefree feeling right now, and I'm not ready for it to end anytime soon.

"You lucky, shit," Slade spits out while yanking the darts out of the board. "That was luck not skill, so stop that smiling bullshit."

Cale tilts back his bottle of beer and grins even bigger, clearly enjoying this. "Oh trust me, that was all skill, bro." He holds up his free hand, showing it off. "My hand is talented as fuck, Slade."

"Nah . . ." Slade throws his first dart, hitting the bull's eye. "That's skill. Might as well give me your dick shaking tips now."

Ignoring Slade, Cale walks over to me and wraps his hands into the back of my hair, pulling me in for a kiss. His lips are soft and sweet, tasting of the chocolate dessert that he recently ate. "I can't wait to get you alone. As soon as I win this asshole's money, I'm taking you to the nearest bed and letting you have your way with me." He smiles against my lips when I grab his ass and squeeze.

"Oh, is that right?" I run my hands up his strong back and dig my nails into his shoulders. "So I can do anything that I want?"

He pulls my bottom lip into his mouth and nibbles it. "Anything," he breathes. "You're the only one with that power, so I would abuse it if I were you."

Cale clenches his jaw when one of Slade's darts comes flying at his head. "Seriously?"

Aspen wraps her arm around Slade's neck and pulls him down to her level so that she can kiss him and whisper something to him.

"You both want to play now, huh?" I grab one of Cale's darts and throw it at them. "I think us girls should get in on this game. Double it."

We're all standing here bickering, trying to decide on what to do when the doorbell rings.

A few minutes later, my mom walks in and takes one look at me in Cale's arms, before clearing her throat and looking around awkwardly. "Riley . . . Tyler is at the door. He said he's here to talk to you."

I just about pass out when Tyler steps into the room, looking at me as if he's waited forever to see me again.

His blonde hair is cut short and slightly messy, and he's dressed in a pair of old jeans and a white shirt. I almost forgot just how cute he is, and seeing him standing here . . . for me . . . makes my heart sink.

Holy. Fucking. Shit.

CHAPTER THIRTEEN
Cale

FUCK ME. . . . MY EYES MEET Riley's and I can see her being emotionally pulled in different directions, about to lose her composure. This is not good. Not good for me at all.

Knowing that he's here to win Riley back makes me fucking sick. Now that I know what he looks like, it's easier to picture him putting his hands all over her and I don't like it. Not one bit. In fact . . . it makes me hate him.

"Tyler . . ." Riley places her hand over her mouth in shock, looking him up and down as if she doesn't know whether to slap him or run to him. "What are you doing here?"

Tyler swallows and looks around the room. Riley is standing close enough to me that I'm sure there's reason for him to question our intentions. "I miss you." He looks at me as he says the next part. "I need to talk to you, Riley. Can we talk in private?"

Everything in me is screaming for her to say no, but I know Riley. I know her more than anything, so I already know her answer before she says it.

"Uh . . . yeah." She looks around the room and stops when her eyes land on me. "I'm sorry. I need a few minutes."

I place my hand on her hip and give it a small squeeze, before nodding my head and turning away. I can't stand to watch her walk away with him. I can't fucking do it.

"Well fuck," Slade says after they walk away. "Just keep your cool, man."

I grip the pool table until my knuckles turn white. "I'm cool, man." I feel Aspen's hand on my shoulder. "I'm good, Aspen. I'm good."

It feels like a lifetime has passed since she's been alone with him talking. I know for a fact that me being here is making it harder for her. I hate that feeling. I hate feeling like I'm the *other* guy.

After about twenty minutes, I can't take it anymore. I feel like I'm about to burst into that room and rip his fucking head off. I keep imagining different scenarios, replaying over and over in my head, and that's when I realize that I need to get out of here before I do something I'll regret later.

"I need to leave," I grind out. Pushing away from the pool table, I turn around and give Slade and Aspen one last look. "I'm about to lose it."

Slade grips my shoulder, but I shake it off and rush out of the room before he can try to stop me. Slowing down for a quick minute, I smile when I reach the living room where Riley's parents are watching a movie. "Thank you so much for dinner."

Kay stands up and kisses my cheek. "Promise me you'll come back soon." I get ready to pull away, but she squeezes my arm, stopping me. "Promise me, Cale," she says firmly. "You know Riley more than anyone. You remember that."

Nodding my head, I pull away and give my respects to her father before hurrying out the door and to my truck. As soon as I close the door behind me, I slam my fist into the dashboard until it's covered in blood. Why the hell does this feeling kill me so much? Why do I want to kill this man?

"Fuck me," I growl.

I may give her a day to get her head on straight, but there's no way in hell I'm giving up and letting him have her back. Riley is mine. She has been from the very first day we met.

It's time that I show her that . . .

Riley

WE'VE BEEN STANDING HERE FOR almost twenty minutes, yet Tyler hasn't said a word. He always does this when he's upset and trying to think of the best way to start the conversation.

"Tyler, just talk." I take a seat on the foot of my bed and look up at him. "What are you doing here? We broke up. Remember?"

He runs his hands over his face before looking at me. "I know, Riley, but damn. I've missed you so much." Looking me in the eyes, he walks over to stand in front of me and reaches out for my hands. "I've been going crazy without you. You haven't answered any of my calls and it's been killing me. Killing me, Riley."

I swallow back the guilt and pain that his words bring and try to keep in mind that *he's* the one that decided to break it off at the last minute. *He's* the one that said it would be better to just be friends.

"I'm sorry, Tyler, but I needed time. I can't allow myself to just sit around and mope over you. I have friends and family here that want to spend time with me and I needed to keep a clear head for that."

"I see that," he says stiffly. "Looks like you've been enjoying your *friend* out there quite a bit."

Looking away, I run my hands through my hair and swallow. I never meant to be intimate with someone, and especially so quickly after the breakup, but Cale is an exception. He deserves my time and attention more than anyone I know.

"Look, Tyler. Cale has been my friend for over ten years. I never meant for things to turn into something more, but . . ."

Tyler bends down and places his thumb to my lips, shutting me up. "I don't care about that. What I care about is making you mine again." He points down at the floor. "I'm here. I have enough bags packed to stay for a week. If we can make it work then I will fly back home and pack up all of my shit if I can't get you to come back home with me." He leans in to kiss my lips, but I turn my head. "Riley, I still love you. I've given you two years of my life."

His words cause my chest to ache. He's right. Two years means something. Maybe just throwing it away is a shitty thing to do. I'm so damn confused right now and all I want to do is scream.

"Do you still love me, Riley?" He grabs my chin to make me look at him when I don't respond. "Answer me, Riley. You can't tell me that you don't have any love left for me after just a short time of being apart. Tell me the truth."

I hesitate before answering him, because I don't want to give him too much hope, especially when I'm this confused. "Tyler . . ."

"Just give me a yes or no. I don't want an explanation of buts or maybes. Just a simple yes or no."

"Of course I do, but–."

"That's all I want to hear, and that should be good enough to at least try while I'm here." Standing up, he pulls me to my feet. "Tell me that I've got a chance, Riley. Please."

I feel my heart beating out of my chest as I think about Cale and what he must be thinking right now. I don't want to think about me without Cale, but Tyler flew all the way here from Mexico. That has to mean something too. I don't want to be a shitty person to the people that care about me.

I can't do this right now. I can't think straight. My breathing picks up and it's getting harder and harder to breathe. "I need time. I need to get out of here." I begin backing out of the room. "I'm sorry, Tyler."

Turning around, I rush out of the room and down the stairs, gripping the railing a little too tight. My chest feels extremely tight as I make my through the house.

My parents both look up at me as I rush to the game room. My heart stops when I poke my head inside to see only Slade and Aspen.

"He's gone," Slade says stiffly.

My throat burns when I hear those two words. "He left?" I whisper, mainly to myself. I stand there frozen for a moment, before rushing outside. Cale's truck is gone and my heart feels completely shattered.

What the hell do I do?

I want to scream, but instead I walk. I just keep walking, needing to get away from everyone and everything. This is so messed up right now and I have no idea what I'm going to do to fix this. My heart aches for Cale, but my head is telling me that I need to at least give Tyler a chance after coming all this way. I hate this so much.

In the end . . . someone always gets hurt. I just hate that I have to be the one to do it.

CHAPTER FOURTEEN

Cale

IT'S BEEN TWO DAYS SINCE I've talked to Riley and I'm on the verge of losing my shit. She called me a few times the night that I left her parents' house, but I forced myself not to answer it. I want her back, but I want to give her time to get her head on straight first.

The thought that she's possibly been spending time with Tyler has been killing me, but a real man will hurt for the woman he fucking loves.

He's had two days now to prove his fucking point. Now it's my turn, and you better believe that I'm going to give her all that I have. The thought of another man pleasing her will never cross her mind. All she will be able to see is the two of us together.

I snap out of my thoughts when Hemy comes into the room

shirtless, looking for me. "The show is about to start, man. You ready or what," he asks while throwing on a fresh shirt. "Get your shit together."

I let out a frustrated breath and slam back my beer. "Yeah, man. Let's do this shit. Where are Stone and Kash?"

"They're coming out of the other room." Hemy pulls his long hair into a man bun as *Earned It* by The Weeknd starts playing from the speaker. "Fuck yeah."

He pushes the door open and dances his way out first, before I follow behind him a few seconds later, followed by Stone, and then Kash from their rooms.

All at the same time, we find a girl in the crowd and pull her chair to the center, before straddling her chair and grinding our hips.

I made sure to pick someone that I've never met so that I won't give off the wrong idea. It just so happens to be a cute brunette that reminds me of Riley with her big, beautiful eyes.

It distracts me for a moment, but I manage to not skip a beat, moving right into the next move. Tilting her chair back until her back is almost to the floor, I walk over her until my cock is in her face, before I grind my hips as if fucking her mouth nice and slow.

I feel the girl's hands grip onto my ass and squeeze, but I don't let it distract me. I can't. I need to stay in the moment as much as I can.

Maneuvering my way off of her face, I put her chair back into sitting position and make my way up to the stage, meeting the guys in the middle.

We all drop down to the ground, gripping our jeans in the front and pulling as if undressing ourselves, while thrusting in a slow, torturous rhythm. Every girl in the room starts screaming and whistling, wishing that they could be the ones below us. The simple fact that we could have *any* girl in this room used to get me hard, but not tonight, not even a slight chub.

Instead, it gives me a sick feeling in my stomach, reminding me that the one and only girl I want might be with another man right now. The thought causes me to work my hips hard and aggressively, while biting down on my lip to ease my anger.

Keeping balance with one hand, I reach behind me, pulling the back of my jeans down until my full ass is on display. Then, I replace my other hand and grind the stage, giving all of the screaming women a full view of what my ass looks like while fucking.

I can feel the sweat drip down my body with each movement, but that only makes it seem more like fucking, giving the women the image that they come here for.

Standing up, we all reach for our shirts and slowly rip them off, before rubbing them over our cocks and throwing them out into the crowd. A bunch of hands fly up, fighting to get to them first. I almost die when I see Riley walk to the front of the crowd, holding my shirt in her hands.

Her eyes meet mine and pull me in, making it hard for me to concentrate on the rest of the dance. All I can think about is the fact that she's here . . . at *Walk Of Shame.*

Running my hands down my body, I look her in the eyes, biting my bottom lip as I shove my hand down the front of my jeans and thrust the air. Watching the way she looks at me has me running my hand over my slightly hard cock, imagining it was hers instead.

I can see the lust in her eyes, making it very clear that she's been thinking about me over the last couple of days. That pleases me. That means she most likely hasn't been sexual with that prick.

The end of the song is coming, so in rhythm we all turn away from the stage and drop our jeans, cupping our packages with both hands, before turning back around and kicking our jeans off the stage.

The women go crazy, practically fighting each other to climb onto the stage. I look out into the crowd, searching for Riley as we make our way off the stage, but she's lost in the pile of screaming bodies.

Hands grab at us, groping and slapping our asses until we dodge into the back room. I go from seeing the woman of my damn dreams to being closed off in a room with three naked assholes.

Opening my locker, I reach for a pair of fresh jeans and a shirt and quickly get dressed, while the other guys start bickering about who did the best.

"Where the hell are you rushing off to," Hemy asks, while pulling up a pair of jeans.

"Riley's here," I say stiffly. "I'm going to find her."

Lynx walks in with a handful of cash, but I brush past him, not giving a shit about getting paid. I just want to get to my girl before she leaves.

As soon as I walk back out into the club, a few girls walk over and start rubbing their hands on me, saying sexual things, but I don't listen to a thing they're saying. Instead, I push their hands away and look over their heads for Riley.

I spot Riley across the room, slamming back a shot by the bar. Setting her empty glass down, she tosses money in front of her before heading toward the door, dodging out as if she couldn't escape soon enough.

Rushing through the crowd, I run to the door and shove it open, trying to catch Riley before she can drive off. By the time I make it outside, she's already shutting the door to her car.

Running my hands through my hair, I let out a frustrated breath and walk over to knock on her window.

She looks up from the steering wheel, surprised to see me standing outside.

Looking me in the eyes, she rolls down her window and releases a breath. "Cale . . . what are you doing?"

Reaching through the window, I rub my thumb over her bottom lip. "Trying to catch you." I breathe. "Where are you going?"

She looks away for a second, before turning back to face me. "I don't know. I just . . . I just need to get away, Cale. I'm so lost right now. I can't stop thinking about you and what goes on here. It's driving me fucking crazy, but I also have Tyler trying to prove to me that two years isn't worth throwing away. I can't breathe, dammit."

I wrap both of my hands into the back of her hair and lean inside the window. "Here," I whisper. "Let me help you with that." Wetting my lips, I press them against hers, showing her just how much I have missed her.

I feel her breath escape her as she wraps one of her arms around my neck and breaks our kiss. "Cale . . ." she says while fighting to catch her breath. "Are you trying to kill me?"

Smiling, I open her car door and reach for her hand. "Come with me, Rile." She gets ready to say something, but I cut her off. "Please don't say no to me."

She looks at me for a second, before pulling her key out of the ignition and letting me help her to her feet. "You know that always works on me," she says defeated. "Not fair, jerk."

I grin, knowing that she's right. "I know. Now let's go."

About ten minutes later, we pull up in my driveway, parking in front of the garage, and she follows me outside to stand by my side of the truck. She's staring at me as if trying to figure me out.

If she wants to know what it is that I want or that I'm thinking, then I'll tell her. I'm not afraid to.

"I want to fuck you, Rile." Stepping up to her, I grip her ass in my hands and run my lips up her neck. "I want to be deep inside you right now, making you scream my name and forget about that asshole. Is that what you want to hear? I'll always tell you what's on my mind if you just ask me."

Leaning her head back, she lets out a soft moan. "I don't know if that's a good idea, Cale. I'm already confused enough as it is."

Gripping her thighs, I pick her up, wrapping her legs around my waist. "Then let me make it less confusing." I brush my lips under her ear and whisper, "Let me show you what I have to offer you. This can be yours. I can be yours. Every. Fucking. Day."

As soon as her body trembles in my arms, I know that I have her, at least for the moment, and I'm going to consume her in a way that no other man will even come close to.

Riley will see the things my body can do that no one else can . . .

CHAPTER FIFTEEN

Riley

I PROBABLY SHOULDN'T BE HERE right now, but I couldn't fight it. My chest has been aching since the moment I realized that Cale walked out of the door the other night.

I went to *Walk Of Shame* just to watch him from the crowd, just to get a small glimpse of him, but seeing him up there on stage and knowing that every girl in the room was most likely thinking about him fucking them was messing with my mental state even more. I couldn't make myself leave. I had to stay until the end.

I was just supposed to leave after that. I was supposed to drive home and be alone in my thoughts, but instead I'm here . . . with Cale. No matter what was going on in the past, just like now, I've always ended up with Cale instead of being alone. He's always been capable of drawing me to him and making me spend my time with him. The problem is, he's even better at it now.

Gripping him as tightly as I can, I feel a moan escape me as his soft lips brush right under my ear. There's no denying how much I want him right now, and I know he can feel it too.

"Has Tyler been inside you, Rile?" Gripping my ass, he presses me against the side of his truck, causing me to moan out.

Of course not, I want to scream out. We haven't even hung out yet, although I did promise him at least one dinner. I plan to talk to Cale about it before I leave tonight. I just hope that he will understand why I have to do it . . .

I shake my head. "No, but we need to talk . . ."

"Not right now," Cale says sternly. "We have all night. Right now . . . I need you."

Cale

I DON'T HESITATE BEFORE SETTING her down with her back pressed against my truck. Her dress rides up in the front, exposing her pink panties, and all I can think about is ripping them off with my teeth. This woman makes me want go fucking wild.

She watches me with lust in her eyes as I pull my t-shirt off and toss it over the truck, good and ready to have her hands all over me. I wasn't lying when I said I want her right now. I. Want. Her. Right. Now. I grip the bottom of her dress and wrap it in my hand, pulling her to me. I can't hold back anymore and I'm hoping she can handle it. "Fuck, Riley," I breathe against her neck. "I want to take you right here. I want to fuck you everywhere."

She lets out a gasp and reaches for the button of my jeans, clearly wanting me as much as I want her. "I really want you too, Cale. I have no idea what I'm doing right now, but I know I've been thinking about this for the last two days." Her fingers work fast on undoing my jeans, while biting her bottom lip. "It's almost crazy how much I want you right now."

I look down at her, my chest heaving up and down as I grip her neck and make her look me in the eyes. "You can have me anytime and anywhere that you please. Not having you touch me is what's driving me fucking crazy." I press my erection against her stomach and she grips it with her hand, running her slim fingers along my length. "Right now I just need you to forget about him. It's just you and me, Rile."

Her breath comes out ragged as her eyes lower to land on my rock hard cock. Her eyes fill with a want that I've never seen from her, and I know for a fact that Tyler will never see that look from her. I'll make sure of it.

She swallows hard, bringing her eyes back up to meet mine. "I don't want to think about Tyler right now. I'm not. I won't. You're all I've been able to think about."

I bite into my bottom lip, before picking her up and setting her on the bed of my truck. "That's all I fucking need right now."

Her legs willfully spread as I slowly pull her dress up, exposing her delicious body that is just dying to be licked and tasted by me.

I grip her hips with force and pull her down to the edge of the truck bed, so her ass is barely hanging on the surface. Then, I bend down and run my tongue up the length of her inner thigh, stopping right by her panty line. "Mmm . . ." I moan against her flesh.

I can tell by the soft moan coming from her lips that my mouth being so close to her pussy is driving her mad. That only seems to make me harder. Moaning, I pull her panties aside and run my tongue over her wet pussy, causing her to grip my arms and squirm. One taste and I'm ready to take her right this second.

I close my teeth around her delicious thigh, giving it a playful bite before pulling away and working my mouth up her belly, my hands pulling her dress up on the way. When the dress reaches her head, I pull it off and throw it into the back of the truck.

With urgency, I position my face between her spread legs again, biting her clit through the thin fabric of her panties. During mid moan, I grip her thong in both hands, ripping each side open, surprising her.

Her legs tremble as she runs her hands over my chest and throws her head back. "I still can't believe we're doing this," she says softly. "People might still be awake."

A soft rumble comes from my throat as I quirk an eyebrow and grip both of her wrists in my hand, pulling her up to meet my abdomen. "Take my jeans all the way off, Rile." I grip the back of her neck and suck her bottom lip into my mouth. "Forget about everyone else."

She slides my jeans all the way down to my knees, looking me in the eyes the whole time. The look in her eyes somehow makes me want her even more. I feel like a beast about to lose control.

I yank her legs, pulling her towards me so my cock is resting above her belly. With one hand gripping her neck, I pull her hips up to meet my stiffness, gently sinking into her heat. I slowly thrust in and out a few times, loosening her up to make room, before giving her my full on thrust that is sure to make us being here known to the neighbors.

She screams out while wrapping her legs around my waist, causing me to thrust harder, rolling my hips in and out, giving her the pleasure that she deserves.

Her hold on my bicep hardens as I grip the back of her neck, wrapping my fingers in her hair and pounding into her with as much force as I can. Being inside her feels so damn good that I almost lose it, releasing myself inside of her right then.

Without pulling out, I grip both of her hips and flip her over so her ass is facing me. I reach down with one hand and rub my finger over her wet clit while pounding into her with fast, consistent thrusts, tugging her hair with my free hand. "Scream for me, Rile. Let it out," I demand.

She lets out a low scream as I slow my pace and wrap my arm around her waist, pulling her up so my chest is pressed against her back. "I don't want to get caught, Cale. Your neighbors . . ."

I bend down so my lips are hovering over her ear before I whisper, "Fuck my neighbors. It's you I want to please."

Locking my eyes with hers as she turns her head to look at me, I pound into her, causing her to scream out this time. She screams so loud that she covers her own mouth, too afraid to be seen or heard.

I quicken my pace while moving my fingers up and down her wetness, knowing that at any moment she's about to clamp around my cock and release her juices. I want to feel it surrounding me and covering me.

With one last thrust, she screams and her legs begin to shake as she struggles to not fall over. "Cale . . . Cale . . . Oh shit . . ."

I support her body with mine and pause for a second, allowing her body to clamp around me as she shakes. "That's it, baby." I kiss her neck and hold her until she's done shaking below me, then, I grip her hips, pull out, and slam back into her.

I do this a few more times, holding her as close to me as possible, before wrapping an arm around her neck as I release myself as deep into her still throbbing pussy as I can. We both let out a satisfied moan as I twist her neck closer and press my lips to hers. "You're so beautiful," I whisper against her lips.

She smiles and hides her blushing face as I pull out of her and clean her off with my shirt.

We're both silent as I climb into the back of my truck and lay down, pulling her onto my chest.

We lay here for what seems like hours, before I finally break the silence.

"Remember laying in the back of my truck outside your house late at night?"

She laughs and wraps her arm tighter around me. "Of course I remember. I lived for those nights, Cale. Do you realize how many times I wanted to crawl into your arms just like I am now?"

Smiling like a fool, I grip her tighter and run a hand through her hair. "I wish you would have, Rile. I definitely wouldn't have pushed you away."

"Good to know," she says with a laugh.

We go back to laying in silence, just staring at the night sky. It's so damn peaceful that I never want to move from this spot.

"Cale . . ."

I press my lips to her forehead. "What's up?"

She hesitates, clearly afraid of my reaction. I can tell by the way she's breathing so heavily.

"Say it, Rile," I say gently. "I never want you to hold back from me."

She sits up and searches for her dress, quickly pulling it back on, making sure that she's covered up. "I promised Tyler that I would let him take me out on a date." She lets out a small breath and repositions herself to get comfortable. "I had to after him coming so far. It just didn't seem right to deny him that small request." She looks up at me, focusing on my lips for a brief moment, before meeting my eyes. "Are you mad?"

Inside I feel like I'm fucking dying. The last thing I want to think about is another man taking her out on a date when I haven't even had the chance. I fucking hate it, but I'm trying my best to not be selfish when it comes to Riley. If she needs to do this, then I need to let her.

"No," I admit. "I'm not mad. I'm jealous as shit and not wanting to share you with another man." I pull her back to me and gently kiss her. "One date. I don't think I can handle more than that without wanting to kill him."

"I think I should go home for the night, Cale." She runs her fingers into the back of my hair. "I'm going out with Tyler tomorrow. It won't be right if I stay here."

I swallow back my anger as my chest tightens in pain. As much as I don't want this, I know that nothing with us will be able to move forward until he's out of the picture. Then, I'm going to make her all fucking mine and hold onto her until I take my last breath. That's a promise.

"I'll drop you off." I hop out of the truck and grab Riley's hand, helping her out and on her feet. "Let's go."

This hurts like a bitch, but there's no way I'm giving up on her. Fuck that . . .

CHAPTER SIXTEEN

Riley

GETTING DRESSED AND READY TO go out to dinner with Tyler is stirring a ton of emotions inside of me. Just a couple of weeks ago it was me and Tyler, and now it's me and Cale, with Tyler fighting his way back into my life. It makes everything a lot more complicated than I hoped it would be. I always thought if Cale and I were to end up together that it would be easy and nothing else in the world would matter, but right now . . . it feels far from easy.

"Riley," my mom screams from downstairs. "Tyler's here. Are you ready?"

Sighing, I grab my purse and slip the strap over my shoulder, before making my way to the stairs. I look down at my mom and shrug my shoulders. "Yeah, I suppose so. I just want to get this dinner over with."

My mom watches me with concern as I slowly make my way down the stairs, passing her without another word. I just have so much on my mind right now that it's making it hard to think straight.

Here I am going out with Tyler while Cale is at *Walk Of Shame*, taking his clothes off for a bunch of horny women. He could have any one of them. Why would he want to wait around for me . . . again?

"Are you okay," my dad asks, snapping me out of my thoughts.

I look up at him and smile. "I'm good. I'm fine. Just tired." *Not really, but . . .* 'I'll be home later. I don't plan on staying out too late."

"Alright, honey," Mom says to my back as I'm walking to the door. "I'll wait up for you. I have a feeling we're going to have a lot to talk about when you get home."

I look over my shoulder at her. "I guess we'll see."

When I open the screen door I look up to see Tyler leaning against his rental car. He's too busy messing around on his phone to notice me approaching. It's probably a good thing, because right now it seems extremely hard to hide the disappointment of what I have to do tonight. One look at my face and it's a given.

I take a second to compose myself before stopping in front of him and clearing my throat.

Tyler looks up from his phone and quickly shoves it in his pocket to show me his full attention. Smiling, he says, "You look really nice." He reaches for the end of my favorite shirt and fingers it. "I've missed seeing this old thing."

I smile small, appreciative of his compliment, before pulling away a bit. "Thanks."

We both stand here in an awkward silence before Tyler holds up his keys and dangles them. "I guess we should get going. We'll discuss the restaurant on the road. Sound good?"

I nod my head and reach for the door handle. "Sounds like a plan."

As soon as I shut the door behind me, my heart starts racing at the realization that this isn't Cale's truck. This is another man's vehicle. My ex's to be more specific; the man that I slept next to for two years. It feels so wrong being here with him and every bit of my body is telling me this.

I sit stiffly, lost in my thoughts as Tyler hops in and shuts his door. Without any warning he reaches over and grabs my hand, pulling it into his lap like old times.

My first instinct is to pull away from him. It doesn't feel right. Not like it used to. "No," I say softly. "We're not a couple anymore, Tyler. Please no touching."

His face registers hurt, but he just nods his head and agrees. "Understandable. Sorry, it just comes so natural with you. I don't want to do anything to make you uncomfortable. No more touching unless you ask."

Relief washes through me that he understands the boundaries of this dinner. The thought of him touching me or trying to kiss me has been eating at me ever since I agreed to this dinner with him. I don't need anything else making me feel more guilty and confused than I already do.

"I know where we can eat at." I sit up and point down the street and over to the left side of the road. "I haven't been there since I was a kid."

Tyler looks over to where I'm pointing and pulls into the left lane. "I'm down."

The only reason I haven't been there since I was a kid is because Cale hates the place. We had one bad experience with some douche giving me a hard time and Cale decided that he never wanted to go back. It reminded him of that issue and always made him want to punch something.

I'd rather take Tyler here to eat dinner than a place that Cale and I enjoy together. It somehow makes me feel a little better about this whole thing.

We don't say much more as we head inside and find an empty booth to sit down in. The waitress nods at us as we take our seats, so we both just reach for a menu from the back of the table and skim over the choices while waiting.

After a few minutes, Tyler sets his menu down and stares at me. I can feel his eyes on me, distracting me from the menu.

"Just say it, Tyler. . . . You know I hate it when you just stare at me like that."

I set my menu down and look him in the eyes. He searches my face in silence before speaking.

"How could you do it?"

We both look up at the waitress as she walks over to take our order. We quickly give her our food and drink order as she jots it down then disappears, leaving us alone in what I'm sure is going to be an uncomfortable conversation.

"What?" I ask, feeling a bit uncomfortable. "What are you getting at?"

His facial expression changes and he suddenly looks angry. "Have sex with that Cale guy."

I suck in a deep breath and bite my tongue. I don't like him questioning me like this, and that look on his face makes me want to slap it off of him.

"Why would you ask me that?" I stop talking and smile up at the waitress as she drops off our drinks, then wait for her to walk away before talking again. "I don't think this is something we should talk about, Tyler."

He reaches for his cup and takes a long, desperate drink. "Oh . . . it's definitely something we should talk about, and your response just confirms my suspicions. Why would you sleep with him? We were together for two years; two years, Riley, and you wouldn't let me make love to you. You've been *here* for less than three weeks and you decide to let that loser in your bed."

Sitting up, I slap the table defensively and get closer to his face, letting him see the anger in my eyes. "I don't want to *ever* hear you call Cale a loser again." I grind my jaw, trying to hold myself back from screaming. "Cale has been in my life a lot longer than you have, and he's always been there for me. You don't even know him, so don't you dare judge him."

The conversation comes to a halt again when our plates are set down in front of us. I'm so angry right now that I almost let my mouth run, not caring that someone else is listening to our conversation. No one gets to talk shit about Cale without getting an earful from me. This man has been everything to me for as long as I can remember.

The waitress smiles at us and tells us to enjoy, before walking away.

I shove my fork into my food and start eating as fast as I can. The faster I eat, the faster I can get this stupid dinner over with. I don't know what he expected to accomplish out of this dinner, but I hope he didn't expect to win me back, because this definitely isn't working.

"Calm down, Riley." Tyler reaches over the table and grabs my fork out of my hand. "Talk to me for a minute. I'm not trying to piss you off. I just want answers. You don't think this hurts me? I'm hurt right now. This hurts me."

I lean back in my seat and take a few breaths to calm myself. "I don't want to fight, okay, but if you keep running your mouth and saying things about Cale then I'm going to leave and never speak to you again. He doesn't deserve you bad-mouthing him when he has done nothing but take care of me."

Tyler's jaw flexes, as he looks me over. I can tell that he's fighting really hard not to tell me how he feels about my words.

"Let's forget about this *guy* for a minute then and talk about us. What about us? Are you really willing to just throw two years away as if it meant nothing to you?"

I sit up and let out a humorous laugh. I can't believe he's going there right now. "Oh . . . I don't know, Tyler. I was wondering the same thing when you decided to back out of our relationship right when we were supposed to get on a damn plane. Apparently our two years together didn't mean shit to you, so why should it mean anything to me now? Tell me!"

Tyler stands up and rushes over to my side of the table, scooting his way onto my bench. "I made a mistake. A huge mistake." He reaches for my face, but I turn away from him. "Riley. Please look at me. I love you. I'm in love with you. After you left, it made me realize how much of an idiot I was for not going with you. I'm here now and we can be together."

I shake my head and run my hands over my face. I don't want to be hearing this right now. I've waited for what seems like forever to hear him tell me he loves me again, and now . . . now here he is at the worst possible time ever and it doesn't mean anything to me.

"I don't want to hear that now, Tyler. I'm sorry, but I'm over what we had. This dinner and conversation are confirming that for me. I don't feel anything. I'm so sorry. I want to be with Cale. I always have."

Tyler stands up and starts pacing in front of the booth. "He's a fucking stripper, Riley." He narrows his eyes at me when I give him a surprised look. "Yeah, I've done my research on your little boyfriend. Is that what you really want? Huh?" He sits back down, but on his side of the table. "A man that takes off his clothes for other women and then comes home horny and ready for you? How do you know what he does at that club? What makes you think that he's not getting off on these women touching him? Open your eyes, Riley. He could have any of those women, all of the ass he wants. He'll *never* be faithful to you and you're stupid if you think he will be."

My heart stops and anger that I've never felt before takes over. Standing up, I walk over to stand in front of him. "Fuck you!" Unable to stop myself, I slap him across the cheek and storm out of the restaurant, needing to get away from him before I break down.

As soon as I'm about a block away from the parking lot, I break down and lose it. My chest aches and I can barely catch my breath. As much as I hate to admit it . . . Tyler's words had an effect on me.

I don't want to think about Cale with other women. I don't want to believe what Tyler said, but what if it's true? What if more goes on at that club than I know?

The thoughts running through my head make me just want to scream. It hurts so damn bad just thinking about Cale possibly wanting one of those girls. I hate it. I fucking hate it.

I hate it, but I love Cale. I've been in love with him for longer than I was willing to admit. There's no hiding it now. This man is going to ruin me . . .

CHAPTER SEVENTEEN
Cale

THE GIRLS HAVE BEEN EXTRA grabby tonight and I can't wait to just get the hell out of here. Here I am . . . with all these women pulling at me and touching me, and *all* I can think about is the fact that *my* woman is out with another man. We might not have a title, but I know without a doubt that she is mine.

No one can make her feel the way that I do for the simple fact that no other man can love her and care for her as much as I do. Actions speak louder than words, and my actions will always be to take care of Riley and *show* her how much she means to me. This Tyler guy needs to hit the fucking road and realize that she's taken. He lost his chance, and these women need to watch their damn hands before I lose it.

The song playing over the speakers slows down, so gripping

my hair I roll my hips, slowing down my rhythm to match the music. *Wicked Games* by The Weeknd is playing, so every girl in this room is hanging on my every move, just wanting me to fuck them to this song later. I can see it in their eyes and it makes me feel fucking guilty.

I don't know what made me think that Riley would be okay with this lifestyle, but the more I'm here, the more I worry that she will start pulling away from me when she sees just how bad it truly can get here. Tonight is one of those nights that would probably push Riley over the edge. Lynx seems to be pushing it to get as dirty as fucking possible.

Doing as Lynx instructed, I strip out of my briefs and cover as much of my cock as possible with my free hand, before replacing my hand with my boxer briefs. Dropping to the ground, I hold the thin fabric over my dick and start grinding on the ground as if fucking someone, long and deep. I feel one of the guys pour water over me, soaking me and making it even harder to cover myself with my white briefs.

I can feel hands grab and slap at my ass as I continue to thrust in a slow rhythm, waiting for this fucking song to end. Every woman in this room now knows what my naked ass looks like while fucking. I don't feel comfortable knowing that Riley should be the only one to witness this dirty moment.

As the song comes to an end I grind my hips one more time, before making my way to my feet. A slim brunette with huge tits instantly plasters herself to the front of my body and grabs my cock. Her other hand reaches around my back side and grips my ass as she starts sliding her hand over my shaft.

"Stop," I growl out, while gripping her wrist and pulling her hand away.

Throwing herself at me, she ignores my demand and grabs at my fucking dick again. "Mmm . . . someone's packing," she slurs.

"Show us your dick, baby, and I'll let you put it anywhere."

I grip her wrist a little tighter this time and get in her face, showing her that I'm not interested. "I'm not going to *fuck* you so just stop."

Pushing past her, I look up just in time to see Riley looking at me from the across the room. I can see the shock and hurt on her face and all I want to do is scream for her to come to me so I can make her feel better.

She shakes her head and starts backing away as I begin making my way through the crowd. I get just a glimpse of Lynx walking her away before a group of girls walk in front of me, blocking my line of vision.

My skin heats up in anger at just the thought of Lynx being with her, so I don't think twice before brushing the group of drunken women off and pushing through them.

By the time I get to where Riley and Lynx are, over by the door, I stop dead in my fucking tracks when I see Lynx pinning her against the door in between his arms. He's whispering something in her ear, but it looks as if she just wants to leave.

Without even giving it a second thought I grip Lynx's shoulder and spin him around, swinging my right fist into his mouth.

"What the fuck!" Lynx screams out in shock. "Did you seriously just fucking hit me, you crazy asshole?"

Keeping my eyes on him, I reach down for my boxer briefs that are now on the ground and quickly slide them back on, before walking over to Riley and grabbing her chin. "Are you okay?" I grip the back of her hair and look her in the eyes. "Did he touch you?"

I feel someone grab my shoulder. I turn around defensively to see that it's only Stone. "You got this, bro?" He asks, while looking back and forth between me and Lynx.

"I'm good, man." I shake his hand off my shoulder and give Riley my full attention. "Did he touch you? Tell me."

She shakes her head and pushes me away, looking hurt and more confused than I've ever seen her. "No . . . but it looks as if *everyone* gets to touch you, Cale."

She pushes me away again, so I back up a bit, giving her space. I never want to make her feel uncomfortable, but I want nothing more than to touch her right now. It leaves me in a fucked up situation.

"Rile, I'm fucking sorry." I grip my hair and growl out in anger at the fact that she had to witness some other girl touch me like that. "I don't want that shit, trust me, but please don't walk out on me without talking to me. You've never just walked out on me. Don't start now."

I feel my heart fucking get ripped out of my chest when I notice that her face is wet. She's been crying. She's been fucking crying while I've been here taking off my clothes for other women and fulfilling their damn fantasies. I'm a dick.

"I'm sorry, Cale, but I can't . . . I just can't." She starts walking toward the door. I grab her arm to stop her, but she pulls it away and gives me a dirty look. That's how I know she needs time alone. "I need to leave right now. Please just understand that. This is so much more than I thought. So much . . . worse."

"I'm sorry," is all I can say. I reach out and rub my thumb over her lip, but she backs away and looks around the room as the women start screaming for Stone.

"I can't handle this, Cale. I thought I could, but I can't. I need time to think." Without another word she rushes out the door, leaving me on the verge of going crazy. I want nothing more than to go after her, but I respect her more than anyone in this world, and if she needs time then I can't take that away from her. I know that and I hate myself for it.

"Fuck!" I slam my fist into the wall repeatedly while yelling out a string of cuss words. "What did you say to her?" I bark at

Lynx as his eyes size me up.

He smirks with a confidence that makes me want to fuck him up even more. "Just told her how it truly is here. How dirty all the women get. The truth. That's what."

"Fucking, piece of shit." I start walking to the back to get my shit and Lynx instantly follows me, talking shit the whole way.

"You're lucky I don't fire your ass for that shit. I don't know who the fuck you think you are."

I ignore him, knowing that if I say anything I'm probably going to break his pretty little face.

Bursting through the door of the locker room, I start pulling out my shit to get dressed.

"Can you fucking hear me, asshole? One more mistake and you're gone. You're lucky that you've been here for as long as you have and that you bring me money, you sorry son of a bitch, or else you'd be so done."

I take a few seconds to breathe and calm down after I pull my shirt over my head. This asshole is lucky that I have a lot of willpower.

"I'm fucking bleeding and it's all because I was talking to that bitch that wants nothing to do with either of us. That's fucked up . . ."

Turning around, I swing out, knocking his ass on the ground. "I fucking quit."

Stepping over him, I rush outside and to my truck. I get in, gripping the wheel for dear life. All I can think about is Riley possibly running to Tyler for comfort, and it's all I need to lose it.

"Fuck! Fuck! Fuck!"

Time . . . how the hell can I give her time when that's the one thing that could possibly make me lose her? Well double fuck . . .

CHAPTER EIGHTEEN
Cale

IT'S BEEN THREE DAYS. THREE damn days and Riley hasn't responded to any of my messages. I feel like I'm going crazy. Riley has never gone this long without responding to me. I've tried giving her time, but I just can't wait anymore. I need to make a move before I lose her completely. I can't let that happen and I won't.

I called her work yesterday and booked every single appointment that she had available today. I've been sitting here in the parking lot on Slade's motorcycle, waiting for them to open. I didn't want her to know I was showing up and I knew that if she noticed my truck in the parking lot that there was a chance she'd freak out and leave.

She isn't due in for another thirty minutes, but I already told Kylie that I'm waiting in her damn room until she gets here, and I don't give a shit what anyone says.

A few cars pull into the lot, so I look down at my phone to check the time. They opened a few minutes ago.

Hopping off of Slade's bike, I set the helmet on the seat and rush over to the door, walking inside. Kylie looks up from her desk and smiles when she notices that it's me.

"Hey, stud," she says sweetly. "Are you sure you don't want to keep me company until *she* gets here?"

I walk past her, ignoring her completely. I don't have time for her shit. I don't want her shit. All I want is to show Riley how much I love her. She may be pissed to see me at first, but I don't care. I have to do this.

About five minutes before Riley is due to arrive, I strip out of my jeans and shirt, before getting comfortable on my back. I was in so much of a hurry that I didn't even bother throwing on any boxer briefs. It's not like I'd be wearing them for long anyways. I plan on spending most of my day, here, naked.

My heart speeds up when I hear the sound of the door opening. I've been fucking dying to be close to Riley, and knowing that she's about to be in the same room is making it very difficult to not just pull her down onto the table and take care of her.

I can hear her shuffling around and getting ready. I'm watching her, but she hasn't even bothered to look at the table yet. She's so damn beautiful that it causes my chest to ache. All I want to do is wrap my hands into that brown hair and pull her lips to mine.

"Good morning," she mumbles. "My name is Riley and . . ." Her words trail off when she finally looks to see who her client is. "Cale," she says in almost a whisper. "What are you doing here?"

Sitting up, I grab her arm before she can walk away. I can see the confusion and hurt written all over her face, and I know without a doubt that she wants to run away and not face me right now.

"Come here, baby." Throwing my legs off the side of the

table, I pull her between my legs and wrap them around her so she will listen to me. "Just hear me out, Rile. Please."

She swallows hard and closes her eyes as I wrap my hands into the back of her hair. "Cale . . . I'm scared. I'm so fucking scared when it comes to you."

"Shh . . ." I gently kiss her neck, enjoying the sweet scent of her skin. Nothing else will ever feel this way and I know that. Now I just need to show her. "I'll never hurt you, Riley. Ever. I want you to know that. Haven't I always been good to you?"

I kiss her neck again, causing her to moan out. "Yes," she whispers. "But if you ever hurt me, it would kill me. Do you get that, Cale? That's why I can't do this. I can't get too deep and allow that to happen."

Running my lips up her neck, I stop below her ear and whisper, "I'll never let that happen, Rile." I suck her earlobe into my mouth and nibble it. "Do you know why?"

She lets out a small breath and shakes her head. "No . . ."

I press my lips against her ear and tug at her hair, getting as close to her as possible. "Because I'm in love with you," I whisper. "I always have been, Rile. I fucking love you."

She lets out a small gasp and presses her hand over her mouth. Pulling away, I look her in the eyes and repeat myself. "I'm in love with you. I will always put you first. I will always make you happy and think of you before anyone else. That is a promise." I pull her forehead to mine. "Do you understand that?"

She doesn't respond, so I ask her again. "Do you?"

"Cale, I can't ask you to do that. I can't . . ."

"You don't have to," I say honestly. "I've been doing it since we were kids. It comes natural to me now. Not doing it wouldn't feel right to me. I quit my fucking job, Rile. I'm going to focus on you." I place her hand on my chest. "This body will only be touched by you. I can promise you that on my life."

I cup her face and run my thumbs over her wet cheeks. "None of that matters to me. This is me showing you how much I love you. Words don't mean shit unless you have the actions to back it up. This is me doing my part. This is me showing you that I fucking love you."

A half laugh, half sob escapes her throat as she rubs her hand over my chest, taking me all in.

The silence in the room is making my heart work overtime. I need her to speak. I need to hear that she's willing to be mine.

"Talk to me, Rile. Please say something."

She reaches her hand up and wraps it into the back of my hair like she always does. Then, her eyes lock with mine, causing my chest to ache in anticipation. "I'm in love with you too, Cale. God, I love you so much that it hurts."

I pull her onto the table with me and crush my lips to hers, just wanting to taste her and feel her against me. "I love you, baby," I whisper against her lips. "I'm your man for as long as you will have me. Only yours."

"Show me," she says with a smirk.

I suck her bottom lip into my mouth and bite it. "Oh trust me . . . I plan to. All fucking day."

She laughs as if she doesn't believe me. "I do have other clients booked today, Cale."

I raise my brows and slide her hand down to my rock hard cock. "Not for the next five hours." I turn us, laying her down on the bed to hover above her. "I'm a greedy asshole today and didn't want to share you for longer than I had to." I smile against her lips. "Fuck everyone else. You're mine until then."

She grips my neck and pulls me down to kiss her, long and hard. "I fucking love you so much."

"Fuck I love hearing that," I growl. Letting my excitement take over, I yank her dress up and over her head, before pulling her panties down her legs and tossing them aside. I need to be inside my woman right now, and I need to show her how much I love her.

Laying her back down from removing her clothes, I get down, in between her legs, and allow my tongue to trail up the inside of her thigh, slowly tasting her. I can already see her juices dripping and all I want to do is lick her clean, tasting her on my tongue. She smells so damn sweet, and I can only imagine her pussy tastes even sweeter right now, just waiting for me.

Grabbing her thighs, I push her legs toward her breasts. "Fuck, I've been waiting for days to do this, Rile." I slowly trail my tongue up the wetness of her pussy, torturing her clit with the tip of my tongue, before slipping my tongue deep inside, getting a better taste. She moans and her whole body shakes with pleasure as I spread her moistness to her clit and slip a finger into her tight little pussy; my tight little pussy.

I swirl my tongue around before sucking her clit into my mouth, being sure to be gentle with her. I suck and lick while moving my finger in and out in a slow, consistent motion, never losing rhythm. I know how much rhythm means to a woman's sexual needs and I will be fucked if I don't give her the greatest pleasure she's ever known. Tyler can fuck off. He's never made her come like I'm about to.

It doesn't take long before I can feel her already starting to clamp down around my finger. It doesn't surprise me though. If I'm good at one thing, it's definitely using my tongue, and I've saved my best for her. I slowly run my tongue in between her lips before sucking them into my mouth and then her clit. When I feel her starting to clamp again, I run my tongue over her thigh, before softly biting down on it. "Come for me, baby," I whisper. "Don't worry about anyone hearing you."

Her body jerks as she clamps around my finger and screams out softly. It's so fucking tight that it almost hurts my finger. It reminds me that I've been the only one to be inside of her.

Right as she's coming, I pull my finger out, replacing it with my tongue. I want to taste her when she comes. "Fuck yeah, Rile." Her breathing comes out in heavy bursts as she continues to scream and moan below me. "Cale . . . Cale . . ." She runs her hands through her hair before biting her bottom lip and looking up to meet my eyes. "Make love to me. Please . . ."

Snaking my arm around her waist, I move up to press my body between her wet thighs. I kiss her, wanting to taste every fucking inch of her. Her lips are the best tasting thing in the world to me, and I swear that I will never be able to get enough.

She moans and leans her head back, pressing it into the massage bed. I love seeing her come undone below me, knowing that I will be the only one. She had her chances and didn't take them. It only makes me love her more.

Gripping her thigh, I slip inside of her, causing her to moan out and dig her nails into my back. "I've missed you inside of me, Cale."

"Say it again," I whisper against her lips.

She leans up and sucks my lip into her mouth, turning me on even more. "I've. Missed. You. Inside. Of. Me." She wraps her legs around my waist and squeezes me hard. "You are my best friend, the man that I love. You and only you."

Her words set me off and before I know it, I'm grinding my hips in and out of her, taking her slow and deep, deeper than I've ever taken her.

With each thrust her nails dig deeper and harder into my flesh, her moans becoming louder in my ear. Something about this moment feels so different than all of the other times we've had sex. Everything seems so much more real.

Maybe it's the fact that I know she loves me now, and this is me proving to her that I love her too. This is us making love.

My hand slips under her neck to grip her hair as I press my lips to hers and continue to make love to her, knowing that this moment is special to both of us. This is the moment that I make my best friend so much more: my woman. This moment I have been waiting on for far too fucking long.

Knowing how this feels, I would wait all over again if I had to. This is a feeling that many men aren't lucky enough to ever experience and I wouldn't give it up for anything . . .

AFTER TALKING AND MAKING LOVE for about the fifth time, I help Riley get dressed before getting dressed myself, then pull her into my arms and press my lips to her forehead.

"Come home tonight, baby," I whisper. "Let me take you out on a real date."

Smiling, she grabs my face and looks me in the eyes. "You making me dinner and taking care of me would be the realest that a date could ever get. If you ask me, you're the only one that has taken me on a *real* date."

My heart swells from her words and a sense of pride swarms through me. "This is why I love you so much, Rile."

Pressing my lips to hers, I kiss her long and hard, not wanting to say bye for the next three hours. I just want her home and in my bed. "Hurry home so I can make you dinner and make love to you all fucking night. I have a lot of making up to do. I'll never again lose time with you."

She smiles and pushes me away as someone knocks on the door. "Okay," she laughs. "I'll hurry back. I promise."

"Home," I say, correcting her.

She kisses me once more and smiles. "Home. I'll hurry home. Better?"

I grip her face and bite her bottom lip. "Much fucking better, baby."

The person at the door knocks again. Smiling so damn hard that I feel as if my face is about to rip, I open the door and step out.

Kylie looks up at me and then at Riley, before grunting and motioning for me to get going. "About time. Damn! Your next client is here." She turns back to me. "Move along now."

Grabbing the back of Riley's neck, I pull her to me one more time and kiss her. "Love you, baby," I say, making sure that Kylie gets the fucking hint. "See you in a bit."

Rolling her eyes, Kylie storms past us and goes back to her desk without another word.

"Love you too." She slaps my ass and gives me a shove. "Now go, before I get fired."

I throw my hands up and start backing away. "Whoa now. Keep spanking me and I won't be going anywhere." I wink at her and then turn around to leave before I'm unable to stop myself.

Fuck me, I love this woman . . .

CHAPTER NINETEEN

Riley

TWO WEEKS LATER . . .

I'M STANDING IN FRONT OF the mirror when I feel Cale wrap his arms around me from behind. Like always when he's around, my heart starts pounding and I feel this rush. That feeling has only intensified since we have become official, and I seriously cannot get enough of him touching me.

"You look fucking beautiful, Rile." Grabbing my arm, he spins me around and whistles. "So damn beautiful."

Blushing, I wrap my arms around his neck and pull him down for a kiss. "Mmm . . ." I run my tongue over my lips, tasting the sweet strawberries that he just got done eating. "Save some of those for later," I say playfully. "If you keep eating them outside of the bedroom then we'll never have enough."

Grinning, he picks me up, wrapping my legs around his waist. His hands grab for my ass and squeeze. "Do we really have to go?" He questions, while pushing his erection against me. "I want to fuck my woman so bad right now that being with those assholes is the last thing on my mind. I'll call Slade back and tell him that we're not coming."

"No!" I scream as he starts rushing into the bedroom. "Don't do it, Cale." He stops in front of the bed and I grab onto his neck tighter, holding on for dear life. "We're going. We already said we would. My sister is waiting for me."

Growling against my lips, he wraps his hands into the back of my hair. "Well shit." He kisses me and smiles. "We don't have to stay long though, right? I've waited all damn day to get you home to me." He kisses me again, his lips lingering against mine. "Fine, let's go," he grumbles in defeat.

He sets me down to my feet and kisses the top of my head, before walking away and letting me finish getting ready.

The last two weeks have been the best days of my life and there's no denying it. Cale is so much more than I ever thought he could be. If I thought he made me feel special before, the feeling is double that now. This man hasn't let me go one second without a smile on my face and I have a feeling that if it's up to him then he'll never let that happen. Cale truly is the perfect man for me.

My love for him has grown so much that my chest aches just from being away from him. It keeps me happy knowing that he's always waiting for me, just like he used to before I left. It only proves to me exactly why he waited all these years for me. When Cale loves someone, he loves them with everything in him.

I'm just lucky to say that that girl is me.

Right as I'm in the middle of throwing my hair up, Cale rushes back into the bedroom and picks me up, throwing me over his shoulder. "I told you how beautiful you looked, Rile. You don't need to change anything. Trust me. Let's go!"

"I'm not done." I playfully slap his ass, but he keeps walking, not caring. "Damn you, Cale."

He doesn't set me down until we're outside next to his truck and he's opening the door for me. "We gotta go, baby. The sooner we get there, the sooner I get to bring you home and make love to you in our bed. I don't know how long I can hold off."

I bite my bottom lip and sit back in my seat as Cale shuts the door behind me and then runs over to his side of the truck.

I swear I have to be the luckiest girl in the world to have Cale. My Cale . . .

AS SOON AS WE STEP inside the bar, Stone jumps up on his chair and starts whistling for us to come over. "Dude! Over here."

I laugh as Hemy reaches over and punches him the leg. These guys will never change, and oddly, I'm good with that. Even though they drive me insane half the time, they're like family to me. No fuck that . . . they *are* family to me.

Now that I have Riley back here with me, my family is complete. There's no better feeling in the world than that. Tyler has gone back to Mexico where he belongs and Riley is here with me, where she has always belonged.

Placing my hand on Riley's ass, I guide her toward the table in the back and whisper in her ear. "Remember . . . we're not staying long. I'm spending the night pleasuring my fucking woman."

I see her cheeks turn red from my words, but she plays it off as Aspen walks over to her and hugs her, pulling her away from me and over to where her and Sage are playing darts.

Pulling out a chair, I take a seat next to Slade, across from Hemy and Stone. "What the fuck, dudes? Stop looking at me like that."

Slade tilts back his beer and grins like an idiot. "I just can't get over it, man. Shit." He takes another drink of his beer, before sliding one over to me. "One day we will be related."

"Ah, fuck." I grab my beer and bring it to my lips. "Ain't that some shit." I smile and nudge his shoulder. "Related to the fucking man whore. I never in a million years would've thought that could be a possibility. Shit is changing, man. Things are becoming real."

Hemy slaps Onyx on the ass as she stands up, nods at me, and goes to join the other girls. "So what's the deal," Hemy asks, before finishing his beer and pushing it aside. "Heard you punched the fuck out of Lynx and quit."

I nod my head and steel my jaw at just the thought of him trying to steal my woman out from under me. "Yeah, man. He had it coming."

"Hell yeah, he did," Stone agrees, tilting his beer to mine. "That asshole deserved it. Now he's all going crazy and shit, trying to find someone as good as you to take your spot. I mean Kash has been doing pretty good, but I don't know about this Stax guy. He looks scared as shit. The vultures smell fear. They may very well eat him alive."

Everyone around the table laughs. It's crazy how much things have changed over the last few months. I'm proud of every single guy at this table. I've never seen any of them happier than what they are right now, and I know for damn sure that I can now say that about myself as well.

Next week I start my management position at *The Anchor*, a bar that Riley and I can feel comfortable with me working at until I can decide what I really want to do. Slade is settling into his stiff

new office job, wearing his suits and shit, Hemy has quit completely at *Walk Of Shame* and is working full time at his buddy's mechanic shop. I even heard that Onyx is getting a job with Aspen at
the salon and that Sage is working on writing a book or something.
Everything in life is fucking good to me. My people are good and
so am I.

When I look over at the girls, I catch Riley smiling and looking
back over at me while talking to Onyx about something. It makes
me feel so damn good seeing her getting accepted by everyone in
the group. I even have a feeling that Onyx finds her attractive. As
wild as that girl is sometimes, I wouldn't be surprised if she hasn't
thought about being with my girl. Of course there is one wild couple out of every group. Hemy and Onyx are that for us.

Grabbing my beer, I sit back in my seat and just enjoy this moment for what it is. This is the only group that I would want to be
doing this with. My *Walk Of Shame* family became my real family,
and I love all these fuckers to death.

*This is all that a man needs to be happy. She is all a man needs to be
happy. With these people, my life is fucking perfect . . .*

THE END

BONUS CONTENT

ONE YEAR LATER

Slade

TODAY HAS BEEN FILLED WITH endless phone calls, meetings and bullshit, yet all I can think about is getting home to my woman and hearing her moan beneath me. She's been on my mind all damn day, making it impossible to concentrate on all my cases.

Finally getting a chance to relax after a ten hour day, I loosen my tie, spin my chair away from my desk and bite my bottom lip in need when Aspen's sexy voice comes through the speaker of my office phone. Hearing her is exactly what I need to remember that my life isn't shit anymore.

"Hey, baby . . . you there?" She sighs when I don't respond, probably aware of the sound of my pants slowly unzipping. Might as well take this as a time to get comfortable and tease her at the same time. "What are you doing, Slade? Was that your zipper? Please tell me that was not the sound of your pants coming undone."

"If that's what you heard, then that was definitely my fucking zipper, baby."

Smiling to myself, I slide my hand into the waistband of my boxer briefs and grip my hard cock, getting harder by the second as Aspen's breathing picks up, working me up.

"Slade, you asshole. Are you seriously teasing me right now? That's not cool."

"You miss my hard cock, baby?" I loosen my tie some more and roll up my sleeves, getting more comfortable. "If you were here right now, I'd bend you over my fucking desk and fuck you so hard that the whole office building would get off on your screaming. How loud would you scream for me?"

I can tell by her loud breathing that she's completely sexually frustrated right now and fighting with everything in her not to explode. I love it. Makes my long work day more worthwhile when I get to come home to her. "Slade . . . leave that office and get your ass home. Now."

Smiling in victory, I run my tongue over my lips, wetting them. "Why?" I push.

She growls into the phone, not wanting to give in. She never wants to, but I'm working on that. "Slade . . ."

"Tell me," I demand.

"So you can fuck me. Dammit, you play dirty. This doesn't count. You know my weakness."

Standing up, I zip up my fly and start gathering up my all my shit. I swear I can't get out of this stuffy office soon enough. "It definitely counts. I'll be there in ten. Be ready."

Before Aspen can respond, I hit end on the phone call and rush out the door, locking it on the way out.

I don't even bother looking anywhere but straight ahead of me as I make my way through the building and outside to the parking lot. The last thing I need right now is someone thinking that I want to stop and chat. Not when my woman has finally broken down first. She's getting it. Fucking hard and dirty.

Just as I said, I pull up in the driveway of our new house, ten minutes later. I might have even ran a couple stop signs.

Not even bothering to grab my crap, I step out of my car, undoing my tie completely on the way to the front door.

I can barely even contain myself when I push the door open to see Aspen leaning over the kitchen island, wearing nothing but a thong and a very tight tank top. I can tell by the way that she doesn't even bother to look at me that she's reading one of Sage's books. Well that book is about to be put on hold until further fucking notice.

"Fuck me . . ." I step up behind her and run my hands along the curve of her ass, causing her to close her book and lean her head back to lay on my shoulder. "Everything in this house is brand new, yet you're the only thing I want to play with."

Gripping the counter, she perks her ass up, rubbing it against my cock. "Is that so?" she questions with a sexy growl. She rubs her ass in a circle, before turning to face me and gripping ahold of my shirt, tugging me closer to her. She knows that I'm on the verge of exploding and is taking this opportunity to torture me, but I guarantee that she will still be caving first.

She undoes the top two buttons on my black dress shirt, before biting her lip and walking over to pull out one of our new kitchen chairs. Her heated eyes stay on me the whole time. "There's a little something that I've been missing from you, Slade." Taking a seat in the chair, she spreads her legs and grips the seat between her thighs, looking sexy as sin. "Strip," she demands. "Nice and slow."

I feel my cock twitch from her demand. I love the playful Aspen and it's been a long time since I've been able to strip for her. This is bound to do the trick. She may not admit it, but this is how

I got her in the first place.

Steeling my jaw, I yank her chair so that she's sitting right in front of me. It's time to get serious now. You ask Slade Merrick to strip . . . and you'll get a damn good show. "You asked for it."

Pulling my phone from my pocket, I scroll through to the music and hit play on the first slow song that I come across. To me it's not about the music; it's about how you move to it and I'm about to give her a glimpse into the Slade that she fell in love with.

After I set my phone down, I look her directly in the eye, making her squirm in her seat, as I empty my keys and everything else out of my pants. I don't want anything poking her except for my cock.

Biting my bottom lip, I step in between Aspen's legs and grip the top of her chair, grinding my hips as I work on undoing the rest of my shirt buttons.

Once I get to the last button, I yank my shirt off and toss it aside, before gabbing her hands and running them along my chiseled chest.

Moving in closer, I take a seat on her lap, grinding my hips to the slow rhythm. I can already see her starting to crumble and come undone beneath me. She wants this just as badly as I do.

"Slade . . ." she says in a shaky voice.

"Yes," I push. "What?" I move her hands lower, until she's stroking the length of my hardness through my dress pants.

She swallows hard and looks up to meet my gaze. "This is too damn hot and you know it . . ." she pauses as I stand up and start to undo my belt.

"You want me to keep going, baby?" After undoing my pants, I slide my hand down the front of my pants and stroke my cock with a moan. "I can keep going . . . or I can fuck you. What do you want?"

Aspen's legs slowly close and her grip on the chair tightens when I start to remove my pants. "I can do this," she whispers. "Stay strong."

Removing my pants completely, I stroke myself for her to watch, knowing that she can never handle when I touch myself. I give it less than two minutes.

"I'm so fucking hard, Aspen." I walk forward, stopping right in front of her. "I'll let you touch it . . . just say it."

Letting out a deep breath, Aspen growls, before reaching out and grabbing me by my cock. "I'm done. You win. I'm the first one to ask for sex in our new house. There. Happy?"

Wrapping a hand into the back of her hair, I pull her up to her feet and suck her bottom lip into my mouth. "Extremely fucking happy."

Pressing my lips to hers, I walk until we're back by the kitchen island, where she was when I first walked in. Then in one movement, I spin her around and bend her over the counter, slapping her ass with my free hand.

"It feels good, baby," I moan into her ear. "I'm about to fuck you in the house that we own together. It's you and me. This is just the beginning of our life together." Wrapping my arm around her neck, I pull her back so that I can kiss her. "I love you."

She smiles and licks her lips. "I love you too. Now hurry before I go crazy. It's already been three days."

I laugh because I love that we've only gone three days without having sex and this woman . . . my woman, already misses me inside of her. I never would've thought that day would come when I first met her over a year ago. It hardly feels like a month has passed. Every day with her feels fresh and new and I couldn't be happier.

Unable to hold back any longer, I yank her panties aside and enter her wet pussy in one hard thrust, making her scream out from the intrusion.

"Slade!" Her breathing picks up as she waits for me to move.

"I can't take this. Do you see how sexy you are in those damn suits? No more teasing. I. Want. You."

"Anything you want is yours." With that, I pull out and thrust back into her, causing her to moan out as I continue to take her deep and hard.

I'm rough at first, before slowing down and being gentle to remind her how much she means to me. This woman is everything to me and I never want her to forget.

It's not long before I feel her clenching around me, bringing me to my own orgasm as well. I push inside of her as deep as I can, giving her every last drop of me.

"Well the new house is broken in." I laugh into her ear, before kissing her neck, trailing my way around to her lips. "Now I never want to wait three days again. I was so fucking close to caving in."

"Are you serious?" She pulls away from me and spins around to face me. "How close?"

I smile and bite her bottom lip. "About ten minutes close." Gently, I press my lips against hers and catch her hands with mine. "Now go take a shower and I'll make you dinner."

"Slade . . ." she starts.

"Go," I say sternly. "You've taken time off work to help put our home together. Making dinner for my woman is the least I can do as a man." I tilt my head toward the hallway. "Hurry."

Shaking her head in disbelief, she smiles, before kissing me long and hard. "Never change," she whispers, then walks away, leaving me alone to clean up a bit and cook dinner.

ASPEN APPEARS FROM THE SHOWER about twenty five

minutes later, dressed in one of my white button down shirts. She takes one look at me by the stove, in my boxers, and growls.

"This might just be sexier than seeing you in a suit. Almost naked, cooking. I dig it," she teases.

Running my hands through my hair, I look at her and feel like the luckiest man in the world as I watch her take a seat in our kitchen.

I've been wanting to ask her to buy a place with me for months now, but I wanted to make sure it was the right time. Last week when I watched her walk out the door for work, I realized that I never wanted her to come back home to a place that wasn't ours together. I knew right then that the time was right. I'm just lucky that she has as much faith in me as she does.

Sometimes I feel as if I don't deserve it, but she always finds a way to remind me just how much she thinks I do. When the time is right, I will make her my wife and I will love her with everything in me. I may have had a hard past, but I'm ready for a new future and I know without a doubt that future is her . . . Aspen.

"I'm the luckiest asshole in the world," I admit.

Aspen walks into my open arms and smiles against my chest as I hug her to me. "Yeah . . . and you're my asshole. I'm not giving you up for anything."

I feel Aspen jump in my arms as my phone starts vibrating next to us. Looking over, I see Hemy's name flash across the screen. "Shit . . ." That's tonight.

Reaching for my phone, I answer it and grunt, before speaking. "Yeah, man."

"Don't forget, dude. We're meeting Cale and Riley at Walk Of Shame in two hours. Don't be late again."

I hear some loud noise in the background and Onyx cheering, before the phone goes silent. Sounds like they're at the club already. No surprise there.

Tossing my phone down, I kiss Aspen on the top of the head. "Looks like we have a couple of hours . . ." I lift my eyebrows in suggestion and Aspen slaps my chest.

"We'll see how good dinner is," she teases.

I may sound like a pussy, but my heart skips a beat from the sight of her smile. I'll never grow tired of seeing it every day.

I'll never grow tired of us. Slade and Aspen. She is exactly where I need to be and I'm going to show her in every way that I can . . .

I HUNG UP WITH SLADE over an hour ago, and Onyx has been pushing me ever since to go show the new guys how it's really done. She said the idea of me being back here makes her want to jump all over me and take me for a ride. Well fuck me . . .

I have to admit that watching the guys sort of has me wanting to go up on the stage and show them what's up, just for the fucking rush.

Peeling my eyes away from the stage, I cup Onyx's face in my hands and pull her in for a rough kiss. All I need is five fucking minutes to show these dicks how it's really done. "Fuck it," I say with a smirk. "I'll be back."

Taking a quick swig of my drink, I slam it down and make my way over to where Kash is dancing. This is sure to get his ass laid at least.

Stepping up behind Kash, I push him forward, stopping him right in front of the sexy little blonde that has been eyeing him up and down ever since he stepped on the stage.

Leaning in to his ear, I whisper, "Make love to her fucking face. Show her what you can do." I slap his back and wink at the girl as she grins at me.

Kash gives me a look as if he's uncertain if he should do it or not. "Seriously, dude?"

"Fuck . . ." Grabbing the back of the girl's neck, I slowly push her down to her knees in front of him. "Grab the back of her head." I place my hand on the eager girl's chin, making her look up at me. "You want this?"

She smiles at me before turning back to Kash and looking

up at him with a sexy grin. Her eyes are practically begging for his cock in her face. "Very much. Kash . . ."

Kash runs his tongue over his lips, before reaching down and gripping the back of the girl's neck, slowly thrusting his hips to the music.

Stepping behind the girl, I grab her hands to guide her, placing one on Kash's ass and the other on the button of his jeans.

So much better . . .

"Fuck . . . that shit isn't hard," I mutter while making my way back over to where Onyx is waiting for me.

When I take a seat, I am taken by surprise when Onyx jumps into my lap, pressing me into the back of the leather couch.

With a grin, she wraps her hand around my neck and leans down to whisper in my ear. "I'm extremely hot right now, Hemy." She bites my earlobe before releasing it. "Do you know why?"

Gripping her hips, I lift her up, pulling her as close to me as humanly possible. Then I grip the back of her neck and yank her face to mine, brushing my lips over hers. "Because you're in my lap," I say with confidence. Getting turned on, I thrust my hips into her, showing her just how hard I am. "And because of my newest piercing."

She runs her tongue over her lips, seductively and nods her head. "Bingo!" Reaching in between us, she grabs my cock through my jeans and squeezes. "And that fucking man bun turns me on. It makes me want to do very naughty things . . ."

Swallowing hard, I lace my fingers with hers and lean in, pressing my lips against the ring on her left hand. Seeing that rock, gets me both excited and extremely turned on, knowing that this woman has agreed to be my wife.

"Fuck . . . I love it when my fiancé wants to be naughty." Yanking her to her feet, I stand up and walk her backward, until we're lost in a dark corner, away from the loud screaming by the stage. I just hope that Stone and Kash can keep the room busy long enough so I can please my woman and finally test out this new piercing.

Slamming Onyx against the wall, I slide my hand up the front of her skirt, shoving a finger inside of her already wet pussy. "So fucking wet, baby," I whisper against her neck, about to lose my shit.

Moaning, she throws her head back as I begin to pump my fingers inside of her.

"Faster, Hemy," she demands.

I shake my head and pull my fingers out, sucking them into my mouth. "Nah . . ." Reaching in between us, I pull my cock out of my jeans, faster than I ever have in my entire life. Not being able to have sex without a condom for the past five weeks has been making me crazy to be inside of her again.

Before Onyx can react from my cock being out, I grip her leg, wrap it around my waist and slam into her. Deep and hard.

I feel her nails dig into my back as I still myself inside of her. "Fuck, Hemy!" She screams next to my ear. "Why do you have to be so big?" She takes a few deep breaths to compose herself. "I can take it," she breathes. "Go."

Cupping her chin, I force her to look up at me. "You okay, baby?" My eyes lock with hers, searching for the truth. "I didn't mean to hurt you, but fuck . . . I can't hold back right now."

"Don't," she breathes. She squeezes me with her leg to get me moving again. "Just a little warning next time so I can prepare. Now move before I go crazy."

Grinning, I wrap one hand around her throat and grab onto her leg with my free hand. "Here's your warning . . ."

I pull out and slam back into her, causing her to dig her nails into the back of my neck and scream out. "Keep going," she breathes.

Resting my forehead to hers, I begin to pound into her, fast and hard, giving her everything that I have. With this woman, I can't hold back. She drives me fucking wild in the best possible way. She always has and that's exactly why I asked her to marry me a few months ago. The truth is, I can't live without this woman. I've tried it once and barely survived. I won't do it again.

The faster I go, the louder her breathing becomes, showing me just how close she is to coming undone. As much as I want to make this last, everyone will be here soon and the last thing we need is for them to come looking for us.

"Yeah, baby," I growl into her ear. "Come for me. You feel that?" I sway my hips in a circle, letting her feel every last inch of my cock.

She nods her head and digs her teeth into her bottom lip. "Just a little bit," she says breathless.

I squeeze her thigh tighter and push in even deeper, before slowly pulling all the way out. "Now?" I ask again.

"Yes," she moans. "Fuck, I love your cock and the rings. All of it Hemy. I love all of you."

I can never grow tired of hearing those words from her lips. When I come home from a long day at the shop, she's always right there, telling me how much she loves me.

Nothing can ever compare to that and I make sure that my body and actions always show her that. She is the only one that I want. The only one I've ever wanted.

I slam into her and stop. "I love all of you too, beautiful." I pull out and thrust back into her, stopping to kiss her lips. "Especially because you love this so much. Now hold on."

Understanding what's coming, she holds onto me as tightly as she can and leans her head into my shoulder.

Gripping her thigh for support, I bury my face into her neck and fuck her fast and hard, not stopping until we've both reached orgasm, her screaming upon release in my ear.

I press my forehead to hers and smile in satisfaction as we look into each other's eyes. "I love you so fucking much. Never forget that, got it?"

Onyx nods her head and runs her hands through the loose strands of my hair. "I love you too." She lifts her hand with the ring. "Always."

"Good," I say in relief. Stepping away from her, I pull my shirt over my head and clean Onyx of her light sheen of sweat, before cleaning myself off and tossing it into the nearest trash can.

"Let's get back before the group shows up." Grabbing Onyx's hand, I pull her against me and walk us back through the crowd and to our area by the couches. The V.I.P section is ours for the night and I have to admit that it feels nice being back here, knowing that the whole group will be here soon.

Right as we're about to sit down, my phone starts vibrating in my pocket. I don't even have to look at it to know who it is. Cale has been on our asses for the last week, making sure that every one of us is here tonight at nine.

It's a little past eight, so I don't know what his deal is. Have a little faith in us, damn.

I pull my phone out and answer it without even bothering to look at the screen. "We're already here, man. And I called Slade about an hour ago and reminded him."

"You're there?" Cale questions. "Is everything good there?"

I let out a small breath and look around the bar at everyone having a good time. The guys are shaking their dicks and the women are having the time of their fucking lives. He worries too damn much. "Yeah, man. It's all good here. No worries. We'll see ya soon."

Right as I'm hanging up, Onyx jumps from her seat on the couch and runs over to greet Sage. Those two have become inseparable and I have to say that it makes me extremely happy.

Onyx has been treating her like a sister for longer than I have and if anyone ever hurts her, I have a feeling that Onyx would get to them before I would even have a chance to.

"Love the hair," Sage says, while grabbing a handful of Onyx's hair.

Ever since Onyx has been working at the salon with Aspen, she has been experimenting with different hairstyles and colors. I have to say that this is my favorite so far. It's almost black, but looks purple in some lighting. It's fucking sexy on her.

Giving me a quick hug, Sage pulls away and walks her way up to the stage to greet Stone. It's as if the screaming, groping girls has no effect on her. She just pushes right through them, wraps an arm around Stone's neck and slams her lips against his, showing them who he's going home with tonight.

It's been a year and those two have managed to stay friends with benefits. Sage says it's what she wants at the moment, but I have to admit that it still drives me crazy. He just better hope that he never hurts her. I'd hate to have to break his pretty face. Well maybe . . .

Stone sees me looking up at him as Sage walks away, making her way back over to us. Stone throws up his middle fingers and sticks his tongue out while thrusting the air. Fast.

"Fucking dick," I grumble.

I feel a bony fist hit me in the ribs. "Be nice, big brother." Sage bites her lip and winks over at Stone. "He's so fucking cute. How can you be so mean to him?"

"It's not too hard. Trust me," I growl out.

"Oh stop it," Onyx jumps in, like the big sister to protect Sage. "Try to have some fun instead of bitching over Stone. You spend over nine hours a day busting your ass on those cars and crap. Loosen up. No worries."

Sage smiles at Onyx before turning to me and wrapping her arm around my neck. "Yeah, what she said big bro. It could be worse," she teases. "I could ask you to read one of my books." She smiles real big at me, knowing that I hate the idea of that.

"I've heard the shit you write and there's no way in hell I'm going to read about your sexual adventures."

Onyx and Sage both slap me at the same time. I just smile because I'm used to it. This is my life now. These women are my life.

I grip my beer and sit back and relax as the girls fall into some deep girl talk conversation. This somehow makes me wish that the assholes would hurry up and get here, but then I look over and notice the smile on both of their faces and I fall apart like a fucking pussy.

I have the two most important women in my life here and will be damned if I ever mess that up . . .

LACING MY FINGERS WITH RILEY'S, I lean in and smile against her lips, before kissing her soft and deep. I can never get tired of tasting this woman's lips. Especially after waiting as long as I did. I never want to wait again.

Her legs tighten around me as I thrust into her, quickening my speed. The way that she squeezes me, pushes me in even deeper, making me about ready to lose my shit right now.

Truthfully, I should have lost it over ten minutes ago. I've been on everyone's ass to make sure that they aren't late tonight, yet here I am still making love to wife.

Being inside of her, hearing her soft moans as I bury myself between her thighs is all that matters at the moment. Here with her is where I belong.

"Cale . . ." She digs her nails into my back and moans as her body starts trembling from below me. I love feeling her come undone because of me. "Oh my goodness . . . Oh my . . ."

Thrusting into her a few more times, I push in deep, releasing myself inside of her. "Fuck me, baby."

Wrapping my arms around her, I roll over, pulling her on top of me. "You're so damn beautiful." I wrap my hands into the back of her hair and pull her in for a kiss. "You know that, right?"

Smiling as if she's the happiest woman in the world, she nods and presses little kisses into my neck. "You never let me forget." She kisses me one more time, before pulling back and running her hand through my hair. "Everyone's going to hate us. You know that, right? By the time we get there, we're going to be over thirty minutes late."

Sucking my bottom lip into my mouth, I grip Riley's ass, lifting her up and off of me. "They won't hate us for long. Trust me." I slap her ass as she stands up, causing her to yelp and look back at me. "I love you," I say to soften her up.

Shaking her head, she smiles and starts walking backward, toward the bathroom. "Dammit! I love you too, but not so rough next time. Especially when we can't stay home and play." She winks at me and then disappears into the bathroom to get ready.

We pull up in the parking lot of Walk Of Shame thirty minutes later, us both rushing out of the car. In a hurry, Riley speeds up, walking ahead of me, but I grab her arm, slowing her down.

Whistling, I spin her around, checking her out in her little black dress. "Perfection."

She gets that look on her face that she's gotten for the last eleven years whenever I do this and it brings me back to the beginning, reminding me exactly why I fell in love with her in the first place.

"Cale . . ." She slaps my chest and I spin her into my chest, pulling her in for a kiss. "Let's go." I kiss her again, not wanting to let her go. "God, you're so adorable," she breathes, "But we need to hurry. I'm so anxious!"

Placing my hand on the small of her back, I guide her to the door and inside to where the crew is waiting in the V.I.P section. The first person I spot is Slade.

He nods at me and then hits Hemy in the side, letting him know that we've arrived. I can already see them talking shit about us being late and it only makes me want to laugh. Those two are usually never on time so fuck it.

Sara and Jules wave at us from behind the bar, letting me know that they're fine. Eight months ago, Lynx had some shit go down and Hilary took the club away from him. I was the first person that she asked to take over. I was hesitant at first, but let the fact that most of the people here are my family, talk me into agreeing.

Stone, Kash, Styx, Sara and now Jules have become a big part of our crew and if I can help them out in any way, then that's what I plan on doing. Plus it's good money and we're definitely going to need it now . . .

"Look who's late," Slade says with a sly grin. "Good thing I took my time getting here."

"Ass." I slug him on the shoulder and take a seat on the couch, pulling Riley down with me.

As soon as Lila sees us join the group, she rushes over to take our drink order.

"Just a beer." I hand her a twenty, before she turns to take Riley's order. Unfortunately, it's going to give everything away.

"I'll take a water," she says softly.

Almost everyone in the group stops what they are doing and turns to gawk at us.

"You're pregnant," Onyx shouts. "Aren't you!"

Lila whisper, "Congratulations," to Riley, before walking away to grab our drinks.

"Dude," Slade pushes.

"Well?" Aspen chimes in. "Tell us!"

Standing up, I pull Riley up with me, placing my hand over her belly. "Eight weeks," I say with the biggest smile on my face. "Looks like we're adding a new addition to our family, guys."

Everyone watches me in awe as I drop to my knees and kiss Riley's belly. My baby is in the woman that I love. Our baby.

"Well . . ." Riley says nervously. "Say something. You guys are too damn quiet."

Aspen bursts into tears while reaching out to pull Riley into her arms. "I'm going to be an aunt." Being sure not to hurt Riley, she shakes her, pulling her in as tight as she can. "Holy shit! I'm going to be an aunt, guys!"

Jumping to his feet, Slade throws his arms around the both of them and kisses the top of their heads. Then he reaches over and grabs the back of my head. "Congrats, man. I'm so fucking happy for you guys."

I can see him fighting hard to hide his emotions. I know his past still hurts him, but the time will come for him and Aspen to start their own family. Hopefully soon. I know they're both ready.

Sage, Onyx, Hemy . . . everyone takes turns giving Riley a hug, showing their love and excitement. Seeing all the support from them almost brings tears to my eyes, but I fight it.

Somehow knowing that I'm about to have a baby has made me more emotional. It makes me more appreciative of the love and support we have, knowing that our child will have the same.

After all the excitement is done, everyone falls into conversation about whether or not it's going to be a girl or boy. Hemy and Slade actually make a bet on it. Hemy says a dude and Slade says a girl.

I'm happy either way. I just want to hold the love of our lives and show him or her how much we're going to love and take care of them.

Hemy holds up his drink, interrupting everyone. "You should all know that if it's a dude that he's going to take after uncle, Hemy. You should be so lucky."

All three of the girl's eyes go wide, before Onyx and Sage start talking at the same time about how badly that shouldn't happen.

"The girls don't need any more dirty boys like you Hemy," Onyx says, before whispering, "Only me," and winking.

Slade grips my shoulder and squeezes. "I'll take care of that child as if it were mine. Never forget that, bro. I love you, man."

I can feel the truth is Slade's words and it warms my heart. It's taken time, but Slade is one of the best men that I know. He's protective and gives his all. It makes me happy to know my kid will have an uncle like him. "Love you too, bro."

Riley and the girls are in the middle of a conversation, but I pick Riley up, pulling her into my lap. Knowing that she is carrying my child makes me want to be as close to her as possible. The truth is . . . I just may never let her go now.

Eleven years ago, she became my life. Seven months ago, she became my wife and now she'll become the mother of my children. I will always show her her worth and how much she means to me. My family will always come first.

Snuggling into my arms, she smiles against my neck as I place my hand over her stomach. "I love you, daddy," she says with a small laugh.

Pulling her face up to reach mine, I press my lips against hers and rest my forehead to hers. "I love you too, baby. Always have and always will. Never forget that."

She smiles and looks me in the eyes. I can see by the way she's looking at me that she knows it's the truth. I would never lie to her. "I know, baby. I've always known."

A few minutes later, I look up to see Stone dancing while watching us from across the room. He knows something is up.

Standing up, I pull Riley to her feet and place my hand over her stomach, like I have almost every day since we've found out.

Stone's eyes widen and a grin takes over his face. Without much thought, he hops off the stage and runs over to us.

"Holy shit!" Grabbing Riley's face, he presses a kiss to the top of her head, before turning to me and doing the same. "Congratu-fucking-lations. I knew it! You've been acting different, man. That's awesome."

He pulls me in for a one arm hug as I squeeze his shoulder, thankful to see he's just as excited as the rest of us. "Thank you, man." I pull away from him. "Now get back on the fucking stage." I smile, showing my appreciation as he rushes back over to the stage surrounded by a bunch of confused looking chicks. He doesn't even miss a beat, falling back into his routine.

Just wanting to be close to my wife, I pull her into my arms and kiss her long and deep, pretending that it's just the two of us. As much as I want to spend time with these guys . . . my family, the excitement of going home to work out the nursery is tugging at my heart. I don't think I'll be able to sleep until I know my baby is going to have the best fucking room ever.

Leaning over Riley's head, I grab Slade's shoulder. "Hey, man. I think we're going to get going."

He looks at me, searching my eyes. He knows that feeling. He knows what it's like to want to be the man and take care of things. It's too bad that he never got that opportunity. "You need any help man, let me know. Any free time that I have, you know you have Aspen and I. We're just a call away."

"I know, man." I squeeze his shoulder. "I'll definitely be calling too. Just not tonight, man. Now that everyone knows, the excitement of it all is kicking in. We have a lot of thinking to do."

"Hell yeah," Slade responds, before turning to Aspen and picking her up, pulling her to him. "I know the feeling." He kisses Aspen's neck and squeezes her as if he never wants to let her go. "One day, man. One day . . ."

When I look over to say bye to Hemy, he's standing with his arm around Onyx, them both laughing it up and talking to Sage as if there isn't a care in the world. I swear I hear baby talk.

In this moment, I know that everyone is right where they belong. Slade has the love of his life, a new home and a good job. Hemy has his fiancé, their home and I have my wife, a baby on the way and a business to run with the love of my life.

The Walk Of Shame family couldn't ask for anything better . . .

ABOUT THE AUTHOR

VICTORIA ASHLEY GREW UP IN Rockford, IL and has had a passion for reading for as long as she can remember. After finding a reading app where it allowed readers to upload their own stories, she gave it a shot and writing became her passion.

She lives for a good romance book with tattooed bad boys that are just highly misunderstood and is not afraid to be caught crying during a good read. When she's not reading or writing about bad boys, you can find her watching her favorite shows such as Sons Of Anarchy, Dexter and True Blood.

She is the author of Wake Up Call, This Regret, Slade, Hemy, Get Off On The Pain and Thrust and is currently working on more works for 2015.

CONTACT HER AT:

www.victoriaashleyauthor.com
or on
Facebook
Twitter
Instagram

BOOKS BY VICTORIA ASHLEY

Wake Up Call
This Regret
Thrust

WALK OF SHAME
Slade (#1)
Hemy (#2)
Cale (#3)

PAIN
Get Off on the Pain
Something for the Pain (#2) Coming 2015

Made in the USA
Charleston, SC
29 September 2015